Praise for Pam Weaver

'What a terrific read – saga fans everywhere will love it and be asking for more from this talented author'
Annie Groves

'An engaging and gripping post-war saga . . . a hard-hitting story of female friendship tested against the odds'
Take a Break

'A heart-rending story about mothers and daughters'
Kitty Neale

'Pam Weaver presents us with a real page-turner – with richly drawn characters and a clever plot'
Caring 4 Sussex

'The characters are so richly drawn and authentic that they pull the reader along through the story effortlessly. This book is a real page-turner, which I enjoyed very much'
Anne Bennett

'An uplifting memoir told with real honesty'
Yours

Come Rain or Shine

Pam's saga novels, *There's Always Tomorrow*, *Better Days Will Come*, *Pack Up Your Troubles*, *For Better For Worse*, *Blue Moon*, *Love Walked Right In*, *Always In My Heart*, *Sing Them Home* and *Come Rain or Shine*, are set in Worthing during the austerity years. Pam's inspiration comes from her love of people and their stories, and her passion for the town of Worthing. With the sea on one side and the Downs on the other, Worthing has a scattering of small villages within its urban sprawl, and in some cases tight-knit communities, making it an ideal setting for the modern saga.

Come Rain or Shine

PAM WEAVER

PAN BOOKS

First published 2019 by Pan Books
an imprint of Pan Macmillan
20 New Wharf Road, London N1 9RR
Associated companies throughout the world
www.panmacmillan.com

ISBN 978-1-5098-5720-3

3 5 7 9 8 6 4

A CIP catalogue record for this book is available from the British Library.

Typeset by Palimpsest Book Production Limited, Falkirk, Stirlingshire
Printed and bound by CPI Group (UK) Ltd, Croydon, CR0 4YY

Visit www.panmacmillan.com to read more about all our books
and to buy them. You will also find features, author interviews and
news of any author events, and you can sign up for e-newsletters
so that you're always first to hear about our new releases.

This book is dedicated to four wonderful people who have always been there to encourage me: Eric and Pat Harvey, Nikki Sheeran and Penny Cheal. Thanks guys and hope you enjoy reading this one . . .

CHAPTER I

Findon, near Worthing, 1915

The light level was changing over Cissbury Ring. In another half-hour the first rays of April sunshine would bathe the prehistoric hilltop fort, highlighting the ring of trees planted in a previous century. In the dull silence of early morning, Amos McCabe was sitting on the steps of his shepherd's hut enjoying his first pipe of the day. Before long, his flock would stir from their sleep to feed on the chalky downland pastures. They had grazed in the same area on the South Downs close to the villages of Wiston, Washington and Findon for years, and because the land was not naturally fertile, they had played their part in keeping it well manured. If the soil was well prepared by his flock, the following year the land could be turned over to wheat.

Bess, his sheepdog, came out from under the hut and shook herself. Amos lowered his arm and she came to his side. He didn't speak. He didn't need to. The bond between them was strong. She sat under his right hand and he fondled one of her ears.

As soon as the first rays of sunlight streamed across the trees on the hill, Amos rose to his feet. He'd count his sheep to make sure they were all there and then he'd return home. Lambing was over and he'd stayed long enough to make sure every animal was sturdy. After six weeks out on the hills and living in his shepherd's hut, he was looking forward to sitting by his own fireplace and listening to Molly singing as she prepared their meal in the kitchen. Of course, he'd still have to come out twice a day to check on the flock, but he could enjoy a little free time at last.

In years gone by, his father and grandfather before him would have had the occasional company of other shepherds, but that was in the days when the Sussex Downs were home to more than three hundred flocks. The Great War was changing everything. Once farm workers and shepherds had been sent to the front, the countryside was denuded of labourers and the huge flocks disappeared. These days, Amos would be lucky to find two hundred flocks on the whole of the Sussex Downs, which stretched from the Itchen Valley in Hampshire to Beachy Head, near Eastbourne.

To the sound of the dawn chorus and the tuneless song of a distant cuckoo, Amos and Bess rounded up the sheep and pushed them through a small gate. This enabled him not only to count the sheep but also to do a quick check for any signs of sickness or injury. Occasionally he'd stop to smear a little tar on a scratch or a superficial cut to stop the flies attacking the animal and to give the wound a chance to heal. The whole exercise didn't take long, but by the end of it, he'd noticed one ewe was missing.

He knew exactly which one it was. He'd nicknamed her Slippery Sybil because whenever she found a gap in the hedge or a weakness in a fence, she'd push her way through to the other side. It didn't seem to matter to her that she'd left behind good pasture and now she only had barren woodland or weed-covered soil, she made a habit of wandering away from the others all the time. Under normal circumstances he would have got rid of her, but she was a delight to the eye with her beautifully proportioned body and an exceptional coat of wool. Amos sighed. Now, instead of going home, he would have to scour the hillside for Slippery Sybil.

He found her high up on a large patch of scrubland. She had walked across a platform of last year's brambles, which spanned a small ditch, become stuck and rolled to one side. She remained forlornly waiting to be rescued, two of her legs dangling between the branches, the others in the air. If he hadn't found her, she would have died. Once she had been 'cast' she couldn't have righted herself and the gases building up in her rumen would have eventually cut off the blood supply, firstly to her legs and then to other parts of her body. For all that, she wasn't completely stupid. Sybil trusted him absolutely and stayed perfectly still while he leaned over her to release her fleece and lift her out. Once she was freed, Amos stood astride the animal, talking softly to her as he rubbed her limbs to bring the sensation back. When he finally let her go, she walked unsteadily at first, but then broke into a trot which quickly became a run to join the rest of the flock.

Bess had wandered away as Amos set about his rescue. A minute or two later she began to bark. With Slippery Sybil on her way back to the rest of the flock, Amos set off down the hill. Bess was still barking. He shouted a command and although the dog stopped for a second or two, she refused to obey. Instead, she cocked her head on one side and began barking again. It was then that he noticed the magpies. There were several on the ground and a couple in the branches of a tree looking on. What did you call a gathering of magpies? He'd read it somewhere but he couldn't quite recall . . . a congregation of magpies or was it a murder of magpies? The thought of murder made him feel uneasy. Bess seemed to be keeping them away from something. She was an intelligent animal, and Amos felt obliged to return and see what was troubling her.

As he drew near, Amos heard a reedy cry. It made the hairs on the back of his neck stand up. He'd been working on Sussex sheep country for years. He knew the Downs like the back of his hand. He was familiar with the sights and sounds of animals in the night, like a hen harrier swooping down on a foraging field mouse, the call of a vixen, the smell of a fox's lair or the cry of an owl. Pathetic as it was, this wasn't the usual cry of any animal that he'd come across, whether in distress or otherwise.

4

Bess was still staring into the thicket, her flanks shivering, when Amos crouched down and, looking under the hedge, spotted a tiny arm.

'Dear Lord alive,' he murmured. 'It's a baby.'

He parted the foliage to get a better look. She was naked but she lay on a dirty piece of yellow-edged blanket. Her skin was blue with the cold and she still had her umbilical cord. The placenta was beside her. Tugging at the blanket, Amos got her into a better position, and whipping off his shepherd's waterproof cape, he wrapped it around her tiny body. Her cry was getting weaker all the time, as feeble as a kitten's meow. He knew he had to get her to a place of safety and quickly.

Because he often had days on his own, Amos had become a man who loved reading. Years ago he'd read in a book how the eastern shepherd who lived at the time of Christ had a pocket on the inside of his cloak. At lambing time, he would put any sickly or orphan lamb inside that pocket where the warmth of his own body would help it survive until he could tend to it properly. Amos had been so impressed with the idea that he'd persuaded his wife to make just such a pocket on the inside of his own coat. He'd had little opportunity to use it, but now he gently pushed the baby, still wrapped in her blanket, into its folds and tied his belt underneath her so that she wouldn't be swung about as he walked. As he hurried down the hill, the birds descended on the bloody placenta, greedy and fighting.

His mind was in a whirl. Who could have done such a terrible thing? It was obvious the perpetrator didn't want the child to survive, else he or she would have put her somewhere where she was bound to be found. Amos felt sure it couldn't have been the mother. For starters, it was highly unlikely that she could have climbed the steep hill so soon after giving birth, so who was responsible? The father? The midwife? He felt his eyes smarting. What should he do? When he reached the village of Findon he planned to bang on somebody's door in the hope they would know what to do, but judging by the poor little mite's colour, she needed expert help and quickly. There was a hospital in Worthing. Somehow or other, he had to get her there.

As luck would have it, as he came off the hill he saw Jack Ward getting into his builder's lorry. Jack was startled by Amos's request, but moments later they were speeding along the Findon Valley towards Worthing with Bess sitting in the back of the flatbed. By instinct, Amos spent the time gently rubbing the baby's back. He'd do it for a lamb after a difficult birth and for some reason it seemed natural to do the same for this little girl.

They didn't say much. Each man was left to his own thoughts. Being so early in the morning, the roads were clear and they made good time before Jack pulled into the area at the front of the hospital. Having told Bess to wait by the door, Amos hurried inside. The nurses sprang into action as soon as they saw the baby and she was hurried away.

Someone brought Amos a cup of tea while the police were contacted and then he spent some time giving them the details of where and how he had found her.

'Don't suppose we'll catch the blighter what did it,' said the policeman bleakly, 'but if we ever do catch him or her, it'll be attempted murder.'

They let Amos see her before he left. A nurse accompanied him and he stood over the tiny crib. The room smelled of disinfectant and carbolic soap. She was all alone in the room and she was wrapped up in warm blankets. There were two hot-water bottles in the crib, one on either side of her. She stirred slightly as he spoke to her as if she recognized the sound of his voice. Amos laid a hand across her precious little body and said a silent prayer. A minute or two later, he sensed the nurse fidgeting behind him, anxious to get back to her other duties.

'Thank God I got there in time,' he mumbled gruffly as he turned to go.

The nurse gave him a sympathetic smile. 'She's very small,' she said softly, 'and she's had such a terrible start.'

Amos stared at her with a blank expression as she shook her head and added, 'Despite your prayers, I'm afraid there's not much hope.'

CHAPTER 2

Worthing, 1946

'Just go to the end of Station Approach and head down Chapel Road. You can't miss it. It's right opposite the new town hall.'

Sheila Hodges thanked the woman who had given her directions, and hurried off. It was a beautiful day, warm and sunny, perfect beach weather, which was a welcome change. So far the beginning of summer had been wet. Sheila had only just arrived in Worthing, but she hadn't brought her bathing suit. She was on her way to a funeral, which was why she'd asked directions to the Tab.

When she'd got the letter from her cousin Ronnie telling her that their grandfather had died, Sheila had hardly given it a second thought. Over the years, she'd had very little contact with family and in fact she'd struggled for a moment to remember what cousin Ronnie looked like. She remembered that her full name was Veronica Jackson but she preferred to be known as Ronnie and that she had short dark hair. Ronnie's older brother, Leslie, had been a bit of a wimp. They'd all met up a couple of times when Sheila was very young and she and her parents had come to Worthing on holiday. That was long before the war, maybe 1929 or 1930. Their week's holiday was all right, but the weather hadn't been all that great and the beach was knee-deep in rancid seaweed. The second time had been in the following year. She and Ronnie, who were roughly the same age, got on well, but her mother and grandfather had a terrible row about something and the holiday was cut short. Sheila's mother said little about the past, but there was obviously some unpleasant history between her and Granddad. Sheila knew her mother and Granny exchanged Christmas cards, but that was about it.

A few days before, Ronnie had written to say that the funeral was to be at eleven thirty at Worthing Tabernacle, Chapel Road, with the wake at their grandmother's house afterwards. The invitation would have stayed where she'd put it on her chest of drawers had she not had such a dreadful day at work the day before.

Sheila caught the train from Victoria, arriving at five minutes past eleven, in plenty of time to walk to the church. After weeks and weeks in stuffy London it was absolute bliss to breathe in fresh air and not to have to walk by bombed-out buildings, a constant reminder of such awful memories.

She was a pretty girl who had not long had her twenty-second birthday. She didn't have anything black so she hoped her grandmother would forgive her grey pinstriped dress with a white Peter Pan collar under her navy coat. She'd been lucky enough to stumble across them in a Red Cross charity shop and she'd used her vouchers to get them. The coat was slightly too big but having taken the belt and the belt loops off, at a quick glance it might have passed for one of those swagger coats which were becoming fashionable. Her hat was a jaunty little pixie, which she wore at an angle over the left side of her head.

The town bore few battle scars until she reached the church. There the shops next door had been damaged, but work was well underway to repair and rebuild them. Worthing Tabernacle was an attractive building with a pale Bath-stone exterior and a large rose window gracing the upper part of the building. With a quick glance up at the town hall clock on the opposite side of the road, she mounted the steps and walked in. An usher gave her a slight nod as she went from the vestibule into the church itself.

There were few people waiting inside; five, maybe six. They sat on the semi-circular pews below the double-deck pulpit. The door slammed behind her and they all turned round. Sheila made to sit at the back until a woman dressed in a shabby brown coat stood up and walked towards her. As she drew closer, Sheila recognized her. It was her grandmother. She was older than Sheila remembered, but of course she would be. She was smaller too. Her hat had seen better days. The flowers on the band were tired-looking and faded. Her shoes were highly polished, but creased with age.

'Granny.'

It must have been easily sixteen years since she'd seen her. The old lady put out her arms and Sheila walked into her embrace. She smelled of lavender and moth balls. When she stepped back, Sheila was struck by her deep-set eyes and sad expression. The frizzy hair peeping out from under the hat was speckled with grey and badly in need of a decent cut and the attentions of a hairdresser. Granny reached up and stroked her face gently. Her fingers were rough. Hard-working hands, Sheila thought to herself.

'I was so sorry to hear about your mum and dad,' Granny said softly.

Sheila nodded. 'I'm sorry you couldn't get to the funeral.'

Granny's gaze dropped to the floor. 'I would have come, but your granddad . . .' Her voice trailed.

'I know,' said Sheila. She smiled.

Her grandmother linked her arm through hers and led her down to the front and the rest of the mourners. Sheila recognized cousin Ronnie at once. She had grown into what her mother would have called a handsome woman rather than being pretty. She still had the same twinkling eyes and a smile which lit up her whole face.

'So good of you to come,' she said, giving Sheila's arm a slight squeeze.

The couple sitting beside her were Ronnie's parents, Auntie Jean and Uncle Bill, from Warminster. Auntie Jean hadn't changed a bit, although she had gathered a few grey hairs over the years. Uncle Bill was like a different man. Sheila remembered him as robust and with a mop of ginger hair. Now he wore rimless glasses and he was almost bald. They were dressed entirely in black. There was a man sitting next to Uncle Bill, but he didn't stand up as she approached. It was her cousin Leslie. He looked every inch the spiv with his flashy checked suit – hardly the thing to wear at a funeral, she thought – and imitation brogues. His hair was slicked down and he had a Ronald Colman moustache. As Sheila squeezed into the pew beside them, there was no time for chit-chat. A voice behind them said, 'Would you all rise,' and a moment later the vicar preceded the funeral director and his pall-bearers as they brought in the coffin.

By the time they were on their way to the house, everyone was exhausted. The service had been brief, but then they'd had to accompany the coffin up to Durrington cemetery for the burial. There was only one car so it was a bit of a tight squeeze.

'Did he make a will?' Leslie asked as they were being driven to the house. He was wiping his hands with his handkerchief, having made a big fuss when getting some sort of smudge on them as he opened the door.

His mother frowned. 'Not now, dear.'

Leslie glanced at Sheila. 'Why not? No need for secrets. We're all family here.'

Sheila saw the colour rise in her grandmother's cheeks. 'It all comes to me,' she said quietly.

Leslie looked out of the window and everybody

shifted awkwardly. Then, turning back, he said, 'Well, I'll take over the garage if you like.'

Uncle Bill harrumphed.

Auntie Jean, wedged between them both, nudged her son in the ribs.

'What?' he demanded. 'It's obvious, isn't it? I'm the only one here that's suitable.'

'She knows you'd never make a go of it,' said Uncle Bill, leaning forward. 'I doubt that you've ever done an honest day's work in your life.'

Leslie glared at his father with a malevolent look in his eye. 'Don't start that again,' he retorted. 'You can't tell me what to do any more.'

'More's the pity,' said his father. They looked away from each other, Leslie to brush his jacket with his fingers and Uncle Bill to turn his head towards the window of the car. 'Look, son,' he began again, 'if you come back home to Warminster, there's a job ready and waiting for you.'

'I've told you before,' Leslie said, his tone of voice softening slightly, 'I'm not coming back.'

'Why not?' Uncle Bill went on. 'What's so terrible about working in a shop? Don't you know that the day you were born I changed the sign over the door to Jackson and Son?'

'Dad—' Leslie began.

'If it's working with me that's the problem,' his father interrupted, 'as soon as you've learned the ropes, I'll retire. I can't say fairer than that, can I? You'll be your own boss.'

'It's not going to happen, Dad.'

Uncle Bill's expression changed. 'Once upon a time you could have made something of yourself,' he snapped. 'Look at you now. A small-time crook in a jazzy suit. Who do you think you are, Al flippin' Capone?'

There was a sudden movement and Auntie Jean cried out in alarm as the two men lunged at each other in the confines of the funeral car.

'Don't like it, do you,' his father challenged, 'when someone tells you the truth?' He turned to the others. 'He's not much good at thieving either. This is the clever dick who nicked a whole batch of tennis racquets and put them in the groundsman's line-making machine to bring them home. Led the police right to the bloody door.'

Sheila turned away, suppressing a smile.

'Dad, please!' cried Ronnie.

'Leave it out, Dad,' said Leslie, 'or I promise you, I'll thump you.'

'You?' Uncle Bill sneered. 'You haven't got the guts.'

'Please . . .' said Granny.

'For God's sake,' Ronnie cried angrily, 'will you stop it!'

The two men backed down and they all sat in silence. After a moment or two, Granny turned to Sheila. 'What have you been doing since the war, dear?' she said, deliberately changing the subject. 'Have you got a good job?'

'I work for the GPO,' said Sheila. 'I'm a telephonist.'

'Nice,' said Auntie Jean.

'Steady job,' Uncle Bill agreed pointedly as he glared at his son. 'Good prospects.'

'Do you like it?' Ronnie asked.

Sheila considered the question for a second or two, then said, 'I bloody hate it.'

There was a moment of shocked silence until cousin Ronnie threw back her head and roared with laughter.

Granny's house was in Pavilion Road. It was part of a small terrace which backed onto the railway line. As she opened the door it smelled vaguely musty. They walked straight off the street into a small passageway with the stairs immediately in front of them. The sitting room was right by the front door and, further down the hall, they came to the living room and the kitchen. There was nowhere to hang their coats so they threw them onto the single bed in the sitting room, the place where, Sheila supposed, her grandfather had spent his final days.

As they walked into the living room, a little dog jumped down from a chair next to the fire and greeted them happily. Sheila could tell that she was well loved. She had a gentle nature and was pleased to see her mistress. 'This is Milly,' said Granny as she patted her absent-mindedly and invited everyone to sit down.

The room wasn't very big and was sparsely furnished. Apart from two soft chairs either side of the fireplace, there was a small table with two upright chairs and a sideboard next to the wall.

15

'Can I do anything to help?' Ronnie called as Granny disappeared into the tiny kitchen beyond.

'No, dear. Sit down and make yourself at home.'

Leslie took one of the easy chairs, Uncle Bill the other. Sheila and Auntie Jean sat on the kitchen chairs and Ronnie pulled out a footstool.

Uncle Bill glowered at his son. 'What sort of a suit is that to wear at a funeral?'

Leslie flicked a little speck of something from his sleeve. 'A very expensive one.' The barb in his tone wasn't lost on his father.

'And how much did you pay for it?'

Sheila could see Leslie's neck going red, but he stayed silent as he stared straight ahead.

Granny busied herself coming in and out of the room and before long the table contained two plates of sandwiches (one egg and the other fish paste, which she'd obviously prepared beforehand), some fairy cakes which looked as if they'd had a tad too long in the oven and a large pot of tea. Leslie picked up and examined a teacup.

I can't stay,' said Leslie, putting it back into the saucer with a slight look of disdain on his face. 'Things to do, people to meet.'

'I hope you're keeping out of trouble, dear,' said Granny.

'I've learned my lesson, Granny,' he said, flicking some of his cigarette ash from his trouser leg. 'Now I'm as pure as the driven snow.'

His father harrumphed again.

16

Sheila vacated her chair to look at the photographs on the mantelpiece. There was Ronnie wearing a uniform of sorts, standing by a veranda with two small children, a picture of Auntie Jean and Uncle Bill on their wedding day, a wedding day picture of her own parents and a photograph of an unknown girl with short bobbed hair and a whimsical smile.

'Who do those children belong to?' she asked Ronnie.

'That's Ruth and Elspeth,' said Ronnie. 'My employer's children.'

Sheila studied the picture carefully, especially the strange flowers at the side of the veranda. 'That doesn't look like it's in this country. It looks as if it was taken somewhere really hot.'

'Australia,' said Ronnie. 'A place called Geelong.'

Sheila put the photo frame back in its place, disappointed that her cousin wasn't more forthcoming. 'Who is this?' she asked, holding the picture of the girl with the quirky smile.

There was an awkward silence, then Ronnie said, 'That's Aunt Daisy.'

Sheila frowned. 'Who's Aunt Daisy? Have I ever met her?'

For a moment nobody spoke, and as Sheila looked from one to the other, everybody avoided her gaze. Granny squared her shoulders. 'It was a bit before your time, dear,' she said. 'Daisy was my first child. That photograph was taken in 1914 when she was fourteen.'

'I've never seen that picture before,' said Auntie Jean.

'You probably haven't,' said her mother with an air

of mild defiance. 'Your father would never let me put it up, but now that he's gone, I can do what I like.'

'She's very pretty,' Sheila persisted. 'How come I've never seen her before? Did she die?'

Her grandmother took the frame and replaced it on the mantelpiece. 'No, she didn't die,' she said quietly. 'Daisy ran away.'

Granny returned to the table to pour the tea. Sheila opened her mouth to ask another question, but then she felt a hand squeeze hers. She glanced down. Ronnie, sitting on the footstool, was shaking her head.

Leslie rose to his feet. 'So if I can have the key to the garage, Granny, I'll be off.'

Granny sank onto a kitchen chair. 'Leslie, I've already told you, I'm not giving you the garage,' she said wearily.

'But why not?' he insisted. 'It'll be one less thing to worry about.'

Granny shook her head.

'Leave her alone,' said Uncle Bill gruffly. 'Can't you see that she doesn't want you to have it?'

Quick as a flash, Leslie rounded on his father and pointed his finger at him. 'What have you been saying about me?' Leslie barked. Uncle Bill seemed to diminish in size. 'This is between Granny and me.' He looked around the room. 'Working with cars is a man's job,' he said, his voice as soft as butter. 'I don't see any other men in this room, do you? It's obvious that the garage should come to me.' He turned to his grandmother. 'I think it's what Granddad would have wanted.'

The old lady straightened her back and, turning towards him, she said, 'Leslie, I said no.'

He turned away, clearly disappointed, then glaring at his sister added, 'You'd better not do anything daft, Granny. Don't you dare go selling it, will you? That garage belongs to me!'

With that he swept from the room and a moment later they heard the door slam. The tension he'd created left with him and it was as if everyone heaved a collective sigh of relief. Granny sniffed into her handkerchief, then stuffed it back into her apron pocket.

'Sorry about that, my dears,' she said, getting up and passing the plate of fish-paste sandwiches around.

'Leslie was always a little headstrong,' Auntie Jean said apologetically.

Although curious to know more, Sheila instinctively felt this was neither the time nor place.

'So tell me, my dear,' said Granny, looking directly at Sheila as she lowered herself into a chair, 'have you recovered from your illness?'

'I wasn't exactly ill,' said Sheila, munching on her sandwich. 'It was just the shock.'

'Can you tell us what happened?' said Auntie Jean. 'I mean, only if you want to.' She glanced at her husband. 'We did wonder.'

Sheila took a deep breath. Painful as it still was, she could at least talk about it now, so she told them everything. How she'd joined the ATS and been away from home for most of the war. How her parents had survived the Blitz and all the privations that went with it. How her father had been awarded a medal for his work in the fire service. How, on the day they'd died, they'd been invited to a reception at the town hall and it was rumoured that the King and Queen would be there. Her parents had been very excited, but they never did get to see their majesties. When he got up that morning, her father had put the kettle on to make a cup of tea as usual and then there had been an almighty explosion.

'They said it was probably a build-up of gas from a damaged main,' she told them. 'My parents were the only ones who were killed, but the whole house was reduced to rubble and four other houses in the terrace were severely damaged.'

She was aware of the shocked silence that had descended into the room.

'How awful,' murmured Auntie Jean. 'But you weren't hurt?'

Sheila shook her head. 'I wasn't there. I'd gone to Peckham to stay with a friend who was celebrating her twenty-first.'

'Thank God for that,' said Granny.

'But you lost everything?' said Auntie Jean.

Sheila nodded. 'I only had the clothes I stood up in. They gave me vouchers to get clothes from the Red Cross shop, and the neighbours, bless them, had a whip-round.'

They'd all gone quiet again when she'd finally finished telling them.

'Ironic, isn't it?' she added bitterly. 'Mum and Dad

went through all that, then just as peace came, they were taken. Not a very happy start to 1946, eh?'

'I'm so sorry,' Ronnie said quietly.

Auntie Jean turned away and blew her nose loudly. Granny was staring at the floor, her eyes brimming with tears and her chin quivering. It was only then that it occurred to Sheila that they were grieving too. They might not have seen much of each other over the years but Mum was still Auntie Jean's sister and Granny's daughter – although her middle child, not her eldest as she'd always thought. Poor Granny had not only lost her husband but two of her children as well. She wondered why Daisy had run away. And why had her own mother never spoken of her sister? Granny pulled the handkerchief from her apron pocket again and blew her nose. Auntie Jean gave Sheila a hug and her uncle muttered something incomprehensible.

'Where do you live now?' Ronnie asked eventually.

'I have a tenement room,' said Sheila with a sniff. 'I should look for somewhere else, but up until now, to be honest, I couldn't be bothered.' She saw Ronnie and her grandmother exchange glances. 'When I get back, I'll look for a proper flat or digs. It's pretty awful.'

Granny slapped her thighs and rose to her feet. 'Let's make a fresh pot of tea, shall we?'

It was when they were helping with the washing-up that Sheila suggested going to the beach. 'It seems daft coming all this way and not seeing the sea,' she said.

21

'In that case,' said Ronnie, tossing the tea towel aside, 'we could catch the next bus.'

'You'll have to get a move on,' said Granny, glancing up at the clock and slipping a pound note into Sheila's pocket. 'It's due in five minutes.'

Dashing along South Farm Road and just managing to jump on the platform before the bus moved off only added to their sense of fun. A little while later they were walking along Marine Parade.

Now that peace had come, Worthing was once again a mecca for coaches. They were parked all the way from Splash Point to the pier and beyond. The beach was packed and the deckchair attendants were doing a roaring trade. People strolled along the newly renovated pier for tuppence or gathered near the Lido to watch the Punch and Judy show. A man handed Sheila a small card. She hadn't noticed him in the crowd but he'd taken a photograph of the two of them as they'd walked along.

'Ready by ten tomorrow morning,' he said. 'Half a crown.'

She passed the card to Ronnie. No point in keeping it. She wouldn't be here – more's the pity.

'What time is your train?' Ronnie asked.

'I'd like to be home before it gets too dark,' said Sheila. 'I'll catch the six o'clock.'

They had just over an hour and a quarter so they walked over the pebbles onto the sand, down to the water's edge, and lifting their skirts, they paddled in the shallows. The water, which sparkled like a million diamonds, was still quite warm.

When they'd had enough, they hurried back to the top and, finding an empty bench, dried their feet with their handkerchiefs.

'We talked for ages about me,' said Sheila as Ronnie leaned back to soak up the sun. 'What about you? I noticed in that photograph of you and those children in Australia that you were in a uniform. Did you have a good war?'

Ronnie opened her eyes and stared out to sea. 'I'll tell you about it some other time,' she said. 'We've had enough sadness for one day.'

Embarrassed, Sheila felt her face heat up. She hadn't meant to pry, but surely if she'd been in Australia Ronnie would have been relatively safe. Apart from that awful raid on Darwin in 1942 which reached the newsreels, and the raids on the Northern Territories, the rest of the country had escaped enemy fire. She tried to remember where Ronnie had said she was based – Geelong, wasn't it? Where was that exactly? The Battle of Darwin had been huge, with the main aim to prevent the Allies from using the base. They said more Japanese bombs had been dropped on Australian shipping than on the Americans in Pearl Harbor, but thankfully the loss of life was about a tenth.

'I'm sorry,' said Sheila. 'I didn't mean to be nosy.'

'You're not,' said Ronnie with a shake of her head. 'It's me.'

Sheila gave her a watery smile. 'Your brother seemed a bit upset that he didn't get the garage.'

'He might like the idea,' said Ronnie, 'but Granny

knows he'd make a hash of it.' She looked at Sheila and grinned. 'You know what he's like. Leslie doesn't like getting his hands dirty.'

'He did look rather swish,' said Sheila. 'I think he even polished his nails.'

Ronnie chuckled. 'That wouldn't surprise me either.' She pulled up her stockings and did up her suspender discreetly. 'Leslie gets himself all mixed up in these hare-brained schemes to make money and they never seem to work.'

Sheila pulled a face.

'Like the time he broke into some bloke's house, got drunk on his whisky and passed out on the sofa.'

Sheila laughed. 'He never did.'

'Oh yes,' said Ronnie. 'He got off lightly with that one, but when he was called up, they sent him to the Army Pay Corps and he fiddled the wage packets. He got kicked out for that.'

'Oh dear,' said Sheila, even though she was smiling.

Ronnie stared at her for a second or two, then said, 'How would you fancy coming back here to live?'

'To live!'

'Granny wants to make the garage a going concern,' said Ronnie. 'It's in a good position on the Littlehampton Road, near the Thomas A Becket pub, but it's been empty for ages.'

'Why won't she let your brother have it?'

'Because Leslie wants to sell it,' said Ronnie, 'and if he did, he'd only waste the money.'

'But why me?' asked Sheila. 'Where do I fit into all this?'

'We thought that seeing as you were in the ATS, you'd have a good understanding about all things mechanical. I'm good at bookkeeping and we could diversify as well.'

Despite her initial misgivings, Sheila felt a tingle of excitement. 'Like what?'

'A little shop for a start,' said Ronnie, 'and maybe even a taxi service?'

'Big plans,' said Sheila, 'but would Granny agree? Who's ever heard of two girls going into business in a garage?'

'It was Granny's idea,' said Ronnie rather smugly.

For a moment, Sheila held her breath. 'Moneywise I've got nothing to offer.' She laughed sardonically. 'I'm just a penniless orphan, remember? We'd need some sort of capital, wouldn't we?'

'Granny has money but she's not a bottomless pit,' said Ronnie. 'She's willing to give us a new start. She'd remain a sleeping partner.'

Sheila blew out her cheeks. 'I'm not sure I'm clever enough to mend every type of car,' she said. 'I'd be good at army lorries and such-like but I'm not sure I could tackle a Rolls-Royce.'

Ronnie pulled a face. 'I'm not too sure we'd get many of them, and anyway, I think Rolls-Royce mend their own, don't they? Look, I'll admit that the place is a bit rundown and it'll take a lot of hard work, but why don't we give it a go?'

'Where would we live?'

'There's a flat above the workshop,' said Ronnie. 'It's not big, but there are two poky little bedrooms and a kitchen area.'

Sheila looked out to sea. It was very tempting, but after all that had happened, did she have the energy to start all over again? This was a radical plan. She was right. Who'd ever heard of two girls running a garage? What if she and Ronnie didn't get on? The scene in front of her was certainly inviting. Because it was Ascension Day, the children had a day off school. Sheila remembered how special it had been when she was a girl. You'd go to school as normal in the morning, walk crocodile fashion to church for a short service and then you could go back home. Clearly, the mothers of Worthing made the most of the occasion, especially now that the war had been over for a year and the beaches were once again accessible. Most deckchairs were occupied. A few fathers and grandfathers sat with their sleeves rolled up and a handkerchief knotted in each corner on their heads. Some had used their newspaper as a sun hat. Mothers helped their children to dress or dished out sandwiches, and everywhere she could hear chatter and laughter. It had been so long since she'd had a good laugh. She sighed inwardly. Turning to look inland, a boy on a bicycle with a large basket on the front rode by. The sign on the side read, 'Stop me and buy one'. Further up the road, 'Kiss me quick' hats fluttered in the breeze outside a gift shop.

Sheila glanced at her cousin and, for the first time,

noticed how thin Ronnie was. Once again, she wondered what sort of war she'd had. Most likely they could both do with a new start. Perhaps Ronnie was counting on her. All at once, helping to run a garage suddenly felt more of a responsibility. Was she up to the job? Could she really be a career woman? Most girls her age were married or at least getting married, but now that the Allies had gone back to Canada or America, there was a shortage of decent men. Sheila desperately wanted to marry and have children but supposing she never met anyone?

'Oh, Ronnie,' said Sheila, 'it sounds wonderful, but it's a big thing. What if we fail? What if we don't get on? Oh, I'm not sure.'

'Tell you what,' said Ronnie, glancing at her watch and getting to her feet, 'why don't you think about it and let me know? Right now we'd better head to the station for your train.'

Ronnie bought a platform ticket and came onto the platform to wave her off.

'I'm sorry about Granddad,' said Sheila as she leaned out of the carriage window, 'but apart from all that and the funeral, I've had a lovely time today.'

'You will think about the garage, won't you?' said Ronnie as the train began to move.

Sheila nodded. They waved to each other until they were out of sight, then Sheila sat down. She was alone in the carriage, so she had plenty of time to think. After all that lovely fresh air, did she really want to stay in London? Life in the capital was difficult enough with all its hardships. She'd glibly said she would get another flat or some new digs, but she knew that so soon after the war, it was almost impossible to find anything decent. If she came to Worthing, she'd have a ready-made home. She'd got on well with Ronnie in the past, so it was perfectly possible they would get on well in the future. Or would they? She chewed her bottom lip thoughtfully. Back then they were only children. She sat back and closed her eyes as she recalled her parents as holiday-makers gliding towards Lancing on a pedalo. The town was attractive and what could be better than to have the beach on the doorstep? It would be nice to swim in the sea or take a bus onto the beautiful Sussex Downs, which were only a mile or two away. Of course, not every day would be as sunny as today. Earlier this year, the weather countrywide had been awfully wet. It was a big step, moving away from all that was familiar, and yet she'd done it once before – when she'd joined the ATS, there'd been no choice but to go where duty called. But running a garage? Did she have it in her to take on such a big challenge? Supposing Granny invested her money and they lost it all? Oh dear, it was so difficult trying to make up her mind.

Back in Norbury, Sheila felt her depression fall back over her shoulders like a heavy cloak. It didn't help to hear a humongous row going on as she walked up the street. Mrs Dawber was leaning out of one of the upper windows yelling at Mrs Perkins; one accusing the other of stealing some washing from the line. The language, as her mother would have said, was enough to make a sailor blush.

Sheila walked up to her room on the first floor, her feet sticking to the lino as she went. The other women in the tenement thought it beneath them to wash the stairs. Sheila got a mop and bucket out now and then, but she hadn't done it for a while. As she made her way wearily upstairs, the hallway smelled of boiled cabbage and of something a little more dubious.

A child, a little boy with a runny nose, came out of an upstairs room and flew down the stairs. Dressed in a holey vest and a pair of trousers two sizes too big, he barged past her. At the top of the landing, his mother, a large woman with bleached blonde hair, leaned over the banister. 'Colin, you come back here, you little tyke, or I'll tan you into the middle of next week.'

The two women eyed each other as they passed on the landing, and whatever Colin had done, they both knew he wouldn't be coming back for a while.

As soon as she walked through her door Sheila knew someone had been in her room. A quick backward peek at the area around the keyhole told her someone had been picking the lock. There was a small fresh scratch on the dark wood. Whoever had done it probably wasn't alone. Others living in the house must have known about it. It would have been impossible to stand by the door picking the lock without attracting some attention. She closed the door behind her before turning slowly. At first glance everything looked the same, but then she noticed that the corner of the counterpane on the bed wasn't tucked in properly. That meant they'd looked under the mattress. One of the drawers on the dresser was slightly open. The suitcase on top of the wardrobe was more to the right than usual. They must have bumped it against the wall as they took it down. One of the pictures was slightly crooked. She had left two coins on top of the gas meter to save having to hunt for a shilling if it should run out when it was dark. They were gone. She took a deep breath. That settled it. She'd take up cousin Ronnie's offer straight away. She wouldn't stay in this dump a minute longer than was necessary. Just the thought of someone rifling through her stuff made her skin crawl. She'd pay the rent and go. Her heart went to her mouth as she felt the panic. The rent money! Don't say they'd found the rent money.

When she'd joined the ATS, her father had taught her a trick or two.

'You can't expect to be in the company of strangers without one or two of them being a bit light-fingered,' he'd cautioned. 'You've got to learn to protect yourself.'

She'd only listened with half an ear but he had been right. The girls she lived with were from all walks of life and there had been the occasional theft. One girl lost her birthday money and another time an expensive watch went missing. Nobody owned up, of course, but it left a nasty taste in the mouth. Sheila often found herself looking over her shoulder if she had something nice. Fortunately, having put her father's advice to good use, she'd never had anything pinched.

'Don't hide anything in the wardrobe,' Dad had told

her. 'It's the first place they go to. And forget about shoving something under the mattress as well. Hide your stuff in plain sight. That's what I'd do.'

She walked to the small marble-top washstand in the corner, lifted the jug and tipped the water into the bowl. Turning the jug upside down, she was relieved to see the rent money still fastened to the bottom. But what of her Post Office savings book? It was obvious that whoever had come into the room was aware of the creaking floorboard by the bed. The mat which covered it was slightly turned up on one corner. She pulled it away and lifted the loose board. Crouching down on her knees, she looked inside the hole. The mousetrap she'd left there had been sprung, though not by a rodent. It was empty but there was a speck of blood on the wood. Uncharitable as it might be, the thought that whoever had put his hand down there had got a shock pleased her. She hoped his finger damn well hurt. Resetting the trap, she put the board back and stood to her feet.

Taking the suitcase down from the wardrobe, she decided to start packing. Everything in her drawers had been disturbed, but the Post Office book was still there. It was possible the would-be thief had taken each drawer out and turned it upside down to look at the bottom of the drawer itself, but he hadn't spotted her hiding place. She turned towards the shelf and lifted the tin of castor oil capsules. Following Dad's advice, she had created a false bottom in the tin and strapped her Post Office book underneath.

She packed quickly. She didn't have much anyway. There wasn't time to catch another train back to Worthing tonight, and besides, the Post Office would be closed by now. She'd have to use some of her precious savings to buy another ticket.

Downstairs, she could hear shouting. Mr Timberlake had obviously come home from work having spent half his wages in the George and Dragon again and Mrs Timberlake was getting the usual treatment. The kids were crying too. The garage might not be up to much, but at least she wouldn't have to listen to this day and night. Up above her, Babs had a client. She heard their voices, then his boots clattered on the bare boards and a moment later the bed springs began their rhythmical squeak.

She'd almost finished packing when there was a thump on the door. She opened it cautiously. Mr Karalis, the landlord, stood on the landing. Two large men, one as broad as he was high, stood right behind him.

'Oh,' she said, 'I'd forgotten it was rent day.'

She opened the door wider and Mr Karalis walked in. She handed him the rent book and the money. Putting the cash into a pouch on his waist, he handed the book back. 'Wish they was all like-a you,' he remarked. 'Pay on time.'

'I won't be here next week,' she said. 'I'm leaving.'

His eyes narrowed. 'You have to give a week's notice,' he said coldly, 'or pay another week.'

'But I paid two weeks up front when I came here,' she protested. 'It's all in the book.'

'The rooms have to be rented all the time,' he said. 'I have expenses.'

What expenses? she thought bitterly. You never do repairs, the place is a pig-hole and overcrowded. 'I don't know if I have it right now,' she said. 'Give me your address and I'll send it on.'

'You pay now,' he said menacingly.

'But—' she began.

One of the heavies moved into the room alongside Mr Karalis.

She reached for her handbag, although she knew her purse was virtually empty. Her fingers were trembling. She'd seen what Mr Karalis and his thugs were capable of. When Sam Hawkins defaulted on the rent, he'd ended up in hospital with two broken ribs. Of course, he told everyone he'd slipped on the stairs but they all knew he'd been on the receiving end of a fist. It was at that moment that she remembered the pound note Granny had slipped into her pocket. She went to her coat hanging on the back of the door and pulled it out.

Mr Karalis took the money and gave her five bob change. 'Make sure you leave room clean and tidy,' he growled.

When he'd gone, she wedged the chair under the door handle. Then, sitting on the bed, for the first time in months she wept with relief.

A dense haze of blue tobacco smoke swirled around the room. It was so thick it was hard to make out people's faces. A couple of men looked up from the snooker table as he walked in, but apart from them, his entrance went unnoticed. Leslie wrinkled his nose. This might be one of the most popular clubs in Brighton, but the room smelled of beer, sweaty bodies and testosterone.

He made his way to the bar and ordered a pint of bitter. Perching on the bar stool, he was tempted to put his elbow down, but the wood was sticky with spilled drink and he didn't want to spoil his suit. He took out his packet of Player's Navy Cut and put a cigarette between his lips. As he fumbled for his lighter, someone struck a match in front of him. Without looking to see who had offered the light, he drew on the cigarette until the aroma filled his mouth. His heartbeat quickened, but he knew it was important to appear unruffled. His benefactor shook the match and threw it into the overflowing ashtray in front of them.

'Well now, Les,' said a gruff voice. 'How did you get on?'

Leslie picked a piece of tobacco from his tongue and tried to appear nonchalant. 'Not so good, Gerry,' he said casually, turning his head. 'Things didn't quite work out as I'd hoped, but don't worry. I'll get there.' He flashed a smile and for a moment he held his breath, until Gerry Carter, leader of the Carter gang, slapped him heartily between the shoulder blades.

'We're counting on you, Les,' he said. His tone was more of a threat than an encouragement and Leslie knew it.

34

He'd been with Carter's gang for a few months now. They were mostly into black marketeering and smuggling – rackets which brought in a reasonable amount of money with low-level risk – but now they wanted to move more upmarket. The plan they'd just put together, which included him, was far more ambitious than stealing a few cigarettes. If this came off, Leslie had dreams of being leader of his own outfit. His idol was Billy Hill, the Bandit King, a London mobster who, everyone agreed, looked so much like Humphrey Bogart it was creepy. Leslie emulated his snappy dressing, his smart suits and his trilby hat, but Billy was ruthless too. Compared to Billy Hill, Carter was small fry.

Leslie had been the one to come up with the idea but Carter and his gang had the manpower to put the plan together. They were taking most of the risk; Leslie simply had to find a suitable place to stash the haul until the heat died down, which was why he was so keen to have his grandfather's old garage. The place was an absolute wreck, but out on the Littlehampton Road, and only a few miles from Worthing, it was ideal. No one would take any notice of any unusual activity on the site if he was supposed to be renovating the property. Of course, he'd have to prepare a suitable room. Goods like that had to be looked after, and to that end he planned to get someone to clean up one of the bedrooms. The thought of handling dust and dirt with his own hands made Leslie shudder.

Gerry stared into his face. He was obviously waiting for some sort of explanation but Leslie wasn't going to be intimidated. 'Can I get you a drink?' he said. Damn, his voice was an octave higher than normal.

'I wanna know what the hold-up is,' said Gerry.

Leslie swallowed hard. He'd been so sure that by now he would have been able to give Gerry the go-ahead, but he hadn't counted on his stupid grandmother digging her heels in and refusing to let him have the garage. 'There's no hold-up,' he said, dragging on his cigarette again and blowing a smoke ring above his head. 'As soon as she's up to it, my grandmother is going to sign my grandfather's garage over to me.'

'A garage?' said Gerry, his eyebrows raised and a greedy smile on his lips.

'It's not up to much,' Leslie said quickly. He didn't want Gerry thinking he'd inherited some swanky place and he certainly didn't want him muscling in on it. The garage was his. He had plans for that place. 'But it'll make an excellent hiding place.'

'In that case,' Gerry said with a smile, 'I'll have a Scotch, and seeing as you've got everything in hand, you'd better make that a double.'

CHAPTER 3

When she first set eyes on the place, Sheila's heart sank. Ronnie had warned her that it was in a bit of a state, but she hadn't expected it to be almost derelict. Built in the heyday of British motoring in the 1930s, it had an attractive art deco half-dome over the doorway, but that was where its appeal both began and ended. The wooden double doors were splintered and broken in places and the hinges rusty. Old painted posters hung in shreds all over them and someone had drawn a chalk 'Kilroy was here' on the wall. Once she'd unlocked the door, they both had to use all their strength to push it open. A plank of wood clattered noisily to the floor. A bird, obviously trapped inside, flew up in panic and threw itself against the window.

Their first impression was one of clutter. Nobody had been in here for years. Granddad had bought the garage in 1939 and he'd worked there every day up until he'd had his first stroke in 1943. He hadn't stepped foot in the place for the past three years, but looking around at all this mess, it was hard to see what the old man had been doing in the years before.

It didn't look like a working garage; it was more of a dumping ground.

'Blimey,' said Ronnie. 'It's going to take an age to get this lot sorted out.'

The bird was still hurling itself at the window, which was covered with sacking. Sheila headed towards it in an attempt to get it to fly in the opposite direction and out of the open door. As she picked her way to the far end of the garage, she knocked her head against a couple of rusty bicycle wheels hanging from the rafters. The bird flew up towards the roof and rested on a paint shelf. Sheila reached up and pulled down the sacking to let the daylight in and then she opened the window. There was some shelving alongside the window, a storage area for small boxes of bits. Underneath the window and buried under bits of old engine parts, she came across various other boxes containing seven-pound tins. She picked one up, but she didn't recognize the brand.

'They look Canadian,' said Ronnie, coming up behind her. 'There was a Canadian camp near Lancing until they all went home last year. They must be black market or knocked off.'

The girls picked their way through old bicycle parts, a radiator from an Austin Seven Box Saloon from around 1933, a pram with only three wheels, a Bakelite radio, various jerry cans, orange boxes and broken chairs, old kettles and even a couple of road signs. The floor was covered in mouse and rat droppings. Something had been chewing up an old newspaper on the desk and the spiders had been busy everywhere. As they headed for the stairs, the bird finally flew out.

They had to brush their way through years of cobwebs to get to the first floor but they found the accommodation more or less as Ronnie had said. The bedrooms had been used for storage, but they could get two single beds or one double in each room or make one room into a sitting room. Because of the severe shortages after the war, what furniture they managed to get hold of would depend on what was available. The only real snag was that the glass in both windows was broken, which meant that pigeons had got in and left plenty of calling cards. The smell was awful.

The small kitchen area had an upright gas stove with a meter on the wall. It wasn't working, which was just as well because the whole place would have to be thoroughly cleaned before they could safely use it. Ronnie looked out of the window to discover that the back area behind the garage was a lot larger than they'd first thought. There was plenty to keep them busy and already she was imagining their vegetable plot and flower border next year. What a perfect way to forget what she'd left behind. At the far end of the property there was a building of some sort. At first glance, it looked like a pretty substantial shed.

Behind her, Sheila asked, 'Where's the bathroom?'

They found a bath under some boards in the kitchen area. To their astonishment, it was full of seven-pound tins like the ones they'd seen downstairs. Some had labels: strawberry jam, peaches and vegetable stew. The rest were a mystery, but every tin had a stamp on the lid, 'Property of the Royal Canadian Army'.

'So he must have been dealing in the black market,' said Ronnie.

'What on earth are we going to do with them?' asked Sheila.

'Well, we can't give them back, that's for sure,' said Ronnie. 'The Canadians are long gone.'

'It would be a criminal waste to dump them,' said Sheila. 'I can't remember the last time I ate peaches in syrup.'

'If we opened one of those tins for ourselves we'd be heartily sick of peaches by the time we'd emptied it,' Ronnie laughed, 'but they might be useful to keep as favours.'

Sheila frowned. 'Whatever do you mean?'

'It's going to take a lot more than scrubbing to sort this lot out,' said Ronnie with a wave of her hand. 'We can't afford to take too long before business is up and running and we may need to call on people with a bit of expertise to do the things we can't manage.'

'Like putting the gas back on?' said Sheila.

'Like putting the gas back on,' said Ronnie with a grin. 'We haven't got much money, so a little flutter of your eyebrows or a tin of peaches for the wife might be just what we need.'

'You crafty devil,' Sheila chuckled. 'I think it's a brilliant idea.'

Back downstairs, they found a toilet in the yard

outside, but it was only a bucket under a scrubbed wooden seat and it stank to high heaven.

At the end of the wilderness which had once been a garden, the shed was locked. Granny had only given them the one key so it looked as if they wouldn't be able to get in. They looked around until Ronnie found a key under the guttering above the door. Together they yanked open the unwieldy door. Inside there was a Morris 8 commercial van dating from 1934. Covered in dust, it had obviously been laid up for the duration. The back and front axles were jacked up and, unfortunately, at some time an animal had made a nest on the front passenger seat. The wooden flooring was in a poor state, but when Sheila looked under the bonnet, she was pleasantly surprised.

'Fan belt looks a bit dented,' she remarked, 'but otherwise it seems in reasonable shape.'

Behind the car, they found a couple of holdalls full of cigarettes. They were all British brands and it vaguely crossed Sheila's mind that they were in remarkably good condition considering Granddad must have left them there ages ago.

'I think these ought to be handed in,' said Sheila. 'There's far too many and if we start giving some away, we might end up being accused of receiving stolen goods.'

Ronnie agreed. 'But I suppose if we do, we'll have the police snooping around everywhere.'

Sheila wiped her hands together briskly. 'Probably.'

'Damn,' said Ronnie. 'Bang go our thanks-for-the-favour tins.'

Sheila looked thoughtful. 'We don't have to tell them everything, just give them the fags.' And so it was agreed.

As they came back up the garden to the garage, they were aware that they were being watched. A man sat at a bedroom window in the house opposite. He didn't react at all when they looked up, so Ronnie told Sheila to ignore him. 'He's probably just some nosy old sod,' she remarked.

They decided Ronnie should tackle the domestic area and Sheila the garage. 'You're more likely to know what's a tool and what's junk than I am,' said Ronnie.

Both girls were excited. For Sheila, it was her first opportunity to have a home of her own, albeit a shared one with her cousin. For Ronnie, this venture was making her think that she could finally put the horrors of the past behind her and maybe even assuage just a little of her guilt.

'Our main problem is water,' said Sheila, skilfully wrapping a scarf into a turban around her head. 'We can't clean without it.'

Although the garage was fairly near some shops while Granny's place in South Farm Road was a fair distance away, to keep asking for water from either source either meant troubling strangers or a tidy walk with a bucket, so neither option was ideal.

'There's an old mug of tea on the bench so there must be a source somewhere on the premises,' said Ronnie. 'Let's go back up to the flat and look for a stopcock.'

Twenty minutes of searching drew a blank and by

that time they'd realized they had no method of heating water even if they found it.

'Hello there.'

They were startled by a man's voice and clattered downstairs to find the village bobby standing in the workshop. The policeman was the wrong side of fifty, portly and with a slightly florid complexion. Sheila noticed that there were beads of perspiration on his top lip and that he had bicycle clips on his trouser legs. He probably wasn't very fit, but he had a pleasant face and spoke in a fatherly tone.

'I was just doing my rounds,' he said, 'when I saw the door was open. Do you mind telling me what you're doing here?'

'Actually, we're getting ready to open up again,' said Ronnie. 'The garage belonged to my grandfather.'

'So you're Agnes and Tom's girl?' he asked.

'Agnes and Tom were my parents,' Sheila interrupted.

'Sheila is my cousin,' said Ronnie. 'My parents are Jean and Bill.'

The policeman beamed. 'I went to school with Tom,' he said. 'I don't know if he ever mentions me. Cecil Longfellow. How is the old rogue?'

There was an awkward silence, then Sheila said, 'He and Mum died earlier this year in a gas explosion.'

Sergeant Longfellow looked both shocked and embarrassed. 'I am sorry, girl,' said. 'Me and my big mouth.'

While Sheila waved her hand dismissively, he cleared his throat. 'So you're planning to start the business up again?'

'We are,' said Ronnie. 'Sheila is a fully trained mechanic.'

'Actually—' Sheila began, but she was interrupted by Sergeant Longfellow.

'Well, that'll be a first,' he chuckled. 'I can't say that old Basil ever put in much effort to make it a going concern and you say you're going to do it all on your own?' There was a hint of admiration in his voice.

Ronnie glanced at Sheila. 'We'd like to, but the only thing is,' she said, shaking her head sadly, 'we can't find the stopcock.'

An hour later, they had their first bucket of hot water. Not only had Sergeant Longfellow located the stopcock (under the garage floor and covered by a metal lid), but he had also persuaded Mr Hurst, who ran a nursery just down the road, to loan them a paraffin primus stove. While the water was boiling, the girls had taken Sergeant Longfellow down the overgrown garden to show him the holdalls and cigarettes.

'They're nothing to do with us,' Sheila said cautiously.

'The wily old fox,' said Longfellow, searching through the bags. 'I had an idea he was dealing in the black market but I could never pin anything on him. I must have gone through that garage a dozen times but, fool that I was, I never once came down here.'

The girls helped him strap the holdalls onto the back of his bicycle and he set off. 'We won't get into trouble, will we?' Sheila asked.

'Bless your life, no,' he said, checking once more

that they were secure. 'And if you need any more help, just let me know.'

As soon as he'd gone, the girls shook hands and had a bit of a laugh. After that, Ronnie tackled the bedroom and kitchen while Sheila cleaned and tidied the garage itself. They worked steadily until three thirty when hunger and fatigue finally got the better of them.

They were dog-tired when they finally went to bed. For the time being, they had a couple of camp beds on the garage floor. It was far from ideal, but Sheila was asleep almost before she hit the pillow. In the middle of the night, she was startled awake as Ronnie cried out in her sleep. She began making incomprehensible noises and she sounded in distress. It only lasted a minute or two and then she turned over and began a gentle snore.

At breakfast, Sheila wondered whether to mention Ronnie's dream, but by then it didn't seem so important.

The next few days were exhausting, but tremendously fulfilling. They began first thing in the morning and kept going until hunger or the need for a break forced them to stop. Thanks to Cecil Longfellow, they didn't lack helpers either. Some were a little more welcome than others. Neither of them liked the look of the man who watched them from above the newsagent's, but thankfully he never came down into the street. In the evenings, they found themselves with off-duty policemen, a shopkeeper's wife, Lily Harris, Elsie Tunnock, who lived on the corner of Highfield Road, a few young lads and a couple of boys from the orphanage, who were all still at school. In no time at all, Sheila had made a pile of junk ready for the rag-and-bone man. Rusty screws, bent nails, old washers and various lengths of old piping would no doubt be melted down to use for something else. He'd also taken the broken chairs which were beyond repair or too big a job to make a profit, but quite what he would do with them was beyond her. Years of bird droppings were scrubbed from every surface and the shelves left tidy with labels on all the boxes. The lads made a start on cleaning up the old van and pushed the stuffing back into the seat.

Upstairs began to take shape as well. Before long, the kitchen was looking more like a kitchen and after using loads of bleach and elbow grease, Ronnie had made the toilet in the yard look as clean as a hospital bathroom. One evening, some men from the pub set to work at the very bottom of the property digging a deep hole to use as an earth closet until the girls could afford to install a proper chain-pulling loo.

'Take my tip,' one old boy told them confidentially, 'a little drop of wee does wonders for yer tomatoes.'

It became obvious that the previous owner, the one before Granddad, had used his equipment for more than simply mending cars. They found old kettles and saucepans waiting to be repaired, although presumably the customers had long since given up on their items. Still, finding the old welding gear gave Sheila another string to her bow. Not many people owned their own car, but everyone had a kettle or a saucepan, and if the metal sprang a leak, the shortages in the country meant that it was very hard to find replacements. She stacked any decent lengths of wood against the shed at the bottom of the garden when they had run out of space in the garage. They might come in useful for something too.

They also unearthed an old paraffin dispenser. One of the off-duty bobbies cleaned it out for them, ejecting a nest of slow worms and a pile of debris in the process. Come the winter, there would be plenty of people who wanted to fill their paraffin heaters.

After much deliberation, they decided to buy a pint for each of the policemen at the pub, and when they had departed, they gave a mystery tin to the other helpers. It caused quite a stir when they were sharing them out, and for a couple of days afterwards they heard stories along the lines of, 'My wife shook the tin when I gave it to her. She was so sure it was peaches, but when we opened it up we were sitting at the table with a jug of custard only to find we had a seven-pound tin of peas!' The schoolboys shared out a stack of ancient books and comics Granddad had saved for some reason and left in a big trunk under the double bed. They looked as pleased as punch as they set off with a pile of *Dandy*s and *Beano*s under their arms, although one boy wasn't interested in anything else except a book of watercolour butterflies. Finally, on June 13th, after a week and two days, the place was ready to go. The small table in the kitchen had scrubbed up well, as had the bath under the wooden boards. There was only one usable kitchen chair, but Sheila said she'd fix the chair in the garage as soon as she could. 'It only needs to have the leg put back on and straightened out a bit,' she assured her cousin. They had bought two single beds, a small chest of drawers, a kitchen cabinet, a meat safe and two easy chairs from a second-hand repository by Worthing Central station. They didn't have any pictures on the walls, but taking pride of place on the dresser was the picture the street photographer had taken the day of Granddad's funeral. When they stood before it, it felt like it marked the start of a brand-new life and perhaps an adventure as yet unknown.

'All we have to do now,' said Ronnie as they waved goodbye to the last of their helpers, 'is to get the petrol pumps up and running, and then the Becket garage will be open for business.' Sheila went indoors. Ronnie glanced up at the window in the building opposite. The man had lifted the curtain and was watching them again. Ronnie frowned crossly. He'd been nosing at them for most of the day. All at once, they made eye contact. Ronnie stuck out her tongue, tossed her head and went inside.

CHAPTER 4

As soon as the work on the garage was completed, Granny decided to go and live with her daughter Jean, Ronnie's mother.

'Are you really sure about this?' Ronnie asked.

'I've got nothing to keep me in Worthing,' she said, 'only memories, and I'd rather leave all of them behind.'

Ronnie and Sheila were understanding and they also felt a sense of relief. If they were to make a go of the garage, they would have little time to keep an eye on Granny, especially in winter. Winifred Peters was a capable woman at the moment, but she was no spring chicken. Her only remaining daughter, Jean – Ronnie and Leslie's mother – lived in Warminster in Wiltshire, and it seemed sensible for Win to move in with her. At first Jean's husband, Bill, had refused to take Milly, Granny's little dog, but in the end she'd said she wouldn't come without her.

The girls decided to give Win a bit of a send-off with a small tea party so she could invite a few old friends and neighbours in before Bill and Jean came back to Worthing to collect her. To their great surprise,

Leslie said he would come to say goodbye to Granny too.

Win rented her cottage, so once she'd given notice it only remained to call in the house-clearance people. She kept a few bits and pieces and gave her grand-daughters first pick of what was left. Granny's kitchen table was in much better condition than the one at the garage, so they had asked for that. Added to this, they took the best pick of cups and saucers, and the pots and pans she was leaving behind. By the time they'd finished, Ronnie and Sheila had everything they could possibly need.

That night, Ronnie had another bad dream. Sheila woke to the sound of her crying. It sounded as if she was in genuine distress. Should she mention it or would it only embarrass her cousin? Obviously something was playing on Ronnie's mind.

On the day before the party, Ronnie made sandwiches and cakes with the meagre ration allowance they had now. In some respects, life was even more frugal than during the war. There was talk of bread being rationed since the awful summer weather was ruining the coun-try's wheat crop. All this was on top of the bacon ration being cut to three ounces a week and cooking fat being cut down to one ounce a week. Ronnie biked to Granny's house and laid the table ready for the afternoon.

'I shall miss you both,' Granny said as Ronnie was leaving. 'I don't know if I'll ever see you again.'

'Of course you will,' said Ronnie, giving her a hug.

'Sheila and I will pop up to Warminster to see you before Christmas, I promise.'

The old lady's eyes filled with tears.

'Come on now, Granny,' Ronnie cajoled. 'You'll be fine. We'll all have a lovely time this afternoon and then you'll be off for your next adventure.'

Win chuckled. Those were the very words she used to say to Ronnie when she was upset at the thought of going back home after her holidays. Now, twenty or so years later, the tables were turned.

'You know, you never did tell me what happened to you during the war,' said Granny.

Ronnie felt her face colour. 'Best left dead and buried,' she said stiffly.

'Did you have a young man?' her grandmother asked.

'He died,' Ronnie said, the lie slipping easily off her tongue.

'Oh, my dear, I'm so sorry,' said Granny.

Ronnie shrugged her shoulders. 'It happens.'

Win gave her a hug. 'Better to have loved and lost than never to have loved at all,' she said sagely.

Ronnie nodded. Had anyone else given her that old cliché she would have blasted them into next week. Granny meant well, but what would she say if she knew the truth? What if she knew about the lies and the deceit? Ronnie felt the guilt sliding back onto her shoulders. When would this ever end?

Putting a big smile on her face, Ronnie got onto her bike. 'See you later,' she called cheerily.

51

'Did I tell you Leslie is coming?' Win called after her.
'Yes, that'll be nice,' Ronnie called back.

Leslie hated his grandmother's place. It always smelled.
He wasn't sure what the smell was – a mixture of
boiled cabbage, fish and Jeyes Fluid; an old people's
smell. He'd never enjoyed coming to stay when he was
a child, even if the beach was less than fifteen minutes
away. Now that he was here, the worst of it was that
he'd have to butter her up or she might cut him out
of her will altogether. It was bad enough that she'd
refused to let him have the garage. He'd had high
hopes with that one and he was determined to persuade
her that giving it to his sister was a really bad idea.
He'd tell her straight. Ronnie didn't know the first
thing about cars. She was more interested in baby's
nappies and wiping candlestick noses. He shuddered.
Ugh. Young kids were so revolting.

He knew he'd overstepped the mark with his
outburst at Granddad's funeral. That's why he'd stayed
away for a while. It had given a chance for the heat
to die down, but he'd have to sort something out pretty
darned quick. The job wasn't far off now and Carter
was breathing down his neck all the time.

He rattled the door knocker and waited, flowers in
hand. They'd cost him a ruddy fortune, but the florist
had done them up like a dog's dinner and when Granny
opened the door he was all warm smiles and tender
looks.

'Oh,' she cried, 'you're early.'

'Am I?' he said innocently. 'I thought you said half past two.'

'Half past three,' she corrected, 'but never mind, you're here now and I've got you all to myself for once.'

The expression on his face hadn't changed. 'How are you bearing up?'

'I'm fine.'

He thrust the flowers at her.

'Ooh, they're lovely,' she said as she led the way inside. 'You know, we didn't get to have a proper chat at Granddad's funeral, but now you can tell me all about yourself. What are you doing these days? Have you got a girlfriend yet?'

She made to give him a hug, but Leslie took off his coat first. He didn't want anybody's greasy fingermarks on his expensive camel-hair coat. It cost an arm and a leg. Of course, he hadn't paid a bean for it, but that wasn't the point.

She showed him into the sitting room and insisted on making a pot of tea. 'Would you like a sandwich now?'

'No, no,' said Leslie. 'Please don't trouble yourself on my account.'

While she was gone, Leslie rummaged around in the drop-drawer dresser. He was looking for the deeds to the garage, but he was out of luck. He did, however, find a Post Office savings book with twenty-two pounds in it. He slipped it into his pocket and rushed to sit down again as he heard his grandmother coming along the corridor. When she came back into the room with the tea, it took a few minutes to get around to talking about the garage.

'I hope you don't mind me saying,' he began, 'but I wonder if you realize Ronnie doesn't know one end of a car from the other. I know she's full of good intentions, Granny, but you really need a man on the job.'

'Ronnie might not know about cars,' his grandmother conceded, 'but Sheila is a mechanic.'

Leslie spluttered into his teacup. 'But she's a woman!'

'I know,' said his grandmother, a smile tugging at the corners of her mouth. 'And you should see the difference those girls have made. The place looks as good as new.'

Leslie's nostrils flared. His bloody interfering sister again. How dare she? She knew he'd wanted that garage. It was always the same. Whenever he made plans, she always had to stick her oar in and ruin everything. He stared at the carpet, struggling to control his temper and hardly hearing what his grandmother was saying about getting the petrol tanks cleaned out and maybe opening a small shop on site. This wasn't what he'd planned.

'Are you all right, dear?' she suddenly asked. 'You look rather pale.'

Leslie looked up sharply. 'Fine,' he said. 'Look, I'm sorry but I can't stay any longer. I've just remembered I have to meet someone this afternoon.'

'Oh,' she said, clearly disappointed. 'But you can't go yet. The others will be here soon.'

He stood to his feet. 'Sorry. Another time maybe.'

* * *

The two girls had flopped into bed exhausted after another hectic day. The petrol tanks had been professionally cleaned and tomorrow the tanker would be here with the first consignment of fuel. They'd had a few orders for kettle repairs and somebody wanted their bicycle stripped down and rebuilt. Under the huge bramble bush at the bottom of the garden, they'd found a small caravan. It was in a bit of a state, but Sheila wanted to set up a small shop inside. As things were still a bit quiet, Ronnie planned to get the bucket and mop out and start cleaning it up.

Their lives were now perfectly organized. They had arranged to have their groceries and meat delivered to the door, which saved having to go down to the town each day to shop. Mr Price of Oakland Dairies, who delivered milk in the area, would include them on his rounds. He was a pleasant-enough fellow to talk to but Sheila guessed he must begin his rounds without bothering to wash when he got up. By the time he reached the garage, especially in the warmer weather, he smelled quite whiffy. Jokingly, and only behind his back, Ronnie called him Armpit Price.

The little tea party that afternoon had been a great success. Their grandmother had shed a tear or two, but everybody agreed she was doing the right thing. Ronnie's parents would take her back with them tomorrow.

They'd said their goodnights and fallen asleep almost at once. In the middle of the night, Sheila was woken up by a strange sound. It made her jump and, as she became fully awake, she found her heart was pounding. The noise was scary, but as yet she didn't understand why. It took a few seconds to realize that it was Ronnie. She was writhing in her bed, throwing herself all over the place, obviously in the grip of some terrible dream.

Sheila sat up, supported by her elbow, and called out, 'Ronnie!'

Her cousin slept on and then began to scream. The bed was too far away to reach, so Sheila called more loudly. 'Ronnie, wake up, you're having a nightmare!' But Ronnie's cries only got worse.

When Sheila put on the light she was thoroughly alarmed by what she saw. Her cousin was bathed in perspiration. Her face was contorted and she was begging someone to stop. Sheila got out of bed and padded over. 'Ronnie,' she said gently. 'Wake up. You're having a bad dream.' She shook Ronnie's arm, then when there was no response, she shook a little harder. 'Ronnie!'

Her cousin let out another cry and, pushing Sheila away, she sat bolt upright, her chest heaving and her eyes wild.

'It's all right,' said Sheila. 'You're quite safe. It was only a dream.'

Ronnie turned her head as if seeing Sheila for the first time and burst into tears.

It took some minutes to calm her. Sheila sat on the edge of the bed. 'Would you like to talk about it? It's obviously distressed you a lot.'

At first Ronnie shook her head, but eventually Sheila

managed to cajole her into saying what was wrong. 'Is it because of what happened to you in the war?'

Ronnie nodded miserably.

'I thought you said you were in Australia,' said Sheila. 'Whatever happened to you that you should be this distressed by a dream?'

'It's a long story,' said Ronnie.

'I'm a good listener,' said Sheila.

'You'll hate me,' Ronnie said bleakly.

'Of course I won't,' said Sheila.

They stared at each other.

'Look,' said Sheila. 'Something is clearly upsetting you. I promise I won't judge you or anything. Let me help . . . please.'

Ronnie pulled the pillow onto her lap. How could she tell her the whole truth?

'Ronnie?'

'I thought I was really lucky to be able to go abroad as a nanny,' Ronnie began. 'I was only eighteen. Usually people have to be ages old before they can travel with a family, but we all got on so well that Mrs Lyle offered to take me with her to Singapore.'

'Sounds like an amazing opportunity,' said Sheila, although hearing the word 'Singapore' she had an inkling of what was to come.

'Her husband was an army officer.'

Putting the pillow under her head, Ronnie pushed herself further up the bed and tugged at the counterpane over her knees. 'It was incredible in the beginning,' she went on. 'I had a day off a week and they let me go to dances on the base sometimes. I met some lovely people.' She began picking at the fringes around the edge of the counterpane, suddenly aware that she might be saying too much. If Sheila knew the half of it, she would hate her. She glanced up at her cousin's face. 'There was no one in particular,' she said quickly, 'except perhaps Wally. He never actually asked me out, but we used to enjoy dancing together.'

'Was he in the army as well?'

Ronnie nodded and sighed. 'When the war reached Singapore, everyone was evacuated,' she went on. 'I went with my employer and the two children – Ruth, she was three and a half, and her sister, Elspeth, was twenty months.'

'Couldn't they have come back to England?' asked Sheila. 'Or maybe gone to Australia?'

'Yes, yes, they could have done if . . .' The words died on her lips and Ronnie took a deep breath. 'At first, Mrs Lyle refused to go,' she began again. 'I supposed it was out of loyalty to her husband.' The voice in her head said, *You know darned well that wasn't the reason*. Ronnie chewed the side of her cheek. 'But she did make arrangements for the children to be sent home with me.'

'So what happened?' Sheila asked quietly.

Ronnie swallowed hard, her eyes filling with tears. Now was the moment to tell her. *Go on, tell her . . .* But she couldn't. She just couldn't. 'Mrs Lyle had sent me to the club as her husband had arranged, but we couldn't find the permits . . .' *Liar.* She broke off and stared into the far distance before clearing her throat and beginning again. 'When the Japs came on the fifteenth of February, the police and army came to the bungalow and told us that we had to leave as quickly as we could.' *Half-truth . . . liar, liar.*

'That was in . . . ?'

'1942,' said Ronnie. She was talking more quickly now. 'When we got to the jetty, we found a steamship waiting for us. I persuaded Mrs Lyle to come on board with her children and we left Singapore that night.'

'Thank God for that,' Sheila breathed.

'But we didn't make it,' said Ronnie. She stopped to blow her nose. 'A Japanese warship found us within moments of setting out to sea. The captain had no choice but to surrender. They had their guns pointing right at us and we were all taken as prisoners of war.'

'It must have been awful,' said Sheila. It certainly sounded far more terrifying that anything she had experienced. She reached out and laid her hand on Ronnie's wrist.

Her cousin, still staring into the middle distance, carried on. 'When they put us ashore, we were terribly overcrowded. We had no proper bathroom and we had to sleep on concrete slabs.' She searched her hanky for a dry area on which to blow her nose, and Sheila stood up and went to get a clean handkerchief from the drawer. 'Thanks,' said Ronnie. 'Every time we moved,' she continued (telling the truth was so much easier), 'they shoved us around in cattle trucks and barges. I looked after the children as best I could, but it was very hard.'

Her eyes suddenly flashed with anger. 'Did you know, those bloody Japs confiscated all the medicines from the Red Cross parcels. We didn't even have quinine for the malaria.' Her voice was rising as she became more and more angry. 'They starved us and we had to scrounge what we could from the jungle. We ate weeds and grass – we even boiled banana skins to get a bit of nourishment. Everybody got beriberi and my periods stopped. I didn't have one for two years.' Her voice drifted. 'The shock and malnutrition, I suppose.'

'Oh God, Ronnie, that's awful,' said Sheila. 'What about the children?'

'They had their fair share of illnesses, but it was far worse for their mother. She just gave up. I nursed her as best I could, but in the end she died.' Ronnie suppressed a sob. Her mind was in turmoil. Where was the harm if her cousin thought of Mrs Lyle in this way? The truth was too shocking and for all her faults the poor woman deserved better than that. Sheila moved to the other side of the bed and pulled her cousin into her arms. 'I tried so hard, but it was too much for her,' Ronnie choked. 'It shouldn't have happened. Goddamn it, it never would have happened if she'd had proper food and medicine.'

Sheila held her until she'd finished crying, then Ronnie sat up and blew her nose again. 'I'm sorry I'm making such a song and dance of it,' she said. 'It's just that I've never really spoken about this before. All I wanted was to forget all about it, get on with my life and rid myself of this awful guilt.'

'What on earth have you got to feel guilty about?' cried Sheila. 'I've never gone through anything as bad as that. You cry all you want. My mum always used to say if you're upset, it's better out than in.'

Ronnie was beginning to regain control. 'Mrs Lyle was only about forty-five. We had to dig her grave and bury her there.' *It should have been you* . . . the voice said.

Sheila shook her head in disbelief. 'What about the children?'

'Amazingly,' said Ronnie, 'both her children survived.'

'Then you did a fantastic job,' said Sheila, hoping it would bring some comfort, but Ronnie only waved her hand in despair.

'And what about you?' Sheila went on. 'You must have been quite ill when you were released.'

'I was,' said Ronnie. She lifted the hem of her night-dress and Sheila stared in horror at her ugly scars. 'I had ulcers all over my legs and I only weighed four and a half stone.'

'Four and a half stone?' Sheila squeaked.

Ronnie nodded. 'They kept me in hospital in Singapore for two weeks. I had to have vitamin injections and lots of other treatment.'

'I can well believe that,' said Sheila. 'How did you get home?'

'My employer came to the hospital,' said Ronnie, her cheeks burning. 'He was so grateful that I had looked after Ruth and Elspeth that he offered me my old job back.'

'So he survived,' Sheila gasped. The horrors of Japanese prisoner-of-war camps were legendary and it was unusual to hear of someone surviving internment for so long.

'He hadn't exactly had a picnic,' said Ronnie. 'He'd spent some time in Changi Prison. It came as a great shock to him to learn of the death of his wife.' She closed her eyes as she remembered his strangled cry when she'd told him.

'Was that when you went to Geelong?' Sheila asked.

Ronnie nodded. 'But I couldn't stay. I just couldn't.'

'So you came back home on your own?' said Sheila.

Ronnie nodded. 'It was far too expensive for someone like me to fly, so Major Lyle got me a passage on a cargo boat,' she said. 'He found this ship which was bringing wool back to England. They had twelve passengers on board and I was one of them. I arrived back at the beginning of this year.' She reached out and squeezed Sheila's arm. 'I'm so sorry to have woken you up like this.'

'No, no, not at all,' said Sheila. 'I only wish I could do more to help.'

'You know the most galling thing of all?' said Ronnie, a hint of bitterness creeping into her voice. 'Because I was a civilian and not in the military, I got sweet bugger all from the government by way of compensation. The Yanks gave their ex-POWs twenty thousand dollars each. Twenty thousand! But not me. Not even a thank you. For me it's: so what, you came home, didn't you? Just get on with it.'

'I got nothing for my parents' house either,' said Sheila. 'If they'd been killed by a bomb, I might have been entitled to two hundred pounds or so, which at the very least would have helped me buy a small place of my own.'

'Weren't they insured?'

'The policy didn't cover explosions,' said Sheila. Their eyes met and then she added light-heartedly, 'Sometimes life is a real bummer, isn't it?'

Ronnie smiled through her tears as she looked up at the ceiling. 'You might be right there.' And the voice in her said, *Maybe that's all you deserve.*

Sheila yawned. 'But now, thanks to Granny, we've got this place.'

Ronnie squeezed her arm, her eyes glistening. 'And no matter how hard it is, we're going to make a go of it.'

'Absolutely,' said Sheila. There was a small silence, then she added, 'Fancy a cup of tea?'

CHAPTER 5

The little caravan proved to be quite a surprise. It had been almost totally hidden by the brambles and at first glance Ronnie thought it had remained untouched for years. However, on closer inspection the bramble was easily lifted off and although the outside of the caravan was very dirty, inside it had been totally gutted and was reasonably clean. The floor was a bit bouncy, but apart from that it seemed watertight and sturdy. If they were going to use it for a shop, they'd have to move it up towards the entrance and closer to the road. Customers couldn't be expected to wander all the way down the overgrown garden through the weeds to get to it.

'Without a car it's far too heavy for us to move on our own,' said Sheila. 'We'll have to ask for more help.'

By this time the girls had gained a bit of a reputation. When they queued for the sparse supplies at the shops, the local housewives who lived near Thomas A Becket would gossip about the plucky young women who were living over the garage. By the time those stories had reached the pub itself, there was no disguising the admiration they had inspired in others, so once the request was voiced, Ronnie and Sheila had plenty of offers of help and new friendships were being forged. One thing was odd, though – Ronnie noticed that whenever the people from the Becket gathered, the man opposite watched from his window.

Their first social invitation came a few days later. Peninnah Albright, Elsie Tunnock's daughter, had tickets for a play being put on in the Archbishop's Palace in Tarring and in the evening the four of them set off at six forty-five to walk down to the village. They came to a T-shaped building with a gable end and Peninnah told them something of the building's history. Apparently, the Archbishop's Palace had been the original manor house way back in the thirteenth century. Over the years, it had been used as a home, then a charity school, and around 1910 it became the parish hall for St Andrew's church. Tradition had it that Thomas Becket, the archbishop martyred in the twelfth century by Henry II's men, had visited the area, and some said St Richard of Chichester, the patron saint of Sussex, also came. Certainly, the village of Tarring was very old with several ancient buildings still standing and in use.

'You'll have to excuse my daughter,' Elsie said good-naturedly as they listened to Peninnah's story. 'Once she's got a bee in her bonnet, there's no stopping her.'

'It sounds fascinating,' said Ronnie. 'You certainly know a lot about it.'

'I always loved history,' Peninnah said. 'Even at school.'

Peninnah was what Sheila's mother would have called a sturdy girl. Stocky, with dark curly hair, she had a ready laugh and was always looking for a bit of fun. She was married to a railwayman, and even though she had two boys, Alan, aged twelve, and Geoffrey, who was six, she didn't look a day over twenty herself. Ronnie fumbled over her name a couple of times. 'Call me Pen,' she said with a laugh. 'Everybody does.'

'It's a lovely name,' said Sheila. 'Is it Welsh?'

'Dear Lord, no,' said Pen. 'It's a Biblical name. Most people know the story of Hannah, the woman in the Old Testament who was desperate to have a baby. Well, Peninnah was the other wife of the same man.' She put her hand to her mouth to shield what she was saying from her mother, who had gone on ahead of them into the hall. 'I reckon Mum got the two names muddled up because Peninnah was a nasty piece of work, and d'you know what – I've been trying to live it down ever since!' She threw back her head and cackled loudly.

The play was great fun and they had a good evening. The St Andrew's Players were excellent and Ronnie said she found it hard to believe they were only amateurs. During the interval, tea was served in the hall and Sheila and Ronnie got to meet some more of the people who lived locally. There were a couple of war widows, out for the evening because someone had set up a babysitting group which took turns to give single mothers a night off. It was thanks to Pen that they met Mrs Edwards, who ran the children's home along Offington Lane. Sheila took the opportunity to thank her for letting the boys help when they'd moved in. Everybody admired her because, unlike the popular image, she ran the home as closely as she could to a normal home, and when the children were old enough to leave, she made it clear that they always had a place to come back to. Cecil Longfellow was there too and eager to hear how well they were getting on at the garage. Sheila found herself talking to Mr Hurst from the nursery and before the evening was out she had secured an order to supply him with paraffin for his glasshouse heaters. 'You're a lot closer than Broadwater,' he told her, 'and I need a reliable and regular supply, especially when the spring comes and I start planting.'

'And we'd be pleased to have your custom,' said Sheila.

The girls linked arms as they walked home.

'I think we're going to be all right here,' said Ronnie.

'Course we are,' said Sheila with a grin.

The day they moved the caravan, Ronnie and Sheila had rolled their sleeves up to help, but of course the men treated them as if they were far too fragile to lift anything heavier than the kettle to make the tea. They would rush to their side with a 'Here, let me. You don't want to go straining yourself. That's much too heavy for a little thing like you.'

Ronnie and Sheila were grateful, but they also enjoyed a giggle about their over-protective neighbours. However, one person who managed to impress Sheila was PC Keller. He was one of the off-duty policemen who had been sent up to the garage by Cecil Longfellow. Tall, dark and handsome, with a dashing smile, Matthew Keller was the kind of man who made Sheila's knees go weak every time she looked at him. Perhaps this was the man of her dreams. She flirted a little and it didn't take long before he'd invited her to the pictures, although it proved a little difficult to find a time when they were both free. Sheila was working every day except Wednesday afternoon and Sunday, and Matthew had erratic shifts.

'We policemen have to be available seven days a week,' he reminded her, but as it turned out, he was free on Wednesday evening. Sheila was already looking forward to her date.

The caravan looked quite good on the forecourt. Ronnie put a notice on the side saying 'Opening Soon' but as yet there was no hint as to what they were going to sell inside. It didn't matter too much. As she painted it up, it only added to the mystery and kept the customers watching out.

In fact, Ronnie and Sheila had no idea what to sell in the caravan. They were indebted to the people of Thomas A Becket so it seemed churlish to market something which could be bought in one of their shops. That ruled out sweets, bread and groceries. Ronnie suggested starting a lending library, but that idea didn't really catch on.

While Ronnie had been sorting out the caravan, Sheila had bagged her first real customer. Doctor Rodway, who lived in Tarring village, needed a service on his car very quickly. Sheila turned it around in a morning and he went away singing her praises. That evening they banked their first cheque and Ronnie entered it in the books.

Now that the Becket garage was well and truly open, people came to them with all sorts of requests. Some were unusual, like the one from Pen's mother, Elsie Tunnock.

'I need a bit of space,' she told them. 'I've been given a pile of redundant ARP blankets. I'm planning to dye them a lovely shade of blue in the old tin bath out of doors, but I don't have enough room to hang them up to dry. Can you help?'

Ronnie and Sheila were only too pleased to return a favour. By tying a rope between the old apple tree and the fence post at the bottom of the garden, Sheila and Ronnie managed to rig up two long washing lines. Soon after Pen's kids went back to school after the summer holidays, Elsie and her daughter managed to pick the first warm and dry day in weeks. By lunchtime no fewer than eight pretty blue blankets were on the line, flapping in the breeze.

'I reckon I could make some lovely kiddies' coats out of that lot,' said Elsie.

Sheila agreed. 'At first glance you might even think they were velvet.'

'Only if you had a speck of dust in your eye,' Ronnie chuckled.

It was Wednesday and half-day closing at the garage. They were sitting on kitchen chairs out the back, drinking tea and doing their best to soak up the sunshine. Pen glanced at her watch. 'I've got to get Geoffrey from school.'

'I'd better get going too,' said Elsie. 'If I'm going to make a start on those coats, I'll have to bike into Broadwater for some cotton.'

Ronnie frowned. 'Why Broadwater? Won't the Tarring shops do?'

'There isn't a haberdasher down there,' said Elsie. 'Woolworths in Broadwater is the nearest place, and you have to go right down into Worthing if you want to buy wool and knitting needles.'

A slow smile drifted across Ronnie's face. 'Thanks for that, Elsie,' she said.

'What?'

'You've given me a good idea,' said Ronnie. 'Now I know what we're going to sell in the caravan.'

Matthew took Sheila to see *Way to the Stars*, a war picture about an RAF squadron starring Michael Redgrave and Basil Radford. It was more the sort of film a man would enjoy, but there were moments of romance, especially when Matthew held her hand in the darkness. Afterwards he walked her home. The nights were getting chilly, but she threaded her arm through his and they walked briskly.

'So tell me about yourself,' he said. 'Have you always lived in Worthing?'

'Heavens, no,' she cried. 'I was born and brought up in London.'

'Is this your first time away from home?'

'I left home in 1942 when I was called up into the ATS,' Sheila said. 'What a shock that was.'

Matthew laughed. 'Bit of a rude awakening, eh?'

'I should say,' said Sheila. 'I was sent up country for basic training. Six weeks of medicals, injections, general knowledge tests, and all the dos and don'ts of army life. It was worse than school: lights out at ten and reveille at six.'

Matthew navigated her around a free-standing board outside a shop.

'I can't tell you how much I hated those first few weeks,' said Sheila. 'Even the underwear was awful.'

Matthew laughed again.

'One good thing,' Sheila went on, 'when we were done, we were allowed a weekend home before moving on to our new billets.' She looked up at him. 'What about you? What did you do in the war?'

'I was called up in '41,' he said. 'We had to go to Yorkshire for our basic training. Beautiful countryside, but when you're on a ten-mile route march with a full pack on your back and wearing brand-new boots, I can assure you it's not much fun.'

'Did you go abroad?' Sheila asked.

He shook his head. 'I was a Red Cap. Not very exciting although I did once capture a German parachutist.'

'Sounds terrifying.'

'Not really,' said Matthew. 'He'd bailed out of his plane and injured his ankle, so he didn't put up much of a resistance.' Sheila chuckled. She liked this man.

She could do a lot worse than him if she were looking for the marrying type.

They had come to the railway crossing and had to wait for a train to pass. 'I was part of the D-Day landings, but only on this side of the channel,' Matthew went on. 'I spent my war mostly guarding military equipment and arresting men who had gone AWOL.'

'And now you've joined the police force,' said Sheila.

'Kind of got the taste for it,' he said with a smile.

You're good company too, she thought to herself, returning his smile.

When they reached the garage, he looked down at his watch. 'My landlady is quite strict even though I'm a copper,' he said apologetically. 'I have to go. Would you like to do this again sometime?'

'Yes,' said Sheila, doing her best not to sound too keen. 'That would be lovely.'

He gave her a peck on the cheek and set off back to town. Sheila stood by the open door for a second or two watching him until he turned the corner of Rectory Road and disappeared. What a nice man. What a lovely evening.

Something made her shiver and she looked around nervously. What was that? Just for a second, she had the feeling she was being watched. Ridiculous, she eventually told herself. Why would anyone be spying on a country garage?

Their grandfather had been lazy with his bookkeeping. The pile of papers on his desk, the shelf and in the drawers took them ages to sort out. He'd left some debts as well, but they dated back to 1939 when he'd first acquired the garage. Clearly his creditors had long since given up any hope of getting their money back. In fact, it looked as if he had let the business slide fairly early on. Ronnie was left wondering what he was actually doing on the premises and how he earned a living.

It was while Sheila was at the pictures with Matthew that Ronnie started going through the books. She came across a chequebook and a letter which was rather puzzling. She read and reread it, trying to make sense of it. She'd have to reply to it, but she decided she needed to talk to Sheila before she did anything.

Sheila woke with a start. What was that noise? She turned her head towards Ronnie's bed, but her cousin was sleeping like a baby. She still had the occasional nightmare though they were nowhere near as awful as before. Talking about her experiences seemed to help, although Ronnie found it very hard. The memory of the camp always reduced her to tears – the cruelty, the wasted lives. 'A lot of good people gone forever,' she would say, 'and for what?'

Sheila felt slightly guilty whenever she felt the need to weep for her parents. They may have passed away but they would have known nothing about it. One minute they were a happy middle-aged couple, glad to have survived the war, still in their own home, and the next they were no more. At least they hadn't suffered like Ronnie's employer. At least they had known that their daughter had come through the war safely. Her only wish was that they could have seen her happily married and settled down. Her lovely dad would never walk her down the aisle and her wonderful mum would never be mother-of-the-bride. Sheila sighed. Most of the girls who had served with her in the ATS were getting married or already married. If she didn't find someone soon, she'd be an old maid.

She heard another crack and froze. There. That noise again. It sounded as if someone was out back. Slipping out of bed, Sheila padded over to the window and stared out. The garden was shrouded in an eerie half-light, the area where they'd cleared the bramble bush dark and forbidding. The branches of the old apple tree stood out against the moonlight like the claws of some terrifying phantom. She leaned forward and peered a little harder. Just beyond the broken fence she could see the outline of something . . . or somebody. She became aware of Ronnie standing beside her.

'What is it?' Ronnie whispered.

'I don't know,' said Sheila. 'I think somebody is down there.'

All at once they saw a pinprick of light. It was followed by a dark shape coming into the garden. Sheila gasped. 'That's someone with a torch.'

'Looks like they've been in the shed,' Ronnie gasped.

Sheila was only aware that she was trembling when she felt her cousin slip her arm over her shoulder. 'It's okay,' said Ronnie. 'I reckon they came in through the gap in the fence and now they're going back out the same way.'

'He must have made that hole a bit bigger,' said Sheila. 'I heard it crack when he broke it.'

Just as Ronnie had predicted, the person with the torch headed towards the fence and disappeared.

'I don't understand,' said Sheila. 'What on earth did he want? There's nothing down there except that old van.' She took in her breath noisily. 'Oh my gosh! I bet he's come back for all those cigarettes we found squirrelled away!'

'Oh dear,' said Ronnie with a grin. 'In that case, he must be one very disappointed burglar.' They both giggled.

'Do you think he'll try breaking in downstairs?' Sheila asked nervously as she climbed back into her bed.

'I'll go down and put the lights on,' said Ronnie.

Sheila got out of bed again and grabbed her dressing gown from the back of the door to follow her cousin downstairs. 'I guess we should think a bit more seriously about security,' she said as she came into the kitchen. 'We've been a bit naive and too trusting, haven't we?'

'We could do with some better doors for a start,' said Ronnie.

'And a decent lock,' Sheila added.

Ronnie had put the kettle on and was reaching for the tea caddy. 'Want one?'

Sheila nodded. There was no point in going straight back to bed anyway. She was wide awake and her nerves were jangling. 'Do you think we should tell the police?'

'I suppose so.' Ronnie yawned. 'Sergeant Longfellow would know what to do.'

'And I could mention it to Matthew when I see him again,' said Sheila.

Her cousin grinned. 'So the date went well?' she teased.

'Yes,' said Sheila, doing her best to appear nonchalant. 'It turns out that he's quite nice.'

Leslie stripped off his gloves and swore loudly. He should have gone back sooner. When he got into the shed, he couldn't believe his eyes. The stash was gone – the whole bloody lot. When he realized the holdalls had been moved, he'd hoped he'd find them in the van, but there was no sign of them. His sister must have taken everything. He should have sold them on straight away, but he'd had high hopes that the depressed market would make them more profitable if he hung on to them for a bit. He'd promised the lot to Carter, who had almost bitten his hand off to get them. He was going to look a right fool now, wasn't he?

Chucking his clothes in a heap, he filled the sink for a strip-down wash. He hated being dirty. It made him feel physically sick. That was why he couldn't go back to his father's butcher's shop. He hated the texture of the meat; hated the fact that his hands were never properly dry; hated the way bits of animal flesh got stuck under his nails. He knew he was luckier than most. He'd been offered a good living, a job for life. Had he been cut out for it, he would have stayed in Warminster and taken over the shop when his father retired. He would have courted a local girl, maybe someone he'd met at school. They would have got married and had children, two or maybe three, and then he would have changed the sign over the door. Instead of 'Jackson and Son' it would have read 'Jackson and Sons'. But it wasn't to be. Just the thought of handling offal or handing a customer an animal heart made his stomach churn. It wasn't so much a love of animals that made him feel that way. It was the blood, the slime and the smell.

As he soaped his flannel he realized he'd look even more of an idiot when he told Carter that the caravan hidden under the thicket was gone too. A rage filled his head as he did his best to concentrate on his wash. After all the trouble he'd gone to, it was unbelievable. Pulling on his pyjamas, he reflected that it had cost him a hell of a lot to get that caravan ready. Hating muck and grime the way he did, he'd spent a whole day cleaning the damned thing. Stripped to the waist, wearing rubber gloves and with a tea towel over his hair, the day before his grandfather's funeral, he'd ripped out the guts of the caravan and washed down all the walls. He'd been so confident back then; confident that he would soon be out of this poky little room found for him by the probation service, and in his own place. Of course, when he saw the state of the garage, he knew he'd have to employ a whole army of cleaners to get it right, but it would have been worth it.

Anyway, now he had another problem. The raid was less than a month away. Where was he going to find a place big enough to store fifty or more fur coats until the heat died down? It was only as he'd made his way back to his car – stolen, of course – that he'd noticed that Ronnie and Sheila had put the caravan on the forecourt. Fat lot of use it was there. Far too public. He pulled on his silk dressing gown and, lighting a cigarette, threw himself into a chair and ran his fingers through his hair. That caravan would have been ideal. Where could he find anything like it? It was one in a million. A sudden thought crossed his mind and he sat bolt upright. Why not? Yes, yes, that was what he would do. Now that he'd thought about it, it was obvious. He'd steal it back.

CHAPTER 6

Reginald Webster, garage proprietor and member of Worthing Borough Council, stepped out of his car and straightened his waistcoat. Throwing his half-chewed, half-smoked cigar into the gutter, he raised his eyebrows as Sheila emerged from the garage wiping her hands on a piece of rag.

'Petrol, sir? How many units?'

'Two.'

Reginald eyed her up and down and reached into his back pocket for his wallet, but it wasn't there. He was a neat dresser in smart trousers with turn-ups. Under his waistcoat he wore a crisp white shirt. His tie was a regimental tie and his suit jacket was thrown casually across the back seat of the car. He leaned in to search for his wallet in the inside pocket.

Since the end of the war, petrol coupons had been exchanged for units. It amounted to the same thing, but now civilians were allowed to have petrol for their own private use. One unit was equal to one gallon, and each person was issued with two books of units. Since 1945, private motorists had been allowed five gallons a month. There had been a forlorn hope that Manny Shinwell, the Minister for Fuel and Power, might scrap the fuel allowance, but so far the government had kept it in place. As a result, motoring remained the prerogative of the rich, black marketeers and people whose livelihoods depended on being mobile.

Reginald handed Sheila his motor spirit allowance book.

Sheila checked the book carefully first and then reached for the pump. Everyone had to use the allotted units within a specified time and you were not allowed to save them from one month to another. If you didn't buy petrol within the time specified, the unit was lost, but it was surprising how many people tried to hoard them for a special occasion.

'You're new to this place,' Reginald remarked.

'We opened three months ago.'

Her customer walked to the big double doors and peered inside. There was plenty to see. Sheila had been down in the pit fixing an exhaust on a 1931 Vauxhall Cadet, a cart from Ham Farm was waiting for two new tyres and several bicycles were lined up by the wall waiting for punctures to be fixed or twisted frames to be straightened.

'That's four and tuppence,' she said, coming up behind him and handing back the ration book with its remaining coupons.

He handed her five bob. 'Keep the change,' he said, waving his hand magnanimously. 'Where's your boss?'

'I am the boss,' she replied with a smile.

'You?' He sounded incredulous.

'Yes, me,' she said teasingly. Why did men always think women couldn't possibly be a mechanic?

'What – on your own?'

'I have help,' she said, 'from my cousin Ronnie.' She could tell by the expression on his face that he thought Ronnie was a man.

'Is he here?'

'No, *she* isn't,' Sheila grinned. 'Ronnie is a girl, like me.'

'So there's only you two girls running the show?'

'That's right.'

He fished in his pocket and drew out a card. 'I own a string of garages around here,' he said. 'You may have heard of Webster and Sons. This isn't the sort of life for a pretty girl like you. If ever you consider selling up, I'd give you a very good price.'

'No thank you,' Sheila said coldly. Up until this point, she'd quite enjoyed the light-hearted banter but now the atmosphere between them had taken on a completely different vibe. She wished Ronnie was around but she had biked into Worthing. There was a rumour that a consignment of meat had arrived, a gift to the British people from Canada, so she had gone to get some. It would mean queuing for most of the morning, but the thought of a nice bit of beef was too tempting to ignore. Her cousin wouldn't be back until lunchtime.

'I'll give you three hundred and fifty pounds,' he persisted as he waved the card in front of her.

'This garage is not for sale,' she said, drawing herself up to her full height. It didn't make a lot of difference considering she was only five foot four.

He turned to go, but then came back and stood in front of her. 'All right, you've encouraged me to offer a little bit more. Four hundred and that's my final offer.'

Sheila shook her head defiantly. 'I've told you, it's not for sale.'

He took a step towards her and took her arm. 'Look at your poor hands,' he said, feigning sympathy, 'all covered in oil. You could do with a nice manicure and a bit of pampering.'

Sheila snatched her arm back angrily. 'If that'll be all . . . sir,' she said tartly, 'I'll bid you a good afternoon.' She turned to leave.

'Promise me you'll think about it,' he said.

Sheila frowned. She didn't like him being inside the garage. She didn't think he would hurt her, but she didn't like his overbearing manner. She could tell this was a man who was used to getting his own way and wouldn't take no for an answer.

They were interrupted by the sound of a dog barking and, moments later, a scruffy-looking hound bounded into the garage. As it rushed towards them, Reginald Webster let go of Sheila's arm and stepped backward. Eyeing the dog nervously, he edged away from it and headed back towards his car. The dog, which had lost interest in him anyway, ran around the garage, sniffing in every corner. Outside, Reginald turned the key in the ignition and his car roared into life. 'Don't forget my offer,' he called, full of confidence once more. 'You've got my card if you change your mind.'

Sheila watched him disappear in the direction of Findon, then turned back. The dog stood by the bench watching her, his tongue lolling.

Sheila smiled. 'Well, thank you, Mr Dog,' she said. 'I really must thank you for coming. I think you might have saved me from a fate worse than death.'

The dog barked twice, but he looked so friendly that Sheila walked forward with her hand outstretched to stroke him. He was quite large, about twenty-five inches tall. His feathered tail thumped against the leg of the bench. His grey coat looked like a cross between an old army blanket and an overgrown lawn, and he looked slightly odd with one blue and one brown eye. 'So who are you and where do you come from?'

At just this moment, Ronnie swerved into the garage on her bike. 'Ah, so you two have met. This is Nelson. He's our new security guard.'

The garage was now ticking along nicely. Trade picked up and they had quite a few day trippers out with their cars coming in for petrol. The backlog of repairs was finally completed and the garage was now neat and tidy.

Sheila and Matthew continued seeing each other. They had fallen into a comfortable pattern of meeting for a walk, going for a bike ride or to the pictures and occasionally visiting tea rooms. Sheila would have liked to do something a little more adventurous, like take a trip on the bus to Brighton, but Matthew seemed content.

'You seem rather preoccupied,' he said one evening.

'I wish we could do something a bit different,' she said.

He seemed surprised. 'I thought you liked the pictures.'

'I do,' she said, her tone measured, 'but we don't do anything else.' She chewed her bottom lip anxiously. She didn't want to annoy him. 'I'm sorry,' she added quickly. 'Take no notice of me. I'm just being silly.'

'No, no,' he said, drawing her close to him. 'You're quite right. We'll do something different next time.' He leaned forward and kissed her lips. 'I only want to make you happy, my darling. That's what I'm here for.'

Ronnie seemed more interested in being an entrepreneur than meeting men. She had made a sign which stood outside on the forecourt. It listed almost everything they were prepared to turn their hands to or to sell: acetylene welding, car and motorcycle repairs, prams re-tyred, spare parts, chimney wicks, batteries, flash lamps, pumps and locks fitted. There was more than enough to keep the pair of them busy. When she had time, Sheila worked on the old van in the shed, but it was hard to get parts. The country was still on its knees. The high days of summer were over and the deprivations seemed as harsh as ever. When would it all end? When would those 'good times' promised for so long finally come around the corner?

* * *

On October 11th, it was as quiet as the grave as the lorry drove into Montague Street. At two in the morning one would hardly expect anything else. The driver kept it in low gear until it came to a silent halt outside Levy & Sons furrier. The driver and his mate, both dressed in dark clothing, slipped out of the cab silently. Had they even been awake, no one in the street would have recognized the window cleaners who had done such an abysmal job on the building the day before. The pair had no idea how to clean a window, but what onlookers didn't realize was that while they'd been up the ladder they'd discreetly wedged a cloth between the bell and its clanger. The driver's mate now went behind the lorry to open the back and let a third accomplice out while the driver went to the shop door to effect an entry. A quick wrench with a jemmy had them inside the shop in no time. Even if the alarm bell was ringing, it only hit the rag.

Earlier in the week the owners had received a long-awaited delivery. The thieves, well versed in furs, knew exactly which ones to take. They would only bother with the fox furs if they had room in the lorry. The ones they were really after were the Persian lamb, the astrakhan and sable. These furs were lightweight, very warm and luxurious. Women were willing to pay big money to have such coats and, because of that, they were worth thousands of pounds. Winter was on its way and the shop was full of them. As they helped themselves to coats, jackets and stoles, the men worked quickly and quietly. By the time they drove away fifteen minutes later, the furrier had lost a fortune and the happy thieves had a bumper haul.

Ronnie stirred in her sleep. The dog was barking. She sat up and listened but, apart from Nelson, there was only silence. She rolled over in bed, thinking he would stop in a minute. Perhaps something had unsettled him. When she acquired him, she hadn't intended that they should have a dog. In fact, it was the last thing on her mind. It was difficult enough feeding themselves on their meagre rations, let alone an animal with such a big appetite. She'd gone into Worthing to queue for Canadian beef, but on the way she'd bumped into Cecil Longfellow. When she'd told him about the man they'd seen at the bottom of the garden, he'd taken down the details, then beamed from ear to ear.

'I've got just the thing for you,' he'd said, but he wouldn't be drawn as to what it was until she'd arrived at the police station. As soon as she'd seen Nelson tied up next to the counter, her heart had melted.

'Picked him up this morning when we got a call to an address in Shakespeare Road,' the sergeant had said. 'Some old chap found lying in his garden, dead as a doornail. Neighbour called us in. If she hadn't heard the dog howling, the old boy would probably still be there.'

'How awful,' Ronnie had cried. 'Whatever happened to him?'

'Doc says it was natural causes,' Cecil Longfellow had reassured her, 'but the poor old dog needs a good home. I'm told he'll make a really good watchdog.'

Nelson was still barking. Sheila moaned in the bed next to Ronnie and murmured sleepily, 'What on earth is the matter with that stupid dog?'

'I don't know,' said Ronnie. 'He'll settle down presently.'

'You did lock the door?'

'Of course I locked the door.'

They lay quiet for a few more seconds until Ronnie said, 'I suppose I'd better go and see what's spooked him up.' She climbed wearily out of bed, but as she reached for her dressing gown they both heard a sort of clatter, as if someone had dropped a spanner onto a concrete floor. Sheila sat bolt upright and the two girls stared at each other. 'There's somebody outside.'

Now Sheila was out of bed. They turned on the light and rushed down the stairs. Nelson was standing by the door, his hackles raised and still barking. Ronnie picked up a wrench from the work bench. Sheila, standing right behind her, armed herself with a rubber mallet. Ronnie slid the lock on the garage door as quietly as she could, but as the door began to open, Nelson became demented. She looked back at her cousin as she put her hand on the doorknob. 'Ready?' she asked.

Sheila nodded. Ronnie yanked the door open and Nelson flew outside as the sound of an engine roared away from the forecourt. The dog gave chase. The girls rushed after him, but almost at once they realized they were far too late. Ronnie threw her hands on top of her head and wailed. 'Oh no! The cheeky blighter's made off with my caravan.'

Sheila stared up the road in disbelief. The newly painted caravan, Ronnie's pride and joy, was being towed away at breakneck speed. They stood watching until they saw the last of it as it followed a slight bend in the road and disappeared into the distance. A light went on in the upstairs room of the house opposite and the bedroom curtain was lifted.

'Who on earth would want to steal that?' cried Ronnie helplessly.

'I've no idea,' said Sheila, 'but it should be easy enough to track down. It's not exactly invisible, is it?'

'What's up?' a wavery voice called from across the road.

'Someone's nicked my caravan,' Ronnie called back. It was only then that she realized it was the man who lived above the newsagent's. They hadn't seen him for a while and if she had twigged that it was him she would have ignored his comment. At the same time she realized that although she was wearing her dressing gown, Sheila was in only her nightie and with bare feet.

The man was staring. 'Want me to call someone?'

'No, no,' said Ronnie, giving Sheila a push to go inside. 'There's nothing we can do anyway.'

Sheila hurried indoors. Nelson, panting and out of breath, returned to Ronnie's side and she patted him. 'I should have trusted you, boy,' she said as she followed her cousin. 'If only I had believed you.'

Arthur Philips struggled to get comfortable. He was used to sleeping rough as he had done since the end of the war. Somehow or other he'd found it really difficult to readjust back into civilian life after the things he'd seen and done overseas. It was the people. He knew they meant well but he'd lost the art of communication. As soon as the questions began – what did you do in the war? What happened to your family? Where were you posted? – he found it difficult to cope. He couldn't hold down a job either. The moment someone spoke sharply or wanted him to do something a particular way, the thumping in his head would start and he'd have to go. And the fact that he liked a drink or two didn't help either. His life became more solitary although he had to go into the villages or the town for food. The Sally Ann were very good. They'd give him a bite to eat if nobody else did and the odd housewife was willing to fill his tin can with its string handle with tea. He never slept in town, preferring to find a quiet place under a bridge or down by the pier, but for the past month or two had made a bed of sorts deep in Titnore Woods. It wasn't easy keeping warm and with winter looming on the horizon it was soon going to be even more difficult.

His sleep was suddenly disturbed by the sound of an engine bumping along the small track which ran through the woods. He looked up to see the headlights of a car followed by a brightly coloured caravan. Who the dickens was moving a caravan at this time of night? He sometimes saw travellers parked up, but they usually stayed closer to the road. He didn't mind them too much. They would only hang around for a day or two and then move on. They were generous too, offering him a drink or the occasional plate of hedgehog stew, but this caravan looked more like something a tourist would use.

A little later a lorry trundled down the same track. Arthur poked his head out of his hidey-hole when he heard men's voices.

'What the hell is this?' The person who spoke was shining a torch onto the caravan.

'Don't worry,' said the bloke with the car, 'there's plenty of room inside.'

'But it's bright yellow!'

'And it's got a picture of a ball of wool and some knitting needles on the back!' Another man was shining his torch on the picture.

'I've brought a tarpaulin. Once we've got them all in, we can cover it over. Nobody ever comes here, believe me. It'll be as safe as houses.'

'I don't think Carter will like it.'

'Let's just do it, shall we?'

Arthur heard the click as the back door of the lorry was opened and the four of them began unloading whatever was inside and putting it into the caravan. The whole operation only took ten minutes. He watched as they pulled a tarpaulin over the caravan, but it was too small to cover it completely. The bloke from the car put a few fallen branches against the sides.

'I'm not sure about this,' said the lorry driver as he climbed back into the cab.

'It'll be fine.'

The lorry backed out towards the road and the car drove a little further into the woods before turning round. Arthur watched them disappear into what was left of the night, then having waited long enough to make sure they weren't coming back, he made his way to the caravan. It didn't take much effort to pull the branches away, but the door was locked. Arthur had no compunction about breaking into the caravan. They were thieves, he was sure of it. Once inside, he gasped. Coats, fur coats, and lots of them.

He put one on and, as he hugged it to his cold body, warmth trickled into his veins. The fur was soft on his skin and as gentle as a mother's caress. Within a minute or two, for the first time in ages, he was lovely and warm. He helped himself to a couple more and found a fur stole to go around his shoulders, then he shut the door and put the branches back. The door refused to close tightly, but it would be all right. The man in the car was right. No one ever came up here.

Back in his own lair, he put the two coats onto his bed and slept warm and comfy for the first time in years. When he got up, he put the stole under his old army coat. Perfect. He'd be all right this winter. His stomach growled. All he needed now was a hot cup of tea. Picking up his tin can, Arthur set off for the village of Durrington.

CHAPTER 7

Sergeant Longfellow was pleasant enough, but not very hopeful that the yellow caravan would be found.

'I'm afraid this will come very low on my inspector's list of priorities,' he said gloomily. 'Worthing police have a lot on their plate at the moment.' He was sitting in the garage, his feet resting on the grass box of a mower which was waiting to be greased. The blades had already been sharpened and the roller repaired. Although the weather was getting much colder, Sheila was preparing for the following spring. Ronnie had given Cecil a mug of tea and he'd taken his helmet off. He slurped the dark liquid loudly and followed it up with an appreciative sigh. 'There's a brick swindle going on for a start.'

Ronnie and Sheila glanced at each other and pulled faces. There was a long silence, then Ronnie said what was expected. 'A brick swindle?'

'Yes,' said Cecil, clearly enjoying himself. 'As you know, the council building sites are only allowed three thousand three hundred bricks at a time.' (In fact, Ronnie and Sheila didn't know that, nor was it of particular interest to them.)

'That sounds an awful lot to me,' Sheila remarked.

The sergeant looked over the rim of his mug with a stern expression. 'My dear girl, that's hardly enough to keep one bricklayer busy for a week,' he said, 'yet some private builders are putting up ten-foot walls around their estates.'

Sheila shook her head in disbelief even though she didn't care a fig.

'So you're telling me that Worthing police are too busy counting bricks to bother about the theft of my caravan,' said Ronnie caustically.

Her sarcasm was noted. Cecil looked up sharply. 'High walls are not new homes,' he said pointedly. 'People need somewhere to live.'

'You're right,' said Sheila, shooting her cousin a look. He might be an irritating old duffer but they couldn't afford to rub him up the wrong way.

The policeman wasn't finished yet. Leaning back on the two back legs of the chair, he began again. 'And then there's all the fighting outside the Food Office.'

Ronnie blew out her cheeks and got to her feet. Did he really think they had their heads in the sand? Everybody knew about that. It was in all the papers and it was happening all over the country.

Since bread had been rationed, everyone had to collect their bread units from the Food Office. The problems began when the government announced that everyone with surplus bread units could swap them for extra points on their ration books. Since the powers-that-be had decided that the basic daily bread ration was six slices from the wartime loaf for a man and slightly less for a woman, not everybody wanted that many slices. As a consequence, long queues of people who wanted to swap units for points built up. This led to arguments and a lot of pushing and shoving. In an effort to keep the King's peace in Worthing, the police had to maintain a presence or risk rioting.

'I must admit, you do sound very busy,' Sheila conceded, 'but surely finding one canary-yellow caravan shouldn't be beyond the skills of Worthing police, should it?'

Cecil gave her a withering stare and cleared his throat. 'I haven't finished yet.'

Ronnie and Sheila felt like giving up.

'I haven't told you the best bit,' said Cecil, taking another slurp of his tea. 'All our detectives are working on the fur robbery.'

'What fur robbery?' Ronnie snapped. She could feel her temper rising. Why couldn't the stupid man understand that without that caravan she couldn't open the haberdashery shop and all the stock was arriving tomorrow! Where was she going to put it? It was so frustrating. Until the theft, everything had been coming together like clockwork. She had planned to stock up and open on Tuesday. Clearly that wasn't going to happen now, even though she'd found a schoolgirl helper. Elsie had recommended the daughter of her next-door neighbour. Julie Summers was fourteen, a sensible girl who had ambitions to be a hairdresser when she left school next year. A Saturday job in the caravan would be good experience for her. She'd learn how to work with people and keep the customers happy. She had good references too. But now it looked like Ronnie would have to disappoint the poor child.

'Levy and Sons on Montague Street was broken into last night,' said Longfellow, determined to finish his tale of woe. He drained his mug. 'They reckon that thousands of pounds' worth of furs were stolen.'

'Thousands of pounds?' Sheila spluttered. 'You're joking! How on earth can a few coats cost that much?'

The sergeant stood up. 'I was told that one sable coat alone cost over a thousand pounds.'

The girls were left with their mouths open. Clearly, with sums like that involved, the theft of a second-hand caravan didn't stand a chance.

'It looks like we'll have to kiss that caravan goodbye then,' said Sheila as the policeman disappeared around the corner. 'I'm sorry, Ron. I know it meant a lot to you.'

'I'm not beaten yet,' said Ronnie stoutly. 'I'll find a way to sell that stuff, don't you worry.'

It was over their evening meal that Ronnie brought up the subject of the letter she'd found amongst Granddad's papers. 'I didn't know what to make of this,' she told Sheila as she handed it to her. 'I would have shown it to you before but it went right out of my mind until I found another one stuck right at the back of the drawer.'

Addressed to a Post Office box number, the writer

was a Matron Fowles. While her cousin was reading it, Ronnie prepared Nelson's meal. 'Tonight,' she told him, 'you're having bread soaked in gravy with a dash of bacon rashers left over from this morning and a couple of bits of gristly meat left over from tonight's offering.'

Nelson barked his approval as Sheila read the first letter, which was dated April 15th 1934.

Dear Mr Peters,

It is with regret that I have to inform you that the workhouse is closing down. Because of our isolated location, we are finding it difficult to recruit staff, and added to that, under the terms of the Local Government Act of 1929, the council has decided on the grounds of cost to close the institution. This will take effect as from May 10th 1934. I would be grateful if you would come in and discuss with us the best course of action for your ward. I'm sure that we can find a solution which is in her best interest.

Yours sincerely,

Matron Fowles

Sheila looked up with a frown. 'What does this mean? What ward? Who is this person?'

Nelson's tail wagged against the chair while Ronnie held her gaze. 'You'd better read the other letter.'

Sheila took the second page from her. This was dated May 1st 1934. It was sent to the same box number and was signed 'Miss G. Porter'.

Dear Mr Peters,

You will be pleased to know that Daisy has settled in nicely. She shares a room with three other girls and has made friends. We would be grateful if you would send more clothes as the workhouse only sent her in what she stood up in. All the paperwork has now been processed and the bank has forwarded your payments.

I remain yours faithfully, etc.

'Daisy?' said Sheila. 'Who is Daisy?'

Ronnie could tell by her expression that as soon as she'd voiced the name, Sheila had answered her own question. 'Aunt Daisy? Oh my God, Ronnie, we've found our missing aunt!'

Ronnie put the dog's plate on the floor and Nelson began eating greedily. 'I worry that he's not getting enough,' she remarked.

As his already-empty plate clattered noisily around the kitchen floor, Sheila regarded their dog with a sigh. 'We're all in the same boat, Ron. Half the country is existing on next to nothing.'

They scrutinized the address on the second letter: Wells House, Home for the Mentally Feeble.

'A mental home,' said Sheila in hushed tones.

'Looks like it,' said Ronnie.

'Poor Granny,' Sheila remarked.

'I'm not so sure she even knows,' said Ronnie.

'Granny said Daisy ran away,' said Sheila. She caught her breath as she looked at the expression on Ronnie's face.

'I got the impression that in her heart of hearts, Granny thinks her daughter might be dead, don't you?'

Sheila nodded. 'Well, if your daughter hadn't been in touch for thirty years, you would, wouldn't you?' She looked at the letter again. 'And all this time she's been in a mental home?'

'I can't imagine Granny hiding something like that, can you?'

'No I can't,' Sheila said slowly. 'But why didn't Granddad say something? It's less than twenty miles away.'

Ronnie shrugged. 'Perhaps he was trying to protect her.'

'Who, Daisy?'

'No, Granny.'

They both became thoughtful.

'Mum always said that when Granny was ill, Aunt Daisy had to look after everyone,' said Sheila.

'When did this happen?' asked Ronnie.

'I'm not sure,' said Sheila. 'I think she got pneumonia or TB or something and had to go away.' Sheila blew out her cheeks. 'Daisy was a couple of years older than her, but I think my mum would have been about eleven.'

'And of course my mother was that much younger,' said Ronnie. 'Nine, maybe ten?'

'Did she say what happened to Aunt Daisy?'

'My mum never talked about her,' said Ronnie. 'Only that one day she was there and the next she was gone.'

'We'll have to tell Granny,' said Sheila.

'There's something else,' said Ronnie. 'I found this

letter from the bank. It's dated March 8th 1946 and it's addressed to Granddad, here at the garage. It tells him that his account is about to be closed because it has insufficient funds. The manager tells him that he cannot honour his instructions and he's to come into the office to discuss the matter.'

'But Granddad had his stroke in 1943,' said Sheila. 'Surely the bank manager knew he couldn't deal with business matters?'

'That's what I thought,' said Ronnie, 'but Granddad must have been dealing with this through that box number and it only came to light when the money ran out.'

Sheila looked up with a puzzled expression. 'I don't understand.'

'That letter was delivered here to the garage,' said Ronnie. 'It didn't go to his home. It wasn't even opened. I opened it. Granddad never saw it.' She leaned forward earnestly. 'I've tallied the receipts and the account number. Wells House must be a private home. Granddad had been sending regular payments since 1934.'

'But that's twelve years!' cried Sheila.

Ronnie nodded. 'When he had his stroke three years ago, there must have been enough money in the account to keep paying the home, but this year it ran out.'

'So where is Aunt Daisy now?' asked Sheila.

Ronnie shrugged. 'No idea. That's why I don't think we should tell Granny just yet. I would hate to raise her hopes and then find out we still don't know where she is.'

Sheila looked thoughtful. 'I suppose it could be another Daisy,' she said. 'I mean, some other relative like an old prune we don't know of?' In answer to her own question, she shook her head. 'No, it has to be someone young. In this letter she was called "his ward".'

'It's possible,' Ronnie said thoughtfully. 'This letter is dated March and it's now October. It's possible that they've already kicked her out.'

'Bit heartless,' Sheila remarked.

'It's business,' said Ronnie, turning the corners of her mouth down.

Nelson had laid his head on Sheila's lap. She fondled his ears absent-mindedly.

'Whatever the reason or the outcome, I think we're both agreed that we can't leave it there,' said Ronnie. 'We'll have to look for her.'

'Absolutely,' said Sheila, 'but where do we start?'

Ronnie shrugged.

'I know,' cried Sheila, the sound of her excited voice making Nelson sit up. 'Why don't you take Granddad's death certificate down to the Post Office and see if you can get access to that box number. There may well be other letters waiting for collection.'

'Good idea,' said Ronnie.

And Nelson's tail thumped against the table leg.

CHAPTER 8

It was Leslie's birthday and he couldn't have had a better present. As he stepped into the club, Gerry Carter called him into the office. When he opened the door he noticed another man sitting in one of the big leather chairs in front of the desk. Dark-haired, and in a well-tailored dark suit, he wore a white shirt with a patterned tie and a matching handkerchief in his breast pocket. The man rose to his feet as he appeared and Leslie had to stop himself from letting out an audible gasp. The man was none other than Billy Hill himself.

'Is this him?' Billy asked Carter.

Carter nodded. He had an early-afternoon copy of the *Evening Argus* in his hand and he pushed it across the desktop.

Leslie glanced down at the headline, '£10,000 fur raid in Worthing', and felt his knees buckle. Ten grand? He knew furs were worth a hell of a lot but he'd had no idea the haul was worth that much. He resisted a smile. Play it cool, he told himself. Don't let him think you're an amateur.

'Sit down, lad,' said Billy affably

Leslie lowered himself into the matching leather chair. It creaked slightly as he made himself comfortable. Billy resumed his seat and Carter handed the cigar box around. Leslie felt pretty important, but he'd never smoked a cigar in his life before. What should he do? Out of the corner of his eye, he saw Billy bite the end off, whereas Carter was using a cigar clipper. He regretted now that he'd never bought one and practised what to do. Leslie always wanted to look the part, but at ten bob a throw it was low on his list of priorities. When he saw Billy picking bits of cigar from his teeth, he decided to wait for the clippers.

'I'm impressed, lad,' said Billy. 'Carter tells me it was your idea. You pulled it off very well.'

Raising an eyebrow, Leslie flicked an imaginary speck from his trouser leg, then leaned forward as Carter held the lighter to his cigar.

'Well hidden, are they?' asked Billy.

Leslie puffed hard and almost at once his head began to spin and he felt sick. The cigar was foul but he sat back in the chair and casually crossed his legs.

'Oh yes,' he said, his voice sounding a little more strangled than he would have wished. 'There's no chance anyone will find them. I've put them in a caravan in the middle of the woods.'

For a second Billy stared at him, then burst out laughing. 'Sure you have,' he said, tapping the side of his nose. 'I like a man who keeps his cards close to his chest.'

'You just remember to keep them cool and dry,'

Carter cautioned. 'We don't want the goods smelling musty when we bring them out.'

Leslie nodded. Obviously Billy and Carter didn't believe he was telling the truth when he said they were in the caravan and the way they'd laughed at the suggestion told him it would be better not to pursue the matter. Right now he had other things to think about. Cigar smoke settled around the three of them like a blue haze, even though Leslie had only puffed on his twice, and he was feeling decidedly queasy. How on earth Churchill smoked these vile things all through the war he'd never know. It was like setting fire to a dirty old sock, or something worse, and stuffing it into your mouth.

'We'll wait a couple of weeks for the heat to die down,' said Billy, 'and then I'll send the boys down from London.' He turned to Carter. 'Meet here?'

Carter shook his head. 'The rozzers will be watching me,' he said. 'Better to find somewhere else.'

They both looked at Leslie. Inwardly, he panicked. They were obviously waiting for him to suggest somewhere they could all meet to pass the goods on, but where? Think, he told his befuddled brain as his stomach churned, think.

'I know just the place,' he said in a voice which he hoped would sound casual. 'There's a small garage at Thomas A Becket near Worthing. What is more natural than to go into a place for some petrol? We could rendezvous there.' Rendezvous – he liked that word. It sounded sophisticated. Leslie closed his mouth quickly. The foul taste in his mouth was making him feel sick.

Billy nodded his head. 'Good thinking.'

'So when do you want the goods?' Carter asked.

'Saturday week?' Billy suggested.

Leslie shifted uncomfortably in his seat and then stood up. He was going to be sick and he knew it, but Carter might not take too kindly to him throwing up in his office. 'Right,' he said firmly. 'Tell your boys we'll meet at the garage at four o'clock on Saturday. After they've filled up, tell them to follow me.'

The two men were staring at him. 'You all right, lad?' said Billy. 'You look a bit pasty.'

'Fine,' said Leslie, forcing a smile. 'You'll have to excuse me, but I've just remembered an appointment and I'm late.'

He walked from the room with as much dignity as he could muster. Once outside, he put his hand over his mouth and made a dash for the Gents. As the toilet door banged against the wall, he heard the sound of laughter coming from the office and then he threw up all over the pan and onto the floor.

It was easy enough to gain access to the Post Office box number once Ronnie had shown the branch manager the paperwork and proof of her identity.

She had to pay a bill of nearly five pounds, which she was forced to draw from her own Post Office savings book because she didn't have enough cash in her purse.

'You're telling me he only died this year, but I'm telling you that your grandfather hasn't paid the rental for more than three years,' the manager explained. It seemed to be lost on him that a person suffering from a devastating stroke would be incapable of doing business and that their grandmother hadn't a clue about it.

When they opened the box, it contained half-a-dozen letters. The manager tidied them with an elastic band before handing them to Ronnie.

'I'm sorry for your loss,' he murmured mechanically as he walked away.

Ronnie was tempted to stick out her tongue to his receding back.

At home, she spent a moment sorting the letters by the date over the stamp before she and Sheila opened them. The contents were very dull. Two letters, one written at the end of 1944 and the other in 1945, informed their grandfather that Daisy had made little progress. Two letters, similar to the one they'd found in the office, reminded Granddad that the fees were overdue. The first in order of appearance was from a member of staff who said Daisy had been ill but was now on the road to recovery. The final letter, and the most recent, informed Granddad that Daisy had been moved, but there was no indication as to where. The two girls looked at each other.

'So,' said Ronnie. 'When the workhouse closed, Aunt Daisy was sent to a mental home somewhere in Horsham in 1934—'

'A private mental home,' Sheila interrupted.

'And Granddad paid the fees.'

'For twelve years,' said Sheila.

Ronnie shifted the letters around. 'It's obvious Granny knows nothing about all this.'

Sheila blew her nose. 'Should we tell her now?'

Ronnie looked thoughtful, then shook her head. 'We won't keep it from her once we've found Daisy,' she said, 'but I think it's best to keep it to ourselves until we know what's actually happened.'

'We've got to find her, Ronnie.'

Ronnie nodded. 'I agree, but all we've got to go on is the headed notepaper from the private home. The only way we'll find out where she is now is to go over there and ask them.'

'Oh, Ronnie, this is so awful,' said Sheila, her eyes filling with tears. 'Why did he do it?'

Ronnie shrugged her shoulders. 'Like I said, I'd like to believe it was because he was protecting Granny, but the more I think about it and the memories I have of him . . .' Her voice trailed.

'I hardly remember him,' Sheila confessed. 'What was he like?'

'I didn't like him much,' said Ronnie.

'Mum and I came here on holiday once,' Sheila went on, 'but there was this humongous row and that was that.' She paused. 'Do you really think Granddad would go on letting Granny believe for all those years that Daisy had actually died?'

'Oh, I don't know,' said Ronnie, 'Perhaps he thought

it was better to remember her as she was rather than what she had become?'

Sheila stared at her cousin. 'You don't really believe that either, do you?'

Ronnie's chin quivered slightly. 'I'm just trying to understand.'

Sheila nodded. 'We'll have to go by train,' she said. 'I'll look up the timetable for next Saturday.'

Matthew wasn't very happy. Sheila had just told him about the theft of the caravan. 'I don't like the thought of you being alone in that garage,' he said protectively. 'If someone can steal a caravan from right under your noses like that, it's not safe.'

He and Sheila were taking a stroll along the beach with Nelson. They'd met at the end of George V Avenue and, instead of heading for the pier, they'd turned right and walked towards Ferring.

Sheila liked being with Matthew, and the dog adored him. His strength and masculinity appealed to her. He always looked smart. It seemed that he only had the one suit, but today he wore a different tie. His hair was neatly slicked down and he had some new shoes, black lace-ups with a brogue pattern on the front. Sheila was wearing her favourite dress, a dusty yellow with white piping along the collar and along the seams on the bodice. The same piping also edged the pockets and it had a small yellow belt at the waist of the A-line skirt. The style was very slimming and because it was quite chilly she'd worn it with a pretty white bolero cardigan.

She looked up at him and slipped her arm through his. 'Don't worry so much,' she said lightly. 'We'll be fine now we've got Nelson.'

Matthew frowned. 'Oh, darling, he wasn't much good when the caravan went missing, was he?' he said rather pointedly.

'That was our fault,' said Sheila. 'He barked and barked, but we took no notice. Besides, he couldn't do much when he was locked in, now could he?' She felt Matthew's arm tense.

'I just think two girls on their own makes you vulnerable,' he insisted. 'It won't take long before people know.'

'What people?'

'Rogues, thieves, gangsters . . .'

Sheila chuckled. 'Now you're being paranoid,' she said. 'This is sleepy old Worthing, not New York.'

Matthew jutted his jaw and stared doggedly ahead. She could tell he was annoyed and decided to change the subject.

'Did I tell you we got the old van going?'

'What van?'

'The one in the shed at the bottom of the garden,' she said. 'It's a bit rusty but it could come in useful. Ronnie is thinking it would be good for making deliveries.'

'That girl is spreading both of you far too thinly,' he said. 'First of all she gets you doing all sorts of weird and wonderful repairs, then it's knitting wool and now deliveries.'

For a moment, Sheila was slightly irritated. Why did he always pour cold water on everything? 'We have to diversify,' she said, using Ronnie's words. 'I haven't got enough work in the garage to keep us going.'

'There you are then!' he cried. 'That's just what I've been telling you.'

Sheila took her hand away from his arm. Really! Sometimes he could be so blinkin' pompous. 'Well, we're quite happy with what we're doing, thank you very much,' she snapped. 'Since the caravan went, Ronnie has rented a few shelves in the newsagent's across the road and it's been a godsend to the women living around the Becket. The wool has been selling like hot cakes.'

Matthew looked contrite. 'I'm sorry, darling,' he said. 'It's just that I worry about you.'

Her expression softened and she slipped her arm through his again. 'There's really no need.'

'I can't help it,' he said. 'You're such a precious little thing. I couldn't bear it if anything happened to you.' He cupped her head in his hands and kissed her.

'Oh, Matthew,' she sighed.

They walked for a while in silence. It was lovely along the coastal path. Although there were a few holiday bungalows along the route, it was the closest to nature that you could get along this part of the south.

The tide was out and the sand looked firm. As they approached Goring Gap, they left the trees behind. With the sea on their left, to the right of them they passed a large area of open farmland and from here they had a fantastic view right up to Highdown Hill. Sheila snatched at Matthew's arm as she spotted a kestrel hovering over the undeveloped ground. Continuing along the path, they came to a narrow lane running along the back of the houses, Nelson running ahead and enjoying the smells along the way. The gun placements were still there, but the guns themselves had been removed earlier in the year. Sheila tried to imagine how it must have felt for the people of Ferring, for that was where they were now, to be so close to a place which must have been earmarked for invasion by the Nazis. Of course, the big troop ships couldn't have come close to shore. The beach was rather shallow but, sandwiched between Dover and Southampton, this isolated spot would have been ideal for an advanced force. Apart from the odd gun battery, there would have been little resistance.

As they approached the Blue Bird Cafe they could see that the beach huts which had been laid on their sides and filled with pebbles to deter any heavy military equipment from coming ashore during the recent hostilities had been put back in situ. Most were locked up for the winter, but occasional families were in their huts, sitting in deck chairs, drinking tea or reading a book as they enjoyed the late October sunshine.

They heard the sound of laughter and Sheila looked across the pebbles. 'Ooh, look,' she said. 'There's Pen Albright with her family. Shall we go and join them?'

'I'd much rather spend my time with you,' Matthew said.

For a moment, Sheila was slightly miffed. She liked Pen a lot.

'Besides,' Matthew went on, 'we might spoil their family time. I'd feel as if we'd be gatecrashing.'

'I guess so,' Sheila conceded as she looked across the beach again. Pen and her children were certainly having a lot of fun. Pen had her skirts tucked into her knickers and she and her husband, whom Sheila had never met, were swinging their youngest boy over the incoming tide. The older boy was scavenging in a rock pool.

Sheila smiled. Maybe Matthew was right and they would be better left alone. Pen had once said her husband didn't get much time off and they clearly loved being together as a family.

'Fancy a cuppa?' Matthew asked as they reached the cafe.

Sheila tucked her arm through his again. They made Nelson wait outside by a bowl of drinking water left for dogs.

The Blue Bird Cafe had been requisitioned as an NAAFI during the war by the Canadian soldiers camped nearby. With the troops gone, it was open for business again although there was a notice on the door reminding customers that they would be closing for winter and reopening at Easter 1947. As they walked in, Sheila spotted a window seat. Matthew followed her. When the waitress came over, he ordered tea for two.

'Look, sweetheart,' he said when she'd gone, 'I'm sorry if I annoyed you back there, going on about the

111

garage, but believe me, I'm only looking out for your best interests.'

Sheila's expression softened. 'I know.'

He took her hand in his. 'Sheila, you must know that I care very deeply for you,' he went on. 'You're my girl and it's my job to protect you.'

Sheila suddenly felt emotional. What a sweet thing to say. 'Oh, Matthew,' she whispered as he kissed her fingers.

CHAPTER 9

Taking an extra day off on Saturday, Ronnie and Sheila made an early start to Horsham. The train left West Worthing station at seven forty-five.

They travelled in silence, each girl left alone with her own thoughts. Sheila was thinking about Matthew. She'd been flattered when he'd said she was his girl. It meant they were officially courting, but she was already having second thoughts. Their relationship had everything going for it. He was good-looking, a hard-working man in a steady job with promotion prospects, the sort of man who offered her the promise of a comfortable life, but . . . There was always a 'but' where Matthew was concerned. He made it plain he didn't like her working in the garage and sometimes it felt like he wanted to wrap her up in cotton wool. She was flattered but, on the other hand, she was being smothered. Did she want to feel like that for the rest of her life? Of course, he hadn't actually asked her to marry him or anything like that. There was no ring on her finger even though everyone knew courting usually led to marriage, but . . . Oh dear, there it was again, the 'but'. The truth of the matter was, she enjoyed her life at the moment. There was always the thought that things could change if Ronnie met someone and got married, but right now she held men at arm's length and because she didn't even have a fella, life was unpredictable and fun. Sheila enjoyed working with the cars and she was learning all the time. They weren't exactly making a fortune, but they were ticking over nicely. Ronnie was never short of enthusiasm or good ideas, and although losing the caravan had been a bit of a setback, they were doing okay. She and Matthew had never discussed it, but she felt sure he would insist she gave it all up if they got married. And as much as she didn't want to end up an old maid, she wasn't so sure she was ready to settle for a pinny and slippers either.

Ronnie was thinking about expansion. She hadn't mentioned it to Sheila yet, but it was obvious that if she didn't do something soon, the business would start to stagnate. According to the books, they were doing quite well, almost well enough to take on somebody else – and therein lay a dilemma. A man might want to take over rather than be subservient to Sheila's leadership and Ronnie was determined not to let that happen. Sheila was brilliant at her job, but she was a bit soft when it came to blokes. Ronnie saw the way things were with Matthew. Sheila always did what he wanted to do even if hers was the better suggestion. She was always giving in to him, so could she stand her ground in a workshop situation with a man working alongside her? Perhaps it would be better to take on a young boy as an apprentice. They could pay him less while he was learning and he would get to do things the way Sheila wanted.

Sheila had told her about Mr Webster. He hadn't come round again, but he had sent several letters, each time upping the offer for the garage – nowhere near the market value, of course, but the old man obviously thought they wouldn't know that and if he kept up the pressure they'd be tempted to take the money. If they had someone else in the workshop, a man or a lad, he could act as a bit of a deterrent if any other would-be buyers turned up unexpectedly.

She glanced across the carriage at her cousin and wondered how long she would be working at the garage. Matthew seemed very keen on her and Ronnie felt sure it wouldn't be long before he popped the question. They'd most likely have a long engagement, most people did these days. As far as Ronnie knew, Sheila didn't have a large amount of savings, but if she married Matthew, they wouldn't have to worry about saving up for a flat: as a serving officer, Matthew would be allocated a police house. Having an apprentice would work on two levels. Sheila would have help while she was still in the garage and, hopefully, by the time she left, the apprentice could be taken on as the garage mechanic. Ronnie smiled to herself, pleased with her plan. She'd talk to Sheila when they got home.

Her mind drifted back to Ruth and Elspeth. They'd be eight and six by now. A small smile edged its way across her lips. Would she recognize them if she saw them? She wondered about their father. How was he coping? He may have been a brilliant officer for his men but, like a lot of his class, he was useless on the domestic front. She could just picture him in that lovely garden in Geelong, pushing the girls on the swing. She sat up quickly. She mustn't keep thinking about them. That life was over. Just like poor Mrs Lyle, it was dead and buried.

They travelled from West Worthing station to Ford and changed trains for Horsham. The journey took just over an hour.

Arriving, they headed down North Street towards the Carfax but at the town hall they were disappointed. The office was only open Monday to Friday between 9 a.m. and 5.30 p.m.

'We should have thought of that,' Sheila said grimly. 'Looks like we've had a wasted journey.'

'We could ask around,' said Ronnie. 'There should be someone who would know where Wells House is.'

They settled instead for a cup of tea in the Honey Pot Cafe nearby, which seemed very popular with ladies of a certain age and their friends, people who had probably lived in Horsham all their lives. As they walked through the door, the buzz of conversation was very loud, suggesting that some of the customers might be a bit deaf.

The waitress who took their order was very helpful. Although she didn't know the place Ronnie was talking about, she pointed them in the direction of a Miss

West and her friend, who were sitting near the fireplace. 'Miss West has lived in Horsham all her life,' the waitress told them in a confidential whisper. 'If anyone knows where it is, it'll be Miss West.'

While they waited for their order to arrive, Ronnie rose from her chair and, with a polite apology, interrupted the two women. Miss West, a generously proportioned woman with straight pepper-and-salt-coloured hair under a rather dowdy hat, looked thoughtful.

'It was a private home for the mentally feeble,' Ronnie explained.

'She must mean that place they closed down,' said Miss West's friend. 'You know, the one where they found you-know-what.'

Ronnie raised an eyebrow. 'Sorry?'

'Oh yes,' said Miss West. 'They closed it down in 1944, or was it '45? Awful scandal.'

Ronnie felt very concerned. 'So what happened?'

The two ladies became quite animated and they lost no time in relating the events with relish.

'Oh, my dear,' said Miss West. 'Very shady goings-on. They were making an absolute fortune on the black market for a start.'

'That's right,' chipped in her friend as she took off her round-rimmed spectacles and polished the lenses on her scarf. 'And pretending they still had patients who had actually died . . .'

Ronnie lowered herself onto an empty chair beside their table.

'Using their ration books . . .'

'Getting medicine and extra blankets – they were up to all sorts, weren't they, dear?'

'Everyone was very cross,' said Miss West. 'Well, they would be, wouldn't they?'

Sheila came over to join them.

'The butcher used to give them a special assignment of beef,' said Miss West's friend, 'when people like us only had the usual ration. In the end, someone complained and that's when it all came to light.'

'Shocking,' said Miss West.

'Really shocking,' her friend agreed. They looked up at Ronnie and Miss West's cheeks flushed. 'Ooh, you didn't have anyone there, did you, dear? A relative perhaps?'

Sheila started to say something, but to spare Miss West's blushes Ronnie shook her head. 'We were just wondering what happened to the patients, that's all.'

Miss West looked to her friend for confirmation. 'They were all farmed out to other places, weren't they, dear?'

Her friend nodded. 'Poor souls.'

'Have you any idea where they went?' Sheila asked.

'The town hall would be the best place to ask,' said Miss West.

'We tried there,' said Ronnie, 'but it's closed on Saturdays.'

'Oh yes, yes, of course it is,' said Miss West.

'The trouble is,' Sheila chipped in, 'we're visitors to the town. Can you think of anyone else who might know?'

The two women shrugged. 'You could try the Post Office,' Miss West suggested. 'After all, they deliver all the letters. They should know.'

Her friend glanced at her watch. 'But they close at twelve today,' she said. 'You'll have to get a move on.'

The telephone rang at Worthing police station just before midday.

'This is Mr Kay,' said the caller. 'I'm the manager of the Midland bank on the corner of Warwick Street. I want to report a tramp who has been sleeping in my doorway.'

'With respect, sir,' said the desk sergeant, noting the time, 'there is little I can do about it. My officers patrol the area and move them on, but unless he is causing a breach of the peace . . .'

'I know all that, sergeant,' Mr Kay said irritably, 'but last night he left some of his bedding behind and I want someone to come and collect it.'

The sergeant rolled his eyes. Did people really think his officers had nothing better to do? 'I suggest you deposit it in the nearest bin, sir,' he replied in a measured tone.

'Normally I would, sergeant,' Mr Kay said tetchily, 'but this tramp has been covering himself with a very expensive Astrakhan coat.'

The Post Office clerk sighed. He had hoped to make a quick get-away today. He wanted to be at the rugby club by two o'clock. After being on the Horsham cricket ground since the 1930s, today would be the first game on the new rented pitch in Horsham Park. For an avid fan and a player such as he was, it was a moment not to be missed.

'We are not permitted to divulge that sort of information,' he said stiffly. 'Go to the library.'

'But surely you can tell us where Wells House is, even if you can't tell us the names of anyone living there?' said Sheila, batting her eyelids like mad.

The clerk busied himself stacking his papers and putting his newly filled fountain pen next to his pencils ready for Monday morning.

'And we have come a great distance,' said Ronnie, emphasizing the word 'great'.

'The house is just off the Market Place,' he said in an offhand manner, 'but it won't help you to know that.' He reached for a board, which he began putting across the window. 'And now, if you don't mind, this Post Office is closed.'

Outside on the street, Ronnie and Sheila looked at each other. This was all very frustrating, but they decided to head for the Market Place anyway. When they got there, they found that the Post Office clerk was right. Wells House was indeed all closed up. The windows were boarded and a few pieces of broken furniture were scattered around the overgrown garden. A creeper of some sort had wrapped itself right across the doorway. It was obvious it hadn't been lived in for some time.

'Looks like we'll have to come back on a weekday,' said Ronnie.

'But we can't close the garage,' said Sheila. 'That would be bad for business.'

As they turned to go, Ronnie threw her arm around Sheila's neck. 'Ah, now you've said that, there's something I'd like to talk to you about.'

When Ronnie and Sheila turned the corner from Rectory Road into Littlehampton Road, they saw a police car outside the garage. 'Oh Lord,' cried Sheila. 'Don't tell me we've had another break-in.'

Two policemen stood on the forecourt. Ronnie began to run.

'What is it? What's happened?' said Sheila as she saw one of the men was Matthew.

'This is Inspector Dawson,' said Matthew.

'Why are you here?' asked Ronnie. 'Don't tell me we've been robbed again.'

'Perhaps we could go inside first, miss?' said the inspector.

They could hear Nelson barking his head off and as Ronnie turned the key in the lock and opened the door, he flung himself at the men. Sheila grabbed his collar and calmed him down while Ronnie invited them in. 'So what's this all about?'

'We've found your caravan,' said Matthew.

Ronnie let out a whoop of delight, but the inspector raised his hand. 'I'll handle this, thank you, constable,' he snapped.

Sullen-faced, Matthew stepped to one side.

'Where was it?' Ronne wanted to know. 'Is it damaged?'

'Can you tell me where you were on the night of the eleventh of October?'

Ronnie frowned. 'Here. Why?'

'To be more precise,' the inspector went on, 'at 3 a.m. in the morning.'

'Here,' Ronnie repeated. 'In bed.' She resisted the temptation to point out that 3 a.m. was always in the morning.

The inspector turned to Sheila.

'The same,' she said, without waiting for the question.

'Can anyone else corroborate that?'

Sheila looked indignant. 'We are two respectable single women,' she said. 'Who else would be here?'

'Hang on,' Ronnie blurted out. 'That was the night the caravan got pinched, wasn't it? I hope you're not suggesting that we had anything to do with it, are you?'

'Can anyone corroborate your story?' the inspector repeated.

The girls looked at each other.

'You see,' the inspector went on pompously, 'I think you removed the caravan yourselves and then reported it stolen.'

'You what?' Ronnie exclaimed.

'We didn't!' cried Sheila in unison.

'It was found near here,' said the inspector.

'Where?' Ronnie demanded to know.

'I am not at liberty to say,' the inspector replied.

'Well, wherever it is, we didn't put it there,' said Sheila.

'Was the vehicle insured?' the inspector asked.

'It was just a manky old caravan, painted up,' Ronnie said irritably, 'so no, it wasn't insured.'

The inspector gave her a dark look.

'Anyway, how could we have taken it?' said Sheila. 'We don't have a motor.'

'You've got that old van in the shed at the end of the garden,' said Matthew. 'You told me you'd got it going.'

Sheila put her hand on her hip. 'And how am I supposed to drive that?' she snapped. 'It's only got three wheels.'

'Three wheels?' the inspector repeated.

'I've been trying to get another tyre for it,' said Sheila tetchily, 'but what with all the shortages and the fact that it's more than twelve years old, the motor may be ticking over but it's still on the jack.'

'The man opposite,' Ronnie blurted out. They all turned to look at her. 'He saw us that night. I remember now, he was ogling out of the window.'

'That's right,' cried Sheila. 'I rushed downstairs without thinking. I was only in my nightie and I had bare feet. He'll remember. He had an eyeful. Lecherous old—' She stopped herself just in time. Matthew didn't like women who swore.

The inspector took down the details.

'Whoever took that caravan,' said the inspector, snapping his notebook shut, 'used it for storing the furs from that robbery in Montague Street.'

'What!' Ronnie gasped.

Sheila glared at Matthew. 'And you thought we had something to do with it?' she said crossly.

'We are duty bound to follow every line of enquiry,' the inspector sniffed. He turned to go.

'So when can we have it back?' asked Ronnie.

'We want it to stay where it is for the moment,' said the inspector. 'We shall inform you of its whereabouts in due course.'

CHAPTER 10

'Why on earth did you did you tell him about the van?' Sheila asked crossly.

She and Matthew had been on their regular date at the pictures. Even though they would be sitting in the dark, Sheila had gone to a lot of trouble to look good. She was wearing a pretty red skirt, gathered at the waistband. The material had white 'V' shapes with the Morse code (dot-dot-dot-dash) stamped along one side of the 'V'. Both stood for victory. She had coupled the skirt with a hand-knitted twinset Granny had made for her in white wool.

'You look super,' said Matthew as he helped her to take her coat off.

Sheila felt a warm glow of satisfaction as he pulled the cinema seat forward for her and she sat back down.

'I like it a lot better than that yellow outfit you wore the other day,' he smiled.

The lights went down and he reached for her hand. She let him hold it, but her mind was in a whirl. Why did he say that? She was glad he liked what she was wearing tonight, but why did he say that about her yellow dress? She really liked that dress. It was her favourite. Disappointed, she sighed. She wouldn't be able to wear it again.

The film was mediocre. It was on the bus on the way home, and because she'd been brooding on it ever since, that she brought up the subject of the van at the bottom of the garden.

'You knew we had nothing to hide,' she said, 'so it seems a bit disloyal to even bring it up in front of the inspector. Did you really think for one minute that Ronnie and I would be capable of robbery?'

'Of course not,' said Matthew. 'But he would have found out about it eventually, so I saved you the embarrassment.'

'What embarrassment?' Sheila demanded. 'We haven't done anything.'

'Darling,' Matthew said smoothly, 'you mustn't forget that I have to be very careful who I associate with. It wouldn't do for me to mix with people on the wrong side of the law.'

'I don't know what you mean,' she said haughtily.

'I was thinking about Ronnie's brother,' he said confidentially.

She gasped. 'What, Leslie? Oh, Matthew, you can't think that he—'

He took her hand in his and leaned towards her. 'You did once tell me he'd been in trouble with the police.'

'That was a very long time ago,' she said indignantly.

Matthew shook his head. 'I was only trying to help.'

An awkward silence hung between them.

'Sweetheart, all I want is to protect you and keep you safe.' She looked up at his face with its hangdog expression. 'You do see that, don't you?'

She nodded sullenly, confused. He kept saying that, but she couldn't help wondering if it was more a case of looking after his own reputation.

'My sweet Sheila,' he whispered and all her irritation melted away.

The bus was stuck at West Worthing crossing.

'I can't think how we're going to get the caravan back,' she said, trying to lighten the conversation and avoid the curious stares of the other passengers. 'How did you find it?'

'Somebody reported an old tramp who was sleeping in a doorway,' he said, 'and when they caught up with him, he had a fur stole under his vest.'

Sheila gasped. 'You mean the shop was robbed by a tramp?'

'No, silly,' Matthew said. 'The tramp saw the robbers hiding their stash, and when they'd gone, he went in and helped himself.' He grinned. 'Of course, by the time the sergeant had finished with him he was only too eager to tell us where he'd found it.'

Sheila frowned. 'You don't mean that he was beaten up?'

Matthew didn't answer. 'Unfortunately, a lot of the coats are ruined. The silly old fool left the door open and a fox got in.'

'A fox?' She waited for him to elaborate but, judging

by the pink creeping up his face, he already knew he'd said too much.

The bus drew up outside the Thomas A Becket pub and they got off. Matthew reached for her hand and tucked it into the crook of his arm. 'Promise me something,' he said earnestly. 'Promise me you'll get out of that awful garage as soon as possible.'

Sheila felt her cheeks flame.

'It's no place for a girl like you,' he went on. 'In fact, you were very lucky that whoever took that caravan didn't break in and ravish you both, especially if you were running around in your nightie and bare feet.'

Sheila snatched her hand back and stuffed it into her pocket. 'It wasn't like that and you know it,' she said crossly. 'Besides, Nelson would have seen them off if anyone had attacked me. And even if I did come outside in my nightie, I did nothing improper.'

He stopped walking and pulled her close to him. 'I'm sorry,' he said. 'I didn't mean to upset you, but you are such an innocent little thing.'

'I'm tougher than I look,' Sheila retorted.

'You look beautiful when you're cross,' he said as his mouth closed over hers in a tender kiss.

At the start of November, a few days of warm weather brought the last of the day trippers to Worthing and being on the outskirts of the town meant that, after a long drive, the Becket garage was the ideal place to fill up before the journey home. If they could have been open for seven days a week, they could have picked up even more custom, but the Sunday Trading Laws meant that everything was closed for the day. Saturday was by far their busiest day and although there still weren't that many cars on the road, Ronnie's suggestion of having their half-day on Wednesdays meant they could capitalize on it.

They'd had a particularly busy morning. Young Andrew Graham came to collect his bike. Sheila had met his mother a while back and agreed to put new brake cables on and replace the back tyre. She had knocked a bit off the bill because she knew Drew, as everyone called him, had saved up for the repair out of his own birthday and pocket money. Drew had lost his father in the siege of Tobruk.

At around twelve thirty, Sheila announced that she was gasping for a cup of tea. 'Can you man the pumps for me?' she asked Ronnie. 'I need the lav as well. I'll bring down a tray of something.'

Ronnie nodded and she was kept on her toes from that moment on. First came Doctor Rodway, their regular customer from Tarring. He was followed by Mr Beale. 'Taking the wife and kidlets to Crawley to see the mother-in-law tomorrow,' he confided as Ronnie filled his tank and wished him a safe journey. Janet Munday was next. She brought her little Ford in for a couple of gallons. As Ronnie handed Janet her change, a flashy-looking chap sounded a very noisy two-tone horn as he pulled into the forecourt in a two-seater MG. At the same time, Sheila came out with two cups of tea and a couple of small cakes on a tray and put them down by the pumps. The driver jumped out, leaving his passenger powdering her nose. 'Fill her up, darling, and where's the Gents?'

Ronnie seemed rooted to the spot, so Sheila pointed him in the direction of the outside lavatory. She was staring at the passenger, a peroxide blonde in her mid-thirties wearing some very expensive-looking clothes. It seemed that although her cousin was staring at her, the woman hadn't even noticed Ronnie. She was still looking into her powder compact mirror. She replenished her lipstick, wet her finger and drew it over her eyebrow and fiddled with the front of her hair. It was only as she finished that she became aware of Ronnie's stare. She turned her head sharply and their eyes met.

'Veronica,' she cried. 'Is that really you?'

Ronnie beamed. 'Angela Lyons. I never expected to see you here. You look amazing.'

'And you look . . .' Angela faltered as she took in Ronnie's messy hair, her smudged face and dirty overalls, 'busy.'

They both laughed.

'I often think of those wonderful evenings in the jazz club,' Ronnie said. 'I had the best time.'

'Me too,' said Angela, tossing her head. 'God, that seems like a lifetime ago, doesn't it? Are you well?'

Ronnie smiled and they paused to regard each other for a few moments. Angela had been her only friend in Singapore. They made the most of their times off together, doing the rounds of the more respectable clubs where the lower ranks met. She sighed. All of those men might be God knows where, but thank goodness her old friend had survived. Not only that, but she was looking as beautiful as ever. However had she done it? Ronnie frowned thoughtfully. 'I never came across you on the boat.'

'Oh, I flew out a couple of days before . . .' Angela began. Her voice trailed.

Sheila saw her cousin's face pale and the woman's cheeks turned scarlet. The driver came back. 'How much do I owe you?' he said, reaching into his inside coat pocket for his wallet and ration book. Ronnie seemed to be transfixed, so Sheila pushed the nozzle into the car. 'What did you want, sir?'

'I said fill her up,' he said tetchily. He turned his attention to his passenger, who was pulling on a head-scarf. 'Can I get you anything, darling?'

He seemed unaware of the awkward silence. Angela shook her head and turned her face away.

'It was you, wasn't it?' Ronnie said quietly.

Angela turned back and gave her a defiant stare. 'I have no idea what you're talking about,' she said, but her voice had an edge to it.

'You know exactly what I mean,' Ronnie said coldly. She put her hands onto the door. 'How could you, Angela? How could you do that?'

'Here,' the man cut in angrily. 'What is all this? Get away from my wife.'

Sheila was dealing with the ration book and his money, but she saw him push Ronnie out of the way as he climbed into the driver's seat. Coming between them, Sheila handed him his change and returned the book. He started the engine.

'You would have done the same thing,' Angela shouted above the engine noise. 'I was desperate. We were all desperate.'

The car began to move. Ronnie walked beside it, her hand still on the door. 'Because of you, two little children lost their innocence and went to hell and back,' she said.

'What about you?' Angela cried defiantly. 'I don't remember you being so bloody perfect either. Everybody knew about you and your lover.'

Ronnie's face went white.

'Get away from my car,' the driver shouted. 'What the blue-blazes is the matter with you?' He glanced back at Sheila. 'She wants bloody locking up, she does.'

They paused at the edge of the forecourt while the driver checked to make sure nothing was coming before he pulled out onto the road.

'You do realize that Mrs Lyle died in that camp, Angela,' said Ronnie.

Angela covered her ears with her hands and cried out, 'Don't, don't.' And as the car sped off, they saw her slump forward. Ronnie watched them disappear into the distance. Her face was ashen and her shoulders were shaking with rage and grief.

'Ronnie,' Sheila said gently, but her cousin only waved her away and ran indoors.

CHAPTER 11

Later that afternoon, Leslie rolled up in a red Morris 8 roadster with black trim and a soft top.

'Nice car,' said Ronnie. 'Is it new?'

'Good Lord, no,' Leslie chuckled. 'Borrowed it from a friend.'

Ronnie was very pleased to see her brother, making what Sheila thought was a rather over-blown show of it when she came onto the forecourt, and she knew better than to ask which friend he'd borrowed the car from. She and Ronnie were tiptoeing around each other as it was. Ronnie still hadn't said anything more about Angela, and Sheila knew better than to ask questions. Ronnie would tell her when she was ready to talk about it – or maybe she wouldn't. Cousin Leslie was, as usual, looking very smart, this time in a camel-coloured wool coat over his suit, and he was wearing a fedora hat.

'What have you been doing with yourself?' Ronnie smiled.

'Oh, you know, this and that,' said Leslie. 'Two gallons please.' He took out a silver cigarette case and helped himself, but he didn't offer it around. 'So, how's the garage business going?' he said pleasantly.

'Very well, although we did have a theft,' said Ronnie.

'Blimey!' he gasped. 'Did they take much?'

'A caravan,' said Ronnie. 'It was parked right here on the forecourt and somebody nicked it during the night.'

'That's awful,' Leslie sympathized. He shook his head and tutted. 'It seems like you can't keep anything safe these days without nailing it down.'

Sheila lifted the nozzle to give him the petrol he'd ordered.

Ronnie was frowning. Could Leslie have had anything to do with the caravan? Inwardly, she shook her head. Nah, what on earth would Leslie want with a bright yellow caravan?

'Ugh,' cried Sheila, almost dropping the pump, 'what on earth is that?'

Ronnie followed the direction of her pointed finger. Hanging from the edge of the nozzle was a tail. Sheila pulled it gingerly. The tail was followed by a very dead mouse, which she dropped on the floor.

Leslie roared with laughter. 'So much for country garages.'

'How on earth did that get there?' Ronnie gasped.

'Search me,' said Sheila, dispensing the petrol into Leslie's car.

Nelson had come out and was sniffing the mouse so Ronnie scooped it onto a shovel and deposited it in the rubbish bin. 'Can you stop for a cup of tea?'

134

she asked her brother as Sheila was wiping her hands on an old rag.

A lorry pulled up behind him on the pumps. The driver leaned out of the cab and asked for an oil check.

'Afraid not,' said Leslie, casually adding his usual, 'places to go, people to see.'

Ronnie took his money and his petrol coupon, then gave him a peck on his cheek. As she did so, she whispered in his ear, 'Stay out of trouble, won't you?'

'*Moi?*' he said, keeping a safe distance from her dirty overalls. 'I'm completely legit now, sis.'

'No hard feelings about the garage?' she said cautiously.

He smiled. 'None at all.'

Sheila had finished the oil check. She slammed the bonnet and the lorry driver started his engine. Leslie climbed into his car. 'I may not be around for a while,' he called as he drove off. 'Don't worry about me. Taking a bit of a break.'

The lorry followed him onto the Littlehampton Road. Sheila went straight back into the workshop, but Ronnie watched her brother, even though the lorry right behind him almost obscured the car, until he was out of sight.

'Fish and chips tonight?' said Sheila as Ronnie came back inside.

'Why not?' she smiled.

She was far too confident, that was the problem. A woman needed looking after; protecting. He liked it

135

when she let him take the lead. That was when she was at her most attractive.

Matthew was sitting in the police canteen on his break when his thoughts drifted towards Sheila again. He was alone. He preferred not to mix with the others and so he'd picked the only empty table. The room was filled with raucous laughter as his colleagues shared stories of their dealings with members of the public, but Matthew was lost in his own thoughts. What was he going to do about Sheila? It was hard to steer her in the right direction when she was annoyed with him over the smallest thing. If only she'd take a job in a shop or as a domestic or something. He didn't hold with girls doing a man's job. One good thing, she was always clean and tidy when he took her out. He would have put his foot down if she'd turned up with grease under her fingernails, for instance, but it wasn't right for a young good-looking girl to spend her working day dressed in overalls and wearing a turban on her head. Oh, he knew factory girls did it, but then they were – factory girls. And you could argue that a couple of years ago women did it all the time, but that was wartime. Girls should look pretty now.

And then there was the company she kept. Earlier in the week, during a spare moment, he'd checked up on Leslie Jackson. Probation, borstal and a spell in prison: it was hardly ideal for the girlfriend of a serving police officer, was it?

She couldn't even make sensible decisions. What was

she thinking, running about the street in the middle of the night, dressed only in her nightie? He could just imagine the street light behind her shining through the flimsy material and showing everybody her legs; her legs apart and she'd have no knickers on. He squirmed in his chair as he felt his erection getting bigger. Bloody hell; he'd better think of something else. Somebody came to the end of his story and everybody roared with laughter. Now was his chance. He stood up to leave. God knows what the others would think if they saw the state of him now.

By the time they turned off the Littlehampton Road and into Titnore Lane, it was already getting dark. Leslie led them towards the small turn-off which took them deeper into the woods and away from passing traffic. It wasn't long before they saw the outline of the caravan, but as he parked up, Leslie felt uneasy. Something looked different. He couldn't quite put his finger on it, but something was not quite right.

The lorry came right up behind him and the men jumped down from the cab. One went to the back of the lorry and pushed up the roll-down door. The silence of the woods was shattered by its shrill rumbling sound.

'Right, let's get this done,' said the driver. 'This place is too quiet for me. It gives me the creeps.'

Leslie tossed his fedora onto the front passenger seat and pulled on his leather gloves. He might be handling expensive furs, but they'd been here in the woods for three weeks. Even though the caravan was locked, spiders and all manner of creepy-crawlies might have got in by now.

'Got the key?' someone asked.

Leslie nodded confidently, but as they walked towards it, they could see that the caravan door had been forced open. 'Oh my God!'

The driver shone his torch inside. The caravan was completely empty. He turned to Leslie. 'What is this?' he growled.

'I don't know,' Leslie gasped desperately.

One of the lorry's passengers was right behind him. Leslie could feel his stale breath on his neck. 'You taken them somewhere?'

'No,' Leslie squeaked.

'Cos I'm telling you, when Billy hears about this, he'll have your guts for garters.'

'I'm as surprised as you are,' Leslie protested. 'I haven't been here since the day we stashed them. I don't under-stand.'

'Billy reckoned as 'ow they was werf ten grand,' said the man who had pushed open the roller door.

For the first time, Leslie was aware of how big they were. The driver was as wide as he was tall and one of the passengers had a broken nose and a cauliflower ear. The back-door man was standing right next to him, cracking his fingers one by one in a menacing way. Leslie felt sick and afraid – no, terrified.

'Honestly,' he said. 'I don't know where they are. I'm sorry.'

'You soon will be,' growled the driver. As they turned

towards the lorry, Leslie suddenly felt a stinging blow on the side of his head. He staggered sideways and cried out as a fist hit his ear a second time. As he fell onto the bracken-covered woodland floor, the back-door man kicked his thigh.

'Leave him to Billy,' said the driver, climbing back into the cab and starting the engine.

For a second Leslie thought they were going to leave him there, but then the other two stood over him and manhandled him towards the back of the lorry. A moment later, he felt himself being picked up and tossed through the air. He landed heavily inside the lorry, hurting his hip and elbow, and then he heard the roller door slam and it all went dark. 'Hey,' Leslie shouted, 'let me out!' but nobody came and, shortly after that, the lorry began to move.

Leslie pulled himself into a sitting position. It was dark inside the lorry, his head hurt and his ear was ringing. He put his hand up to feel it and it came away wet. He must be bleeding. As the lorry bounced over the rough ground the pain in his hip was almost unbearable. His heart rate had gone through the roof and he was trembling from head to foot. Dear God, this was his worst nightmare. What was going to happen to him now?

'I've written a letter,' said Ronnie as they finished their fish and chip meal. She handed it to Sheila to read. It was quite formal, addressed to Horsham District Council, and was a request for information about Miss

Daisy Peters, aged forty-six, who had been incarcerated since 1934. Ronnie went on to explain that Miss Peters's father had recently died and the family wanted to make contact. She had included a copy of his death certificate along with the letter.

'Brilliant,' said Sheila, handing it back. Ronnie put it into an envelope and licked it down.

That night, Ronnie's dream was the most violent yet. By the time Sheila was fully awake Ronnie had thrown all the bedclothes onto the floor. Sheila put her bedside light on and found her cousin sitting on the pillow with her knees drawn up towards her face. 'No,' she wept. 'That can't be right. No.'

'Ronnie,' said Sheila, crossing the floor. 'Wake up, Ronnie. You're having a bad dream.' She reached out and gently touched her cousin's arm, but Ronnie recoiled as if she'd been scalded. Even though her eyes were wide open, it was obvious that she was still trapped in her nightmare. Her face was white and she was trembling.

Suddenly Sheila felt scared. How was she going to get her out of this? 'Ronnie,' she repeated, only this time a little more firmly, 'Wake up. It's only a dream.' She rubbed Ronnie's arm and gradually a sense of the here and now came back into her eyes. She blinked, leaned forward, put her hands over her face and began to cry.

'It's okay,' said Sheila. 'It's over. You're safe now.'

'Oh, I'm sorry,' said Ronnie, becoming aware that

her nightie barely covered her and that she was exposed. She pulled her nightdress down and grabbed the fallen bedclothes to pull them up. 'I didn't mean to wake you up.'

'Please,' said Sheila, shaking her head, 'I don't mind at all. I only wish you didn't keep having these dreams.' Her cousin looked away. 'Is it something to do with that woman who came today?'

Ronnie wiped a tear away angrily. 'It doesn't matter.'

'I think it does,' Sheila said gently. 'You told me what happened in the camp, but I think you held something back. And seeing that woman has triggered everything off again.'

Ronnie stared at her for a second, then shook her head. 'It was all her fault,' she said. The voice in her head repeated *liar, liar* until she shook it away. She looked at her cousin helplessly. 'Oh, Sheila, I feel so bad and I can't do a damned thing about it.'

CHAPTER 12

'So who was that woman?' said Sheila, coming back into the bedroom.

Ronnie cupped her hands around the mug of hot tea she was offering. 'Angela Lyons,' she said. 'Like me, she worked for the wife of an army officer in Singapore.'

Sheila had put her own mug of tea onto her bedside table and was clambering back into bed. The room wasn't very warm, so she kept her plaid dressing gown on.

'Were you friends?'

'I thought we were good friends,' Ronnie said miserably.

Sheila reached for her tea with a frown. As soon as her cousin had agreed to talk, she'd gone into the kitchen to make a hot drink, leaving Ronnie space to cry for a bit. She seemed a little more composed now. After hearing about the horrors of prison life and the death of poor Mrs Lyle, Sheila wondered what on earth was coming next.

'You have to understand how things were out there before the war,' Ronnie said, staring down at the blanket in front of her. 'There were places you weren't supposed to go; people you couldn't mix with.'

'Because they were all upper-class snobs, I suppose,' said Sheila.

'Something like that,' said Ronnie. She hesitated. No, no, she couldn't tell her everything. Not yet. She wasn't ready for this much confession. 'I . . . I . . .'

'Let me guess,' said Sheila. 'You fell in love with someone you shouldn't have.'

Ronnie nodded, the expression on her face softening. 'He was a lovely man. So kind and gentle. We met up whenever we could; lovely long drives, that sort of thing.' The voice in her head was saying, *Go on, tell her. Tell her everything*, but she looked away to avoid Sheila's eye.

'There's something else, isn't there?' said Sheila. 'Go on, Ronnie, you might as well tell me.'

Ronnie's voice became very small. 'He was already married.'

'Oh.'

'I know what you must be thinking,' said Ronnie, 'but it wasn't like that, really it wasn't. He and I had something special.' She paused to sip her tea, hardly daring to look at her cousin. 'We had to keep it a secret otherwise they would have sent me home in disgrace.'

Sheila nodded. 'I don't know what to say.' There was always an unwritten rule that adultery was the worst of betrayals. No decent girl wanted to be responsible for the break-up of a marriage.

143

'There's nothing you can say,' said Ronnie. 'I can only hope you don't hate me too much.'

'I don't hate you, Ronnie,' said Sheila. 'I'm just a bit . . .'

'Disappointed,' Ronnie said defensively, 'that I'm a home wrecker?'

'Surprised,' said Sheila. 'That's all.'

Ronnie blew her nose.

'Anyway, what happened next?' said Sheila.

'When the call came to get ready for evacuation,' said Ronnie, stuffing her handkerchief under her pillow, 'the Major arranged for all of us to fly out on one of the last available planes. Mrs Lyle sent me to the offices to get the paperwork.'

'I thought you said you got out of Singapore by sea.'

'And we did,' said Ronnie, 'but before that, as I said, in the beginning we were supposed to fly out.'

'So why did it all change?'

Ronnie picked at the bedclothes. 'I set off but then I realized I would probably never have the chance to see the man I loved again, so I told the taxi driver to go to his little flat first.' She pulled her handkerchief from under the pillow and blew her nose again. Nelson stood up and laid his head on the bed near her hand.

'And did you see him?' asked Sheila.

Ronnie nodded. 'It was all very upsetting, but we said our goodbyes and then I went straight to the office. At first they wouldn't let me go in and when I finally did –' she paused to stem fresh tears – 'it wasn't there any more.'

'I don't understand,' said Sheila, confused. 'What wasn't there?'

'The permit, our exit papers, the tickets for the plane,' Ronnie wailed. 'Mrs Lyle's passport . . . everything. It was all supposed to be in one envelope, but it wasn't there.'

Sheila frowned.

'There was such a terrible flap going on,' Ronnie went on, 'and they went through every damned filing cabinet in the place.' She blew her nose again. 'Then this man came in and said somebody else had already collected it.'

'And you think that was Angela?'

'As soon as she blurted out that she'd flown home a couple of days before, I knew. I don't know why I didn't put two and two together before. Her surname is Lyons. Lyons, Lyle – with the mad panic that was on, it would have been easy for the person dealing with her to misread a name.'

'Oh, Ronnie, that's awful.'

The voice in her head was back: *But that wasn't all, was it? Go on, tell her.* Ronnie hung her head. 'One mistake, one stupid mistake, and I killed my employer.'

'Whoa, hang on a minute,' said Sheila, coming to sit on the edge of Ronnie's bed. 'You can't blame yourself for that. Anyone in your position would want to say goodbye to a special friend. It wasn't your fault. Angela was a thief and she knows she's in the wrong, Ronnie. That's why she couldn't even look at you.'

The voice was saying, *Now's your chance to make*

a clean breast of it. 'But I feel so responsible,' Ronnie said brokenly.

'Well, don't,' Sheila said firmly. 'Life happens. Wanting to see the man you loved was the most natural thing in the world. You're not a clairvoyant. You couldn't possibly have known the way things would turn out.'

Her cousin shook her head, but she was still upset. Sheila put her arms around her until she had calmed once more.

'So what happened to him?' Sheila asked as she climbed back into bed.

Ronnie stiffened. 'No idea,' she said quickly. 'I never saw him again.'

In the run-up to Bonfire Night, the streets around the Becket had become a frenzy of activity. The actual day was Tuesday, but because that was a normal working day, someone had organized for a bonfire to be set up on an area of waste ground opposite the Becket garage on Saturday November 9th. As Ronnie put a big notice up on the garage door she looked up and saw the man opposite staring at her through the upstairs window again. Funny, she thought, I haven't seen him for a while. For a second, she wondered vaguely where he had been and wished he hadn't come back. He seemed to spend his life spying on them. Didn't he have anything better to do?

The local children began collecting any combustible material which was no longer wanted or useful. Sheila and Ronnie had quite a bit of old rotten wood, especially broken fence panels, as well as old crates with no bottoms and some unusable furniture they'd found when they'd moved in. As Alan Albright and his friends Michael Hetherington (Hethy), Steven Kennard and Drew heaved it all onto their wheelbarrows, an old pram and a home-made trolley with wheels, the girls were glad to see it go. The men – dads, granddads and a couple of German POWs who had been working for Len Hurst in his greenhouses along Terringes Avenue – supervised the building of the bonfire and the local boys were delighted to hear that it was reported to be the biggest in the area.

Ever since the beginning of November the younger children like Geoffrey Albright had hung around every street corner asking for a penny for the guy. The shops had a much better selection of fireworks than last year. Catherine wheels, rockets, golden rain and jack-in-the-boxes were readily available, and of course, nobody minded how much light filled the skies.

Elsie Tunnock and Pen Albright had organized the local women into preparing food for the crowd. There would be baked potatoes and hot chestnuts, which would be roasted in the dying embers of the fire. The vicar's wife had several apple trees in her garden and offered the windfalls, so Sheila and Ronnie decided to make toffee apples for the children as their contribution to the fun. They had also been asked to man the tea table. People could have tea or Bovril on the night at thruppence a mug (bring your own mug), the profits going to the children's home on Offington Lane.

On Saturday, the men nailed Catherine wheels onto

posts and set up temporary shelves so that everybody could see the display. They used empty milk bottles to keep the rockets upright and pointing towards the sky. One man had the bright idea of putting a large rocket in an old kettle filled with soil. When he finally lit the blue touch paper on the night, it whooshed up into the air and lifted the kettle with it. As it headed towards the Littlehampton Road, everyone waited with bated breath for an irate yell or perhaps the sound of breaking glass, but fortunately none came.

Someone had bought some atom bomb bangers which were about six inches long. 'That made one hell of a bang,' said the vicar as one thundered into the sky and everybody laughed. There were plenty of sparklers for the little ones. An old three-piece suite was placed beside the fire, waiting to be lobbed on the top when it was safe to do so, but until then the older folks used it for one last time.

The whole occasion was a wonderful opportunity for friends and neighbours to get together and although they had been enemies only a year ago, even the Germans were made to feel welcome. Ronnie and Sheila met so many new faces and they certainly did a roaring trade on the tea and Bovril table.

Nelson had been left indoors. He probably wouldn't have liked the bangs, and in such a large crowd Sheila was afraid that someone might accidentally step on his paw. People were very complimentary about the garage and although they never intended to, the girls soon found themselves drumming up new business.

'Ever since you fixed Dad's mower, it's been going like the clappers. Can you fix new valves in the wireless?'

'Do you do paraffin deliveries?'

'We've only just taken the covers off my husband's old car. It's been holed up since the war. Can you come and have a look at it?'

Matthew came for a while, but he had to report for duty at eight so he couldn't stay. Sheila was disappointed for him because the jacket potatoes were nowhere near ready, but he didn't seem too perturbed. He bought some Bovril although he had to borrow Sheila's mug. After giving her a kiss, he went on his way.

When the fireworks were finished, everyone stood around the bonfire roasting their faces while their backs were like ice, but that was half the fun. The POWs, both young Germans, handed round the food. It was tricky trying to hold a hot baked potato and eat it at the same time, especially if you didn't have gloves.

Towards the end of the evening, Pen called Ronnie over to meet someone.

'My name is Mrs Edwards,' she said, cutting to the chase. 'I understand you might take on a young school leaver?'

'Yes,' said Ronnie. 'My cousin is our mechanic and there are times when we need an extra pair of hands. We'd be willing to pay a small wage and we'll give the person on-the-job training.'

'Excellent,' said Mrs Edwards.

'Do you think you might have someone in mind?' said Ronnie, ducking to one side as Pen suddenly called out, 'Bedtime, you little tykes,' and dashed past them as Alan and Geoffrey tried to escape.

'Most definitely,' said Mrs Edwards. 'One boy in particular. Derek Milne. I'm sure he'd be a hard worker, but he's still at school until Christmas.'

'Why not send him round at the weekend?' said Ronnie. 'Perhaps we could offer him a Saturday job and see how it pans out.'

Mrs Edwards beamed. 'Thank you, Miss Jackson, that would be wonderful.'

'Ronnie, please.'

They were joined by an attractive young girl aged about thirteen or fourteen who was dressed in a red coat. The girl slipped her hand through Mrs Edwards's arm. 'What would be wonderful?'

Mrs Edwards paused to introduce them. 'Miss Jackson, er, Ronnie, this is my granddaughter, Trixie. Ronnie and her cousin run the Becket garage.'

'Pleased to meet you,' said Trixie politely.

'Ronnie is offering Derek a Saturday job,' said her grandmother.

Trixie chuckled. 'Oh, Granny, you are truly amazing.' She turned to Ronnie. 'If my grandmother has her way, every single one of those kids will be settled in their own jobs.'

'Everyone deserves a fair crack of the whip,' Mrs Edwards said stoutly.

Trixie smiled. 'Can you sing?'

Ronnie laughed. 'After a fashion, I suppose, but I'm not competition material if that's what you mean.'

'I only ask,' said Trixie, 'because we'll be starting our choir practice in a couple of weeks' time.'

'I'm not much of a churchgoer,' said Ronnie apologetically.

'Oh, this isn't for the church,' said Trixie. 'We do the odd concert, but mostly we go around the villages at Christmas time singing carols. You must come. It's great fun.' Her shining eyes and her enthusiasm quickly won Ronnie over, so despite her reservations, she found herself agreeing to come.

'Oh good,' said Trixie, 'I'll tell Mum.' Struggling to see in the gloom, Trixie wrote Ronnie's name and address in a little book.

'What about you, Sheila?' Clearly Trixie wasn't going to let anyone slip through the net.

Sheila nodded. 'And after saying all that about your gran,' she chuckled, 'you must be a chip off the old block.'

Trixie and Mrs Edwards looked at each other and smiled. 'That's the nicest compliment we've ever had,' said Mrs Edwards, drawing her granddaughter into a hug. 'You see, Trixie's mother is adopted.'

The evening was virtually over by nine although Sheila and Ronnie stayed behind to help with the clearing up. Everything had gone smoothly despite the fire brigade turning up at eight o'clock with a threat to douse the flames. The men let them on site but several women brandishing long-handled brooms chased them away. The fire was big, but, they insisted, it was well built and perfectly safe. The firemen left, only to return later in the evening, though this time in the hope of finding some left-over food. As soon as the three-piece suite was tossed to the flames, most of the kids and the older folk left for home and Ronnie and Sheila weren't far behind.

When they got to the garage, Sheila let out a cry of alarm. The door was wide open. 'Oh no, we've been broken into again!'

It looked like the whole place had been turned over. Cupboards had been emptied; the contents of an old trunk lay strewn over the floor. The trunk itself had been turned upside down and everything had been pulled off the shelves. Upstairs, the beds had been pulled apart and their wardrobes had been emptied out as well. The squeaky floorboard had been broken open with a jemmy. Splintered wood was everywhere. 'I don't understand,' said Ronnie. 'Who would do this?'

Sheila shrugged. 'Whoever it was, they were obviously looking for something.'

'But what?' Ronnie cried. 'There's nothing of any great value here.'

Sheila went back downstairs. A second or two later she called to Ronnie. 'There's worse,' she said. 'There's blood on the floor by the door and Nelson is missing.'

CHAPTER 13

The police, in the form of Sergeant Longfellow, turned up on Sunday morning. The night before, Sheila and Ronnie had spent some time trailing around the local roads, calling for Nelson, but he was nowhere to be found. Completely exhausted, they finally hauled their mattresses back into place and fell onto their beds at two in the morning. By the time Cecil Longfellow arrived, Sheila had already trekked around the same area again and now they were both in the middle of what was obviously going to be a mammoth clear-up. Everything had to be ready in time to open up on Monday.

'Any idea who would have done this?' said Longfellow, pulling his leg over the saddle of his bike.

Ronnie shook her head. 'As far as we can see, nothing has been taken.'

'We think someone was looking for something,' said Sheila.

Sergeant Longfellow looked thoughtful. 'And what would that be?'

Ronnie shrugged.

'Have you girls by any chance been dabbling in the black market?' he enquired.

'No we jolly well haven't!' Sheila cried.

Of the two of them, Sheila was the one who was the most affected by the break-in. Although she put a brave face on it, her eyes were permanently red-rimmed and she kept blowing her nose. 'I'm more concerned about poor Nelson,' she said. 'He must have been terrified.'

Cecil Longfellow told them there wasn't a lot he could do about it. Nothing had been stolen, and although the blood was most likely Nelson's, the police had more pressing things to attend to. Frankly, no one at the station would give a hoot for a missing mongrel. 'You might think about getting a telephone put in,' he said sagely. 'Two women on their own, you may need to summon help quickly.' He smiled. 'Now, how about a nice cup of tea?'

Having enjoyed the tea and a little rest, he went on his way.

'I think he's right about the telephone,' said Ronnie as they went back to the task of clearing up. 'It would be good for business as well. I'll look into it.'

Matthew turned up during the afternoon and Sheila went into his arms as he comforted her for some time. Ronnie left them to it and kept out of their way. She didn't much like Matthew, but she knew her cousin could do with the attention as she had been quite emotional about it all. Ronnie wasn't sure why she felt uneasy about her cousin's relationship with Matthew. He was always polite and, as far as she could see, he treated Sheila well enough.

The thing that worried Ronnie more was how detached she herself felt. Since she'd been imprisoned by the Japs, apart from the emotional turmoil in the wake of her dreams, she'd found it hard to show any sort of feeling. She supposed it was because of three years of keeping it all stuffed inside, but now that she was free to show her emotions, she just couldn't do it. She was efficient, hard-working and level-headed, but inside she was switched off and cold. She tried, but she couldn't conjure up a feeling that wasn't there. That was the way she was now. Upstairs, she nailed a new piece of board over the one which had been splintered. Then she folded everything neatly and put it back into the cupboards. Her mind was in a whirl. Whoever had done this must have known they were all at the fireworks and yet she couldn't imagine any of their neighbours being responsible. What on earth could the intruders have been looking for? And if they'd wanted some particular thing, why trash the upstairs rooms and vice versa? They must have made quite a noise chucking everything around, but she supposed the people in the surrounding area were all on the waste ground watching the show and eating baked potatoes. It was a real puzzle.

Downstairs, Matthew was gentle. He stroked Sheila's hair and told her everything would be all right and eventually her tears subsided. He felt a glow of satisfaction as she rested in his arms, grateful that she had someone so strong and dependable. They had sat down by the desk in the garage.

'By the way,' he said, 'you'll be pleased to hear that the police have released the caravan.'

'Really? So where is it?'

'Titnore Woods,' said Matthew. 'They had to keep it secret in case the criminals came back. It was being used to store stolen property.'

'And did they?'

'What?'

'The criminals. Did they come back?'

'Oh yes,' said Matthew.

'So you caught them red-handed?' she said eagerly.

Matthew licked his lips. She liked him, didn't she? She admired him. 'Not exactly,' he confessed, 'but they did find an abandoned get-away car. A Morris 8 with a soft top.'

Sheila didn't move but he saw her face flush. She chewed her top lip thoughtfully. Wasn't Leslie driving just such a car when he called by last weekend? 'But you didn't catch the driver?'

'Not yet.' And when she let out a sigh of relief, he frowned and added brightly, 'But don't worry, we will. It's all part of the plan; little minnows catch bigger fish.' There was a small silence. Sheila sat up and he let his arm fall. 'I finish my probation at Easter,' he went on, eager not to miss the moment. 'After that, will you marry me?'

'Oh, Matthew,' she whispered.

He caught her hand and squeezed it, then kissed her fingers tenderly. 'So first things first,' he said. 'We have to find you somewhere else to live.'

Sheila regarded him for a moment. 'What? But I already have somewhere to live.'

He could feel her irritation and shot her a wounded look. 'I'm not going to argue with you,' he said, his voice tight and controlled. 'But I've told you before. I only want the best for you and I don't want you staying here. Surely you can see more than ever now that it's not safe?'

She took her hand back. 'But I don't want to give up the garage,' she said stubbornly. 'This is my home.'

His mouth became set in a thin line.

'I would like to marry you,' she said in a measured tone, 'but I think we should wait a while, don't you?'

He resisted the desire to hit her. 'Why?'

'It all feels a little rushed,' she said, 'and so much has happened in the last few months.' She looked away. 'I just need some time to catch my breath. I'm sorry.'

He smiled awkwardly. 'Fair enough.'

'Oh, Matthew,' she sighed as she sank back into his arms. He kissed the top of her head. 'You really mustn't worry about me being in the garage,' she said into the folds of his coat. 'I don't think for one moment those men will come back. Whatever they were looking for, it obviously wasn't here.'

'You're probably right,' he said quickly, careful that

157

she didn't see his nostrils flare or the impatient expression on his face.

Nelson came back two days later. As he limped into the garage, Sheila cried out in delight. He came towards her, doing his best to wag his tail, but she could see at once that something was wrong. He had earth on his snout and one of his front paws was bleeding. They offered him water and some leftover scraps. He was ravenously hungry and very thirsty.

'I want to take him to the vet,' said Sheila.

He seemed exhausted, so they put him into an old pram and Sheila wheeled him there straight away. Normally he would have jumped out of the pram as soon as it moved, but today he was lacklustre and in pain. The vet was unequivocal in his diagnosis.

'I would say he's been shut up somewhere,' he said. 'It looks to me as if he was trying to dig himself out.' He pointed to the damage on Nelson's front pads. 'I suggest a good rest and plenty of food should do the trick.'

'What about his side?' Sheila asked.

'It's badly bruised,' said the vet. 'Someone most likely kicked him.' Sheila felt a moment of absolute rage.

They were confident that once Nelson was well again and the garage was tidied, things would get back to normal, but the morning post brought two letters. The man from the GPO was coming tomorrow to install the telephone, so at first Ronnie thought it was something

158

to do with that, but one turned out to be a poison-pen letter. Made up of newspaper cuttings, it had no postmark, but it said, 'Get out or I'll come back.'

It was disconcerting, but they were determined not to let it upset them.

The other letter came from a Mr Pulsford of Horsham Borough Council. He thanked them for their enquiry regarding Aunt Daisy and said he would be coming to Worthing next month. 'I would be very grateful if you would meet me in the new town hall on Monday December 2nd at 2.30 p.m.,' he wrote. 'I believe I have some information which may be of use to you, but I prefer to speak to you in person rather than write a letter.'

'Oh dear,' said Ronnie with a sigh. 'It sounds as if he's going to tell us she's died.'

Sheila nodded. 'Well, at least we tried,' she said, 'and if he tells us where she's buried, we can take flowers.'

The two of them were sitting at the breakfast table. A busy day lay ahead of them. Sheila had a couple of new tyres to fit on some farm vehicle and the paraffin delivery would be coming in the afternoon. Ronnie had to replenish the wool stock in the newsagent's and she was due to meet up with Mrs Edwards to discuss further the arrangements for their apprentice. With no extra accommodation on site, and Mrs Edwards being forced to evict the young lad as soon as he turned fifteen, they had to find somewhere for him to live. Fortunately, Elsie had a spare room and even though she would only get a pittance, she was happy to give the boy a roof over his head. They still hadn't found a way to retrieve the caravan, but Ronnie hoped that when their business was over, Mrs Edwards might be persuaded to either lend her car or agree to help them tow it back.

Sheila stood up to wash the breakfast things – two eggs cups, two plates, two cups and saucers and some cutlery – while Ronnie wiped down the oil cloth on the kitchen table. The radio was on, but it was only the weather forecast so they were hardly listening. Just before the news, the announcer, Alvar Liddell, began an SOS message.

'Would Mrs Peters, last seen in Worthing, West Sussex, and now believed to be in the Warminster area, please contact the Royal Sussex County Hospital where her grandson is dangerously ill.'

The two girls froze. 'Was that about Leslie?' Ronnie asked.

'I think so,' said Sheila. 'Your mum and dad live in Warminster, don't they?'

A look of terror crossed Ronnie's face as she grabbed her purse from her handbag and raced downstairs to the call box on the corner of the road.

CHAPTER 14

It turned out to be a long day. Sheila was struggling to get the tyres onto the wheels of a builder's lorry and at the same time she was having to deal with a steady flow of customers at the pumps. The numbers of cars on the roads were growing all the time. Halfway through the morning, Sally Emmet turned up with an old pram. The bodywork was sound, but the straps were broken and one wheel had been damaged in a bomb blast in 1943. Sally's husband had returned from the war earlier in the year and, like a lot of married women of her ilk, Sally was pregnant. Fortunately, Sheila had a small collection of pram parts, including old straps and wheels, which she kept on the premises – if she couldn't repair a pram she would cannibalize it for another.

A bit later, Len Hurst turned up with a couple of German POWs. Sheila recognized them from the night of the bonfire. They were in uniform, but they had a large letter 'P' sewn on the back. Len had been allocated several such men to help him in the greenhouses. Even though the war had ended in 1945, the country still had a large number of German POWs. Some were in camps, but the majority had been put to work on the land, mending the roads and working on building sites. Several hundred were earmarked to begin working on the new housing estate which was to be started shortly near Durrington-on-Sea station. 'I heard you're on your own,' said Len, 'so they may as well give you a hand. Helmut could be a general handyman, but young Gerhard here tells me he's done a bit of garage work. Shall I leave them with you for the day?'

Sheila could have kissed him. Mr Hurst stepped back and shouted at the men, 'You stay here. You help in garage. Okay?'

Helmut gave her a sullen look, but Gerhard nodded politely. When Mr Hurst had gone, Sheila discovered that although Helmut struggled, Gerhard's English was excellent. They both looked very young, maybe only eighteen or nineteen years old.

Getting the tyres off and on was a piece of cake with an extra pair of strong hands and they helped her with several other heavy jobs. She didn't even have to feed them as both men had been sent with their own sandwiches. While she made them some tea, Nelson sat at their feet salivating until she sent him indoors. Nelson and Gerhard appeared to be firm friends already. In the afternoon, she sent Gerhard down to the shed at the bottom of the garden. A couple of weeks ago, she'd managed to get hold of a wheel for the old van but hadn't had time to fit it as yet. Gerhard seemed to think it would be no trouble at all so she left him to it. Helmut was put to work sweeping the floor and generally tidying up, but he was slow and not very thorough.

It was getting dark and the shed had no light, but to her utter joy, at about four o'clock she saw the old van moving sedately up the garden towards the forecourt.

'You got it going!' she cried. 'Oh, thank you!'

Gerhard jumped out of the driver's seat and smiled sheepishly.

'What was wrong with it? I got the engine to turn over, but I couldn't sustain it.'

Gerhard opened the bonnet and explained what he'd done. Once he'd gone through the sequence of events, it became blindingly obvious. She turned to him and smiled. 'You are amazing,' she said. Their heads were very close together and up until then she hadn't noticed how handsome he was. Blond with twinkling tawny eyes and a dimple on the left side of his face which only showed when he smiled. He smelled of car engine oil, but underneath she sensed a hint of Lifebuoy soap. His breath was sweet, probably because he didn't smoke. As she caught his eye, he moved towards her.

They heard a sound behind them and Nelson let out a soft growl. Gerhard stood up so quickly he bumped his head on the lid of the bonnet.

It was Matthew.

'Oh,' Sheila said guiltily as Gerhard walked away. 'What are you doing here?'

'I've just come off duty,' Matthew said with a dark

look on his face. He reached out to pat Nelson, but the dog backed away. 'There was an accident on the Findon Road and I was assigned to traffic duty until the upturned car could be removed.' He stared at Gerhard's receding back.

Sheila felt a tinge of frustration. If only they had their own recovery vehicle they could have collected the car for repair. It annoyed her that, despite all their hard work, she and Ronnie still operated on a shoestring.

Matthew leaned over to kiss her cheek. 'Where's Ronnie?'

'She's gone to Brighton,' said Sheila, closing the bonnet.

'What, and left you here on your own with these two?'

'They're all right,' she said. 'And Ronnie had to go and see her brother.'

Matthew pulled a face. 'What's he been up to now?'

Sheila could feel herself beginning to prickle. She knew he had already put two and two together and made five when he'd seen Gerhard and her so close together, but why did he always have to make snide remarks? 'As a matter of fact, he's ill,' she snapped, 'and there's a possibility he might even die.'

Matthew pulled a face. 'Well, if he does, that'll be one less criminal, I suppose.'

Sheila felt a rush of righteous indignation. She opened her mouth, but they were interrupted by a ruddy-faced British soldier on a bicycle. Nelson barked and then sniffed at the soldier's outstretched hand. 'Hello there. Is Fritz ready?'

On the forecourt, Gerhard snapped to attention, clicking his heels smartly. The soldier, a man in his late forties, got off his bike and came towards them. 'Mr Hurst told me he'd lent you a couple of them for the day. Been behaving themselves, have they?'

'They've been a great help,' said Sheila, deliberately giving Matthew a sideways glance. 'In fact, I couldn't have managed without them.'

'That's good then,' said the soldier, and turning to Gerhard he said, 'Come along now, Fritz. Get your stuff together. Where's the other one?'

'In the garage,' said Sheila, putting her hand out for Gerhard to shake.

'There's no need for that,' said the soldier, adding quite unnecessarily, 'he's only a POW.'

Slightly embarrassed, Sheila opened up the bonnet again as she watched all three of them go. Helmut appeared annoyed about something. He was jabbering away in German, but Gerhard didn't seem to be taking much notice.

Matthew hovered, clearly waiting to be invited to come in. Sheila busied herself doing nothing in particular under the bonnet of the van until he said awkwardly, 'There's something I want to ask you.'

She re-emerged with a look of disdain on her face. 'Oh? And what's that?'

'I wanted to ask you to come with me to the Police Ball,' he said. 'It's in the Assembly Rooms on New Year's Eve.'

Sheila's eyes lit up. A ball! She'd never been to

165

anything like that before. Her crossness forgotten, she beamed. 'I'd love to.'

'All the women wear ballgowns,' he said cautiously. 'Will that be all right?'

'Of course,' she said. She was already planning what colour to have.

'Well, I guess I'd better be off or I'll be late for tea.' He paused, expecting her to respond.

Sheila had turned away and was checking the oil level.

Matthew was disappointed. He'd expected her to be overcome with excitement. 'Coming to the pictures tomorrow night?'

She stood up to wipe the dipstick on her rag before putting it down the chamber. 'I might do, but I can't make any promises,' she said. 'Not until I know how Leslie is, and besides, Ronnie may not even be back by then.'

'Of course,' he said, and giving her a wounded look, he swung his leg over the saddle of his bike and rode off.

The Royal Sussex County Hospital in Brighton was an impressive building on a hill overlooking the sea. Built in the Georgian style, it was a beautiful cream-coloured brick, which had been designed in the previous century by no less an architect than Charles Barry, the one who had redesigned the Houses of Parliament. Ronnie hardly noticed as, almost demented with worry, she hurried through the main doors of the Barry Building.

After making the call from the phone box at the end of the road, she had raced back to the garage to tell Sheila where she was going, then run all the way to West Worthing station. She was lucky. The Brighton train was due in five minutes, which gave her just enough time to cross the line, buy her ticket then cross back again in time to catch the train. It was an all-stations-stop so the journey seemed endless. Once she arrived in Brighton, the hospital was too far to walk, so that meant a bus ride.

When Ronnie had phoned the ward, they had been sparing with the details. All she knew was that her brother had been brought into the hospital unconscious and remained in a critical state. As soon as he was able, the police wanted to interview him, although nobody thought he would name his attackers. The custom of honour amongst thieves meant that the cops were faced with a wall of silence. When Ronnie arrived on the ward, the sister was slightly surprised. After the SOS on the radio, they had been expecting to see Leslie's grandmother. Ronnie had to explain who she was and that Granny lived a long way away and it would take a while for her to get here. The ward sister led her to a small cubicle. 'You must prepare yourself for the worst,' she said before they went in. 'He is not a pretty sight.'

She was right. Leslie's normally handsome face was so bloated, bruised and swollen that he was hardly recognizable. It was obvious that he'd been beaten to within an inch of his life. His arm was in plaster and there was a cradle over his leg. Ronnie resisted the urge to cry out or burst into tears.

'Can I sit with him for a while?'

The sister smiled kindly. 'Take all the time you like,' she said.

Ronnie knew how strict hospitals were with visiting times, afternoons two till four, evenings six till seven, no exceptions. That's when she understood just how seriously ill Leslie was. They obviously didn't expect him to survive. She wished she had stopped long enough to telephone Mum. There was nothing for it but to ask the hospital to get in touch with them. The sister took down the details and, with a squeak of her shoe on the mirror-like linoleum floor, she hurried away.

Ronnie sat down beside the bed. She'd never been particularly close to her brother, but now that this moment had come, all the angst and resentment she'd once felt towards him melted away. She found herself reliving small memories of childhood. She recalled the time he'd tied the belt of her school dress to her chair in assembly and how when she'd stood up to sing the hymn, she'd lifted the chair behind her and dragged half the row as well. It made an awful clatter and she'd got into trouble.

The first time he'd pinched something, half a crown from their mother's purse, their father gave him a terrible thrashing. Afterwards, Leslie had run away. He didn't reappear until teatime and their father had knocked him about again. That was the day the vendetta between them began. If the truth were told, Ronnie didn't much like her father either. He could be a hard and vindictive man. Leslie did everything he could to provoke his father, whereas she chose to avoid confrontation and keep out of his way. That was why she'd jumped at the chance to work for Mrs Lyle. 'Abroad' was just about as far away as she could go to get away from him. As they got older, Leslie seemed to enjoy going out of his way to antagonize their father. The more his father retaliated and ridiculed Leslie, the worse it became. Just to spite him, petty crime became a way of life and her brother began his downward spiral. He was always caught. To begin with it was a severe reprimand from the police, but that quickly escalated to six strokes of the birch and eventually led to borstal and then prison.

She knew when he'd turned up at Granddad's funeral in his flashy clothes that he was still at it, but what could she do? Granny was the only member of the family Leslie could relate to. He often went to stay with her as a boy and they had been very close, but now even she had apparently turned her back on him by giving Ronnie and her cousin the garage. Granddad had been so like her father. It always amazed her that they weren't blood relatives. They certainly came from the same stable. Why on earth, when her own father had made Mum so unhappy, did she marry a man so much like him? It was a question which couldn't be answered. Even when she was a young girl, Ronnie was convinced that, given the same set of circumstances, she would have chosen a man who was completely opposite – and of course, she had done. Her heart constricted as she thought of him again. She shook her head. She must stop doing this. It was over. She should never have allowed it to happen in the first place and she hated the person she had become.

Her brother's hand lay on the top of the sheet. Ronnie reached out and touched it. It was as cold as ice. She rubbed the skin gently to try and get some warmth back. She glanced around. They were quite alone so she did something she hadn't done since she was at school. She prayed.

The sister came back a few minutes later. 'I've spoken to your parents,' she said quietly. 'Your father tells me if your brother is still with us at the weekend, they will journey down.'

Ronnie nodded grimly. Trust Dad. Anyone else would drop everything and come right away, but not him. He would think of the expense and keeping the shop open first.

The sister left. Ronnie rubbed Leslie's hand again. 'Leslie,' she whispered. 'Come on, love. Defy the old man one more time. He thinks you're not going to make it.' And just for a moment, she could have sworn she felt his fingers flicker.

CHAPTER 15

The day after the SOS message, Granny turned up at the garage with her little dog and Ronnie's mother. Apparently they'd jumped on a train while her father was at work. Nelson regarded them with a slightly suspicious stare, but quickly became friends with Milly.

'Did Dad say you could come?' Ronnie asked as she made her mother and grandmother a cup of tea and a sandwich. They had already made plans to go with her when she went to see Leslie in the evening.

Her mother shook her head. 'He'll go mad,' she said, 'but I can't help it. He's my son and I want to see him.'

'We didn't hear the SOS message on the wireless,' said Granny. 'That's why we were so glad to get the call from the hospital.'

'Are you going back home tonight?' Ronnie asked. It would be quite a struggle to get them onto a train which could take them all the way back to Wiltshire before midnight.

Granny shook her head as she folded Nelson's ears. 'My old neighbour, Mrs Roberts, has offered to put us up for a couple of days.'

Jean Jackson was pinning her brooch back into place where it had come undone on her cardigan. 'Do you know what happened to Leslie?'

'Only that he was beaten up,' said Ronnie. 'He hasn't said who did it or why.'

'At least he's conscious now,' said Granny.

Ronnie nodded. 'He came round early this morning.' She reached out and grasped her mother's hand. 'I have to warn you, he looks a bit of a mess.'

Jean Jackson pulled a handkerchief from up her sleeve and dabbed her nose. 'I just don't understand why he gets mixed up with such awful people.'

'Yes you do, Mum,' said Ronnie as she propped up a card on the dresser inviting her and Sheila to choir practice in the Archbishop's Palace in Tarring on December 2nd. 'You know you do. It's because of Dad.'

'Oh, Ronnie,' Granny cautioned.

'No, Granny,' said Ronnie. 'It needs to be said. Just because Leslie doesn't want to work in the shop, Dad has always put him down. He's never got a good word to say about him. Leslie makes out he's tough and that he doesn't care, but he does. He's hurt.'

'I despair of that boy,' said Granny. 'I've tried and tried to help him.' She let out a sigh. 'I've lost count of the times he's had a brush with the law. I don't know why you blame your father. You were both brought up in the same home and look at you. You turned out all right, didn't you?'

'Only because I got out as soon as I could,' said

172

Ronnie. 'And I got as far away as possible when I went to Singapore.'

Jean made a small noise.

'I'm sorry, Mum,' said Ronnie, 'but I'm sick of pretending it doesn't happen.' She put her hand on her mother's arm again. 'You need to get out and all.'

'Ronnie!' her grandmother gasped and Ronnie rounded on her. 'Stop defending him, Granny, or things will never change. No offence, Mum, but you're not going to sit there and tell me that you're happy.'

The two women looked uncomfortable. 'Your dad says he's washed his hands of Leslie,' said Jean. 'The day after the funeral he called the sign writer in and changed the sign over the door. He's always prided himself that he was carrying on the family business and that he would pass it on to his son, but he got them to take off the "& Son". Now it just says "Jackson Master Butchers since 1842".'

'You should have given him another son, Mum,' Ronnie quipped.

'Good Lord, no!' Jean blurted out. 'I put a stop to all that nonsense years ago.'

All three of them were slightly embarrassed by the outburst and Ronnie quickly changed the subject. 'Granny, why don't you come back to Worthing? All your friends are here. Since they heard that SOS message, no end of people have walked up from Pavilion Road to ask about Leslie and you.'

Her grandmother turned her head away, but not before Ronnie saw a tear in her eye. 'I don't know what's got into you, my girl,' she said. 'Really I don't.'

'Perhaps it's seeing Leslie like that that's made me think about what's really important in life,' she said. 'I've spent too many years doing what other people expect me to do and far too long pretending everything will be all right tomorrow. Well, not any more. I'm happy here. I've put the past behind me.' Ignoring the voice in her head, she went on, 'I may not have much, and Sheila and I have had a few knocks on the way, but I like my life now.'

'They look nice!' Sheila burst through the door and grabbed an egg sandwich. 'This one for me?' she said as she sat down with a bright smile.

Ronnie got to her feet and, getting another cup and saucer from the cupboard, she poured a cup of tea for her cousin. 'I'm taking Mum and Granny to see Leslie tonight, is that all right?'

'Fine,' said Sheila. She hesitated. 'I'm sorry. Did I interrupt a family conflab?'

'No, no,' said Ronnie, sitting back down.

'Good,' said Sheila, 'then look at this.' She threw the local newspaper onto the table. The headline, big and bold, screamed across the front page: '£10,000 haul of furs found. Gang members caught.' Underneath, there was a picture of the caravan looking forlorn and empty.

'Flippin' heck!' cried Ronnie as she grabbed the paper.

A sudden wave of panic swept over Sheila. Was Leslie involved in that robbery? Was that why he was beaten up?

But Ronnie was beaming. 'What a stroke of luck!' she cried. 'Don't you see? With that caravan out front, we'll attract customers for miles.'

Jean was appalled when she saw Leslie's condition and she lost no time in telling the nursing staff that she hardly recognized him. As soon as he heard her voice, he opened one eye as much as it would allow and croaked, 'Mum.' She saw a tear trickle down the side of his cheek and he was her little boy again.

Jean had always been a woman torn. Friends told her she was too soft, but her chief aim had always been to keep the family together. It was not easy when her husband and son were at loggerheads and her daughter was twelve thousand miles away. Bill and Leslie were like two peas in a pod. Bill would put his foot down and Leslie seemed to enjoy antagonizing his father. When Leslie was younger, it was manageable. Bill would insist and, of course, being that much bigger, always got his own way. It was only as their son grew older that the real trouble started. Leslie was every bit as stubborn as his father. They argued and fought all the time until Leslie decided he didn't want to work in the shop and told his father he didn't give a fig for the family business. Of course, Jean understood why. Leslie had a thing about being clean, but for Bill, it was like a slap in the face and things went from bad to worse.

The constant rows drove Ronnie away. Jean was broken-hearted when she went off to Singapore of all places. There was no doubt that it was a fantastic opportunity for a girl like Ronnie, but it was halfway across the world.

The war years had been agony for Jean. Her daughter had been captured by the Japanese and who could tell what horrors she faced. Maybe she was dead? As for Leslie, while other women's sons were fighting for freedom from tyranny, he'd ended up in trouble with the law and was locked up in prison. The end of the war brought the promise of a better life. Ronnie came home safe and sound, albeit terribly thin, and Leslie was released, but when her own father died, the fate of the garage had led to more rows. As Jean pulled up a chair, she looked down at her son and took his hand in hers. Where was this all going to end? She'd kept quiet and tried to keep the peace all these years. Could Ronnie be right? Was it time to stand up for herself or was it already too late?

Sheila was beginning to worry about the Police Ball. She had nothing in her wardrobe which could be remotely considered suitable. There was no time to go to Worthing apart from half-day closing. They couldn't afford to let her take a day off at the moment because Ronnie's time was taken up with her brother, so Sheila had to resort to dashing down on her bike after four o'clock when things were quiet. By the time she got there, she was hot and sweaty and there was barely an hour before the shops closed at five thirty.

It was a disappointing task. Everything was either

wildly expensive, or desperately old-fashioned and frumpy. It was beginning to look as if she'd have to tell Matthew she couldn't go.

'I'll make you one.'

Sheila had just bumped into Pen Albright waiting at the bus stop. Today it had been chucking it down with rain so she'd decided to take the bus rather than getting completely soaked on her bike. It gave her even less time to look around, but at least she could stay reasonably dry if she kept under the shops' awnings and under an umbrella.

'Make one?' said Sheila.

'Why not?' said Pen. 'I'm a dab hand with the needle, even if I do say so myself.'

'So what do I do?' said Sheila.

'Go into Fabulous Fabrics in Warwick Street,' said Pen. 'That's the best place. Look for a dressmaking pattern you like, then choose the material. I'm popping down to pay the gas bill. If I wait until tomorrow it'll be overdue. I'll come along when I've finished.'

Sheila looked at her watch. 'There's not a lot of time,' she remarked.

'You can do it,' said Pen confidently.

By the end of the week, Leslie's condition had improved beyond all recognition. He was still battered and bruised but the swellings were going down and he was able to get out of bed and sit in a chair. With her mother and Granny taking up the slack, Ronnie was able to reduce her visits to Monday and Saturday, but the vexed question as to where he should go once he was discharged loomed large.

Their father had sent a couple of letters demanding that their mother come home immediately and making it abundantly clear there was no room at home for Leslie. Leslie wouldn't have wanted to go back anyway. The doctors insisted that he couldn't possibly be allowed home on his own. How could he look after himself when he still had an arm in plaster and he found it hard to walk? During the attack, someone had stamped on his hand, which didn't help either, and it meant that even leaning on a stick was difficult.

Sheila and Ronnie discussed what to do but there was so little room at the garage. They could, at a push, get another bed in their sitting room, but a man sleeping under the same roof, albeit a brother and cousin, was hardly practical. The only option was to empty the storeroom downstairs and put a bed in there, but with winter coming on and no real means of heating the storeroom, that was far from ideal. 'But what choice do we have?' Ronnie said desperately.

Her mother and grandmother stayed on for over a week, much to the annoyance of her father. He motored down the following Sunday with the express purpose of getting Jean back home but, for the first time in her life, Ronnie saw her mother dig in her heels and refuse to go. She was shaking like a leaf as she did so, but she flatly refused to get into the car.

'If you stay here,' her father snarled angrily, 'you needn't expect a welcome when you finally get home.'

'I'll come home as soon as I can,' she said, ignoring the threat.

He got in the car, slammed the door and drove off at high speed.

'We've made a decision,' Jean said later that day. 'Granny and I have taken rooms in Canterbury Road. We're going to look after Leslie when he comes out of hospital.'

Ronnie felt an enormous sense of relief. 'You do realize Leslie might have been mixed up in the theft of those furs?' she cautioned. 'The police will come and talk to him.'

'We'll cross that bridge when we come to it,' her mother said stoutly.

With Mrs Edwards's help, they at last managed to get the caravan back on the forecourt. Gerhard and Helmut were assigned to them for the day and Gerhard helped Ronnie give it a spring clean. She was right: people stopped their cars, got off the bus or walked from the station just to see the caravan that had been involved in the infamous fur robbery. Having looked, they came in and bought something, a new torch, a snow shovel or an outside broom from the shop. The caravan had become a nice little earner.

December 2nd came round very quickly. Their appointment in the new town hall with Mr Pulsford was scheduled for 2.30 p.m. They hadn't mentioned it to Granny or Auntie Jean. Both girls wanted to find out what they were dealing with first. Leslie had become a welcome distraction. Out of hospital now, he was enjoying the undivided attention of both his mother and grandmother. He was able to walk with a stick and, although he still got very tired, everyone agreed that he was making good progress. The police had interviewed him several times but so far no charges had been made against him.

The new town hall was at the top end of the town, right opposite the church where Granddad's funeral had been held. They found themselves in front of a magnificent building. Built in 1933, with ninety per cent of the workforce taken from the unemployed of the town, it had won several prestigious awards for its London architect, Charles Cowles Voysey. They walked up the steps and through the foyer into a bright and airy reception area.

Ronnie explained who they were and the girl on the desk rang somebody on the internal telephone. Shortly afterwards, a man came running down the wide staircase to the left of where they stood on the marble floor.

'Good afternoon,' he said cheerfully. 'Miss Hodges and Miss Jackson? My name is Ian Pulsford.' And they all shook hands.

They followed him down a long corridor to a small room on the left. There was a window in the room, but it was covered over with some sort of outside shutter, giving it a rather dingy feel. The walls were badly in need of decoration, with mustard-coloured paint above the dado rail and brown wood panelling underneath. The ceiling was grey. The room was sparsely furnished with a small tubular steel table and two tubular steel and canvas chairs. Mr Pulsford invited them to sit down and went in search of another chair. Ronnie and Sheila glanced at each other, their mutual disappointment remaining unspoken. Why had they been shown into such a poky little room for what was, for them, such an important occasion? A few minutes later, Mr Pulsford came back and positioned his chair on the opposite side of the table. He placed a tan-coloured folder between them.

He was very young, no more than eighteen or nineteen. His skin was greasy and he had acne scars on his downy face. He wore round gold-rimmed glasses and his faintly ginger hair wrestled against the Brylcreem holding it down. His suit was crumpled and the cuffs of his shirt peeping from under the sleeves of his jacket were slightly frayed.

'Well now,' he said, opening the folder. 'First of all, I have to make sure you are capable of understanding what I may have to tell you.'

Sheila could sense Ronnie bristling. 'Of course we are,' she snapped.

'What I mean to say is,' Mr Pulsford began again, 'what happened to your aunt may not be a fairy-tale ending. Before I begin, I want you to understand that.'

'For God's sake, man,' said Ronnie, leaning forward. 'We have both been through a war, my cousin in the ATS and I in a Japanese prison camp, so you can rest assured that neither of us is a wilting violet.'

Mr Pulsford's face flushed and he seemed slightly flustered. Glancing down at the papers in the folder, he said, 'Miss Peters was admitted to the Horsham workhouse infirmary at the age of fifteen. She remained there for some time.'

'What was wrong with her?' Sheila asked. 'Why was she in the infirmary?'

Mr Pulsford shuffled some papers. 'She was registered as a moral degenerate.'

Ronnie and Sheila exchanged a puzzled look. 'What does that mean?'

Mr Pulsford shrugged. 'I am not a medical man,' he said. 'You will have to ask a doctor.' He turned the page and added, 'As you may know, workhouses were closed in the 1930s. When that happened, Miss Peters was removed to Wells House, a private establishment, in 1934.'

'We know all this,' said Ronnie tetchily. 'We've been there in person. The place is closed. It's all boarded up.'

'The council received a complaint at the beginning of 1945,' Mr Pulsford continued. 'As a result, the police were involved and eventually all the residents were moved.'

'Yes, but where?' Ronnie snapped. 'For God's sake, man, get on with it. Don't keep us in suspense.'

'Miss Peters is currently in a home called Nightingales,' said Mr Pulsford. He'd taken a voluminous handkerchief from his pocket and was mopping his brow.

Ronnie leaned over the desk, but it was Sheila's more measured voice that asked the question. 'Can you tell us where that is, Mr Pulsford? Is it another hospital or some sort of home?'

Mr Pulsford gave her a watery smile. 'Nightingales is a home for the mentally frail.'

'So what you are saying,' Sheila went on, 'is that our aunt is mentally unstable.'

Mr Pulsford nodded miserably.

'And is that what you meant,' Sheila continued, 'when you said we may not have a fairy-tale ending?'

Mr Pulsford nodded again. 'I was trying to soften the blow.'

Ronne made a loud scoffing noise, but Sheila smiled and said, 'Thank you, Mr Pulsford. You are very kind.'

'So where is this place?' Ronnie interjected.

'I have the address here,' said Mr Pulsford. He scribbled something on the corner of the piece of paper in front of him, tore it off, then pushed it across the table towards Sheila.

'Can you tell us anything about her condition?' Ronnie asked. She felt surprisingly unsettled and upset about someone she'd never even met. Poor Aunt Daisy had spent all her young life incarcerated and alone with no visitors, and no chance of being released. How must that have felt? Ronnie knew something of being a prisoner and it was hell. The only thing that had kept her going, apart from the need to survive for the children's sake, was the hope that some day she would be free again. How would you survive with no hope of ever being freed? And all because she was – what was it? – a moral degenerate.

183

'As I said before,' said Mr Pulsford, 'I am not a medical man and we have no such information.'

Ronnie frowned. 'So if she can't look after herself, and I assume that must be the case, who is responsible for her?'

'Horsham District Council,' said Mr Pulsford, 'acting as agents for the state.' He stood to leave. 'I have given you all the information I have, ladies. I'll bid you good afternoon and show you out.'

Outside in the street, Ronnie was angry. 'How dare they send us some spotty schoolboy still wet behind the ears,' she cried. 'What a nerve, asking us if we could cope. Good God, the man was hardly out of short trousers.'

Sheila put a soothing hand on her cousin's arm. She'd never seen her so worked up. 'I'm just as upset as you,' she said. 'Let's find somewhere to get a cup of tea and calm down.'

Fifteen minutes later they were sitting in Lyons Tea Rooms in South Street. The waitress, wearing the iconic black dress with a white apron, had just brought them sandwiches, a cake and a pot of tea. Ronnie seemed incapable of doing anything, so Sheila poured.

'I can't stop thinking about it,' said Ronnie. 'She must be forty-six by now. Imagine being locked up for thirty years.'

'I know,' said Sheila, 'but it might not be as bad as you think.'

Her cousin looked up sharply.

'If she's not normal,' Sheila added quickly, 'she might not be aware of it.'

'Granny never said she was a lunatic,' said Ronnie. Sheila pushed a cup of tea in front of her. 'But we don't know that, do we? Granny only told us she'd run away.' She helped herself to a sandwich. 'I don't think we should jump to conclusions, that's all. We've got the address. Let's go and see her as soon as we possibly can.'

'And that's another thing,' said Ronnie. She took the paper with the address on it out of her handbag and laid it on the table. 'That scrap of paper is about somebody who has been locked up for most of her life. It's about a family separated and a mother grieving for her lost daughter. It's about our auntie and he scribbled it down as if . . . as if . . .' She turned her head away and searched her pockets for her handkerchief.

Sheila reached out and touched her hand. 'I know,' she said. 'He was crass and he was stupid.'

Ronnie's eyes were bright with unshed tears. 'Oh, Sheila, he talked as if she was a "thing", not a person. As if she didn't matter.'

'Well, she does,' said Sheila firmly. 'She matters to us and when we finally tell them, she'll matter to Granny and Auntie Jean.'

They became aware that the two women on the next table were staring at them. Ronnie's back stiffened and she gave them a hostile glare. 'Can I help you with anything?' she asked aggressively.

The women looked away and a few minutes later they got up to leave.

'Why are you so angry?' Sheila whispered. She'd never seen her cousin like this before.

Ronnie pushed her handkerchief back up her sleeve. 'I don't know,' she said quietly. 'I suppose it's the thought of somebody else being locked up for so long with no good reason. An emotional degenerate: what does that mean?'

'Moral degenerate,' Sheila corrected. 'I've no idea what it means, but you're right, being locked away from your family for all those years must have been awful.'

'Believe me, it is,' said Ronnie.

Embarrassed, Sheila shifted in her chair.

'You start off by being upset,' Ronnie went on, 'then you get angry, and once you've worked your way through that, all you have left is hope. If you go to the next stage, you'll never survive.'

'What is the next stage?'

'Despair.'

Sheila didn't know what to say. It was obvious that she was referring to her own incarceration. There were no other customers sitting near them. Ronnie sat facing the window with her back to the rest of the tea room. Sheila decided not to stop her talking. It had been so helpful when she'd been having those terrible dreams.

'The one thing you mustn't let go of is hope,' said Ronnie.

'Do you think Aunt Daisy still has hope?'

Ronnie pulled a face. 'If she's lost hope there's every likelihood she's probably lost her mind as well.'

186

Sheila's hand went to her mouth. 'Is that what happened to Mrs Lyle?'

Ronnie's face darkened. 'What? Oh no. She died of beriberi.'

Sheila stared at her in horror and she was about to express her sympathy when Ronnie added, 'Just as well it happened or the other women in the camp would have done for her anyway.'

CHAPTER 16

Back at the garage, they moved around each other in an awkward silence. Sheila had been dying to ask more, but Ronnie had retreated into her own thoughts. What had she meant when she'd said the other women would have done for her? Aunt Daisy's plight had clearly re-opened an old wound, but her cousin was still unable to talk about it.

They had closed the garage for the afternoon in order to meet Mr Pulsford, so coming back fairly early gave them a chance to catch up with the paperwork and some housekeeping. Nelson was eager for a walk as well, but then they found another white envelope shoved under the door. They knew what it was without bothering to open it. 'Another anonymous note,' said Ronnie sourly. She handed it to her cousin.

'That makes three in one week,' said Sheila.

'Better pass them on to Matthew.'

'I'd rather not give it to him,' said Sheila. 'He's really busy and he seemed a bit put out when I gave him the last one. Besides, it'll only encourage him to tell me to jack it all in.'

'Jack it in? Why?'

'He wants us to get married when he's finished his probation,' Sheila sighed, 'but the more I think about it, the more unsure I am. He's so determined that when we marry I should give up the garage.'

'Most women would want that,' Ronnie said cautiously.

'But I don't,' said Sheila. 'Why should I? Why can't I have both?'

Ronnie shrugged. ''Cos that's the way things are, I suppose. But you're right. Why can't we have both? Look at all the girls who kept down jobs during the war.'

'That's just what I mean,' said Sheila. 'It's a pity they didn't stick to their guns instead of going back to the kitchen sink.'

'If you're not too sure how you feel about Matthew,' Ronnie asked, 'are you still going to the Ball?'

'Of course!' cried Sheila. 'I wouldn't miss that for the world.' She hesitated and gave Ronnie a sheepish look. 'Do you think I'm being awful?'

'Nah,' said Ronnie. 'He'd probably be upset if he had no one to go with.'

Sheila giggled. 'You're right. He would.'

'So if you don't want to give this letter to Matthew, what shall we do about it?'

Sheila shrugged. 'I don't know,' she said irritably. 'But I've got a shrewd idea who might have sent it. Honestly, you'd think Mr Webster would have better things to do. I'd like to ram it down his throat.'

There was a glint of excitement in Ronnie's eye.

'Okay,' she said slowly, 'I feel in the mood for a good old ding-dong. Let's go over there right now and have it out with him.'

Webster's garage, on the Brighton Road, was modern and up-to-date. Bright petrol pumps, four of them no less, graced the spacious forecourt. As Ronnie and Sheila pulled in the van, a petrol-pump attendant in bright blue overalls came hurrying out of the building to greet them.

'Good afternoon, ladies,' he said cheerfully. 'What will it be?'

'We haven't come for motor spirit,' Ronnie said in a superior tone. 'We've come to see Mr Webster.'

The attendant asked them to park at the side, away from the pumps, and then he pointed them in the direction of the office. It was to the left of the garage itself and housed in a new building. As they threaded their way past several new cars, motorbikes and a few brightly polished second-hand vehicles, a man in a smart suit made his way towards them. 'They've come to see the boss, Jim,' the attendant called out and the salesman returned to his desk with a polite nod.

Mr Webster's office was every bit as impressive as his garage and showroom. Sheila knocked on the glass-fronted door and, without waiting for an invitation, the girls walked in. The man behind the desk was a lot younger than the man who had called into the Becket a few months ago. Attractive and about their own age, he was smartly dressed with dark-brown wavy hair and twinkling eyes. The only blemish was a deep scar on the side of his cheek which ended near his ear. It looked as if he'd caught a bullet or suffered some kind of knife attack in combat. If that was the case, here was a man who was incredibly lucky not to have been killed. He looked up with a smile. 'Can I help you?'

'My name is Miss Jackson,' Ronnie said stiffly, 'and this is my cousin, Miss Hodges. We have come to see Mr Webster.'

The man stood to his feet, pressing his wayward tie to his shirt. 'I'm Mr Webster,' he said. 'What can I do for you ladies?'

Slightly flummoxed, Sheila frowned. 'I'm sorry? The man who introduced himself to me as Mr Webster was much older.'

'That would be my father.' The man behind the desk smiled. 'I'm Neville Webster, his son.' He held out his hand and Sheila took it. Ronnie stood her ground, ignoring his outstretched hand. 'We need to speak with your father,' she said tightly.

'I'm afraid that's not possible,' said Neville, indicating the chairs in front of the desk. 'Please, do sit down.'

Sheila did as she was bidden, but Ronnie remained standing. Neville was obviously wanting her to sit so, embarrassed, Sheila stood up again.

'My parents have gone away,' Neville said politely. 'They prefer warmer climes so they will be spending the winter in South Africa.'

'When will they be back?' Ronnie said crossly.

191

'They should return in March sometime,' said Neville, blowing out his cheeks. 'Can I help?'

Ronnie frowned. 'How very convenient,' she said sarcastically. 'When did they go?'

'Their ship sailed from Southampton on the twenty-first of November,' said Neville. 'Look, do you mind telling me what this is all about?'

Ronnie glanced at Sheila. 'So it can't be him,' she murmured as she lowered herself into the chair, adding darkly, 'Not the father, anyway.'

Neville and Sheila both sat down too.

'A few months ago, your father stopped by our garage near Thomas A Becket and bought some petrol,' said Ronnie. 'He expressed an interest in buying the garage, but I told him it wasn't for sale.'

'Ah yes,' said Neville. 'I know the one you mean. A sweet little place. Good position too. My father would be delighted to acquire it. Name your price, ladies.'

'You're not listening,' Sheila chipped in. 'It's not for sale.'

Neville frowned. 'Then why are you here?'

'Your father has written to us several times,' said Ronnie.

Neville stood up and went to the filing cabinet, which stood behind him. As he came back to the desk with a buff-coloured folder, a woman opened the office door. 'Ah, Mrs Hewitt,' he said, 'could you bring us some tea, please?' The woman left as quickly as she'd come in and Neville laid the folder on the desk to open it. Inside were three letters, identical to the ones the girls

192

had received. 'Yes,' said Neville, 'and my father has upped his offer each time. It's a perfectly sound business action. I fail to see the problem.'

'Our problem is this,' said Ronnie. She opened her shoulder bag and took out the most recent anonymous letter. Angrily, she pulled it from the envelope and banged it on the desk.

Neville Webster frowned. 'But I don't understand,' he said slowly. 'Are you suggesting that my father . . . that we . . . that Webster's garages had anything to do with this?' He seemed genuinely shocked. 'Miss Jackson, this amounts to a poison-pen letter. I can assure you that neither my father nor anyone else in this business would stoop so low as to send such a thing. We are a respectable chain and, attractive as your little garage is, in all honesty we don't need it that much.'

'Then who—' Ronnie began.

'I have no idea, Miss Jackson,' said Neville, 'but I strongly advise you to go to the police.'

'The police already have some,' said Sheila. 'This isn't the only one.'

Mrs Hewitt arrived with the tea and placed the tray on the desk in front of them. As she left the room, Neville handed Ronnie and Sheila a cup and saucer each. 'If you have already given them some letters, it puzzles me why the police haven't dealt with this more robustly,' he said, sipping his tea.

'I do apologize,' said Sheila. 'We were so positive they must have come from here, but we had no right to—'

'Please,' said Neville, waving his hand dismissively,

'say no more about it.' He turned the envelope over. 'This has obviously been delivered by hand. Don't you think that rather odd?'

Sheila and Ronnie gave him a confused look.

'I mean to say,' he went on, 'people who write poison-pen letters usually operate in secret. Surely if you hand-deliver your letter, there has to be a great risk of being caught?'

'I never thought of that,' Ronnie admitted.

'So that means someone must be spying on us,' said Sheila, glancing anxiously towards her cousin. 'They have to make sure we're out before they come over.'

Neville leaned forward. 'Miss Hodges, I had no intention of alarming you. Please forget I ever suggested that.'

'There's no need to worry, Mr Webster,' said Ronnie. 'Neither of us are easily frightened.'

'I can see that, Miss Jackson. You certainly came in here all guns blazing.'

Sheila caught her breath and Neville chuckled. 'It's all right, Miss Hodges, but if I might make a suggestion . . . Go back to the police and insist that they do something. I am quite happy for you to use my name if you think it would help.'

Back at the garage, they were grateful to sit down. They hadn't said much in the van coming home. There was a lot to digest. It was peaceful at the garage, but it didn't last long. They hardly had time to kick off their shoes and tuck into a freshly made sandwich when there was a knock on the door. With a long-suffering sigh, Sheila got up to answer it. Young Trixie Rodway, Elsie Tunnock and Pen Albright were on the doorstep. Sheila stared at them with a blank expression.

'Don't tell me you've forgotten,' said Elsie. Sheila pulled a face. 'You have, haven't you? The choir. We start the practice tonight.'

Sheila's first instinct was to cry off, but one look at their happy smiling faces made her change her mind. After the day she'd had, this could be just the tonic she needed. Ronnie had groaned when she told her who was at the door, but she was quite willing to give it a go as well. The girls piled back onto the street and Sheila locked the garage door.

'Just who is that bloke up at the window?' Ronnie was looking at the house across the road and the white face staring down at them. 'He seems to spend his whole life ogling at us.'

Trixie followed Ronnie's gaze and, to her surprise, waved her hand in salute. 'Oh, that's Benjamin Steadman,' she said. 'We all call him Benny. He loves to watch what's going on.'

'Doesn't he have anything better to do?' Ronnie said crossly.

The girls gave her a wounded look. 'Benny is an invalid,' said Pen. 'He's bedridden.'

Ronnie's face flushed with embarrassment. 'I'm sorry,' she mumbled as they all set off for the Archbishop's Palace.

'My mum says he was injured during the Great War,' Trixie went on. 'Mustard gas or something.'

'How awful,' said Sheila. She glanced at her cousin. 'I'm afraid we've done him a great disservice. We thought he was just some dirty old man.'

Someone giggled and Elsie added, 'You needn't worry. There's no harm in poor old Benny.'

Half a mile away, Leslie sat hunched up in front of the open fire. It was lovely to be out of hospital and he was grateful to his mother and grandmother, who had given him somewhere to go. While he was in hospital, the rooms he had rented in Kemp Town, in Brighton, had been trashed and the landlord had taken a dim view of it. He'd been evicted. His clothes had been nicked from outside where they'd been dumped and all he was left with was what he stood up in. It was a dark day. As soon as he thought he was making progress, something always happened and he was back to square one. He felt depressed and miserable. When his mother turned up in hospital and told him she'd taken rooms in Worthing to look after him, he was almost reduced to tears. He didn't deserve that.

He half expected them to nag him about getting a proper job. Certainly, if his father had been around that's exactly what would have happened. His mother and grandmother said nothing. They changed his dressings, helped him walk from room to room, made his meals and brushed his hair. He felt like a little boy again.

The bruises that showed were beginning to heal, albeit very slowly, but his inner turmoil was harder to deal with. He had so wanted to be up there with the big shots, but as Gerry Carter and his thugs had laid into him, Leslie realized he wasn't cut out for a gangster lifestyle. He hated violence almost as much as he hated dirt.

The police had interviewed him several times. They were none too gentle either. He admitted taking the caravan, but insisted it was only because he was angry with Ronnie. He had wanted his grandfather's garage and was upset that it was given to his sister. Yes, he'd hidden the caravan in the woods, but he'd had nothing to do with the robbery. He wasn't a thief. This was about sibling rivalry and revenge, nothing more. On the day in question, his conscience had pricked him so he'd gone to the woods to get the caravan back. 'How was I to know the gang would turn up?' he'd protested. 'They thought I'd taken the furs for myself.' He spread his hands open helplessly. 'As if I'd come back when I already had everything?' No, he'd never seen the men before and he didn't know who they were. He'd just been unlucky to be in the wrong place at the wrong time, that's all.

He could tell the police were sceptical about what he was saying but, with no proof, what could they do? He stuck to his story and, eventually, they stopped coming.

The hall was fairly active when Ronnie, Sheila and the others arrived and it was fun meeting up with old friends again. Their choir mistress turned out to be Trixie's mother, April Rodway, a tall, elegant woman in her thirties, the wife of the local doctor. Trixie wasn't her only child. Her daughter Janice, a year younger than Trixie, was already a gifted pianist and her son Dennis appeared to be a bit of a bookworm. He sat in the corner of the room, reading the latest Richmal Crompton book, *William and the Brains Trust*, and chuckling every now and then throughout the evening.

The choir was made up of both male and female singers. Doctor Rodway, Sheila's first real customer, was a tenor. Mr Hurst, from the nurseries, was definitely a bass baritone and he was placed next to Sergeant Longfellow. Sheila asked after Gerhard because she knew he had a lovely tenor voice, but apparently, because he was a POW, he wasn't allowed out at night.

'Is it possible he could help me out in the garage again sometime?' she asked. 'Only my cousin and I have to go to Horsham about a family matter and I don't want to leave it unattended.'

'No problem at all,' said Mr Hurst. 'I'm glad to keep him occupied and I know he's trustworthy. I shall need him myself in the spring, but if the powers-that-be think they're idle for too long, they move them on to somewhere else.'

April broke up their conversation and put Sheila with the sopranos while Ronnie's more dusky voice was better suited to the altos.

They sang mostly carols, which sounded quite good once they'd all got used to making harmonies. There was little in the way of sheet music. The shortages of the war lingered on. Even if they had the money to get their music printed, what little printing ink was to spare would have been used to get the country back on its feet rather than for such luxuries.

At the end of the evening, April Rodway asked everybody to come back every Monday, Wednesday and Friday evening in the run-up to Christmas. She had, she told them, already got several engagements for the choir including doing the rounds of the hospital wards and a concert on the Saturday before Christmas.

As the meeting broke up, Ronnie heard a few murmurs of dissent, but she had no doubt that, when the time came, everybody would turn up and be counted.

As they walked back to Littlehampton Road, Pen threaded her arm through Sheila's. 'Better come to my place for a fitting of your ballgown next week,' she said.

'You've done it already?' Sheila said, breathless with excitement.

'Almost,' said Pen. 'I need you to try it on before I do any more.'

'Ooh, I can't wait,' cried Sheila.

CHAPTER 17

It took a whole week to make all the arrangements to go and see Aunt Daisy. Ronnie wrote to the matron of Nightingales and she took a couple of days to reply. Once they'd agreed a date and time, Sheila asked Mr Hurst if Gerhard could look after the garage on that day. Mr Hurst was only too pleased to release him and promised to keep an eye on him. Sheila didn't think that was necessary, but Ronnie said it would give them peace of mind.

The four boys biked down to the end of Ringmer Road, past the allotments to Field Place, an old Georgian house which had been requisitioned during the war by the RAF. There had been a Ground Control Interception Radar station at Durrington. The main operation block, a substantial building in the middle of green fields and nicknamed by the locals the Happidrome, had been further north opposite the junction with Terringes Avenue while the house at Field Place had been used as a mess hall and accommodation for the officers.

Hethy had the bigger bike, one which had belonged to his father who, according to his mum, had cleared off with some floozy at the beginning of the war. It was still too big for him to sit comfortably on the seat so he stood to ride. His friend Ian Moore balanced on the handlebars. Alan Albright was on a bike which was a mishmash of old parts his dad had put together for him and bringing up the rear was Drew on the bike Sheila had repaired.

Field Place was a far cry from how it had been during the war. Back then it was shrouded in secrecy and guarded night and day. Rumour had it that there were secret underground tunnels, but so far the boys had been unable to find an entrance.

'My dad says the entrance is inside the house,' Ian had told them. 'He reckons it's massive down there.'

The lads had listened with rapt attention and now, today, they were going to look for themselves. Yesterday, Drew and Steven Kennard had been playing Cowboys and Indians around the Pavilion in Field Place and stumbled across some sort of air vent. Steven, who lived in one of the four houses in Bolsover Road, was waiting for them as they arrived.

The boys lifted the turf and brambles surrounding the vent and heaved open the steel grid which covered the entrance. They all switched on their torches and stared down into the abyss. Drew was the first to go down because he was the smallest. Once he was safely in, the others followed. They found themselves a couple of yards from a staircase going down.

'Blimey,' said Alan. 'It looks like we've found it.'

Their hearts pounding with excitement and fear, the boys made their way down the steps. All at once they were faced with a tunnel. It was beginning to feel spooky. Drew shivered, but not from the cold. After they passed a sign saying 'Radar Room', they came to a fairly large brick-lined chamber.

'Cor,' said Hethy. 'My granddad says smugglers used to use Field Place to store their stuff. I reckon this is it.'

'Looks more like a sort of bunker to me,' said Drew, wiping his finger across an empty shelf. Steven was tugging at an old filing cabinet, but it was firmly locked.

A few wooden racks were fixed to one wall and there were some old tins and a couple of bottles which Alan said looked like his mum's sherry. A thick steel table stood against another wall with some sort of chart nailed above it. Nobody could work out what it said. It was all numbers and arrows. Above the chart, a large clock had stopped at three forty-five.

Ian was larking around with a small gold-coloured Junior Pyrene fire extinguisher which stood in the corner. He turned the handle to the left and began to pump it. Whatever it was that came out smelled bad and, almost at once, Drew started coughing.

'Pack it in!' shouted Hethy. 'You don't know what that stuff is.'

Ian threw the extinguisher to the floor with a loud clatter.

There was a shout from Alan who had found another

flight of stairs. It wasn't very long and at the top there was a steel door which was firmly locked. 'That must be the door that leads into the house,' said Hethy, and they all agreed.

When they turned to look back into the room they realized that behind a small screen there were two other tunnels. By now their confidence and excitement were mounting. Having argued as to which tunnel to try, they grouped together and went down the left-hand side. Further exploration led to a door at the side. It had a barred window but no glass. Steven tried the door handle but it wouldn't budge and, when they shone the torches inside, it was just a bare room apart from what looked like a camp bed. They trudged back and tried the right-hand-side tunnel. This proved to be far more exciting.

After a few yards, they came across some bikes. They were very big, obviously meant for men, but in fairly good working order. For a while they had the most amazing time on the bikes, shouting down the tunnels and following their echo. The tunnels weren't very long and they seemed to link up with other tunnels. One had another locked door at the end, but they didn't care. They soon found themselves being bank robbers chased by the police or British Tommies hunting old Hitler down. It took a while before they realized they hadn't come across the brick room for some time and that they were lost. Panic set in. Drew began to cry.

'Oh, shut up,' Alan snapped. 'Blubbing isn't going to solve anything.'

'But,' Drew protested, 'we might end up stuck down here forever. We might die!'

'No, we won't die,' Ian said angrily. 'Belt up, will you.'

'I want to go home,' said Drew, choking back the tears. 'I want my mum.'

'We should have marked the tunnel when we came in,' Hethy said gloomily.

They tried making a more methodical plan but somehow they didn't get very far. It was another twenty minutes before Ian stumbled across the 'Radar Room' sign and eventually their own entrance.

'Better bring some chalk next time,' said Hethy as he gave Alan a shove up the bum to get him above ground. 'Then we can mark the walls.'

'I don't want to go down there again,' said Drew.

'Ah, poor little diddums,' Ian laughed. 'Are you too scared?'

'No, I'm not!' cried Drew.

'Chicken,' said Alan, making clucking noises.

Steven gave Alan a shove.

'Well, it's up to you,' Hethy said, 'but you're not to tell. This is a secret, got it? We don't want everybody else coming.'

The boys solemnly promised to keep mum and set off for home.

The dress was already looking really good. Pen said Sheila's choice of material, royal blue with a white spot, was inspired. The pattern was ankle length with figure-hugging scalloped Basque points at the waist, a sweetheart neckline and little cap sleeves. The skirt clung to her body yet swished attractively as she moved. It was perfect for the dance floor.

Sheila had found a small clasp-handled clutch bag in the Red Cross shop and although the blue wasn't exactly the same colour, the fact that the bag was beaded meant that she could get away with it.

'When can I take it home?' she asked as she twirled in front of the mirror.

'I still have to finish the hem and one of the sleeves,' said Pen. 'I've only tacked them.'

Reluctantly, Sheila peeled the dress off. It was so gorgeous she was loath to part with it.

'When do you actually need it?' asked Pen.

'The Ball is on New Year's Eve,' said Sheila, reaching for her skirt and jumper.

A man's voice outside the back door called, 'Hello, I'm home.'

Sheila snatched her clothes to her body as Pen called out, 'Hang on a minute, love. I've got somebody in here changing.'

Sheila dressed quickly.

'Hurry up,' said the voice. 'It's perishing cold out here.'

The minute Sheila was decent, Pen let her husband in. He was a jolly-looking man with a gap-toothed smile.

'You finished dressmaking, then?' he asked. 'Can I have me tea?'

'Go and say goodnight to the kids and I'll be right with you,' she said and, turning to Sheila, added, 'Can you come back after the holidays? Only I've used up a lot of evenings getting it this far and I've still got the kids' toys to sort out for Christmas. Is that all right?'

Dick Albright opened the stair door and went upstairs to say goodnight to his boys. 'I don't know what our Alan got up to today,' Pen called after him distractedly, 'but he came home looking like a right mucky pup. As if I haven't got enough to do. His shirt was as black as the ace of spades.'

'After Christmas is fine,' said Sheila. 'December thirtieth will do.'

'Perhaps the twenty-ninth would be better,' said Pen. 'That way, if I need to do some alterations, I'll still have time.'

'You mean if I eat too much Christmas pudding,' said Sheila, pulling on her coat, 'you've got time to let it out.'

'You said it, love,' Pen chuckled.

Matthew was rather annoyed. Sheila was going to Horsham again, but she wouldn't say why. 'Is it something I could help you with?' he'd asked her again and again, but all she'd said was 'No'. This was the second time she'd been there. If she hadn't been going with Ronnie he might have wondered if there was another man. He couldn't understand it. If they were to be married, there shouldn't be any secrets between them. He'd tried to explain that, but she'd just smiled and said, 'You'll have to trust me.' What did that mean? How could he trust her when she wouldn't say where she was going? Who was she meeting? And why Horsham? When he'd first met her she'd said she didn't know anyone in the area. The questions reverberated around and around his head like a bee trapped in a bottle. Why couldn't she see? All he wanted was to protect her, to look out for her, to be her rock. She had confided in him over the anonymous letters and he'd been delighted that she'd turned to him for help. That particular matter was well in hand and he loved it when she'd cuddled up close to him for comfort. The vexed question of the garage hadn't been resolved, though. Why couldn't she understand that it really wouldn't do for the wife of a serving policeman to be working outside the home? Most working women had gone back to their homes now that the war was over. It was a woman's place. It was her job to keep house and raise the children, but Sheila was adamant. 'I love my job,' she'd declare. 'I don't want to leave the garage.'

He sighed. Being a fiancé shouldn't be this hard. He had to make her see reason, but what could he do? She was so stubborn – too bloody stubborn.

Ronnie and Sheila set off for Horsham with mixed feelings. On the one hand, it was rather exciting to be meeting up with a relative who had been out of touch with the family for so long. On the other hand, they were both uncertain as to what to expect. Of course, they knew that after meeting Aunt Daisy they then faced the vexed question of how to break the news to Granny. She and Ronnie's mum were still looking after

Leslie, whose recovery made slow progress. Although Ronnie's father secretly wanted them home, he was too proud after their row to come and fetch them. Besides, Christmas was the busiest time of the year and he couldn't leave the shop for any length of time. He simply couldn't understand why they devoted so much of their time to 'that wastrel' as he called his son.

When Ronnie and Sheila reached Horsham, they took a bus from the station. Nightingales wasn't far and they were pleasantly surprised to find a smart-looking 1930s house at the end of the driveway. Sheila mounted the circular steps and rang the doorbell. They waited nervously until a woman in a green overall and apron opened the door, and a few moments later, they were shown into Matron's office. The office was light and airy and Matron turned out to be a rotund woman with a florid complexion and brown teeth. 'Ah,' she said, peering over her spectacles, 'Daisy's long-lost relatives.'

They went through some formalities. Matron examined the documents proving who they were; then she went through Daisy's history, asking if they were prepared for what they might find when they met her.

'Will she know who we are?' Ronnie asked. 'What I mean is, she won't know us personally, but does she still remember her family? Will she understand that we've come to take her home?'

'I wouldn't advise that just yet,' said Matron cautiously. 'This will be a lot for her to take in. We need to do this slowly, at a pace which is comfortable for Daisy.'

Ronnie hadn't really meant she wanted to take Daisy right away, but it seemed better not to try and justify herself. They couldn't possibly take Aunt Daisy back to Worthing today. They hadn't even told Granny what they were doing.

'Another thing you should know,' Matron began again. 'Daisy was living in a home where they didn't treat her well. We think she may have been the victim of violence. Occasionally she thinks she's still there and she's very frightened.'

Ronnie and Sheila exchanged a glance.

'Please be assured that we are doing all we can to help her feel safe again,' Matron went on.

'Something we both want to ask . . .' Sheila began hesitantly, 'Mr Pulsford told us Aunt Daisy had been admitted to the workhouse infirmary as a moral degenerate. We've never heard that expression before and are confused as to what that might mean.'

Matron dropped her gaze and seemed a little uncomfortable as she answered. 'That was a euphemistic term they used for someone who had been engaging in unlawful sexual intercourse.'

A hush fell on the room. Matron fiddled with the papers in Aunt Daisy's file. 'It is worth noting that at the time Daisy was only fifteen years old,' she said. 'I realize the world has changed a lot since the war, but even we would frown upon a girl of that age being considered promiscuous.'

Ronnie and Sheila looked at each other again, but neither of them wanted to pursue the matter. The questions hung in the air. Who was Daisy sleeping with? Was she messing around with more than one boy? Maybe, young as she was, she'd been hopelessly in love with someone or, perish the thought, maybe someone had forced her into a sexual relationship? Sheila couldn't bear the thought of Daisy being snatched from the arms of the one she loved and thrown into the workhouse infirmary. She must have been broken-hearted. Ronnie wondered what was so dreadful that Granny and Granddad could have sent her away like that.

Matron got to her feet. 'Daisy works in the kitchen now. She's shown a great aptitude for cooking which I have to say has surprised us all.' She walked from the room, indicating that they should follow. 'I want you to see her first in surroundings which are comfortable for her. Meeting you is going to radically change her life and, no matter how gentle we are, it will be unsettling for her.'

Ronnie and Sheila followed Matron down the closed corridor to the kitchen. They heard it long before they reached it. When she opened the door, it was a hive of activity, noise and heat. As they all walked in, someone rushed passed them with a large saucepan of prepared vegetables, a cook was basting a beef joint in the oven and another woman was putting clean cutlery onto a three-tier stainless-steel trolley. In a room beyond, someone else, her sleeves rolled up above her elbows, was washing pots and pans in a huge sink.

'That's Daisy,' Matron said quietly. She gave Sheila

a nudge and nodded not towards the woman at the sink as Sheila had expected, but to a woman working at a table set apart from the others. She was decorating a cake. It wasn't huge, but it was covered in white icing, something which was still comparatively rare in these days of continued shortages. Aunt Daisy was painting roses on the sides with cochineal and some green colouring. It was basic, but beautifully done. 'It's Mabel's birthday tomorrow,' Matron whispered. 'She's a lovely old dear and we thought we'd spoil her. She's got no family now except us and she's never had a proper birthday celebration in her life. We shall have a special tea and some of Daisy's lovely cake.'

Ronnie and Sheila watched their aunt create another rose.

'Our rations won't allow us to make a cake like we used to have before the war,' Matron went on, 'but I think that's a worthwhile substitute, don't you?'

Ronnie and Sheila nodded enthusiastically.

Matron moved towards Aunt Daisy. 'Daisy dear, when you've finished that bit, would you come to the office for a minute? There's something I want to tell you.'

'They're putting up some pre-fabs in Castle Road,' said Win. 'I've put my name down for one.'

Win Peters had just come in. She'd been down the town to do a bit of Christmas shopping when she'd bumped into Mrs Hargreaves, her old next-door neighbour. They'd got talking and Mrs Hargreaves had told her about the pre-fabs.

'They say they've got a back boiler and central heating,' Mrs Hargreaves had said in hushed tones. 'Imagine that.'

Win had been breathless with excitement. 'But surely they're for people who got bombed out in London? That's what I read in the paper.'

'The council is building a whole new estate of them in Castle Road,' Mrs Hargreaves had replied. 'You should apply for a pre-fab, Win. They're only supposed to last ten years, but you could sort yourself something out by then, and in the meantime you'll have a lovely home.'

That had been enough for Win. She'd gone straight to the council offices and seen somebody about it. She hadn't done a lot of Christmas shopping, but she had come home with something better than that. She'd got hope for the future.

Jean frowned. 'But they're only meant for families, aren't they?'

'They've got a couple of smaller ones for old people,' said Win. 'I've lived here all my life so I reckon I stand a fair chance of getting one.'

'Oh, Mum,' said Jean, 'don't get your hopes up too high.'

'I belong here,' Win said defiantly.

'So you're going to stay in Worthing?'

'Yes, love,' said Win. 'I'm sorry to disappoint you, but I was homesick in Warminster. I belong here. And you needn't worry about Leslie. I'll look after him until he's fully recovered and then it's up to him.'

Jean nodded slowly. 'I may as well go back home then.'

'Bill wants you back.'

'Does he?' Jean said sourly. 'Or does he just want an extra pair of hands in the shop?'

Win rubbed her daughter's arm softly. 'You've been very brave. You've shown him you're not a pushover any more and now it's up to you to keep him on his toes.'

'I hate it when he shouts,' said Jean.

'He shouts because he's a bully,' said Win. 'Listen, love, don't make the same mistakes I made. You don't need to put up with it. Stand up to him. If he gets too much, pack your suitcase again.'

Jean smiled. 'He was quite shocked when I refused to go back with him.'

'Exactly,' said Win. 'He's not a bad man, Jean. He's just got into bad habits. I think the man still loves you, but you've let him get away with blue murder.'

Jean put her arm around her mother's shoulder. 'I think you're right,' she said. 'When he kept going on about Leslie, I let it get on top of me and then I couldn't be bothered to fight any more.'

'Start as you mean to go on,' Win said sagely.

Her daughter nodded. 'Will you be able to cope with Leslie on your own?'

Win shrugged. 'I'm under no illusions when it comes to that young man,' she said. 'I'll take care of him until he's back on his feet again and then it's up to him.'

'I'd like to think he could made a go of his life,' said Jean, 'but a leopard doesn't change its spots.'

Win sighed. 'With a bit of luck, he might stick to the straight and narrow.'

They gave each other a hug, but, if they were honest, neither of them held out much hope.

Ronnie and Sheila were back in Matron's office when Aunt Daisy opened the door. She was a plain-looking woman with long hair speckled with grey and scraped back into an unflattering and old-fashioned tight bun. Considering the type of life she'd had, her complexion was good, but her eyebrows were badly in need of some attention. Her eyes were empty and sad.

'Daisy,' said Matron, 'do sit down.'

Aunt Daisy seemed nervous and a little confused, but she sat quietly, head down, and with her hands resting in her lap.

'Daisy dear, this may come as a bit of a shock to you, but these two ladies are your relatives. They have been looking for you.'

Aunt Daisy didn't move, but Ronnie saw her eyes glance towards them. Matron gave Sheila a nod.

'My name is Sheila and I'm your sister Agnes's daughter,' said Sheila. 'This is Ronnie – well, her name is Veronica, but we all call her Ronnie.'

'And I'm Jean's daughter,' said Ronnie.

Aunt Daisy turned her head slowly and looked towards them. The silence in the room became oppressive.

'Ronnie and Sheila have been looking for you for quite a while,' Matron repeated. 'It is their hope that you might all get to know each other.'

'Your mother, our granny,' Sheila went on, 'is still alive. She doesn't know about you yet, but when she does, I'm sure she'll want to see you.'

Aunt Daisy tensed. 'No,' she blurted out in a too-loud voice edged with panic. 'He told me no. He said she mustn't see me.'

Ronnie, Sheila and Matron were shocked. This wasn't the reaction they'd expected. It was very puzzling.

'Is there a problem, Daisy?' Matron's interjection was calm and soothing. 'If you're worried about something, do tell us. We may be able to help.'

Daisy leaned forward and looked around the room as if she was checking that they were alone. 'She mustn't know,' she said, her voice still loud and panicky. 'He said if I told, it would kill her.'

The three women looked from one to the other, totally confused.

'Who, Aunt Daisy?' asked Ronnie. 'Who told you that?'

The corners of Aunt Daisy's mouth went down. 'He did,' she said bitterly. 'Dad.'

'But Granddad is dead,' cried Sheila. 'That is, I mean your father is dead.'

Aunt Daisy looked up sharply, her face full of surprise. 'Dead?'

Sheila was immediately seized with regret. 'Oh, Aunt Daisy, I'm sorry. Me and my big mouth. I shouldn't have told you like that.'

'Granddad died earlier this year,' Ronnie said quietly. 'He had a stroke.'

'And he's dead?' Aunt Daisy repeated.

'Yes,' said Sheila.

'And you saw him dead?'

'Well, no,' said Sheila, glancing at her cousin, 'not exactly, but I saw his coffin at the funeral.'

Daisy looked down. 'So he could still be alive.'

'I'm afraid not,' Ronnie said quietly. 'We all went to the undertakers. I saw him. He looked very peaceful. Sheila only came for the funeral.'

Aunt Daisy's eyes filled with tears. Ronnie leaned forward and put her hand over the top of her aunt's hands in her lap. Matron opened a drawer in her desk and took out a freshly laundered handkerchief and handed it to Sheila, who gave it to her aunt. Daisy took it and used it to cover her face as she gently rocked herself. A few minutes later she looked up and said in a small, almost little-girl voice, 'When can I see my mummy?'

CHAPTER 18

The girls didn't talk that much on the way home. Each was lost in her own thoughts. When they got back, the garage was in darkness and Ronnie slipped on something near the door and almost fell. They shone the torch down and saw a black puddle. It didn't take long to realize that it was an oil leak. The big drum they used to put old oil in when changing the oil in cars had a small hole at the side. Thick sludge was all across the path. Late as it was, it meant they had to don their overalls and deal with it. It wasn't something that could be left. Sheila used the sand from the fire bucket to spread over the spillage while Ronnie, once she had secured the lid, managed to get the drum on its side and stuff a piece of rag into the small hole. Then they scooped the sandy black mess into another container.

'Good job the council lorry is coming tomorrow,' Sheila remarked.

'Somebody did that deliberately,' said Ronnie. She shone her torch onto a mark on the side of the oil drum. 'That hole has been made with a tool of some sort.'

Sheila gasped. 'But who would want to do that?'

'Search me,' said Ronnie.

'You don't think it was Gerhard, do you?' said Sheila.

'Why on earth would he want to do something like that?' cried Ronnie. 'It's more likely somebody who's got a grudge against us.'

'So who?'

'Search me,' Ronnie said again.

On Sunday Ronnie and Sheila went to Granny's. They had both agreed that they should tell her about Aunt Daisy as soon as possible. They walked from the Becket to High Street Tarring and the rented rooms where Granny and Ronnie's mother were living. Nelson was glad of the exercise and they managed to stay fairly warm by walking briskly. There was a real concern building in the country that this coming winter would be a difficult one. The Minister for Fuel and Power, Manny Shinwell, had announced in the House of Commons that stockpiles of coal were sufficient, but the press had other ideas. The papers pointed out that by nationalizing the coal industry earlier in the year, supplies at the depots, which had once been high enough for ten to twelve weeks, had dwindled down to only four weeks' supply. Mr Shinwell was gambling on a mild winter, but the weather was already becoming very cold and sales of electric fires had rocketed.

Nelson and Milly seemed to have a genuine affection for each other. As soon as they met, they danced around, waving their tails and sniffing until Milly broke free and, crouching on her forepaws, barked happily. 'Out you go, you two,' laughed Granny as she opened the back door to let them play in the tiny courtyard garden for a while.

Granny had a lovely fire going in the little sitting room and, a little later, they all gathered around it, including the dogs who lay side by side on the hearth rug.

Leslie looked more like his old self and, although he still had traces of the bruising on his face, his handsome features were beginning to resurface. His walking had improved and his arm functioned normally although he still complained of tiredness towards the end of the day. The doctor had told him the good news that his internal injuries were healing nicely and he should have no further trouble.

Uncle Bill was there as well. He never actually apologised but he seemed contrite and was attentive towards his wife. He had arrived just before lunch to take Auntie Jean back home. He was keen not to stay too long. He wanted to be home before ten.

'I must say, you've made a damned good job of that garage,' he said.

Ronnie looked startled. Her father was never lavish with compliments and he'd never liked the idea of her working rather than getting married. She didn't know what to say. Was he serious or was this one of his barbed comments? She felt herself tense, but then Sheila smiled and said, 'Thank you, Uncle Bill. We do our best.'

'Is it profitable?' Uncle Bill asked.

'Not yet,' Ronnie conceded, 'but we're getting there.' She held her breath, waiting for the put-down, but, surprisingly, it never came.

They enjoyed their meal, then went back into the sitting room to have a cup of tea before Ronnie's parents set off. She was sensing that something between her parents had changed. Her mother gave her the impression that somehow she was stronger. Nothing was said, but her father's attitude was less belligerent and more conciliatory towards her.

When everyone was settled, Ronnie turned to her grandmother. 'Granny, this is a long story, so I'll just cut to the chase. We've found Daisy.'

Granny seemed confused. 'Daisy?'

'Your daughter Daisy,' said Sheila. 'Aunt Daisy. We met her last Saturday.'

There was a collective gasp from the others in the room. Granny's face paled.

'So where is she?' Jean demanded. 'Is she married? Does she have children? Where's she been all this time?'

Ronnie put her hand up. 'Hang on a second, Mum. Like I said, this is a long story and I'm afraid it doesn't quite have the happy ending we'd all wished for.'

Everyone sat in silence as Ronnie and Sheila, sometimes working in tandem, told them the whole story. They began with the letters they'd found among Granddad's effects and moved on to the non-payment of bills.

'I had no idea,' Granny murmured.

'We guessed that,' said Sheila, taking up the story

with their first trip to Horsham and their meeting with the pimply-faced Mr Pulsford in Worthing town hall. 'He gave us the address of Nightingales and that's where Ronnie and I went to see her.'

Auntie Jean dabbed her eyes and blew her nose into her handkerchief. 'You mean all this time and she's only been about twenty or so miles away?'

Her daughter nodded.

'What does she look like?' Jean asked. 'I mean, does she look well?'

Ronnie looked slightly awkward. 'Let's say she looks a little dowdy, but it's nothing a new frock and a bit of lipstick won't cure.'

Granny pinched the end of her own nose with a hanky. 'I don't understand,' she said brokenly. 'Why didn't Basil tell me? I know he was a law unto himself, but he could have said.'

Sheila put her arm around her grandmother's shoulders. 'We thought he may have wanted to spare you.'

'Spare me what?' Granny said bitterly. 'She was my daughter!'

'What did you say was wrong with her?' These were the first words Uncle Bill had uttered. Until that moment, he'd been sitting very still, staring into the fire the whole time Ronnie and Sheila were talking. Ronnie and Sheila exchanged a glance. 'Why are you looking at each other like that?' he demanded. 'Come on, out with it. What's wrong with her?'

'They called her a moral degenerate,' Ronnie said hesitantly.

'And what's that supposed to mean?' her father snapped.

'Before we left Nightingales,' Sheila went on, 'we asked Matron to write it down for us.' She held up a piece of paper which trembled as she read from it.

'Daisy's sexual nature makes it impossible for her to keep out of difficulties should she be allowed to remain in the community. It is considered that although she would never do it for financial profit, she would be willing to indulge in indiscriminate intercourse, with any male, anytime and anywhere.'

Leslie, who up until that time had remained silent, shifted in his seat. 'In other words,' he said, looking languidly at his fingernails, 'she was locked up for being a tart.'

Granny audibly gasped and Ronnie rounded on her brother. 'Well, that wasn't very nice!"

'She was only fifteen!' Sheila cried.

Leslie put his hands up in mock surrender. He made no further comment, but a few minutes later he got up. The rest of the family were still deep in discussion so they didn't notice him creep from the room. Closing the sitting-room door quietly, he lingered a moment in the hallway while he put his coat on. When he opened the front door a blast of arctic air hit him. Grabbing a scarf and some gloves from the hallstand, he went outside.

He was glad to be on his own. Being in the sitting room with everybody else and the fire made him feel claustrophobic. Whilst he was grateful to his mother and Granny for taking him in and nursing him back to health, he preferred his own company. Now that he was on the mend, he needed to think about his future. He'd have to start all over again. As his punishment for losing the stolen furs, his home had been trashed, then rented to another, and his beautiful clothes were all gone. It had taken the best part of three years of ducking and diving to get where he had been and, frankly, he didn't have the stomach to do it again. All he wanted was a quiet life and to be his own man, but how could he do that without money? It always came down to money and the lack of it.

His father had said his sister had made a good job of the garage and Leslie was curious. He hadn't intended to walk as far as the Becket, but, after a while, he found himself rounding the corner of Rectory Road. He stood on the forecourt for a few minutes looking around. The pumps gleamed and the blackboard leaning against the wall offered would-be customers extra services like wheel balancing and paraffin deliveries. He peered in through the window. Inside, where there had been utter chaos, now he could see a semblance of order. The bench was less cluttered and the floor space had been swept. He cupped his hands against the glass. The shelves were a lot tidier than when Granddad had been there. Walking down the side of the building, Leslie made his way to the shed. Someone had spilled something on the path. It was mostly cleared up, but the grass on the edge of the path looked a bit black and gungy. Leslie stepped to the other side rather than risk dirtying his shoes. The garden had been dug over, presumably in preparation for next year's crop. The Morris 8 van was still inside the shed and, even though it was already getting dark, he could see that the bodywork glistened. It had a professionally written sign on the side. It took a while to fathom it out, but all at once he could see BECKET GARAGE ROADSIDE REPAIRS, SALVINGTON 28. Leslie smiled to himself. How typical of his sister. Ronnie was always one step ahead of the competition. He strolled back.

The caravan was still on the concourse. The knitting needles had gone from the back and it had been resprayed all over in bright yellow. What was it going to be used for now? He peered through the windows, but it was already too dark to make out what was on the inside. His feet were getting cold. He'd better go back. He was beginning to feel light-headed. This was the longest excursion he'd had since leaving hospital and he was very tired. Wrapping the scarf around his neck a little tighter, he headed back towards Rectory Road again.

In the window of the house opposite, Benny Steadman watched him go. There were few faces that went un-noticed and that wasn't one of them. He'd seen that man before, but it was hard to remember exactly when. Benny wracked his brains and then it came to him. Wasn't he the chap who had pinched the caravan that night? What was he doing back here again?

* * *

Ronnie, Sheila and Granny were playing rummy. Jean and Bill had already gone. They'd left about three-quarters of an hour ago and Jean had been a bit upset that Leslie had sloped off somewhere without saying goodbye.

'Probably in need of some fresh air,' Granny had said, making light of the matter. After that, they'd all hugged and kissed each other, promising to meet up again in the New Year.

Granny dealt the cards.

'What are we going to do for Christmas this year?' Ronnie asked as she sorted her hand – two spades, the king and the five, two diamonds, the ace and the three, the three of hearts, queen of clubs and the seven of clubs – not much to work with there, she thought bitterly. The show pile had the four of hearts on the top, so she picked up the four and discarded the queen of clubs.

'You're most welcome to come here,' said Granny, taking her turn.

'We could share the meal,' said Ronnie. 'That way it won't be a burden to anyone.'

The game moved on until it was her turn again and she picked up the three of clubs Sheila had just discarded and got rid of the king. Now she had three threes, the five of spades, the ace of diamonds, the seven of clubs and the four of hearts.

'Good idea,' said Sheila. 'Why don't Ronnie and I bring the vegetables and some biscuits?'

'Will you have time to do them?' Granny asked, rearranging her hand.

Ronnie picked up the eight of diamonds from the deck and discarded it.

'I thought you said you had quite a few choir dates around that time?' Granny insisted.

'We'll be fine,' Sheila said.

Granny picked up the eight of diamonds and discarded the three of spades but before Ronnie could pick it up to add to her other threes, Granny laid her cards down on the table. She had the eight, nine, ten and Jack of diamonds and three twos. 'Rummy,' she grinned.

'That's the third time you've won,' Sheila teased.

'Beginner's luck,' said Granny, shuffling the cards like a pro.

The fellow was back. It was getting very dark, but Benny Steadman could just make out a shadowy figure lurking near the bushes at the side of the garage. The man looked around shiftily, then began spreading something on the forecourt. Benny peered through the glass. He couldn't quite make out who it was, but it had to be the same bloke as he'd seen fiddling about with the oil drum. He should have told the girls what he'd seen, but he was afraid he might scare them.

The man looked up and Benny pulled his head back behind the curtain. Had he been spotted? He reached for his diary and pen. When it was safe, he looked out of the window again. The bloke was pulling his scarf up around his mouth and then he began to hurry away. The forecourt was littered with something, but just then something else caught Benny's eye. Something inside the garage was flickering. What was it? It looked like a flame. What would a naked flame be doing in a garage? His blood ran cold. Dear God, it was a fire!

Benny banged on the floor with his stick. Normally his sister, Grace, came straight away because he seldom summoned her. He was grateful that she and her husband, John, had given him a home for all these years. His fate could have been a lot worse. Other men, comrades who had suffered the same fate in the trenches, had been rejected by their families and were doomed to live out their lives in institutions where they were little more than a statistic. True, he only had one room, but Benny had been given the only room which overlooked the main thoroughfare. He had spent so long watching this little community at Thomas A Becket that he really felt he was part of them. The children and young girls would stop and wave up at the window and occasionally the men would doff their caps, salute or nod in his direction.

Benny seldom went out. The damp in winter and the heat in summer played havoc with his damaged lungs, and besides, it was a big effort for Grace and her husband to get him downstairs. After all this time, they were no spring chickens themselves.

He glanced anxiously towards the garage again. There was definitely a red glow around the back of the building. Benny thumped the floor with his stick once more. He could feel his heartbeat quickening as he tried to control his growing sense of panic. The third time he banged the stick he remembered Grace had told him she and John were going to the North Star just up the road for a darts match. No wonder she hadn't come.

The red glow was getting brighter. He got out of bed and, with supreme effort, opened the window. A blast of freezing-cold air swept into the room and almost took his breath away. He started coughing. He couldn't shout for help, so, pushing the stick out of the window, he began to hit the iron drainpipe on the outside wall. It made a ringing sound, but it was hard to keep it up. After what seemed to be a lifetime, a curtain twitched in the house next to the garage and Doris Melville looked up at him. A second later her husband opened the front door and walked into the street. 'What's up, mate?'

Benny couldn't speak. His breathing was far too painful and, although the cold air had chilled his body, he had beads of perspiration on his face. All he could do was point to the garage. Mr Melville turned towards the direction of his pointed finger. At first he seemed confused, but as he took a few more steps in the right direction, he saw the fire. Benny watched him hurry round the back. Doris had followed her husband out of the house and a few seconds later he yelled, 'Go to the phone box and call the fire brigade. The bloody garage is on fire.'

A wave of relief swept over Benny and he dropped his stick onto the pavement with a clatter. He didn't have the strength to close the window so he tried to flop back onto the bed, but instead he found himself on the linoleum floor. His chest was on fire and he was shivering, but he'd done it. He'd warned his neighbours. If that fire reached the pumps . . . well, it didn't bear thinking about. He was too ill to see more neighbours coming out of their homes with buckets of water to try and douse the flames. A little later, he heard the fire engine coming from the High Street in the town, but then he had another terrible coughing fit. It was so damned cold. He wished he had the strength to close the window or even get back into bed. The floor was hard and cold as well. It didn't take long before he could hear the guns. He could taste the acrid smell of dead bodies and cordite in his mouth. He was lying in the muddy damp earth of the trench and someone was shouting, 'Over the top, my boys. Over the top,' but he didn't have the strength to move. He was vaguely aware of someone coming up to him and saying his name, but all the while something was ebbing away from his body and he hadn't the strength to fight any more. Finally, everything faded.

CHAPTER 19

'Do you think they'll let me see Daisy before Christmas?' Win was doing her best to make her question seem casual, but she couldn't hide the longing in her voice. They were in the kitchen where Win insisted they have a hot Ovaltine before the girls walked back home.

'We had a chat with Matron in her office just before we left,' said Ronnie. 'She wanted things to calm down a bit before we went back again.'

'She wasn't trying to put us off,' Sheila added quickly, 'but she was a bit concerned, what with the run-up to Christmas and everything that was going on in the home, that an emotional family visit might be a bit too much for Aunt Daisy.'

Win frowned. 'I don't understand,' she said stubbornly.

'I think Matron was worried about her mental state,' said Ronnie.

Their grandmother turned her back to them, but they knew she was crying.

'You could write to her,' Sheila suggested. 'Matron didn't say anything about that.'

'And if she thinks Aunt Daisy is happy about having a letter,' Ronnie went on, 'she may be more inclined to invite you all the sooner.'

Granny nodded and squeezed the end of her nose with her hanky. The milk had almost boiled over as she whipped the pan from the stove. 'There now,' she said, pouring the milk onto the granules. 'This'll warm you up. It's freezing out there.'

The three of them sat at the table.

'I can't think where Leslie can be,' said Granny, glancing up at the clock. 'He doesn't usually stay out this long for one of his walks.'

'He's looking very much better,' said Ronnie. 'It's done him good staying here with you. You've done him proud, Granny. I hope he realizes how lucky he is.'

Granny sighed. 'He won't stay much longer,' she said. 'I sense the restlessness in him already.'

They finished their drinks and the girls wrapped up for their walk home. Nelson, reluctant to leave the fireside rug and Milly, was persuaded to join them. Hugs and kisses were exchanged and they set off five minutes later. 'Don't forget to come to the Archbishop's Palace for the carol service if you can,' Sheila called from the gate, 'and we'll see you Christmas morning.'

'Looking forward to it, my dears,' Granny called as she closed the door.

The pavements were already glistening with frost as Ronnie and Sheila linked arms. Nelson walked beside them.

'I have a feeling this is going to be a good Christmas,' said Sheila.

'About time we had one of those,' Ronnie said with a chuckle. 'Have you decided what you're going to do about Matthew yet?'

Sheila blew out her cheeks. 'I know I have to make a decision, but I want to go to the Ball first. Is that too awful?'

Ronnie laughed. 'I'm sure he'll survive. I often wonder why you still go out with him. All you two ever seem to do is row.'

'I don't want to be left on the shelf,' said Sheila.

'Don't be daft,' said Ronnie. 'There's plenty more fish in the sea as my mum would say.'

'What fish?' Sheila said scornfully. 'I don't see any around here, do you?'

'Are you sure?' said Ronnie, giving her a knowing look.

'I don't know what you mean,' said Sheila. 'Where are they, then? Go on, name one.'

They became aware of a fire engine coming up behind them. There was virtually no traffic on the road, but the engine roared and someone was ringing the bell like mad.

'Oh dear, don't tell me you left the toast under the grill before we came out,' Ronnie quipped.

'I hope not,' said Sheila, 'and don't duck the question. Name just one of those fishes in the sea.'

Ronnie clicked her tongue. 'Gerhard?'

'He's years younger than me!' Sheila cried.

'Not that young,' said Ronnie. 'What is he? Nineteen, twenty?'

'And I'm an old woman of twenty-two,' said Sheila.

'I'm telling you, he's crazy about you,' said Ronnie.

Sheila was taken aback. 'I've never even thought of him like that.'

'Well, you should,' said Ronnie. 'He really likes you. I can see it in his face.'

Sheila said nothing, but she was glad of her thick scarf and woolly hat as she felt her cheeks go pink. They turned into Tarring.

'Then there's Mr Webster,' said Ronnie.

'Oh, come on, Ronnie, he's as old as the hills and all he wants is the garage.'

'I meant young Mr Webster,' said Ronnie.

Sheila turned her head sharply. 'Do you really think so?'

'Yes, I do,' said Ronnie. 'He couldn't take his eyes off you either.' She paused to allow her cousin to take in what she'd just said and then added, 'I don't see why you should worry about being left on the shelf. You can do a lot better than Matthew Keller *and* keep our beloved garage.'

They'd walked through the village and, as they came back out onto Rectory Road, an acrid smell of burning drifted towards them.

'Wherever that fire is,' Ronnie remarked, 'it must be a big one.'

'What about you?' said Sheila. 'Is there another man in your life? You don't seem to be interested in anyone around here.'

'I'm off men at the moment,' said Ronnie in a flat tone of voice.

'Is that because of your chap in Singapore?' Sheila asked.

Ronnie was non-committal. 'Maybe.'

'Well, seeing as how you're giving me a lecture about men,' Sheila went on, 'I'm going to tell you a few home truths. You shouldn't let your past ruin your life. You need to put it all behind you and start again.'

'Well,' said Ronnie with a chuckle, 'your advice is just as good as Evelyn Home any day.' She paused, then added, 'And thank you, you've saved me buying a copy of this week's *Woman* magazine.'

Sheila gave her a playful shove.

They both looked up at the same time and saw the red glow. Neither girl voiced the sudden chill of recognition that gripped her heart, but instinctively they walked a lot faster. Nelson went ahead of them. They turned into Highfield Avenue and by the time they'd reached Highfield Road they'd all broken into a trot. A small crowd had gathered on the corner by the Littlehampton Road, but a policeman was preventing anyone from going further.

'Oh God,' Ronnie whispered. 'It is, isn't it? It's the garage.'

Just after eleven, Leslie walked through the door. His grandmother was in her dressing gown, her hair pinned to her head with kirby grips. 'You've been a long time,' she said.

234

Leslie walked to the fire and put his hands out to warm them even though there wasn't much heat in the dying embers. 'I stopped off for a drink.'

'Did you see the fire engine?'

He shook his head. 'No. Why?'

'I just wondered where it went, that's all,' she said, packing up her knitting and stuffing the needles through the ball of wool. 'It came flying down the road around quarter to ten.' She stood up. 'Fancy some Ovaltine before you go to bed?'

Leslie shook his head and made to take his coat off.

'Here, let me help you with that,' she said. She supported the coat as it came off his shoulders. 'Goodnight, love.'

Her grandson didn't answer and, as she hung his coat on the hallstand, the sleeve fell close to her face. It smelled of smoke.

The hall clock struck six as he crept back out of the bedroom. He was putting his coat on when the dog came padding up behind him. He took her by the collar and led her back into the kitchen and shut the door, hoping and praying that Milly wouldn't bark.

Back in the hall, he opened the front door quietly, put his bag on the doorstep, then stepped outside, closing the door behind him. He heard it click, but luckily the dog made no sound. The woman was waiting for him in the car. He hesitated for a second, then took a deep breath. Was this a good idea? She repulsed him with her layers of fat and over-made-up face and she smoked far too much, but she was a means to escape.

'Shall I drive?' he asked.

Wordlessly, she got out of the car and walked round the back. He opened the rear passenger door and gave her a slight bow. 'We may as well start off as we mean to go on, madam,' he said.

She smiled. 'You'll look much better in a uniform, Jackson.'

She climbed into the back seat of the Rolls-Royce and he closed the door. On the way back to the driver's door, he threw his bag into the boot.

Sitting behind the steering wheel, he called over his shoulder. 'Where to, madam?'

'Home,' she said.

He started the engine and it purred into life. 'As you wish, madam,' he said, 'but I'm afraid you'll have to tell me where that is first.'

CHAPTER 20

It had been a long night. The fire brigade had the blaze under control fairly quickly, but they hung around to check everything and to make sure nothing flammable had got near the tanks.

'You've been very lucky,' the chief told Ronnie, but it didn't feel much like it when she and Sheila finally stared into the blackened hole that had once been their garage. Everything was charred, melted or smoke-damaged. What had once been a tidy workshop was swimming in black water and the acrid smell of burning lingered in the air.

They spent the night apart. Ronnie went to stay with Maud Butler, who lived in Highfield Road just around the corner from the garage. There was no spare bed so she was given the sofa. It smelled of dog and she slept badly. She managed to hold it all in, but there was a heavy void in her chest which only seemed to grow bigger with every passing hour. How were they going to manage? What was she going to tell Granny? She couldn't stay here indefinitely so where would she live? The questions whirled around her head until the early hours of the next morning when she finally dropped off to sleep.

Sheila went to stay with Pen Albright. Pen was her usual chatty self but Sheila couldn't talk. While Pen made up a bed in the spare room, Sheila sat on the sofa hugging a mug of tea and staring at her beautiful ballgown hanging from the picture rail. They hadn't actually gone upstairs, but the firemen had told her the rooms above the garage were in a bit of a state as well. It seemed ironic that, apart from the clothes she stood up in, the only other stitch she had was an unfinished ballgown.

When she finally laid her head on the pillow, Sheila cried. She cried because she was miserable. She cried for her mum and dad. She cried for the life she might have had. She cried because Hitler had messed up everything good and proper, and in the end she cried because all their hard work at the Becket had been for nothing. Her thought pattern was muddled. One minute she was wondering if they would be able to access their money if all the bank books had been burned and the next she was imagining herself as Mrs Matthew Keller. It looked as if the decision about what to do about her future had been taken out of her hands. Much as she wrestled with the idea of being his wife, at least it would mean she'd have a roof over her head.

Elsie Tunnock took Nelson and, as usual, he accepted his lot with patience and gratitude.

* * *

In the morning, Ronnie and Sheila collected Nelson and headed back to the garage. There was an undertaker's hearse outside the house opposite, and Gerhard and Mr Hurst were already on site throwing anything totally useless onto a pile at the side of the building.

'I've arranged for Don Fisher to bring his flatbed lorry round after work,' Mr Hurst said. 'He'll take it to the council tip for you. Oh, and the insurance man is here.'

Ronnie peered through the open door and saw a man in a raincoat with a clipboard. She recognized him at once as Elsie Tunnock's husband, Morris. They'd been introduced at the concert.

'I'm not sure if I can be of much help,' he said, coming towards her. 'The police will have to investigate, of course, but it looks like a faulty fuse box.'

'How did that happen?' Ronnie choked.

'Just one of those things,' said Mr Tunnock. 'One good thing, I don't see any problem with the payout. Once it comes through, you and your sister can get the place shipshape again.'

'Cousin,' Ronnie corrected. She looked around and her heart sank. It was going to take ages to clean up, let alone do the repairs.

Seeing her expression, Mr Tunnock smiled. 'Chin up. I shall make my report as soon as possible and the money will be sent to you by cheque.'

Sheila had gone to look at the office. The fire had damaged the wood on the desk and everything on the top was charred, but the petty cash tin inside the drawer had fallen to the floor as it burned. It had melted a little but appeared to be intact. Sheila prised it open with a chisel. There wasn't a lot of money but it was in good order. The girls always banked the takings on a regular basis and Ronnie had been into town on Friday afternoon. Saturday's takings hadn't been great, but when she counted it there was £26/13/4. Luckily Ronnie had put one of their bank books into the tin. The current account book and the cheque book in the drawer were burned to ash.

'At least we can prove our identity in the bank,' Sheila said as she divided the cash between them. 'We can pay our outstanding creditors.'

Ronnie took her share of the money but said nothing.

Even though the insurance man had been very quick and the news was positive, she was close to tears. Where to begin? Everywhere was such a mess. She glanced towards the stairs and gingerly made her way up to their living quarters. The fire hadn't reached this far, but everything would have to be ditched. The smoke and water damage was awful. Even the walls were streaked, the chairs smelled and all her clothes in the wardrobe did too.

Sheila followed her up the stairs. Neither girl thought to comfort the other. Each was battling with her own disappointed hopes. Ronnie opened her underwear drawer. She was still wearing yesterday's things and wanted to change her knickers if nothing else. She reached in and took out a clean pair, but when she put them to her nose she threw them back inside and slammed the drawer. 'Everything stinks,' she said bitterly.

'We'll have to go down to the Red Cross shop and get some new things,' said Sheila, 'but I'm not sure if we can get any money out of the bank today.'

Ronnie didn't respond.

Sheila opened a drawer. 'Oh no, look. All my Christmas presents are spoiled.'

Back downstairs a few new faces hovered in the doorway. Mr Hurst was talking to a fresh-faced young man with a camera.

'The press,' Ronnie said scornfully.

Granny had arrived too. 'Oh, my dears, I'm so sorry,' she said as she hugged them both. Sheila wept a little but Ronnie remained as stiff as a board. 'Mrs Brown came on the bus to tell me what had happened,' Granny went on. 'How did it start?'

Sheila dabbed her eyes with her handkerchief. 'They think it was the fuse box.'

'Oh dear,' said Granny. 'Has somebody been fiddling with it?'

'Wouldn't surprise me,' Ronnie said. 'It could have been the same idiot who's been sending us poison-pen letters.' The tone of her voice was flat.

Win Peters looked startled. 'What poison-pen letters? I never knew that. Why didn't you tell me?'

'We didn't want to worry you,' Sheila chipped in quickly. Ronnie's face was as black as thunder. Sheila had never seen her looking so cross. 'Anyway, Mr Tunnock didn't say anything about someone fooling

241

around with the fuse box. He said it was just one of those things.'

Win tutted. 'You should have said something about the letters.' Looking around, she sighed, 'Now what can I do to help?'

'Nothing,' Ronnie said grimly.

Her grandmother gave her a sympathetic smile, but Ronnie moved away. 'You may as well go home, Granny,' she said. 'And take Nelson home with you. He's got nowhere to go.'

'Of course I will,' said Granny.

They heard the sound of bicycle wheels and Matthew came round the corner. Nelson let out a low growl, but Sheila ran to him with open arms. Ronnie saw the look of disappointment on Gerhard's face.

'I came as soon as I could,' said Matthew breathlessly. 'Are you all right? Have you any idea how this happened?'

Sheila shook her head. 'The insurance man thinks it might be the fuse box.'

'Why don't I write a running commentary on the blackboard?' Ronnie said sarcastically. 'We could put it up by the pumps and that would save us going over and over the same thing again and again.'

Matthew was genuinely shocked. 'But that's terrible. Have you reported it to the electricity people?'

'We've only just been told,' said Sheila. 'The insurance man has just left. Oh, Matthew, it's going to take us ages to get all this cleared up.'

'Get it cleared up?' Ronnie said acidly. 'Oh, Sheila,

don't be an idiot. We're never going to get the garage back the way it was.'

Sheila looked hurt and confused. This wasn't like Ronnie. She was the strong one; the rock. Why was she giving up without a fight? 'It might take a while,' she began hesitantly, 'but we've had stacks of offers of help and there's—'

'For God's sake!' Ronnie snapped at the top of her voice. 'The place is a total wreck.'

'Don't speak to me like that,' Sheila said crossly.

'I'm sorry,' Ronnie said forcefully, 'but you don't seem to understand how hopeless it all is.'

Just then, a car drew up on the forecourt and they were surprised to see Neville Webster climb out of the driving seat.

'Oh, I might have guessed he'd turn up,' Ronnie muttered darkly. She turned back to the others, her eyes wide and her hands spread out. 'See how the vultures gather.'

'Ronnie!' Sheila cried.

'I only just heard what happened,' Neville was saying as he walked towards them. 'I'm so sorry. If there's anything I can do.'

'There's nothing anyone can do,' Ronnie said harshly, her eyes blazing. 'As you can see for yourself, the Becket garage is finished. Kaput.'

Sheila touched her cousin's arm. 'Ronnie, listen to me,' she began.

'No,' cried Ronnie, rounding on her, 'you listen to me. There's not going to be any fairy-tale ending to this.

They've won. They've all won. Hitler, the bloody Japs, whoever did this, they've all got what they wanted. They've finally beaten me. It's over. We can't make a living here and I've had it with the lot of you as well. I've already picked myself up twice before, but I can't do it any more. I just can't.'

Nelson barked and moved backward.

'Darling girl,' said Granny, 'you're upset . . .'

'Of course I'm upset,' Ronnie shrieked. She spun round to face Neville. 'D'you still want the garage?'

Neville put his hands up in mock surrender. 'I didn't come—' he began, but she shouted him down, her face contorted with rage.

'I don't know about Sheila, but you can have my share of the garage for tuppence halfpenny. That's about all it's worth and you're bloody well welcome to it.' There was a stunned silence and she turned on her heel to go.

'But where are you going?' Sheila cried helplessly.

'I don't know,' said Ronnie. She kicked out at the pile of rubbish Gerhard was creating and stubbed her toe painfully. Gerhard rushed to help her, but she pushed him away angrily. 'And as for you,' she spat, 'you may be a POW but you don't have to be such a bloody wimp. If you were half a man you'd tell her how you feel instead of letting her go.'

Everyone stared, open-mouthed.

'Ronnie—' Sheila began again.

Ronnie threw her hands into the air. 'Just bugger off and leave me alone,' she said, limping away.

CHAPTER 21

It wasn't until she got home with Nelson that Win realized Leslie was gone too. When she'd left the house that morning, she had surmised that he was still in bed asleep, but with no sign of him around when she got back, she tapped on his bedroom door. The bed was unmade and, as the wardrobe door swung open, she saw the empty coat hangers. There was no note, but his bag was gone as well.

At first she was hurt. It would have been common courtesy to write a note or leave a forwarding address. Win sat down heavily on the kitchen chair. What on earth was happening to her life at the moment? Daisy was alive, but she couldn't go and see her, her grandson had cleared off without even saying goodbye and Basil's garage had gone up in smoke. She looked around. The place was so small. If she'd had another bedroom she could have offered all three of her grandchildren a place to stay. She never should have given up her lovely home to go and live with Jean. What a fool she had been.

Life with Basil hadn't been a bed of roses, but she'd got by. In the early days he hadn't been her first choice,

245

but he'd been all right. He was never what you might call a romantic man. He gave her enough housekeeping and was kind to the girls, but he never paid her much attention except when he wanted 'it'. There were a couple of occasions over the years when he was less demanding. When that happened, he'd go to the pub all spruced up and his hair plastered with Brylcreem, so she'd guessed he'd found some floozie to give him what he wanted. She was only guessing, but she didn't want to ask. When it was over, he'd come back as keen as ever. She never got flowers or even a birthday present, but then he was a man of his time. He went to work, came home for his tea and went to the pub each evening. He regarded it as women's work to keep house and bring up the children, which she had done to the best of her ability.

After years of suffering very heavy periods, the doctor told them she had to go for a hysterectomy and a long convalescence. Basil had been distraught. At first she'd been comforted that he cared about her, but it didn't take long to realize it was the sex he would miss. Well, she'd thought to herself at the time, he's welcome to find another tart. Win had been sent away and she'd taken a turn for the worse. She'd ended up with pleurisy and at one time they thought she might have TB. Daisy had to take over the running of the household, but it was all too much for the poor child and she'd run away. They'd never talked about it and when Win finally came home again it was business as usual.

She guessed Basil had bought the garage as a cover for some of his shady dealings. She knew when he was up to something, but, thankfully, he'd never been caught. The stroke had been devastating, but she'd done her duty for the last three years of his life. She wasn't exactly sorry when he died, but she wasn't over the moon either. She wasn't as callous as that, but it was nice to be able to make her own decisions for a change. She'd bought herself a frock or two, had her hair done once in a while and gone to the pictures. Living with Jean had brought the restrictions back again. Bill didn't give her daughter much spare cash and he constantly wanted to know where they'd been and how much they'd spent. To his way of thinking, tea rooms were a waste of money when you could have a cup at home for quarter of the price and why go to the pictures when you could sit at home and read the book?

Win sighed. 'Well, my girl,' she said aloud, 'moping about the past won't do any good.' She picked up the framed picture of Daisy and kissed the glass. Putting it back, she glanced at the clock. It was time to clear up Leslie's room and make up the bed. When Sheila got in, she would send her back up to fetch Ronnie. Jean had slept on the couch, but the two girls might prefer to share the bed until they could afford another one.

The bank manager was sympathetic. He knew Sheila of course, but as he explained, he had to go through a few formalities before she could get hold of the money in their bank account. 'Seeing as how it's a joint account, Miss Jackson will have to be present,' he reminded her. Sheila booked an appointment for Tuesday January 7th.

'If you need money in the interim period,' he went on, 'the bank would be happy to extend a loan, providing you can find a male guarantor.'

Sheila thanked him, but declined. It seemed grossly unfair that they had to find a male guarantor, and even though he knew exactly who she was, the only practical help the bank could offer was a loan, probably at some exorbitant rate.

It was nearly four o'clock and already getting dark as she headed off back to Granny's place. She'd agreed to have her tea with Granny rather than intrude into Pen's household. Sheila was grateful for the bed, but if she stayed with Pen they would have to come to some sort of amicable arrangement regarding rent and board.

As she cycled by the new gas showroom in Chapel Road, Sheila spotted a card in the window: 'Cooking demonstrator wanted.' By the time she'd reached North Street, she found herself heading back.

Leslie stuck out his chest, his fingers on the inside of his lapels.

'I think the double-breasted jacket suits sir a lot more,' the tailor's assistant said. 'And grey is definitely sir's colour.' Leslie smiled. The mirror can't lie, he thought as he put the peaked cap on at a jaunty angle. He was beginning to feel alive again.

'If sir would allow me,' the assistant went on.

They were standing in a gentleman's outfitters in Regent Street, London, or to be more precise, in the domestic uniform department at the back of the shop. Leslie had been sent there to be fitted for his chauffeur's livery and he'd been having the time of his life. There was nothing better than looking good, looking smart, looking well-dressed. He could hardly believe his luck.

After seeing the Becket garage, he'd been really down. Not that he'd wanted it any more. He hated the thought of greasy overalls and having oil under his fingernails; but it brought what Ronnie had achieved into sharp focus. She'd made a success of her life. He had no money and had to start all over again. Granny was kind enough, but he didn't want to live his life at her level. Her place was small and it smelled because of the dog and he couldn't bear it sniffing around his ankles all the time.

Feeling depressed, he'd crossed over the road and wandered into the Thomas A Becket hotel bar for a drink before he went back home. That's when he'd seen her. While he warmed his hands by the log fire, she was sitting on a bar stool, her fat backside hanging over the edges. Her little feet were stuffed inside a tiny pair of high-heeled shoes which were far too small for her. He'd been thinking how much she reminded him of one of those fat ladies on saucy seaside postcards when he'd realized there was a mirror on the other side of the bar and she was watching him watching her. With a mumbled apology, he'd turned away, embarrassed. A little later, a whisky appeared in front of him.

He'd jerked his head up and the waiter, giving him a meaningful wink, had said, 'From the lady at the bar.'

The whisky mellowed him and made him feel better, so when she came over to join him, he was more than happy to welcome her. He could tell at once that she was moneyed. The rings on her fingers were the genuine article and the fur she had around her neck must have set her back a few thousand. She told him that her name was Mrs Harrison-Vane and she was staying at the hotel.

'My wretched chauffeur has been taken ill,' she'd said unsympathetically. 'I don't suppose you know someone who could drive me back to London to-morrow?' Letting her stole slip enough to reveal her generous bosom, she leaned towards him. 'It's a bit short notice, but I'd make it worth his while.'

Leslie had offered his services behind the wheel, but when she'd invited him up to her room to 'discuss' the terms, he'd declined.

The walk home in the cold air cleared his head. This was an opportunity too good to miss. He might even mange to get a permanent position. How hard could it be driving some fat old biddy around in her Rolls-Royce?

When he'd arrived in London, she'd not only given him ten pounds for his trouble but she'd offered him a job. He was to have his own quarters above the garage, a uniform and ten pounds a week over and above his board and lodging.

'Shall I wrap both the suits for you, sir?' The assistant brought him back to the here and now.

'Not this one,' said Leslie. 'I'll wear it.'

'If you'll forgive me saying so, sir is a man to be admired,' said the assistant. 'The whole ensemble is most becoming on sir.' He pointed to Leslie's old suit. 'What about sir's old clothes?'

Leslie admired his reflection in the mirror once again. 'Umm? Oh, bin them.'

'And how would sir like to pay?'

'Charge them all to Mrs Harrison-Vane's account,' he said majestically.

'I've managed to get a job to tide us over.'

Sheila was in the Thomas A Becket hotel. She hadn't intended to be there, but when she'd got back home, Granny had asked her to find Ronnie and invite her to stay because Leslie had done a bunk. Sheila had been surprised to discover that Ronnie had already left Maud Butler's place and was staying just across the road in the hotel.

'She said she'd come into some money,' Maud said sourly. 'Pity she couldn't have given me a bob or two after sleeping on my couch.'

In fact, Ronnie was standing behind the desk at reception. 'Mrs Butler rather gave me the impression you were staying here,' Sheila said with a chuckle.

'That was what I intended to do,' said Ronnie. Her voice was cold and she avoided Sheila's eye. 'But then Mrs Fford asked me if I wanted a job, so here I am.'

'Oh, Ronnie, that's wonderful!' Sheila cried. 'My new job is working in the gas showroom in Chapel Road.

251

They want me to cook a quick meal every lunchtime to catch the office workers in their lunch hour and if I can get at least six customers gathered around the stove I can do some other cooking during the afternoon.'

'I'm pleased for you,' Ronnie said stiffly. 'Now if you will excuse me.'

'Ronnie, please don't do this,' said Sheila. 'Let's put it all behind us. It couldn't be helped.'

Her cousin glared.

'I've come to tell you that Leslie has gone,' Sheila ploughed on, 'and Granny says we can both live with her.'

A guest stopping by for his keys interrupted them. When he had gone, Ronnie said, 'I want you to go, Sheila.'

'But, Ronnie . . .'

'Why can't you get it into your head?' Ronnie snapped. 'I don't give a stuff about the Becket. I'm not coming back. If you don't go, I'll have to ring for the management.' As she spoke, a tear formed in each eye.

Sheila's heart was thumping and she had a lump in her throat. 'But we're family.' Ronnie picked up the telephone receiver. 'Okay, okay,' said Sheila, putting her hands up. 'I'm going.' She turned towards the door, then turned back. 'Perhaps it's just as well,' she retorted. 'Right now, I'm not even sure I like you any more.'

CHAPTER 22

The Archbishop's Palace looked amazing. Someone had put candles on every windowsill and the hall itself was dotted with paper chains. In the corner by the fireplace, there was a card table with a nativity scene on it. The chairs were neatly arranged in rows and, fortunately, whoever had organized the chairs had left a decent gangway down the sides. Before long the place was packed. By the time the carol singing started people were standing two deep along the sides as well. The children sat crossed-legged at the front and everyone made sure the older folk were able to sit on a chair. This was only the second Christmas since the war ended and the hall was buzzing with excitement. Last year some members of the armed forces were still abroad. Not everyone had been demobbed the minute the armistice was signed. Now, in 1946, just about everyone was home apart from those who had signed up for the regular army.

The choir, including Sheila, filed in from the little room at the back. They had no uniform but April Rodway had asked everyone to wear something red or green. Ancient faded jumpers mingled with brand-new knits, but everyone in the choir had made an effort. Sheila had a blouse which belonged to Granny. It was rather 'roomy' as Granny would say, but at least she was in the right colour.

As soon as she came in, Sheila scanned the room. Granny was there, sitting on the third row near the side, but there was no sign of Ronnie or Matthew. As Mrs Rodway stood up to conduct them, Sheila made a determined effort to shake off her disappointment and sing her heart out. They had practised the old favourites including 'Hark the Herald Angels Sing', 'O Little Town of Bethlehem' and 'Silent Night'. Afterwards there was a short address given to them by the vicar and, just before the concert ended, she saw Matthew slip in through the door. He was in uniform so people made room for him and he grinned at her as he saw her. Sheila's heart soared. Outside might be bleak but here in the hall the Christmas spirit was alive and well.

Afterwards, while Sheila thanked her friends for their kind thoughts and Christmas wishes, Matthew chatted to some of the men.

'I hear you have a new job,' said Pen Albright, coming towards her with a few cups of tea on a tray. 'When do you start?'

'After Christmas,' said Sheila. 'It's in the new gas showroom in Chapel Road. I have to demonstrate how to use one of the new gas cookers.'

'Sounds very impressive,' said Pen. Someone took a couple of cups from her tray.

'Apparently some husbands have already booked their wives in for a session as a Christmas present,' said Sheila. 'All the new houses the council are building near Field Place will have gas cookers.'

'You know your Ronnie is working at the hotel?' said Pen.

Sheila nodded. 'I have seen her, but she's very cross with me.'

'But why?' said Pen, giving the last of her teacups away. 'It wasn't your fault, was it?'

Sheila blinked back a tear and Pen rubbed her arm sympathetically. 'Have you got somewhere to go for Christmas dinner?'

'Yes, I have, thank you, Pen,' she said. 'I'm staying with my grandmother. And, Pen, I want to thank you for all you've done for me. '

'Don't be daft,' said Pen. 'I haven't done anything.'

'I'm so glad I paid you in advance for the dress,' said Sheila.

Immediately Pen looked concerned. 'Oh Lord, I suppose all your money went up in smoke and all. Do you want it back?'

'No, no,' said Sheila, smiling at Pen's anxious face. 'I'm fine. I have money and now I have a job.'

Pen squeezed her arm, satisfied. 'When will you come to collect the dress?'

Matthew had joined them.

'I think we said the twenty-ninth?' said Sheila.

'Lovely,' said Pen, 'but mind you come long enough to stop for a cup of tea.' She gave Matthew a nod and pushed her way through the crowd towards the kitchen to get more cups of tea.

Sheila turned to Matthew. 'Thank you for coming.'

'That's all right,' he said, munching a homemade biscuit. 'Sorry I missed most of it. How did you get here?'

'I came with Granny,' she said. 'I'm living there now.'

'But what about your cousin?' he said, raising an eyebrow. 'I thought he was living with your grandmother.'

'Leslie has gone,' she said.

'Gone!' Matthew seemed shocked. 'Gone where?'

'I've no idea,' said Sheila, 'but we're not surprised. Leslie is a restless sort of person.'

'Bit funny, isn't it?' he said. 'I mean, so soon after the fire?'

Sheila frowned. 'I hope you're not implying that Leslie had something to do with it?'

Matthew's pursed his lips.

'Matthew,' she said, 'it was a fault in the fuse box.'

'Then how do you account for the tin tacks on the forecourt?'

Sheila looked puzzled. 'What tin tacks?'

'The whole area was covered in them,' he said. 'The fire chief wasn't too happy. He had to get his men to change two tyres before the engine could return to the station.'

Sheila put her hands to her face. 'This gets worse by the minute.'

'Don't worry about it,' he said soothingly. 'So long as you're safe, that's all that matters.'

'Well, you'll be pleased to know I have a new job,' she said, changing the subject.

He slipped his arm around her waist. 'So you've finally left the garage.'

'Not exactly,' she said. 'I'll go back when it's all cleared up.'

'Listen, darling,' he said, drawing her to one side. 'I've talked it over with my sarge, and now that you've lost your home, I may be able to get special permission to get married.'

She suddenly felt panicked. 'Let's not get too hasty,' she said.

'You were brilliant,' someone interrupted. 'I loved that arrangement of "Silent Night".'

'Thank you,' said Sheila with a shy smile.

'I know,' Matthew said in her ear, 'we could announce our engagement right now.'

'No!' cried Sheila. 'I'm sorry, Matthew, but I can't do everything at once; not with the fire and losing our home and everything. This has been such an awful year. Please try and understand.'

Turning, she saw someone across the room. 'Oh, there's Mrs Edwards. I must catch her before she goes. Sorry, sorry.'

Matthew was livid. What the hell was she up to? All she was doing was stringing him along. How many times had he told her the blasted garage was unsafe, and even when it had been all but burned to the ground, she still wouldn't have it. He'd been patient, he'd been loving, he'd been kind, but still she wouldn't let him take charge. Didn't it say it in the Bible? Wives submit yourselves to your husband for the husband is the head of the wife. He'd never found the passage himself, but he'd heard a preacher say that once and it had always stuck in his head. He stared after her, his spine prickling. That's when he saw the Kraut sniffing around her. It was all very well letting these POWs do the dirty work and all the jobs nobody else wanted to do but not when they hung around our women and girls. He decided to keep his eye on the man. Just let him touch her, he thought, and I'll have him in the clink faster than you can say 'leave off'.

When Sheila had finally managed to push her way through the crowd, it pained her to have to tell Mrs Edwards that an apprenticeship at the garage was no longer an option.

'Don't worry, my dear,' she said. 'When I saw the damage to your home I guessed straight away. I noticed Mr Hurst was still there with his POWs. I hope you can get back on your feet as quickly as possible.'

'What will you do with Derek?' Sheila asked anxiously.

'Your Mr Webster offered to help him,' said Mrs Edwards. 'And if that doesn't work out, I have a few other people I can harass.' She laughed heartily. 'Don't worry. He'll be fine.' And with that she hurried off to buttonhole the vicar about something else.

Sheila heard someone cough quietly behind her, and

when she turned round, she was surprised to see Gerhard standing next to her. He pulled off his woolly hat and turned it nervously in his hands.

'Oh,' she cried. 'Fancy seeing you. I thought you weren't allowed out after dark.'

'Mr Hurst has permission for us to be here,' he said. She smiled up at him, admiring his natural-looking hair – no Brylcreem. His azure-blue eyes regarded her with an intensity that made her heart flutter. 'I have for you a gift.'

'A gift for me?' He handed her a small box tied with a piece of rag fashioned to look like a ribbon. 'Oh, you shouldn't have.'

'I am sorry,' he said quickly. 'Why is it so, that I should not give you gift?' Someone bumped into them and all at once he was even closer.

She smiled at his puzzled expression. 'Sorry, I didn't mean that. I've confused you. It's just an English expression. What I mean is, thank you for your gift. It's very kind of you.'

Their eyes met as she took the box.

'You have somewhere to go for Christmas?'

'Yes,' she said. 'I'm staying with my grandmother. That's her over there.'

Gerhard followed the line of her pointed finger and nodded. Just beyond Granny, Sheila could see Matthew watching them with a very dark expression.

'This is *gut*,' Gerhard said, unaware. 'You will be happy.'

She nodded. 'I hope you enjoy your Christmas too,'

259

she said. 'It must be hard for you being so far from your home.'

He shook his head. 'There is nothing for me in Germany,' he said sadly. 'It is all gone. Helmut, he is angry with me,' he went on. 'He says I should go back, that I should rebuild the country with him, but for me, it is no longer my home.'

'I'm so sorry,' she said, touching his arm lightly. 'Where will you go for Christmas?'

He smiled and shrugged. 'I shall be locked up,' he said. 'It is better for the soldiers that I and my colleagues are in the barracks.'

'Oh, Gerhard!' she cried.

'It is fine. I do not mind. Apparently we have Father Christmas too.'

They both laughed until she became aware that Matthew had joined them. 'Everything all right here?'

'Yes, fine,' said Sheila.

They heard a gruff voice saying, 'Time to go, lad,' and they turned to see the soldier who was to take the POWs back to camp. Gerhard nodded and made to follow him. '*Frohe Weihnachten, schöne Frau,*' he said as they parted. She didn't understand what he'd said, but the tone of his voice and the sentiment in his eyes told her it was something lovely.

'Happy Christmas, Gerhard,' Sheila called after him. She caught sight of Helmut. He was waiting by the door, ready to go, a sour expression on his face.

Matthew was looking at her hand. 'What's that?'

'A present,' said Sheila, and before she could protest, he'd taken it from her. 'Matthew!'

The rag ribbon fell away, revealing an exquisitely carved box. It was very dainty and she could probably only manage to put a couple of pairs of earrings or a brooch inside. The lid had been fashioned into a rose in full bloom. It was obviously handmade and it must have taken him ages to do it. Some of the other choir members had gathered around to look.

'Oh, that's gorgeous.'

'Lucky thing. Who gave you that?'

'Isn't that smashing?'

Sheila looked up just as Gerhard and the other POWs had reached the door. Their eyes met and she mouthed, 'Thank you,' as he left the room.

When the others had finished admiring the box, Matthew leaned towards her. 'Be careful, darling,' he whispered close to her ear. 'We don't want people to think you're hobnobbing with a Nazi.'

Later, as they were all clearing up, someone found a woolly hat by the door.

'Oh,' cried Sheila, 'that looks like Gerhard's. He must have dropped it.'

'Nobody's got time to get it round to him now,' Pen remarked.

'Put it in the lost-property box for now,' said April. 'I'll see he gets it back after Christmas.'

'I'll take it,' said Matthew, adding with a laugh, 'Can't have the poor man getting a chill, can we?'

CHAPTER 23

Christmas was very quiet for Sheila and Granny. Win had given her granddaughter some perfume and a box of embroidered handkerchiefs. Sadly, the necklace and a pen Sheila had wrapped up for her grandmother had been lost in the fire. Sheila shed a tear as she explained.

Granny hugged her. 'This has been a terrible year for you, my dear,' she said gently. 'What with losing your mum and dad and now your home.'

'And for you,' said Sheila, her voice muffled by her grandmother's jumper. 'You lost your daughter and your husband.'

Granny nodded. 'We didn't see a lot of each other, but I miss your mum.'

Sheila was about to ask about Granddad, but she decided that was a question better left unsaid. 'I can't believe Ronnie has cut us off like this,' she said bitterly.

'Don't be angry with her,' said Granny. 'We all have different ways of dealing with things.'

Sheila harrumphed and sat up.

'It won't always be like this,' said Granny. 'She'll come around.'

It was at that moment that Sheila gave her the card. She had found it on the mat a couple of days before and hidden it as a special present. She hadn't opened it, but the Horsham postmark and the immature handwriting were a dead giveaway.

'It's from the home,' said Granny when she opened it. It was a pretty card with holly and bells. Inside the card it said 'To *wish you a very happy Christmas*,' and it was signed, '*Love Daisy xx*'.

As soon as she saw it, Granny burst into tears.

Later that day, as she had promised at choir practice in the Archbishop's Palace, Sheila went to the children's home to help with Father Christmas's visit. She'd lost the elf outfit they'd wanted her to wear in the fire, of course, which was another thing she had wanted to tell Mrs Edwards. However, Granny had come to the rescue and lent her a floral wrap-over apron and a paper hat. Sheila was now Auntie Christmas just arrived from Lapland to help Mother Christmas (Mrs Rodway) give out the presents.

The children were all gathered in the largest of the nursery rooms when they heard a loud 'ho-ho-ho' coming down the front stairs. A few of the smallest children were a bit scared, but the staff and other friends of the home cuddled and reassured them that all was well. Then Father Christmas (Doctor Rodway) came into the room carrying a large sack over his shoulder. Mrs Edwards welcomed him warmly.

'Have you brought your reindeer?' she asked as she handed him a carrot.

'I left them on the roof, looking after the sleigh,' Father Christmas said gruffly. As if on cue, which it was, they heard a *clip-clop* sound in the distance. Sheila had to turn her head in case any of the children saw her grin as Trixie Rodway made a very convincing hoof noise with two empty tin cans outside the door. 'I shall put the carrots in my pocket,' Father Christmas went on, 'and they can have them for their tea.'

'After the long journey you've had,' Mrs Edwards said with a smile, 'I'm sure they deserve it.'

'Have all these children been good?' Father Christmas said, looking around.

'Very good,' said Mrs Edwards.

'For a whole year?' said Father Christmas.

A few children shifted uneasily in their chairs.

Mrs Edwards turned to look at the adults in the room. 'What do you think?'

Much to everyone's relief, there was a resounding cry of 'Yes!' and Father Christmas swung the sack from his shoulder.

It took a while to distribute the presents. Father Christmas handed each gift to Mother Christmas or Auntie Christmas and they gave them to the children. Each child had a brand-new toy. Mrs Edwards hated the idea of giving them second-hand presents although in the run-up to Christmas they had had quite a few donations.

'Why should I give one of these children a battered

old teddy with one eye or a car with a wheel missing just because they're in a home?' she'd say stoutly and Sheila had to agree.

As the pressie-bash continued, Sheila knew she was absolutely right. She'd never forget the look on Lucy's face when she unwrapped a dolly with long blonde hair and wearing a red riding cape, or Kevin's delight when he took a shiny red fire engine out of the box. She may have lost the garage, but, young as they were, the children in the home had had their share of tragedy too. Lucy's dad was in jail for murdering her baby brother because he kept crying and Kevin had been found abandoned in his pushchair in the waiting room at West Worthing railway station.

Sheila stayed for a cup of tea and a piece of Christmas cake and then she decided to make her way home. Doctor and Mrs Rodway and their daughter, Trixie, offered her a lift.

'Your grandmother and your parents are amazing people,' Sheila whispered to Trixie as they sat in the back seat of her parents' car. 'You're a very lucky girl.'

'We were very sorry to hear about the garage,' Mrs Rodway said, turning round. 'Can I help in any way?'

'You're very kind,' said Sheila, 'but Pen has already mustered the troops.'

'Well, if you change your mind,' said April, 'the offer still stands. What will you do now?'

Sheila explained about the gas showroom.

'I must say, I admire your pluck,' said Mrs Rodway.

'I would be terrified that my cake would get burned or my soufflé would collapse.'

Ronnie plunged herself into her work. The guests at the Thomas A Becket were mostly older people; people with no family and nowhere to go at Christmas. Nobody would be checking in at the reception so she was asked to help make sure everyone was happy. A sumptuous lunch was followed by a visit from Father Christmas (Mr Fford in disguise), who gave each of the guests a present. After they'd listened to the King's speech, those who were left in the sitting room were treated to some music as Ronnie played the piano for them, the songs of yesteryear, which made her a great favourite from that moment on.

When she'd finished, Ronnie bowed as a dozen tearful but happy guests smiled and clapped.

'Make the most of it while you can,' said Mrs Fford as Ronnie came off the piano. 'We've got a wake here in the New Year.'

Ronnie grimaced. 'Oh dear,' she said. 'It sounds like we'll be going from the sublime to the ridiculous. Who is it? Anyone we know?'

'Benny Steadman,' said Mrs Fford, emptying an over-flowing ashtray into a small bin.

Ronnie's jaw dropped. 'Is that the Mr Steadman who lived opposite the garage?' Her employer nodded. 'Oh, I'm sorry,' said Ronnie.

She felt strangely sad about the poor man's demise. Who wouldn't? Here was a man who'd gone to war as a boy in his teens, fit and healthy, with the whole of his life in front of him. One whiff of mustard gas put an end to all that. He'd come home to thirty years of misery. She wondered how she would have coped with breathing problems and being confined to one room for the rest of her life. Benny's world had been reduced to the people in the street below. She'd heard people say that his sister and her husband took him out occasionally, but Ronnie had only ever seen him behind the glass of his bedroom. She'd been annoyed about him watching them at first, but that was only because she hadn't understood. 'I suppose the damage to his lungs finally caught up with him,' she remarked sadly.

Mrs Fford turned towards her with a puzzled expression. 'Over-exerting himself more like,' she said. 'He never should have got out of bed and opened that window to bang on the drainpipe.'

'Bang on the drainpipe?' said Ronnie. 'Why would he do that?'

'It was the only way he could attract attention,' said Mrs Fford.

Ronnie seemed confused. 'If he needed help, why didn't he just call his sister?'

'She and her husband were out,' said Mrs Fford. She frowned. 'Didn't anyone tell you?'

'Tell me what?'

'When the garage caught fire, he was worried that you and Sheila were still inside. He did it to save you both.'

* * *

267

Sergeant Longfellow undid his laces and slipped his boots from his feet. He sighed and a wave of relief swept over him as he rubbed his throbbing bunion and wiggled his toes. PC Willows put a cup of tea on the desk in front of him.

'Arthur Philips all locked up, is he?'

Willows nodded. 'I reckon he'll sleep it off now,' he said. 'If you ask me, he only put the bloody brick through the window to get a warm bed for the night, and he was no more drunk than I'm the man in the moon. You should have sent him off with a flea in his ear, sarge.'

'Now, now, constable, where's your Christmas spirit?' Longfellow said good-naturedly. 'We have every reason to be grateful to poor old Arthur. He was the one who led us to the stolen furs, remember?'

PC Willows scowled. Arthur Philips had definitely pulled a fast one, but the sergeant was right about giving him a bed for the night. Who would want to spend Christmas out in the cold? A bed in the cell, albeit as hard as a board, was preferable to a perishing cold night under the pier.

It was reasonably quiet at the police station. On Christmas Eve, they'd picked up a shoplifter in Woolworths and ruined his holiday plans, but apart from a slight road traffic accident on the corner of Heene Road and Cowper Road, the day had been easy. Aside from relieving the pain in his feet, Sergeant Longfellow had been looking at the reports about the fire in the Becket garage before handing them over to the inspector. PC Keller had raised some suspicions that the fire might not have been accidental and he and PC Finchley had taken statements from the people in the area. Apparently the two girls who lived there, Veronica Jackson and Sheila Hodges, had alibis which had been corroborated. They had no reason to set fire to the place anyway. The business was doing well; perhaps not making serious money as yet, but they were enthusiastic about it and had concrete plans for the future. The books had been damaged in the fire, but the bank manager was willing to testify that all was well.

Finchley and Keller had discovered an eyewitness who had seen Leslie Jackson, a well-known petty thief, hanging around the place before the fire started. Jackson was Veronica's brother and known to have expressed his displeasure when the garage had been given to his sister after their grandfather died. There was a suspicion that Jackson could also be involved with the fur robbery, although nothing could be proved. PC Keller also pointed out in his notes that Jackson had left Worthing on the night of the fire.

The finger of suspicion was also pointing at one of the POWs, particularly a man called Gerhard, who had been sent to help out at the garage. As an ex-Nazi with a grudge, Keller suggested, it wasn't beyond the bounds of belief that he could have sabotaged the garage as a last defiant act against the King's peace. Sergeant Longfellow grimaced as he closed the file. His men had done a good job. Perhaps Keller was a little too opinionated, but the inspector would have no trouble at all in wrapping this one up. All they had to do was locate Jackson and pull the Nazi in and question them both.

'Put this on the inspector's desk for me,' said Longfellow, handing Willows the file. 'Seems to me somebody is going to spend 1947 behind bars.'

The day after Boxing Day couldn't come soon enough for Win. She phoned Nightingales and made arrangements to be there the next afternoon. Sheila offered to go with her. Having to wait yet another day was almost unbearable. After all this time, Win didn't want to be parted from her daughter a minute longer. The bus ride seemed interminable and she was so nervous the first thing she had to do when she got to Horsham bus station was find a toilet.

Sheila waited outside the Ladies while her grandmother spent a penny. 'The next bus isn't for another half an hour,' she said.

Win couldn't wait that long. She hailed a taxi.

The house at the end of the driveway was a pleasant surprise. While her grandmother paid the taxi driver, Sheila ran up the steps to ring the bell. The same woman in a green dress opened the door and when Win said who she was, she stood back to let her in. Ten minutes later, the little fat matron was taking both of them to see Daisy.

Win was struck dumb when she walked into Daisy's room. Daisy was sitting in a chair by the window having a bit of a doze. She was wearing a cook's uniform, the apron of which badly needed to be changed. Her untidy hair stuck out either side of her hat and she had kicked her shoes off.

'Daisy loves working in the kitchen,' said Matron quietly by way of an explanation, 'but she does get rather tired.'

She walked across the room and shook her arm gently. Daisy woke with a jolt and, to Win's horror, she cried out, 'I'm sorry, I'm sorry,' as she cowed away from Matron and protected her head with her arm.

'It's all right, Daisy,' Matron said gently. 'You're safe now.'

'What have you done to her?' Win said crossly.

Remembering what Matron had said when she and Ronnie came the first time, Sheila held Win's arm. 'It's all right, Gran.'

'Don't worry, Mrs Peters,' said Matron, positioning herself in front of Daisy. 'As I explained to your grand-daughters, Daisy was ill-treated in the last home, but in this home we don't hit our patients, do we, Daisy?'

'She seems scared to me,' Win challenged.

A small voice came from behind Matron's back. 'Mum? Mummy?'

Matron stepped aside and Daisy and Win stared at each other for the first time in thirty-two years. Tears sprang to Win's eyes. 'Oh, Daisy, Daisy my love.'

Daisy looked from her mother to a place somewhere over her shoulder. 'Is Dad with you?' Daisy's voice was cold.

'No, darling,' said Win, moving closer. 'Dad's dead. Don't you remember? When Ronnie and Sheila came they told you.'

'Are you sure?' said Daisy.

'Yes, darling. I'm sure.' She was surprised that Daisy seemed so confused by her father's death. 'Dad had a stroke three years ago. He was paralysed. I looked after him and then he died earlier this year.'

Daisy stood up, but she said nothing.

'He didn't suffer,' said Win, trying to be comforting.

Daisy fixed her eyes on her mother. 'He told me I would never see you again.'

As Win fought to control her emotions, she lifted her arms, and with a shaky smile, said brightly, 'Well, he got that one wrong, love, cos here I am.'

A second later, they fell into each other's arms and sobbed.

CHAPTER 24

The boys had come to Field Place several times since finding the tunnels. Despite Hethy's edict that they had to keep their find a secret, it had become a mecca most Saturdays. To avoid getting lost again, they had chalk-marked the original tunnel and the rest were identified by small piles of stones or a blob or two of green paint. Drew's mum was painting the back door at home so when she'd finished he'd pinched the brush and put a few drops of paint in a jam jar.

It was always great fun. One time, Steven Kennard found a bird cage. The seed was still in it but, apart from a bright yellow feather, there was no sign of a bird. The droppings on the bottom of the cage looked very hard.

'They must have kept a canary down here,' he said. 'That's what they do in coal mines.' Drew seemed confused.

'In case of poison gas,' Hethy said. 'If the bird drops dead, you have to get out quick.'

'Oh no!' cried Steven, grasping his own throat and staggering around the room. 'The bird just died!' And several other boys collapsed on the floor, moaning in pain.

Most of the large areas were denuded of furniture apart from the odd broken chair or an empty box or something with wires sticking out of it. They made 'guns' out of anything they could carry and had the best war games.

It was just after Christmas when it all ground to a halt. There were eight boys in the tunnels at the time when they heard a loud shout at the entrance. 'You lot. Out of there.'

Everybody froze.

'This is the police,' the voice bellowed. 'Get out now. Come on, come on.'

Ian groaned.

'This is all your fault,' Hethy hissed at Drew.

'What did I do?' Drew cried.

'If you hadn't told everybody . . .'

'I didn't, I didn't. I only told Ginger and Patrick.'

'Exactly,' said Hethy.

'We never said nothing,' said Patrick.

'If you lot aren't out of that tunnel in two minutes,' the voice insisted, 'I'm sending the dogs in.'

Reluctantly, and with heavy hearts, the boys headed back to the surface.

'Is that all of you?' the lone policeman said as the last boy clambered out onto the grass. Hethy nodded.

'Well, you can't play in there,' the copper said. 'It's out of bounds.'

'We weren't doing any harm,' Alan protested mildly.

'That's as maybe,' said the copper, 'but this is still RAF property. You can't go swanning in there without permission.'

The boys picked up their bikes from the pile they'd left outside.

'It's all very hush-hush,' the copper said, softening his tone. 'And they're coming to brick it up soon. In fact, you're lucky I wasn't a workman.'

Everybody shuffled away.

'And don't let me catch you riding two on a bike either,' said the copper in a more strident voice. 'It's against the law.'

Dragging their feet and silent, the boys made their way back to the road. A minute or two later, Hethy glanced back. The copper had gone.

On New Year's Eve, the Assembly Rooms in Worthing was packed. The organizers had lined the sides of the room with small tables with four or six chairs around each one. Matthew pushed Sheila in front of him, keen to be as close to the top table as possible.

'I need to be visible,' he said. 'If the chief sees me and gets to like me, he'll remember me when it comes to promotions and stuff.'

The dignitaries, men above the rank of superintendent right up to the deputy chief constable, sat close to the stage. Their wives and partners were resplendent in their ballgowns and jewellery. Sheila and Matthew searched for a space nearby, but sadly the tables were full and they were forced to move further away.

'If you hadn't spent so much time powdering your nose,' Matthew grumbled, 'we wouldn't have missed the earlier bus.'

Sheila apologized, but he was unforgiving. It wasn't a good start to the evening. His nose was out of joint as soon as he saw her dress.

'Gosh, it's a bit bright, isn't it?' he'd gasped as she did a twirl in front of him.

'I think the colour suits her,' said Granny.

Matthew pulled a face. 'I thought you said the woman who made it was an expert dressmaker. It looks far too tight.'

'Oh, Matthew!' cried Sheila.

'Can't you wear something plainer?'

'No. I don't have anything else, remember?' said Sheila as she struggled to bite back the tears.

When they got inside, Sheila had never seen so many policemen in one place. They had obviously come from miles around. They were all in uniform, but the women wore a variety of dresses. Some were knee-length, others full-length. Matthew and Sheila were a lot further back in the hall than he wanted to be, but they were joined by two of Matthew's fellow PCs and their girlfriends. While PC Ivan Warwick and PC Mike Finchley went with Matthew to the bar, the girls introduced themselves. Betty, a pretty blonde girl with an hour-glass figure, a hairdresser, was engaged to Mike.

'We're childhood sweethearts,' she said, her grey eyes glistening with excitement, 'and we're getting married at Easter.' She was wearing a very busy multicoloured

276

floral dress with a dropped waist. She had picked out the blue in the material and matched her gloves, a fabric brooch and blue clip earrings.

Laura was Ivan's long-term girlfriend, down from Yorkshire. When Sheila saw her muscular arms and wide hands, she wasn't surprised to hear that Laura worked on a farm. She was wearing a knee-length dress with a gathered bustline and a bow at the neck made in a soft crêpe material with three-quarter-length sleeves. The only jewellery Laura had was a chunky gold bracelet. They both seemed friendly and Sheila warmed to them.

'I love your dress,' Betty said. 'You look fantastic. 'Did you make it yourself?'

'It's a Butterick pattern,' said Sheila, feeling better than she had done all evening. She told them about Pen Albright.

'She should go into business,' said Laura. 'I'd buy a dress off her any day. She's a very good seamstress.'

Sheila laughed. 'I'll tell her that.'

Betty was fingering the material. 'How many has she made for you?'

'Just this one,' said Sheila. 'And I'm lucky to have it.' She explained about the fire.

'How awful!' cried Betty. 'You mean you lost absolutely everything?'

Sheila nodded and Betty gasped.

'You're so brave,' said Laura. 'I don't think I could come to a dance like this if I'd lost absolutely everything I owned.'

Sheila shrugged. 'I can't let the past dictate my future,' she said. The words sounded sagacious and there was a part of her that wanted to believe what she was saying. One thing she knew for sure: she needed to hang on to the idea that things would get better in the future. She'd done her crying and if she kept harking back to the past, it would destroy her.

Getting the famous Eric Winstone band to play for them was a bit of a coup for the organizers and part way through the evening Sheila was delighted to see the darling of Worthing, Alma Cogan. Alma, who had won first prize and five pounds in the Sussex Queen of Song Contest when she was only eleven, was now fourteen and making quite a name for herself on stage. Everyone was talking about her and they said she would go far. It was even rumoured that she'd been recommended for a place in a variety show in nearby Brighton by none other than Vera Lynn herself. As she sang the lovely ballad 'Amado Mío' on the tiered stage, the sprung dance floor was already heaving with dancers. A dark-haired couple in rather less glamorous clothes sat fairly near the front. The chief constable went to speak to them and Sheila guessed they must be Alma's parents, here to chaperone her. The room itself was lit by a glitterball rotating from the ceiling in the middle of the room and hundreds of balloons in a net hung over the dance floor waiting for the moment when they would be let down at midnight.

A bright light suddenly lit up their table. A man with a huge camera with a flash had just taken a picture of them. He grinned and handed Laura a card. '*Worthing Herald*,' he said. 'Any picture is available to buy from the office.' He moved on to the next table.

The three girls stood up and went to the buffet table where they collected a plate of the sort of food they hadn't enjoyed in a long time. They were tucking in when the men eventually came back with their beers.

Matthew handed Sheila a glass of orange. 'It's punch,' he whispered confidentially. 'I didn't think you'd want anything alcoholic.'

Sheila envied Betty her sherry and Laura her milk stout, but she made no comment.

After a while, Ivan and Mike took the girls onto the dance floor, but Matthew was still sulking about the position of their table and he seemed to be drinking quite a lot.

'Come on, Matthew,' she cajoled as she stood to her feet. 'I want to dance.'

'I prefer to sit and watch the drinks,' he said.

Sheila laughed. 'You can't possibly think they'd get nicked at a policeman's ball?'

'I'm not one for dancing,' he said in a bored tone.

Disappointed, Sheila sat back down. This was a side to Matthew she hadn't really seen before and she didn't like it.

The girls and their boyfriends went back onto the dance floor several times. Early in the evening, Alma left the stage to rapturous applause and was replaced by a male singer, but that didn't stop the music being very enjoyable: 'A Sentimental Journey' for a waltz, 'Chattanooga Choo' for a more upbeat dance and 'Chickery Chick', a rather amusing tongue-twister everybody tried to keep up with.

Eventually, when the singer struck up 'I've Heard that Song Before', Matthew got up and excused himself to go to the toilet.

Tears pricked her eyes as Sheila watched her new-found friends enjoying themselves. All at once, Betty left Mike and crossed the dance floor. At first Sheila thought they may have had a tiff, but then she saw Betty talking to the photographer. While her friend went back to her dance partner, the photographer came over to Sheila's table.

'Is that right?' he asked. 'Your place burned down?'

Sheila's mouth went dry, but she nodded.

'I'm sorry to hear about that, miss,' he said. 'Could you stand up, please?'

Puzzled, Sheila did as he asked and he took several pictures. 'Lovely gown,' he remarked. 'Was that in the fire?'

'It was at a friend's house,' she said. She gave a lame chuckle. 'It's the only thing I have left.'

Matthew came back. 'What's going on here?' he demanded.

'*Worthing Herald*,' the photographer repeated as he reached into his pocket for another card.

'Bugger off,' said Matthew churlishly as he sat back down.

The photographer's flash went off again. Matthew

rose to his feet. 'I told you to clear off,' he shouted angrily.

'Matthew,' said Sheila. 'It's all right. I don't mind.'

All around heads turned and the flash went off again.

'Well, I bloody do,' said Matthew as he made a dive towards the photographer. There was a sound of breaking glass as several drinks glasses rolled noisily onto the floor and one of the chairs fell backward.

It didn't take long for the doormen to arrive, and much to Sheila's embarrassment, she and Matthew were escorted off the premises.

Leslie smoothed down his jacket and glanced at his reflection in the mirror. Even if he did say so himself, he looked a proper gent. His suit had cost him the best part of a fortnight's wages, but it had been worth every penny. Maybe there was something in this being honest m'larkey after all.

Of course, he'd still have to keep his wits about him. He didn't know the first thing about cars, but he was expected to keep the Roller purring. Mrs Harrison-Vane was constantly making eyes at him and a couple of times she'd even put her hand over his privates. He didn't fancy her one bit, but if he was going to make a fresh start, he'd have to keep the old duck sweet.

'Once she's got you into her bed,' Effie the maid told him, 'I'll give you two months, three tops.'

They were sitting together in Mrs Harrison-Vane's sumptuous kitchen after sharing their evening meal. It might be New Year's Eve but there was little celebration in this house. The rest of the world was partying, but tonight of all nights, Mrs Harrison-Vane preferred the quiet life. Her only daughter had died of polio on New Year's Eve in 1932.

She had given Leslie the night off, but after ferrying her everywhere in the run-up to Christmas and the New Year, he'd surprised himself by jumping at the chance for a quiet supper with the maid. Their employer was in the sitting room with an old friend and was not to be disturbed.

'Has she done this sort of thing before then?' Leslie asked. 'Sleeping with the chauffeur?'

'She does it all the time,' said Effie.

Leslie liked Effie. She was nothing to look at but she had an open face and she was very understanding. When he'd first arrived, he'd spun her his usual story about being unloved as a child, kicked out of home at fifteen and making his own way ever since. She'd listened, but she was no fool. He soon became aware she was taking everything he said with a pinch of salt.

'The last bloke lasted two weeks,' Effie said, standing up to put the dirty dishes into the sink. 'Apparently he was no good in bed. His dick was too small.'

Leslie almost choked on his beer.

'But she likes you a lot,' Effie went on innocently.

It was a bit disconcerting to hear that his employer was discussing the chauffeur's sexual prowess with her maid, but it was also very useful.

'Then I'd better make the most of it while I can,' he said, reaching for the tea towel to help with the drying-up.

'Rich people always want chauffeurs,' said Effie. 'You'll soon get another position.'

'I don't want to be a chauffeur all my life,' said Leslie. 'I like cars, but only to drive.'

They both laughed at his little joke.

'So what will you do next?'

Leslie shrugged his shoulders. 'Haven't a clue, but one thing is for sure. I don't want to go back to the way things were. I've mixed with some pretty bad people in the past.'

When she turned to him, her eyes were full of concern and something inside Leslie's chest stirred. He looked away quickly. Don't be a damn fool, he told himself. And don't do what you usually do: ruin her life, then move on. She may be a Plain Jane but she's a sweet kid. He carried on with the drying-up until the draining board was clear.

'What about you, Eff?' he said as he sat back down and lit a Capstan.

'What about me?' She was busy stacking the crockery away.

'What are you going to do with your life? Have you got some chap hiding in the wings?'

Effie laughed. 'Good Lord, no,' she said. 'Who'd have me? My brother reckons I've got a face like the back of a bus and a figure like a broom handle.'

Leslie felt strangely disturbed by her remark. 'You

shouldn't put yourself down like that, Eff,' he said. 'Looks aren't everything.'

Placing another bottle of beer in front of him, she pulled a face. 'And a pretty-looking fella like you expects me to believe that?' she said teasingly.

In the distance, they heard the grandfather clock in the hallway chime twelve. Leslie stood to his feet. 'Happy New Year, Eff,' he said, raising his beer glass. 'I hope 1947 brings you joy and happiness.'

She smiled. 'And a Happy New Year to you, Mr Jackson.'

'Leslie,' he corrected as he moved closer to give her a peck on the cheek. 'After such a lovely evening, we're mates now, aren't we?'

And he felt a little glow of pleasure as he saw her face colour.

CHAPTER 25

Sheila woke with a bad headache. It couldn't be a hangover. She'd been forced to stick with orange juice all evening. She moved her foot and winced. She remembered now. When Matthew had been unceremoniously removed from the Assembly Rooms, she'd grabbed her coat and followed him. Unfortunately, she'd accidentally tripped down the circular steps outside. Under the sheets, her ankle felt swollen and tight. A tear sprang to her eye.

Matthew had been furious and he'd blamed her.

'If you hadn't been posing for that photographer like some cheap French tart,' he'd bellowed, 'I wouldn't have lost my temper. I hope you realize you've ruined my whole life.'

'Oh, don't be so melodramatic,' she'd said crossly as she'd sat on the bottom step and rubbed her ankle.

'You don't seem to understand,' Matthew had cried. 'The chief constable was watching us the whole time!' He put his hands to his head and pressed his hair. 'Oh God, I'll be called up before the super tomorrow. What am I going to do?'

'I'm sorry,' she'd said miserably. She didn't know what she was sorry about but it seemed to placate him a bit. Her ankle hurt and she needed help. He'd walked her home but they'd hardly spoken. She kept thinking of what it would be like when all those balloons came down at midnight and the fun everybody would have. Her dress was thin and she was perishing cold even though she had her big coat on. The pavements glistened with frost. When they'd reached the gate, it was past midnight. She'd turned to wish him a Happy New Year and to give him a kiss, but he was already walking away.

She watched him go with mixed feelings. A part of her was sorry he'd had a terrible evening but another part of her was angry with him. The dance hadn't exactly been a success for her either. She wished she'd stayed on and left him to it. She might have had some dances with other men once she was disentangled from a sulky boyfriend. She'd hung on to the relationship, afraid of being on her own for the rest of her life, but was it worth it? She tried to imagine her life in ten or twenty years' time and suddenly the prospect of being with Matthew didn't seem nearly as attractive. With a heavy heart she put her key into the lock and opened the front door.

Granny had waited up, but she was surprised to see her back so soon. Sheila had told her the sorry tale while the two of them bathed her foot in cold water, then Granny dabbed it with witch hazel to bring the bruise out and keep the swelling down.

'I hope Matthew will be all right,' Sheila remarked.

'Well, if he isn't,' Granny said sharply, 'he's only got himself to blame.'

Sheila hadn't said any more. She didn't want to hear Granny say, 'I told you so'. Perhaps she'd been too hasty. Maybe he was just upset. He'd turn up tomorrow morning with flowers and say sorry.

Afterwards, when Granny had put a bandage round her ankle, and they were sitting huddled by the fire, warming their hands around a mug of hot cocoa, the clock on the mantelpiece struck one.

'Happy New Year,' said Granny.

Sheila looked up and laughed. 'It's got off to a flying start, I must say.'

Granny smiled. 'We'd better get to bed. I'm off to Horsham again tomorrow . . . er, today.'

'When do you think Aunt Daisy will come home?' Sheila asked as she hobbled towards her bedroom.

'Matron says she can come for a weekend in the middle of January and we'll take it from there,' Granny said. 'Much as it frustrates me to have it all drawn out, I'm glad she's thinking about what's best for Daisy.'

Sheila lay in bed for a while wondering what she should do about Matthew, but then she found herself thinking about the whole family. Her lovely mum and dad dead and gone; Ronnie, who hadn't even bothered to wish Granny and her a Happy Christmas, let alone a Happy New Year, all on her own just down the road; the garage in ruins and Leslie God knows where.

1946 hadn't been a good year for any of them. She hoped her cousin wasn't in prison again. Then, remembering his terrible bruises, she hoped he hadn't gone back to whoever had done that to him. She wondered about Aunt Daisy too. When she finally came to live with Granny, would she explain why she'd run off all those years ago? That thought gave Sheila another reason to feel unsettled. There were only two bedrooms in the flat. Sharing a room with her cousin Ronnie was one thing; sharing a room with Aunt Daisy was something else. Aunt Daisy was a complete stranger. She was the same age as her mother. She'd probably want the lights out at nine o'clock or something daft. She wouldn't approve of men friends hanging around. The more Sheila thought about it, the more convinced she was that she'd have to find somewhere else to live. Her thoughts wandered back to the garage. She hadn't been back since the day after the fire. Was it possible to clean up the rooms upstairs? Gerhard and Mr Webster's men had tidied up the work area, but as far as Sheila knew, no one had been upstairs. Her new job started on January 6th. That meant she'd got five whole days to sort herself out. If she found some digs, she'd have to pay rent. If she went back to the Becket, she could live there for nothing and save enough money to get herself back on her feet. All at once, she was filled with optimism. Okay, her ankle was a bit sore, but if she was careful, she could make a start on getting the place back to normal today. Maybe her problems weren't so insurmountable after all. Maybe she could go home. She smiled to herself. Yes, that's what she'd do. Clean up and go back home.

For some, the New Year didn't begin well. The newspapers were full of the train crash in Essex where the Peterborough express had collided with a stationary train at Gidea station. The accident happened in thick fog and was so devastating that the rear carriage was flung over the roof of the platform, killing five people and injuring forty-three others. The weather was getting worse all over the country and Worthing was no exception.

Sheila wrapped herself up warmly to go to the garage. Her ankle had been so sore she'd been forced to waste two of her precious days waiting for the swelling to go down. She had hoped that Matthew would turn up and they'd have a wonderful reunion, but it hadn't happened. She was hurt and upset and yet she felt relieved as well. He'd never treated her right, had he? Loading cleaning stuff into the basket of her bicycle, she set off just after it got light, around eight in the morning. It was bitter cold and a sea fog was rolling inland.

The garage was deserted when she arrived, but apart from the obvious damage, it looked a lot better than she remembered. The men had swept out the black sooty water and the pile of rubbish which had been stacked alongside the charred building was gone. Inside, only the pungent smell remained. A freezing draught of cold air came in through the smashed window and she knew if she was going to clean up in here, she would have to board it up. Down the bottom of the garden, the shed containing the old 1934 Morris 8 van was untouched. Sheila remembered stacking some pieces of timber against the wall. Before long, she had selected a few bits and was hammering the boards across the open gap. Outside, above the window frame, she found a piece of wool dangling from a nail. It looked familiar, but she couldn't quite place it. She needed to remove the nail so that the board completely filled the gap. Absent-mindedly, she slipped the wool into her pocket as she pulled the nail out with some pliers and hammered the board in place. Of course, it made the inside of the garage much darker, but she was grateful not to have all that cold air whistling through the building.

Her first job was upstairs. The laundry boxes were still intact although they did need a bit of a wipe to get rid of the soot. She piled their bedding into one box and their smelly smoky clothes into the other. The bill would be huge, but it would save both of them from having to cope with a major wash in this awful weather. Having done that, Sheila decided she would go in search of some hot water. There was no water, heating or electricity on the premises and she needed to tackle the walls and furniture. Everywhere was covered in a thick layer of grime, the walls were streaked and, of course, there was that awful smell.

Pen Albright was more than happy to boil up a kettle or two and she even offered to come and help for a while. 'I've got to go down town to get something for my hubby's tea,' she said, 'but I can give you an hour or two.' Sheila was more than grateful and they were soon carrying two buckets of hot water and a flask of tea to the garage.

As they turned the corner, they heard men's voices. For a second, Sheila's heart leapt. Matthew? But then she realized it was the voice of a stranger. She glanced anxiously at Pen.

'Who's there?'

A policeman peered out from the garage doorway. 'Who are you?'

'Sheila Hodges,' said Sheila, startled. 'I live here. Why are you here?'

Another man came to join him. 'My name is Inspector Sandgate,' he said. 'We're investigating a possible arson attack.'

'Arson!' cried Sheila. 'You can't be serious. The insurance man came and he never said anything about arson.'

'That's as maybe,' said the inspector, 'but when someone makes a complaint, we are duty bound to follow it up.'

'I don't understand,' said Sheila. 'Who made a complaint?'

'I cannot tell you that,' said the inspector. 'Where were you the night of the fire?'

'My cousin and I were with my grandmother,' said Sheila. Her mind was in a whirl. Who had complained and why? 'We arrived shortly after the fire brigade closed Highdown Road.'

'They seemed to think it was a fault in the fuse box,' said Pen.

'And you are?'

'Peninnah Albright; a friend.'

The inspector looked thoughtful. The uniformed officer who had gone round the back as the inspector questioned them, returned and shook his head. 'Somebody's boarded up the window.'

'That was me,' said Sheila. 'We're planning to do some cleaning and there was such an awful draught . . .'

'Do you know a man called Gerhard Müller?' the inspector interrupted.

'Yes,' said Sheila. 'He's a POW.'

'How well do you know him?'

'I know him to be a hard-working man who regrets that his country believed in Adolf Hitler,' she began. 'He's talented and he sometimes comes here to give us a hand.'

The inspector gave her a knowing look. 'Friendly, is he?'

Sheila frowned. Where was this line of questioning going? What was he insinuating? 'He's polite, if that's what you mean,' she said defensively. 'He behaves in a perfectly correct manner and he's a good worker.'

'Who runs this garage?'

'I do.'

The inspector raised an eyebrow. 'But you're a woman.'

Sheila looked down at her own body. 'You know, I believe I am.'

'No need for cheek, miss,' he retorted stiffly. 'Did somebody buy the garage for you?'

'My grandmother owns it,' said Sheila. 'I just run it; well, my cousin and I run it.'

'And he is?'

'She is Ronnie, Veronica Jackson.'

'What about your brother, Leslie?'

'I don't have a brother,' said Sheila. Now she was being obstreperous.

'Oh,' said the inspector, glancing down at his notebook.

'Leslie is my cousin,' said Sheila. 'He's Ronnie's brother and he doesn't live around here any more.'

'I am reliably informed that he didn't like the fact that you got the garage and he didn't.'

Sheila frowned. Who had told him all this? 'That's all water under the bridge,' she said. 'When he was ill, he stayed with my grandmother, but he's recovered and moved on.'

'We may need to speak to him.'

'When you find him,' said Sheila, 'ask him for his address, will you?'

'He's a known associate of villains,' said the inspector.

Sheila crossed her fingers behind her back. 'Not any more,' she said. 'He's learned his lesson and he's a reformed character.'

The inspector gave her a long, hard look. 'Wait here,' he said, going back inside.

When he'd gone, Pen sighed. 'I might have to go back home for another kettle of hot water at this rate,' she grumbled. 'This water will be stone cold soon.'

'Sorry, Pen,' said Sheila. 'I've no idea where he's

getting all this stuff from.' She thrust her cold hands deep into her pockets and the fingers of her right hand touched something soft. She pulled it out and saw the piece of wool she'd taken from the nail. All at once she remembered. It was exactly the same colour as Gerhard's hat. But how on earth had it got there? As far as she could remember, the hat had ended up in the lost-property box. She gave an involuntary shiver. No, it hadn't. Matthew had taken it to give to Gerhard. How odd. Well, Gerhard couldn't have put the wool there. He was under lock and key for Christmas. He'd told her as much at the concert. Her mouth went dry. Did that mean Gerhard had been in the garage before then? No, that was silly. Why would someone take his hat off to climb into a window? If it had snagged on something, surely that would be at the top of the frame, not on the ledge. This could mean only one thing. Someone had planted it. Someone who wanted to get Gerhard into trouble. And that could only be Matthew.

The two policemen came out of the garage. 'I think we'd better call in a specialist team,' said the inspector, 'so I'd rather you didn't do anything in there for the time being. We have to seal it as a scene of crime.'

Pen put her bucket down. 'Oh, for goodness' sake,' she said crossly.

Sheila was numb with shock. 'All right,' she said with as much dignity as she could muster. 'You have to be thorough. I quite understand.'

The inspector smiled. 'I'm glad you're taking it so well.'

'But I don't understand,' Sheila began again. 'If the fire brigade and the insurance people are happy, why do you need to carry out another investigation?'

'We may well have left it there if it weren't for the tin tacks,' said the inspector.

'I must say, I was puzzled by that,' said Sheila. She chewed her bottom lip.

He began to walk away. 'Inspector, can you tell me something?' she called after him. 'The person who raised this complaint, would it happen to be PC Keller?'

'I'm afraid I cannot say, miss,' he called over his shoulder.

'I only mention it because Matthew and I have been courting,' she said, then taking a deep breath added, 'He has absolutely no reason to be, but he can be very jealous.'

The inspector stopped walking and stared at the ground in front of him.

'But, of course, you must do your job,' said Sheila. 'I can only hope it doesn't turn out to be a silly mistake and a waste of police time. You see, Gerhard gave me a Christmas present and Matthew didn't like it.'

The inspector resumed his walk, but when he reached the forecourt he turned his head. 'Tell you what. You do what you have to, but keep well away from that fuse box. I'll get someone from the electricity board to come and look at it.'

'They already have,' said Sheila. 'You'll find his report with the insurance company.'

The inspector didn't look back again.

CHAPTER 26

The mourners were few in number. Over the years, Benny Steadman had lost touch with his friends and contemporaries, so only a few diehard relatives and acquaintances came to his funeral. It was held in St Andrew's, the eleventh-century church in Tarring, famed for its beautiful mosaics. The mourners only managed to fill perhaps three of the pews although, being spread out, it seemed as if quite a few had turned up. The British Legion, a charity which provided support to disabled ex-servicemen and their families, formed a guard of honour, but not everybody accompanied him to his grave. They buried him in the cemetery in Durrington, in a pretty spot halfway up the hill and next to a member of the Home Guard who had died when Hayes Road was bombed in November 1941. Benny would have liked that – to lie in Worthing soil, next to a fellow soldier who, like him, had in Churchill's words, 'defended the survival of Christian civilization . . . British life and the long continuity of our institutions . . .'

By the time the group of mourners, including the

members of the British Legion, arrived at the Thomas A Becket hotel, it was even smaller. Mrs Fford had given them the back room. A cheerful fire blazed in the hearth and there was a buffet on the table in the far corner. Benny's sister and her husband moved around thanking everyone for coming and listening to their memories. Benny's sister was the only one who could recall the days before his injury when he took part in bicycle races to East Preston or ran all the way up Salvington Hill with the Worthing Harriers. The companions who had joined up with him in 1915 were all dead and gone.

As soon as it was practicable, Ronnie asked to speak to Mrs Griffith, Benny's sister. 'I've only recently been told of what your brother did on the night he died,' she began, 'and I wanted to express my thanks and gratitude towards him.'

Mrs Griffith smiled. 'He really admired you girls,' she said. '"Them's got pluck," he used to say. He kept a weather eye on you both from the word go.'

Ronnie's face flushed with embarrassment as she recalled the resentment she'd felt towards Benny when she'd first arrived at the garage and the times she'd stuck out her tongue at him. Back then, she'd regarded him as little more than a lecherous old man with nothing better to do than leer at them from the window. Now, of course, it was a different story. 'I only wish we could have got to know him,' she said. 'People should know what men like Benny did for this country. I promise I'll never forget him.'

'Thank you,' said Mrs Griffith, and the two women shook hands.

As Mrs Griffith turned to go, she hesitated for a second. 'Benny always kept a diary,' she said. 'He started it when he came to live with us in 1921. Perhaps you might like to read it.'

Ronnie felt a stab of panic. She didn't want to disappoint or offend her, but when would she have time to read a diary spanning twenty-five years? 'Um . . .' she began feebly.

'My brother was a keen observer of people,' Mrs Griffith went on. 'I'm sure you'll be in it somewhere.'

Ronnie smiled. 'Then I'd be happy to read it when I've got time.'

Mrs Griffith smiled back. 'I'll pop it over in a day or two.'

Ronnie watched her go. Oh Lord, what had she done?

'You seen the *Herald*?'

Mrs Fford had found Ronnie in the guests' sitting room. Having checked there was enough wood in the log basket, she was plumping up the cushions and tidying the newspapers. The hotel had settled back to normality after Christmas and the New Year. The people who had turned up for the season, either for the company or to be pampered, had gone back home. January and February were always slack, with only a few regulars and a lot of empty rooms.

Normally Mrs Fford laid off the extra staff after

298

the first week in January, but Ronnie was lucky. Mrs Fford liked her and, more than that, Ronnie was a hard worker who was always willing to chip in anywhere she was needed and didn't have to be asked. Having joined the staff as a receptionist, Ronnie had proved herself capable of office work, entertaining the guests and checking that everything was running smoothly elsewhere in the hotel.

Mrs Fford flapped the newspaper in front of her. 'Isn't that your sister?'

Ronnie glanced at the headline and gasped. Under the heavy print, 'Beauty and the Beast', she saw two pictures. One was of Sheila in a beautiful gown and beneath it was a picture of Matthew being ejected from the Assembly Rooms with a very distressed-looking Sheila in the background. 'She's my cousin,' Ronnie corrected as she took the paper from her employer and sat down to read it.

At the Police Ball, local beauty Miss Sheila Hodges poses for the camera despite having lost all her possessions and her home in a devastating fire just before Christmas. 'She's an amazing girl,' said a friend. 'So determined to bounce back and enjoy herself.' We agree and admire her Dunkirk spirit, although apparently others don't. PC Keller took exception to our photographer taking pictures and, having become aggressive, was asked to leave. The *Herald* thinks that the police would make better use of their time fighting crime rather than preventing the people of Worthing from seeing a picture of such a brave and pretty young woman. We are glad to publish her photograph and we are sure our readers will agree. Miss Hodges, wearing an attractive royal-blue gown made by a friend, has all the right curves in all the right places.

'She certainly does look lovely,' Mrs Fford remarked. Ronnie could feel her chest getting tighter and turned away in case her employer saw the tears threatening to fall. What had she done? At the time she'd told herself it was better to walk away rather than face yet another setback. Starting all over again for the third time was more than she could bear, but Sheila had had more than her fair share of troubles too. Ronnie felt herself shudder. She'd been an absolute pig, hadn't she? She looked at the picture of her cousin again. That beautiful royal-blue dress was probably the only decent thing Sheila had left. She glanced at the picture underneath of Matthew sprawled across the steps with two stewards towering over him. She didn't like the man much but it couldn't have been pleasant being ejected like that. What an affront to his dignity. She wondered vaguely what he'd said. She looked at Sheila standing in the background. The expression on her face was one of absolute horror. Ronnie longed to give her a hug and tell her she was sorry. How could she have left her cousin to clear up the mess all on her own?

'Are you all right?' said Mrs Fford, suddenly concerned.

Ronnie nodded dully. 'Can I take an hour off this afternoon?'

'My dear girl,' said Mrs Fford, 'you haven't taken any time off since you got here. Of course you can. Go now if you like.'

'Is anyone there? Coo-ee.'

The sound of the woman's voice brought Sheila to the top of the stairs. Her voice was familiar but Sheila couldn't quite place her. 'Yes?'

'Is Ronnie here?' The woman, a very glamorous-looking peroxide blonde with bright-red lipstick, seemed agitated.

'No,' said Sheila. 'Can I help you?'

The woman held a copy of the *Worthing Herald* in her hand. 'When I saw the paper,' she said, 'it made me think of Ronnie again.'

Now Sheila recognized her. She was the woman who had known Ronnie in Singapore before the Japs invaded; Abigail or Alice something. She was the girl who had left Ronnie's employer to her fate when she'd stolen her plane ticket. Sheila's eyes narrowed. 'What do you want?' Thank God Ronnie wasn't here. The last time she'd come to the garage Ronnie had had nightmares for weeks.

The woman looked at the chaos all around. 'God, this is awful; much worse than I thought. You poor things.'

'I think you'd better go,' Sheila said coldly. 'I know what you did and I don't know how you can live with yourself.'

'She told you?'

Sheila looked away in disgust.

'I didn't mean to do it,' she whimpered. 'Everyone was in such a mad rush and when they asked me my name, someone shoved the papers in my hand.'

'But you didn't see fit to point out the mistake,' Sheila said coldly.

'I thought she'd be safe enough with the Major.'

Sheila didn't answer.

'Tell Ronnie I'm sorry,' said the woman. 'Tell her I'll make it up to her. I know how I can put it right.'

Mrs Harrison-Vane was a lot like Potiphar's wife. She did her level best to get Leslie into bed with her, but thus far he had resisted her. Leslie considered himself a red-blooded man, but he was also picky and strong-willed. He'd had his share of flings and he'd enjoyed them, but to be aroused he had to fancy what was on offer. Putting it quite simply, Mrs Harrison-Vane didn't cut the mustard. He was willing to flirt with her, but as soon as she got what he would call 'fruity', something inside of him died and he backed off. After keeping her at arm's length since he'd come here, Leslie knew that he had a problem. She was becoming bored with games and it wouldn't be long before she found someone better-looking or a bit more randy and gave him the sack.

For the first time in his life, the thought of moving on made Leslie feel unsettled. To begin with, he wasn't sure why, but now he knew it was because of Effie.

He'd always liked her, but ever since New Year his feelings had become much deeper. She looked after him so well. She knew the things he liked and she seemed to enjoy pleasing him. She'd always have a doorstep slice of bread ready for his toast for his breakfast. She made sure he had the jelly at the bottom of the dripping to spread thickly over it. She'd remind him and turn on the radio for the comedy programme called *Much-Binding-in-the-Marsh* that he liked so much. She'd warm his driving gloves over the fireguard when Mrs Harrison-Vane wanted him to go out on a cold night. His favourite paper was always on the arm of the chair when he came back in and she made a fruit cake like no other he'd ever tasted. They enjoyed a laugh together. She thought his jokes were really funny. She made him feel king of the wharf and cock of the hen house, but it was more than that. He found he was thinking about her all the time. Sometimes he only had to look at her and he'd feel his heart beating faster. If he accidentally touched her hand or bumped into her, he'd get a sizzling sensation all over his body. When she smiled at him, he glowed inside. His first thought in the morning was Effie and she was his last thought at night.

She had a wonderful smile and she looked grand in her Sunday best when she tripped off to the church across the green. He even liked her when she was dressed in her old brown dressing gown when she waited up for Mrs Harrison-Vane to get back from the theatre. The first time he saw her lovely brown hair all loose and hanging down her back instead of stuffed inside her maid's cap, his heart skipped a beat. It shone like a jewel and he was almost overwhelmed with a desire to touch it.

'Come to the pictures with me, Eff?' he'd asked.

'Bless your life,' she'd said, giving him a playful shove on his arm. 'What on earth would my brother say if I turned up at the Odeon with a good-looking boy like you?'

'Who cares what he thinks? I'd like to take you,' he insisted.

'I wouldn't mind seeing that new Myrna Loy film, *The Best Years of Our Lives*,' she said. 'They say it's very good.'

He took her, but he couldn't remember a lot about the film. Sitting right next to her, breathing in her eau de cologne and feeling the warmth of her arm against his, sent him into waves of ecstasy. He began to think about settling down, but how could he provide for her? He didn't want her to live in rented rooms somewhere, she deserved better than that. But even though he had some beautiful clothes, he had precious few savings. He was tempted to go back to the old ways, but he knew her well enough to know if she ever found out he'd been on the wrong side of the law, that would be that. In fact, everything seemed against him. If Mrs Harrison-Vane gave him the sack, he might never see Effie again. What if the new chauffeur came in and stole her heart? Just the thought of it made him feel physically sick. One minute he was overflowing with happiness and the next he was filled with misery. He kept thinking about Granddad's garage. Surely it must be making a fortune by now? He didn't deserve it, but maybe, just maybe, Ronnie might lend him a bob or two, just to tide him over, and then he'd make a new start. But no, that wasn't the way to go about it either. If he was to win Effie's heart, whatever he put his hand to had to be honest and it had to make money. He put his head between his hands. Was there anyone else in the world who felt as miserable as he felt right now?

CHAPTER 27

Sheila and Pen had finished for the day. The electrics still weren't restored, so it was becoming difficult to see because the only light they had was a Tilly lamp. They were both cold and there was no heating in the garage, but the living quarters were beginning to take shape. It was tedious and hard work, but they had already washed down all the walls and cleaned the furnishings. The mattresses on the beds would have to be thrown out. They still smelled smoky, so nobody would want to sleep on them. The curtains had to be washed, but the laundry boxes had already been collected. There was no telling when they would be back. Apparently the coal shortage meant that the laundry was only working four days a week and the backlog was beginning to mount.

'I might be able to rustle up a pair for you,' said Pen. 'I've still got stuff in the loft left over from when my granny was alive. They won't be up to much, but you're welcome to them.'

'Thanks, Pen,' said Sheila. 'You're a pal.'

They parted having agreed to come back on Saturday

afternoon to make a start on the kitchen. As they reached the door, they heard a footfall outside. Sheila stopped dead and Pen walked into the back of her. Who would be creeping about in this gloom? 'Who's there?' Sheila called out. 'There's nothing left worth pinching, so shove off.'

She put out her hand and armed herself with a wheel lever lying on the bench. Pen looked into her bucket and armed herself with the brush from the dustpan and brush set. Sheila nodded, then snatched the door open. 'Ronnie!' she cried. 'You gave me such a fright.'

Then Sheila saw the tears in her cousin's eyes.

'Oh, Sheila,' Ronnie said hoarsely. 'I'm so sorry. I've been such a cow. Can you ever forgive me?'

'Come here, you daft bat,' said Sheila, dropping the lever back onto the bench, and as Pen slipped away, the two girls embraced each other and wept for a long, long time.

By the end of the second week in January it was obvious that the country was not only in the grip of winter, but also in crisis. The prime minister finally admitted the government was facing what he called a sticky wicket. On top of the army being called in to deliver meat in danger of going rotten in the warehouses because of the haulage strike, and the dockers blacking other imports, the country was heading for a fuel crisis as well. The weather was deteriorating all the time and for days on end the temperatures struggled to reach two degrees Fahrenheit.

Ronnie and Sheila kept their new jobs, but whenever they had a spare minute they worked at the garage getting things back to normal. The inspector had returned to tell them no charges would be made. The tin tacks on the forecourt, he decided, must have been put there by some prankster. 'Probably some schoolboys mucking about,' he said sagely. 'If I'd have caught the little blighters, I'd have tanned their hides.'

Granny kept going to Horsham and each time she came back a little more content. 'Daisy made me a special meat and veg pie today,' she said, putting the little dish onto the table. 'She called it Surprise Pie.'

'Never heard of it,' said Sheila, 'but it looks good.'

'She calls it Surprise Pie,' Granny said with a twinkle in her eye, 'because if you can find a piece of meat on your plate, it'll be a nice surprise.'

Then she and Sheila roared with laughter.

'I'm so glad Daisy hasn't lost her sense of humour,' said Granny, wiping a tear from her eye.

'Any indication as to when she's coming home?' Sheila asked. She was getting ready to go out with Matthew, who had been up in Yorkshire visiting his parents for a few days.

'I can sign the papers sometime next week,' said Granny. 'Maybe the twenty-third.'

'Thursday?' said Sheila.

Her grandmother nodded and Sheila turned away from the mirror over the mantelpiece to give her a hug. 'I'm so pleased for you,' she said. 'The electricity people reckon they'll have us reconnected next week so Ronnie and I can move back in. It'll give you and Daisy some time to get to know each other again.'

'You won't be able to start straight away, surely?'

Sheila went back to taking out her kirby grips and brushing her hair. 'Ronnie reckons it should take us another couple of weeks. The insurance money is already in the bank and Neville has given us first refusal on some tools he's replacing.'

'What about your cooking job?' asked Granny, sitting back down with her knitting.

Sheila gave her an apologetic smile. 'I feel bad about that, but I'm really not much good at it,' she said. 'I've managed to burn the edges of a couple of cakes and yesterday there was a power cut right in the middle of my demonstration.'

'That's hardly your fault,' Granny said.

'Maybe, maybe not,' said Sheila, 'but Mr Castle knows I'm not an experienced cook.'

'Don't be silly, dear,' said Granny. 'How can he possibly know that?'

'I lost my knife a couple of days ago,' Sheila went on as she patted her hair in place. 'Couldn't find it anywhere, but when I turned the sponge out of the tin, there it was, baked into the bottom.'

Granny chuckled.

'And,' Sheila went on, 'I haven't managed to sell one cooker.' The shrill sound of the doorbell cut across their laughter. 'That'll be Matthew,' said Sheila. 'Will I do?'

'You look lovely, dear,' said Granny.

Sheila took a deep breath. She was wearing her yellow dress with the white piping. She'd been thinking long and hard about her relationship with Matthew ever since New Year's Eve. She knew he didn't like this dress – in fact, he'd been positively rude about it – but this was the new Sheila, a Sheila who was going to stand up for herself. She'd made up her mind to tell him this was their last date and to tell him, as nicely as possible, to sling his hook.

'What do you mean, you don't want to go out with me any more?'

Matthew appeared to be taken completely by surprise when Sheila told him.

'I like you, Matthew,' she said patiently, 'but I think even you must agree this isn't working.'

'Whatever do you mean?' he protested. 'We've been going out for nearly five months.'

'Yes, but . . .'

'And we've had some good times, haven't we?'

'Yes, but . . .'

'Then what's this all about?' His eyes were bulging. 'Is this because of what happened in the Assembly Rooms?'

'Not just that—'

'Because that was all your fault, Sheila.'

'My fault!'

'Of course,' he said angrily. 'That bloody dress for a start.'

'Well, I happen to like that bloody dress!' she snapped,

but inside she kicked herself. She had been so determined not to get angry with him, but it hadn't taken him long to get her all wound up, damn it. Right now she could feel her cheeks blazing and her heart was going like the clappers.

They were in a small cafe having a cup of tea before crossing the road to go to the Rivoli cinema where *Notorious*, a film starring Cary Grant and Ingrid Bergman, was showing.

A man came out of the kitchen. He and the waitress whispered together before he went back into the kitchen. The waitress came over to the table. 'Excuse me, miss, sir,' she said, 'but would you mind keeping your voices down?'

There were no other customers in the cafe, but Sheila said, 'Yes, sorry.'

Matthew made no reply, but stood to his feet so quickly he knocked his chair against the wall. 'Come on,' he growled. 'We're going.'

The waitress hurried back to the safety of the counter while Sheila picked up her cup of tea and sipped the cooling liquid. 'You go if you like,' she said, willing her voice not to tremble. 'I haven't finished my tea yet.'

The next moment the cup had gone flying. There was a sound of breaking as it smashed into the wall and she was left holding the handle. Sheila squealed as she felt his iron grip on the top of her arm. He pulled her to her feet.

'Let go,' she protested. 'Let go of me.'

Behind her, the anxious waitress called, 'Bob! Bob, come back here!' As the man returned, the two of them watched in horror as Matthew half dragged, half hauled Sheila towards the door. 'Shall I call the police?' the waitress cried.

'I am the police!' Matthew retorted.

Outside on the street, he shook her arm violently. 'How dare you?' he hissed. 'Showing me up like that.'

Now she was afraid of him. Her arm throbbed like mad and she felt humiliated. 'Matthew,' she said, her voice small and trembling, 'you really hurt me.'

'It's that bloody Kraut, isn't it?'

'No, it's not,' she protested, her strength creeping back. 'Look, you said yourself I'd ruined your career, so let it go.'

His face suddenly contorted with rage and he lifted his arm. Instinctively, she ducked and shielded her head, thinking he was going to hit her. Instead, he leaned towards her.

'Bitch,' he said, his spittle splashing her face. Then, much to her relief, he strode away.

The door of the cafe slowly opened. 'You all right, love?' The waitress's voice was gentle and full of concern. Sheila felt her whole body relax as the woman put her arm around her shoulder and took her back inside. Bob, who she presumed was the owner of the cafe, turned the sign on the door to 'closed' and locked it.

Sheila silently wept as they sat her back down and Bob poured some whisky he'd got from behind the counter into a small glass. 'Here you are, love,' he said kindly. 'Have a drop of Dutch courage. Looks like you might need it.'

Sheila blew her nose into her handkerchief and took the glass.

'You're that girl from the paper, aren't you?' said the waitress.

Sheila nodded dully as she sipped the amber liquid. It stung her throat, but it warmed her gullet as it went down. Bob began clearing up the broken pieces of cup and wiping spilt tea from the chair and the wall.

'You must let me pay for the damage,' said Sheila, reaching for her purse.

'He wouldn't hear of it, would you, Bob?' said the waitress.

The look of surprise on Bob's face was only fleeting. 'Course not,' he said, flicking his dishcloth over the tea-splattered menu.

'I thought your frock was lovely,' said the waitress, adding, 'In the paper, I mean,' when she saw the look of confusion on Sheila's face.

Bob jerked his head towards the door and for a split second she thought Matthew had come back. 'Is he your husband?' he asked.

Sheila stared at the inky darkness outside and shook her head.

'Then if you don't mind a bit of advice,' said Bob, 'I think you'd best be shot of him.'

Win Peters waited nervously in Matron's office. This was it. After all these years, her daughter was coming home. She could hardly take it in. She'd made three trips to Horsham in the past fortnight. Daisy had been delighted to see her every time and they were beginning to form a close bond once again. The most difficult thing had been telling her about Agnes's death. Daisy had wept on Win's shoulder, but the good news that Jean and Bill would be coming to Worthing at the end of January was a godsend. Daisy asked lots of questions and was beginning to grasp where everyone fitted into the family. 'It's going to be a bit of a squash at home for a bit,' Win told her. 'You and I will be in the same bedroom to start with, but when Sheila finally goes back home, you can have your own room.'

Win smiled to herself. Those girls had been wonderful. Right now Sheila was with Daisy helping her to finish the last of her packing while she took care of the formalities.

'You can't possibly bring Aunt Daisy home on the bus!' Sheila had exclaimed.

The plan had been to use the van at the bottom of the garden, but the girls were struggling to get it going again. As luck would have it, Neville Webster had turned up to see how they were getting on with the repairs.

'You'll never get all the way to Horsham in that old thing,' he said. 'I'll take you.'

'Are you sure?' Sheila had asked uncertainly.

'Of course,' he'd said, opening the back door of his car for Sheila and the front passenger door for Win. 'There's plenty of room. Hop in.'

Neville's car was obviously brand new, probably one

of the first to come off the assembly line in Wolseley's Birmingham factory since production recommenced after the war. The engine purred like a dream and the interior was impressive with soft leather upholstery and a walnut trim on the dashboard. As she settled in, Win smoothed down the leather seats and felt like a queen. She had never been offered such a luxurious ride before. Sheila had leaned forward and chatted amiably with Neville, and by the time they had reached Horsham, they seemed like old friends.

The door burst open and Matron bustled into the room. 'So sorry to keep you waiting, Mrs Peters,' she said, sitting down at the desk and reaching for a folder. 'I'm delighted that Daisy is going home at last, but we shall miss her.'

She worked her way through the papers in the folder, telling Win things she already knew: that Daisy had been admitted into care as a moral degenerate, but she was now a good person, placid and cooperative; that she loved cooking; that at some time she had been ill-treated and still bore the emotional scars.

'I consider her one of life's innocents,' said Matron. 'Since being in the home, Daisy has never had a man friend, but in view of her history I advise you to watch her carefully.'

Win was irritated by that remark, but she held her tongue. If she made waves now, Matron might stop her daughter coming home.

'She may be nearly forty-seven,' Matron went on, 'but in many ways she is still a child. I suggest you treat her as such and, as far as possible, keep her away from men.'

Win clutched the handbag on her lap and nodded.

Matron took a sheet of paper from the folder. 'And finally,' she said, 'all that is required is that you sign the discharge papers. It gives you sole responsibility for Daisy's conduct and welfare from this day forward.'

Win reached for the fountain pen held out in front of her, and with a heart bursting with joy, wrote 'Winifred Alice Peters' on the bottom of the page.

CHAPTER 28

Ronnie was back at the garage full time and overseeing the final preparations to begin trading again. The petrol tanker had restocked the tanks, the paraffin dealer had filled the dispensers and most of the other equipment they needed was in place. Neville had brought some more old tools he said he was getting rid of, although Ronnie thought they seemed to be in such excellent condition they looked brand new. Hardly the sort of thing one would offer to a rival.

It came as no surprise when Neville offered to drive Granny and Sheila over to Horsham to fetch Aunt Daisy either. Now that Matthew seemed to be out of the picture, Neville had seized his chance. Ronnie liked him. He was genuinely kind and considerate. Although Matthew appeared that way to others, Ronnie had always doubted his sincerity.

With the garage exactly as they wanted it after the refit, Ronnie had been looking at other lines. They now had every kind of battery torch imaginable, snow shovels and other farm implements. The nearest blacksmith was Overington's in Durrington. She'd stocked

317

up on lamp oil, petrol cans and batteries of all types and description. Most of it was ex-military stuff, but it was still useful. For a small fee, they would offer a delivery service for paraffin and if there was room on the van, they promised to take any orders to their customers from the local shops. The delivery van was going to be very useful, she was sure of it.

Banking on getting a bit of snow, Ronnie had made a few sleds and she'd managed to bag a couple of pairs of skis from a local auction. Her biggest coup was an old Commer ex-military breakdown and recovery truck. Sheila had wanted one for ages and Ronnie happened to hear a guest in the hotel telling someone he was winding up a business. As a result, she'd acquired a ten-wheel recovery vehicle in a lovely cherry red for just a song.

Of course, all this expansion was going to be far too much for one mechanic, but Ronnie had a solution for that too. A lad from the children's home, Malcolm, had been given a job as a local delivery boy, but he didn't like it much. Ronnie could see he was ambitious and, best of all, keen to do well. With Derek already settled with Neville in his garage, Malcolm was delighted to be offered an apprenticeship at the Becket garage. He and Sheila got on well. He was polite and willing to go the extra mile. He had helped Sheila get the garage into military order, the way she liked it.

But Ronnie's plans didn't stop at Malcolm. She wanted to offer Gerhard an opportunity too, so that afternoon she called him into the office.

'Gerhard, you work very hard,' she began. She was dying to add 'unlike that lazy good-for-nothing comrade of yours', but she kept her opinion to herself. Helmut did the bare minimum of anything he was asked to do.

As she spoke, Gerhard stared at his feet.

'As you know,' Ronnie went on, 'POWs are not allowed to be paid, so here is a proposal for you. For any period of time that Mr Hurst allows you to work for us, we will put a wage into a bank account. As soon as the government releases you to go back home, we shall give you that money as a gift.'

Gerhard stood with his mouth open. 'You are most kind, *Fräulein*,' he said, grasping her hand and shaking it vigorously.

Ronnie brushed him off. 'There's talk that POWs might be returned this year, but certainly by 1948,' she said.

'I do not wish to go back to Germany,' he said, shaking his head. 'I have no family.'

Ronnie was slightly startled by his admission, but hid it well. 'Then the money will give you a good start here,' she said briskly. Their meeting was over but Gerhard lingered. 'Was there something else?'

'If I apply to stay in England,' he went on, 'would you sponsor me?'

'Of course, Gerhard. We'd be glad to.'

They heard a small sound somewhere near the door. Gerhard nodded and went back to his work. Ronnie looked out of the window and saw Helmut kicking one of the tyres on the recovery truck. Ronnie felt uneasy. Had he been listening? Probably. She hoped he wasn't going to give Gerhard any trouble.

It was snowing when they came out of Nightingales, and judging by the state of the road, it had been for some time. Win almost slipped on her way across the car park. It was only Neville's quick reaction that saved her from a tumble.

He put Aunt Daisy's suitcase in the boot of his car and, this time, Win sat in the back with her daughter while Sheila sat in the front passenger seat. As Sheila leaned forward she noticed another feature of the Wolseley: the windscreen could be opened. Not a good idea in this weather, but how perfect for a drive on a warm summer's evening. She turned and caught Neville's eye as he drove onto the road.

'Lovely engine,' she remarked. 'More powerful than the pre-war model.'

'Thirty-three brake-horsepower,' he said with a grin. 'Overhead valve instead of side valves and half-elliptic leaf springs.'

Sheila pulled the corners of her mouth down as she nodded her approval. 'Classy.'

'Don't be too impressed,' he said. 'Sadly, she's not mine. My father ordered her before he set off on his trip and naturally I had to check that his four hundred quid was a worthwhile investment.'

'Naturally,' she agreed with a smile.

'When do you think your garage will be open again?'

'Ronnie is there this afternoon to take the tanker delivery and the paraffin dealer is due to come as well.'

'So back to the grindstone next week?'

'Absolutely,' she said. 'We plan to put Webster's garage out of business by the end of the month.'

Neville made a show of his trembling hands on the steering wheel and they both laughed. The weather was deteriorating all the time. Aunt Daisy stared out of the window, although she couldn't have seen much. The snow was coming down in blizzard proportions and Neville was forced to reduce his speed. The only sound in the car was the *whoosh* of the windscreen wipers.

'Have you heard from your parents?' Sheila asked after a while.

'I had a cablegram from Cape Town when they arrived,' said Neville. 'Having a wonderful time and all that.'

'Right now I envy them all that lovely sunshine,' Sheila chuckled.

'Me too.'

'How long do you reckon it will take us to get back?'

'Normally no longer than forty minutes,' said Neville, 'but with this weather it might be upwards of an hour.'

They had been going for twenty-five minutes already and had only reached Dial Post, seven miles from Horsham. Granny had fallen asleep, her head back and her mouth wide open. They passed several cars abandoned at the side of the road and one man trying to hitch a lift. Neville didn't stop. 'Sorry, old chap. This car is already full.'

By the time they reached Ashington, barely three miles further on, they could only crawl. Sheila was glad Neville was such a good driver. Keeping a safe distance behind other road users, he accelerated slowly and braked with care. He stretched his neck and looked into the rear-view mirror. 'There's a blanket under the front passenger seat if any of you are getting cold.'

There was no response. Daisy was still staring out of the window and Granny only snorted in her sleep and changed her position slightly. Sheila giggled. 'Don't worry. I think she's fine.'

'If this keeps up,' said Neville, 'I shall have to get out and check the exhaust pipe isn't getting blocked up with snow. We don't want to die of asphyxiation.'

On the hill between Ashington and Washington, snowdrifts were beginning to form and the surface on the bend leading to the turn-off for Storrington was particularly treacherous. It was just past here that the car suddenly jerked into a skid. Neville took his foot off the accelerator and, as the car's speed dropped, he regained control. The car coming up behind them wasn't so lucky. They saw it career over the road and come to a halt facing the other way. Sheila sensed Neville tensing as she wondered if they should stop and check that the driver was all right, but then, much to their relief, they saw him reversing slowly to right himself.

'Black ice,' said Neville in a solemn voice. They could hardly see anything in front of them now and the snowfall was even worse. 'It's no good,' he went on. 'I can't risk getting you all killed. I'm going to pull into Findon. If I can get to the Gun, we can stay the night and I'll get you all back in the morning.'

Sheila gulped. How could they possibly afford a night in a hotel?

'Don't worry about paying,' he said as if reading her mind.

'Don't be ridiculous,' she cried. 'I can't expect you to pay for all three of us.'

'Okay then,' he said, teasing. 'You stay in the car and freeze. I'll take your grandmother and your aunt into the Gun.'

'That's very kind of you, but I insist on paying,' she said stubbornly.

Neville glanced over at her and saw the look of determination on her face. 'Fair enough,' he grinned.

Sheila looked away. Oh rats! Why was it that she and Ronnie always seemed to take one step forward and three steps back? This was going to cost an absolute fortune, but Neville was right. They had no choice.

As it turned out, the decision was taken out of their hands anyway. As they inched their way towards the turning for Long Furlong, two lorries and a car had completely blocked the A24. The road was fairly new. Built in 1938, it had borne the brunt of the heavy traffic when the Canadian regiment, the Stormont, Dundas and Glengarry Highlanders, had an observation post above Church Hill, but it was only a single carriageway. Judging by the number of cars waiting behind the crashed vehicles, if they joined the queue they would be waiting for an awfully long time.

'So much for the faster road,' Neville said as he turned onto the old Horsham Road. 'Let's hope there are no hold-ups down here.'

As they turned left and headed for Findon village, Win woke up. 'Where are we?'

Sheila explained the situation. 'Stay the night at the Gun?' Win exclaimed. 'But we're only four miles from home.'

'I can't risk it, Mrs Peters,' Neville said apologetically. 'The only way you'll get home is if you walk, and frankly I don't advise it. I've never seen weather like this before.'

'I suppose you're right,' Win said grimly. 'Let's hope they've still got rooms.' She grasped her daughter's hand. 'Daisy dear, it looks as if we have to spend the night in Findon.'

Daisy gasped audibly. 'No,' she cried. 'No, no.'

The other three occupants of the car were hugely surprised by her reaction. These were the first words she'd spoken since she'd left the home. Neville strained to see her in the rear-view mirror, Sheila turned round and Win tried to pacify her.

'It'll be all right, dear.'

'You said I could go home,' Daisy accused.

'And we will,' Win assured her. 'We'll set off first thing in the morning. It's not far, really it isn't.'

Daisy put her head in her hands.

'Whatever's the matter?' Win asked anxiously.

When she looked up, Daisy's eyes were bulging with fright and she began wringing her hands. 'I can't, I can't,' she said tearfully. 'Oh, please don't make me. Please, please . . .'

CHAPTER 29

Ronnie was woken by loud banging on the garage door and the sounds of Nelson and Milly barking. It was hardly daytime, but there was a strange light in the room. She was alone in the Becket. Sheila was still living with Granny. The plan was that she should move out at the weekend after she'd finished her last day working in the gas showroom. Apparently when her cousin had told them, the management seemed relieved. Sales of New World gas cookers were very slow.

Ronnie, on the other hand, had already finished at the Thomas A Becket hotel. She'd packed her bags at the end of the previous week and was glad to be back home with Nelson.

The banging was very persistent.

She was warm and cosy in her bed, but the atmosphere in the bedroom was so cold she could see her own breath and there was ice on the inside of the window glass. Jumping out of bed, she grabbed her outdoor coat, thrown onto the bed as an extra cover, and going over to the window, she scratched a small porthole with her fingernails. Three men stood by the door. They were muffled up, but she was fairly sure one of them was Pen's husband. Snow lay everywhere and in places was quite deep. Ronnie hurried downstairs and half an hour later she had sold all eight shovels (how she wished she'd taken the chance and bought a dozen), two spades and the skis.

The men told her they had only just managed to get out of their houses, Mr Griffith by climbing out of the sash window, and now they were on a mission to dig a pathway from their front doors to the pavement. Ronnie had never seen so much snow and it was quite clear nothing would be moving along the roads until they were cleared. And, come to think of it, she hadn't heard the toot of the trains as they passed West Worthing station, so the railways must be at a standstill as well.

The people of the Becket were making sure their neighbours were all right. Sally Emmet's baby was due any minute. The midwife hadn't turned up to give her the usual checks, but several of the more matronly women assured her that they knew exactly what to do if the baby came. Old Nobby Clark had plenty of offers of a hot meal and so long as the bar of the Thomas A Becket hotel was open, the men were happy. By midday, pathways had been dug, cups of tea dispensed and the children were having a whale of a time. All the sleds were sold. Helmut, Gerhard and several other POWs were put to work clearing the roads. The Littlehampton Road was open but Poulter's Lane, which was only a small track, had become impassable because the snow was so deep.

Early afternoon, Ronnie decided to try to get to Granny's place because she was dying to know how Aunt Daisy had settled in. It was difficult to avoid obstacles and in places the snowdrifts were so high, she could only see the tops of parked cars. The walk, which should have taken fifteen minutes, twenty if she dawdled, took almost forty-five minutes before she got there. Ronnie knocked on the door and after a minute or two she heard a shuffling sound as someone came to open it.

The door opened slowly and a man's voice said, 'I know I should have asked first, but it was perishing out there . . .' He stopped mid-sentence and stared at her.

Ronnie gasped in shocked surprise. 'What the hell are you doing here?'

Early that morning, Sheila had woken with an elbow pressing gently against her cheek. It took a moment or two to remember where she was, but as soon as she turned her head and saw Aunt Daisy at the other end of the bed and Granny in the middle, it all came back to her.

When they'd arrived at the Gun the previous night, the inn was almost full of stranded travellers. There was only one room still available, a double. Neville snapped it up immediately without even bothering to ask the price. After a cup of warm soup and a sherry, the three women were dying to go to bed, so they were shown upstairs. Daisy was a lot calmer than she had been when they'd first arrived, but she became agitated if they moved about and even more anxious if she lost sight of her mother. The room itself apparently overlooked fields although they couldn't see much as it was dark. It was comfortably furnished and the bed was clean. The landlady had put two hot-water bottles under the covers and the gas fire was on, giving the room a cosy feel. The shared bathroom and toilet was just along the corridor. As they had no nightclothes, they slept in their petticoats. Neville had been given the use of the settee in the lounge. It looked fairly comfortable, though Sheila wasn't sure about spending the whole night on it. She felt certain he was destined to wake up with a bad back, but there was no other choice. As she drew the curtains, it was still snowing.

When they'd first gone into the room, Sheila had said she would sleep on the floor, but Granny wouldn't hear of it. 'It's a big bed,' she said. 'None of us is jumbo-sized. We can all fit in.'

They did, and surprisingly they'd all slept well. Sheila slipped out of bed and lit the gas fire. As it popped into life, she lifted the curtain. The scene before her was Christmas-card beautiful although it had stopped snowing. The whole courtyard was knee-deep in snow and it had drifted against Neville's car. It would be difficult to get the driver's door open and they would have to dig their way out.

Granny opened her eyes. 'Still snowing?'

Sheila shook her head. 'But it's going to be difficult getting home.'

'Then we'll walk,' said Granny brightly. 'Lovely comfortable bed, isn't it? I was as warm as toast.'

'It's the first time I've slept three in a bed,' Sheila said with a grin.

'Reminds me of home when I was a nipper,' said Granny. 'We used to sleep four or five in a bed back then.' She yawned. 'I could do with a wash.'

'The landlady left us some towels and soap on the chair,' Sheila said, 'but I think someone is already in the bathroom. I heard the door locking.'

Aunt Daisy stirred and opened a bleary eye.

'Hello, my darling,' said Granny. 'You slept well.'

Sheila was the last to use the bathroom. When Granny came back after Aunt Daisy, they both went downstairs for breakfast. Sheila, still in her petticoat and wearing her outdoor coat, padded along the corridor in her bare feet. As she tried the door handle, the door flew open and there stood Neville. He seemed pleased to see her.

'Hello, gorgeous,' he said quietly. 'Did you have a good night?'

Sheila felt her cheeks warm. She looked behind herself as if expecting someone else to be there. 'Oh,' she teased, 'you mean me? You need glasses. I look an absolute sight.'

'You certainly do,' he quipped. 'Fabulous.' He stepped to the left at the same time as she did. He laughed and then they both stepped to the right. 'A dancer too,' he joked, and snatching her up in his arms, he waltzed her halfway along the corridor. Sheila was laughing as he let her go. Just as she turned to go back, someone else nipped into the bathroom.

'Oh, I'm sorry,' Neville apologized. 'I hope you're not desperate.'

'Good job I'm not,' said Sheila, pretending to scold him, and he waltzed her back to the door.

He kissed her hand. 'Thank you for a wonderful time, fair maiden.'

Sheila cuffed him playfully on the arm. The bathroom door opened and a man came out. Sheila walked in, and as she turned to close the door, Neville snapped to attention and saluted her.

Ronnie glared at Matthew. She'd just done a quick tour of the rooms, calling as she went.

'There's nobody here,' he said.

'If my grandmother isn't here,' she said crossly, 'how did you get in?'

'I know where she keeps the key.' He was already adopting that supercilious tone of his.

'That doesn't give you the right to walk in uninvited,' Ronnie said sharply. In fact, she was furious. How dare he? Surely this amounted to trespass?

Matthew shrugged his shoulders. 'Where's Sheila?'

Ignoring him, Ronnie hung her coat on the hallstand.

'I said, where's Sheila?'

'I don't see that that has anything to do with you.'

'Sheila is my fiancée,' he said.

'I don't think so,' said Ronnie. 'The last thing she

331

told me was that she didn't want to go out with you any more.'

'That's not true,' he said.

Ronnie walked away.

'Look,' he said, softening his tone and following her into the kitchen, 'we had a little disagreement, that's all. I'm sure I can smooth it over. I just need to talk to her.'

Ronnie filled the kettle with water.

'So where is she?'

Where indeed? Ronnie was as surprised as he was that there was no one at home. She had no idea where Sheila, Granny or Aunt Daisy could be. She could only surmise that they had either decided to stay in Horsham until the weather improved or they had found shelter somewhere else along the way. The fact that Neville was with them gave her confidence that nothing bad had happened, but Matthew's guess was as good as hers. He sat himself down at the kitchen table.

'They've gone to fetch my aunt,' said Ronnie, pointedly placing but one cup and saucer on the table.

'When did they go?'

'Yesterday.'

'Did they go by bus or did they take the train? What time did they leave?' He fired his questions at her like bullets. 'Horsham, was it? Did they go to Horsham?'

'Look, Matthew,' said Ronnie, putting her hand on her hip. 'I have no wish to be rude, but I would rather you left. I'm sure Sheila is fine and there's nothing to worry about.'

Something flickered across his face – something dark and frightening. She wished she'd brought Nelson with her, but she'd been worried that walking through some of the snowdrifts might damage his paws.

'Somebody was with her, weren't they?' he said coldly. 'Who was she with?'

'I've already told you, my grandmother and my aunt.'

'Who else?' he insisted.

As Ronnie reached for the teapot, his hand came crashing down on the kitchen table, making the cup and saucer rattle. 'Who else!' he bellowed.

This was a side of him she'd never seen before. She was used to his smarmy ways, his quiet insistence, his domination of Sheila, but she'd never seen his temper before. Inside, Ronnie was shaking like a leaf, but she was a past master at not showing her true feelings. What was it the Major had once said? 'A bully needs a victim.' Well, she wasn't going to allow herself to be bullied again. When she'd left that awful camp she'd made a solemn vow. No more kowtowing; no more being intimidated; no more being a victim.

She turned slowly to face him. 'I don't know who you think you are,' she said in a superior tone, 'but as a member of His Majesty's constabulary I would have thought—' She didn't get to finish her sentence.

Putting his hands up in mock surrender, Matthew said, 'You're right. I'm sorry. I'm sorry. I never should have spoken to you like that.' He sat back down and put his head in his hands. 'It's just that I love her so much,' he went on, his voice breaking, 'and I've been so worried.'

'I can't think why,' she said coldly as she spooned two scoops of tea from the caddy into the pot. 'You've hardly seen her since the New Year.'

'I went on leave,' he said brokenly. 'I wish I hadn't gone now. Oh, Ronnie, help me with this. Please . . . I'm begging you.'

She watched him running his fingers distractedly through his hair and was tempted to applaud. He was fairly convincing; a bit over the top and not exactly Laurence Olivier, but he'd have made a good leading actor in a local am-dram play.

'I'm afraid I can't help you,' she said in a disinterested tone. His head jerked up. That look was in his eye again. This man is dangerous, she thought to herself. 'I can't tell you where she is because I don't know.'

He frowned, disbelieving. Ronnie poured the boiling water into the teapot. 'I can only imagine they've been delayed by the weather,' she said, sitting back down and pouring herself a cup of tea. He waited for a moment, clearly expecting her to offer him one, but she only sat with her elbows on the table, sipping from her own cup and regarding him over the rim.

'I'd better go,' he said eventually.

Ronnie didn't reply. He rose to his feet again and turned to leave. 'Matthew,' she said, holding her hand out towards him, 'the key, please.'

When it came hurtling across the room towards her,

it took every ounce of her strength not to flinch or duck. The key hit the teapot and clattered to the wooden kitchen table. A moment later, she heard the front door slam.

She still didn't trust him, so she picked up Granny's rolling pin and went out into the hall. Thankfully, she could see him through the glass panel in the door, stumbling in the snow in the direction of West Worthing station. Safe at last, Ronnie bolted the door on the inside. It was only then that she noticed how much her hands were shaking.

CHAPTER 30

It was hard for Leslie to get time off. When he'd taken up the post as chauffeur to Mrs Harrison-Vane, he'd been offered a day off a week, but in truth he only occasionally managed the odd evening at the pictures with Effie and even that was only when Mrs Harrison-Vane had an escort or she was spending the night with friends. During the daytime it was even more difficult. Whichever day he asked for was always inconvenient and he never knew until the very last minute if he could go.

He had been wanting to go back to the Regent Street gentleman's outfitters for some time. When he'd bought his chauffeur's uniform and his own suit, he had ordered a grey-and-black houndstooth waistcoat with its own complementary bow tie and he needed to collect it.

According to the radio reports, the snow was significant in the Midlands and the north, but apart from Kent, which always got it bad, the rest of the country was still moving. The recent snowfall meant that Mrs Harrison-Vane was reluctant to venture out, but Leslie explained that the car needed to be taken for a run in

336

order to keep it in tip-top condition. The roads were surprisingly clear so he quickly found his way into central London.

Fortunately, for all her faults, Mrs Harrison-Vane remembered to give him his wages, so he would be able to put cash on the counter, but he had already decided that this was his last indulgence. From now on, he must save his money, for he had found something far more important to him than beautiful clothes.

The smart doorman held the door open as he entered the shop and he walked straight into the domestic uniform section. The assistant, Mr Archer, recognized him at once and hurried to fetch his order. When he came back, Mr Cranleigh, the tailor, accompanied him and Mr Archer was carrying a blue-and-gold box. Leslie was undressed and dressed, fitted and fussed over until all three men were satisfied that he looked perfect. All that remained was to surrender the correct number of clothing coupons and the money.

'Shall I charge it to Mrs Harrison-Vane's account?' said Mr Archer.

'No,' said Leslie, proud to be performing his first honest transaction. 'I'm paying for this myself.'

When the tailor returned to his workroom, Mr Archer drew Leslie to one side in a confidential manner. 'I think you might remember me saying that sir was a man to be admired,' he said in a low voice, 'and I know sir is in gainful employment, but I wonder if I might ask sir something?'

Leslie was intrigued. Mr Archer looked around

furtively. 'I shouldn't be doing this,' he said, reaching into his inside pocket and taking out a small business card, 'but I told my brother about you and I promised to give you this.'

Sensing the manager was coming, Mr Archer straightened up and handed him the blue-and-gold box. 'I trust sir will enjoy wearing this waistcoat,' he said aloud. 'It is made of the very finest quality material.'

'Thank you,' said Leslie and turned sharply, almost bumping into the manager. 'You've been most helpful.'

The manager bowed. 'Good afternoon, sir.'

'Good afternoon,' said Leslie. He turned at the door and glanced back. The manager had moved on, but Mr Archer was still watching him. Leslie inclined his head.

Mr Archer winked.

When she was nine years old, Sheila's parents had taken her to Southend-on-Sea for a holiday. It was a time she remembered fondly. As if the wide, almost-empty streets, the trolley-bus tour and the amazing electric railway chugging along what seemed to a nine-year-old like the longest pier in the whole wide world wasn't enough, there was the carnival as well. She recalled the marching bands, clowns in funny costumes and the pearly kings and queens from London. The colours, the sights and sounds were all etched in her mind forever. The whole idea was to raise funds for the local hospital, so nurses walked beside the floats with enamel buckets and bowls for the crowds to throw in their loose change. For Sheila, seeing the carnival queen was the stuff of dreams. It became part of her role play for weeks afterwards. Dressed in one of her mother's old nighties, Sheila would stand in front of her big teddy bear as he, like the mayor of Southend-on-Sea, paid homage to her and kissed her hand. Best of all, she would rearrange her chairs so that she was the carnival queen sitting in an old-fashioned brake pulled by two white horses.

Now, thirteen years later and standing on the back of a David Brown tractor fitted with caterpillar tracks was a poor second, but Sheila felt quite regal as they rode through Findon Valley.

Neville had bumped into an old farming contact who worked the land surrounding Monkton Court, a large country house north of the village. He had just been called upon to pull a bus out of a snowdrift and was happy to oblige when Neville asked him to take Sheila, Win and Daisy back to West Worthing. They had to stand on a small platform just behind the driver and it was when the people who were clearing snow from outside their own homes started waving that Sheila's childhood memories came to the fore. It was bitter cold with leaden skies, but Sheila, every inch the queen, waved back gracefully.

Hanging on behind the driver, Daisy was tempted to pinch herself to believe this was real. After all this time, she was free at last. She glanced back at her mother. How many times had she prayed that this moment would come? Of course, she could never tell

Mum everything. She could still hear her father's threat in her ear and she couldn't bear it if it came true.

She was barely sixteen when she'd left the workhouse infirmary and they'd put her in the first home. It was hell on earth. She'd tried to stand up for herself, but the constant beatings and the punishments wore her down. She used to fantasize that her mother would come and rescue her, but she remembered what he'd said – 'If your mother knew what sort of girl you are, she'd be far too ashamed to have you back.'

The bit she hated the most was when they tied her to a chair and threw a bucket of cold water over her. They told her it was to calm her down. The shock of the wet took her breath away and the more she protested, the more they did it. In the end, she realized nobody was coming to fetch her and to be compliant was the only way to avoid being singled out. If she remained quiet and anonymous then some other poor bugger got the treatment instead.

When it first started, she felt like she had no choice. She was only fourteen and he was so big and powerful. He'd said nice things to her, but she'd hated what he'd done. And the worst of it was, he wouldn't stop. She'd begged him, she'd wept, she'd tried pushing him off, but he would hold her down until she submitted. Sometimes he would hit her and tell her to stop snivelling when he was doing it. He even had the cheek to complain that she wasn't being nice to him. But how could she be nice? That first time, every move he made was agony and she honestly thought he would rip her apart. And then there was the shame of it. She'd never been told about the facts of life, but somehow she knew what they were doing was wrong. It was dirty and a secret.

When she started being sick in the morning her father was so angry. He'd called her a dirty little slut and demanded to know how many men she'd been playing around with. She'd protested that she hadn't but he'd locked her in the shed for a whole day until he could sort something out.

Eventually she'd ended up in Findon. He sent her to live with some old tartar of a woman to work as her skivvy until the baby came. Daisy guessed she'd been one of her father's women. She'd heard him arguing with her mother one day and Mum had said, 'Don't touch me. Go to one of your other women.' And he'd hit her.

Daisy's little girl had been born out in the shed on a cold April morning. She didn't have a doctor or a midwife. There was only Dad and the woman. Daisy remembered the pain and being told to keep her mouth shut. She'd been forced to bite down on an old piece of blanket to stop herself from crying out. She smiled to herself as she remembered the exhilarating moment when her baby left her body. She had a strong and lusty cry, but Dad wouldn't let her see her properly. All she'd got was a tiny glimpse of her wrapped in the little crochet blanket she'd made while she was waiting. It wasn't very good because she'd got a bit muddled with the stitches when she did the corners.

'Don't you ever breathe a word of this, girl,' he'd snarled as he'd stood by the shed door in the early hours of the morning with the baby in his arms. 'The shame of it will kill your mother.'

Daisy had wept. The woman had bound her breasts when the milk came and it was so painful, but not as painful as her feeling of loss. A week later, her father took her to the workhouse infirmary. She had no idea what yarn he'd told them and at the time she was too weak to care. When she'd been discharged he'd promised to take her home, but he lied about that too and she'd ended up in that awful place.

'Nearly there,' said Sheila, patting her arm and bringing her back to the here and now.

Her mother smiled. 'Oh, Daisy, love, it's so good to have you home again.'

CHAPTER 31

The whole of the month of February was difficult for everyone. The snowfall was unprecedented and in so many ways it made ordinary everyday life a question of survival. At the beginning of the big freeze, light industries and laundries found their fuel allowance cut by as much as two tons a week. There were constant power cuts, which of course led to employees being sent home and many were given notice. The worry was that by the time some semblance of normality prevailed, the people who had been laid off would have found other jobs. Low gas pressure didn't help either.

The shortages had a knock-on effect and it wasn't just about food. Jack Watts, who ran a well-known shoe shop in the town, complained that his shoe repair service was almost at a standstill. With no power to drive the machines, his workers were forced to stand idle. For those who only had one pair, no shoes meant they couldn't go to work themselves. The sweet factory in Church Road, Tarring, J. Whitehouse & Co., reduced its production to three days a week, something which had never happened, not even in the darkest hour of the war.

Council workers were overwhelmed. In an effort to keep the pavements clear, the council sent loud-speaker vans around the town reminding people that under the by-laws, it was the responsibility of each house-holder to clear the snow from outside their own homes. As the terrible weather continued, the council depot was in danger of running out of grit for the roads and Mr Lambert, the borough engineer, had to fend off numerous complaints.

Buses ran as usual but it wasn't uncommon for a bus to end up 'ditched' and unable to pull away from the kerbside. If this was the case, passengers had a long cold wait until they could be transferred to another bus. Broadwater Bridge was considered unsafe so buses were rerouted along Teville Gate and Worthing crossing.

There was a knock on the door of his room. Matthew's heart raced. Sheila! She'd come at last. He was busy composing his third letter to her. She hadn't replied to the others, so this one was proving a lot harder to write. He gathered the papers quickly and stuffed them into his drawer. He was mixed up and confused. Sometimes he was angry with her and at other times he was convinced she was just playing a game with him.

He went to the mirror and smoothed down his hair with his hand. She'd looked really happy the last time he'd seen her. He hadn't approached her. Just lately he'd developed a taste for watching her from afar. Sometimes she sensed he was there and stopped what she was doing to look around. He knew that was part of the game so he'd duck behind a tree or step back behind the wall. He supposed he should call a halt to it now. After all, he had neglected other things; things which were once important to him.

The person at the door knocked again. He imagined how it would be when he opened it. 'Hello,' he'd say and she'd step forward and lay her head on his chest. 'I've missed you so much,' she'd say.

The knock at the door was louder this time. 'I know you are in there, Mr Keller. Open the door.' His heart sank. It was only his landlady, Mrs Stubbs. 'You need to pay the rent.'

Matthew opened the drawer again and took out the rent book, then he snatched the door open, making her jump. As he came close, she wrinkled her nose.

'There's a terrible smell in your room,' she complained. 'Have you had a wash today?'

'I don't see that is any of your business,' he said, thrusting the rent book at her.

'I'll have you know, Mr Keller, this is a respectable house,' she snapped. 'Your room smells like a doss house.'

Matthew said nothing.

Mrs Stubbs sensed that she had the upper hand. 'If it doesn't smell any better tomorrow,' she said, 'I shall have to ask you to leave.'

Matthew arched his eyebrows in a superior manner. 'You can't throw me out because I haven't washed.'

'Oh, can't I?' she said. 'This is my house and I expect my tenants to behave like decent human beings.'

'I'm working undercover,' he said sullenly.

'Undercover?' Her voice was shrill.

'Yes,' he said, coming so close she was forced to step back, 'and I'll thank you to keep your voice down. You never know who might be listening.'

He focused his gaze just beyond her, making her turn sharply. When she looked back, he was grinning. Mrs Stubbs sniffed and opened the rent book. 'You owe me two weeks.'

'It's all there.'

He looked at her with contempt. She had a nerve telling him to wash, the fat lazy old cow. He stared at her mountainous bosom straining to escape from her wrap-over apron and wondered what she looked like without her suit-of-armour corsets to hold those two monumental bladders of blubber and fat together. The thought of it made him shudder.

Stuffing the cash into her apron pocket, she marked up the book and gave it back to him. He smiled affably.

'When I agreed to take you on,' she said stiffly, 'I told you rent day was every Friday. Make sure you have it next Friday.'

He gave her an exaggerated bow and as she walked away he put up two fingers. She almost caught him as she turned to say, 'The bathroom is free right now.'

'Is it really?' he said as he closed his door again. 'Well I never.'

* * *

In the interests of economy, most people only heated one room in the house and Ronnie and Sheila found their stock of paraffin going down fast as people with little or no coal and reduced gas pressure for their fires turned to paraffin heaters in an effort to warm their homes. The girls had never been so busy. The breakdown truck was a godsend and in constant use. Sheila had put chains over the wheels so, unlike her competitors, she had little problem with the roads whether they were gritted, covered in fresh snow or packed ice.

Gerhard and Helmut still came to the garage to help out, but only occasionally. As the month wore on, Mr Hurst was frustrated because he couldn't start work in his greenhouses apart from making sure the weight of snow on the roofs didn't break the glass. His quota of coke had been severely delayed, and besides, it was far too cold to get the seedlings started. All he could do was hope and pray that the thaw would come soon. There was little sign of that. At the end of February, the observatory on the top of Beach House in the east of the town registered nine degrees Fahrenheit – twenty-three degrees of frost – and as a result, Gerhard and Helmut spent most of their time trying to gain access for the people trapped in isolated farmhouses in the area.

As February faded into March, the electricity cuts were in danger of threatening milk and bread supplies. Stories emerged of fifty employees of Highfield and Oakland Dairies standing idle because there was no power for bottling the milk. At the same time, Ronnie and Sheila experienced a rather odd phenomenon. For two days running, their milk delivery was sour. More than that, it was curdled and solid.

'I don't understand,' said Ronnie. 'It's perishing cold out there. How come the milk is off?'

'It must have been off when Armpit Price left it,' said Sheila.

'I'll have a word with him tomorrow,' said Ronnie.

The next morning, she was looking out for the horse and cart bringing Mr Price and his milk delivery. By the time he was walking towards the door, she was waiting for him, arms folded across her chest.

'Mr Price,' she said stiffly, 'we have had solid milk in our bottles for two days running.' She held up yesterday's delivery for inspection.

'Frozen, innit,' he said.

'This milk isn't frozen,' Ronnie said huffily. 'It's sour. Not to put too fine a point on it, it's rancid.'

'None of my other customers have complained.' Armpit Price squinted at the bottle and shook his head. 'Anyroad, them's not mine.'

'What?'

'Them's from Coronation Dairies.'

Ronnie frowned and to her utter embarrassment, as she turned the bottle in her hand, she could see he was right. The bottle was the same shape as she was used to, but embedded in the glass was the name of a different supplier; not Oakland but Coronation Dairies. Ronnie was left feeling a bit of a fool.

'Do you still want me to deliver?'

'Oh yes,' cried Ronnie, flustered. 'I can't think how this has happened.'

With his usual whiff of sweaty armpit, Mr Price bent down to put the milk on the step. 'Well, it ain't my milk what's off.'

Aunt Daisy had settled in nicely. She and Granny got on really well and it turned out that Daisy was a worker of miracles in the kitchen. She had the knack of making a pie or a pudding taste amazing even though she had only the usual meagre rations. Her baked sausage-meat roll was an absolute favourite and yet all it contained was sausage meat, a few vegetables, herbs and a bit of pickle mixed into some stale bread-crumbs. Win couldn't resist it and she was putting on weight. That was why, when Mrs Edwards advertised for a new cook, Sheila suggested Aunt Daisy apply for the job.

Daisy's eyes lit up the moment Sheila mentioned the children, but Granny was less than enthusiastic. 'Oh no, dear. I don't think Daisy is capable of running a kitchen.'

'I'm sure Mrs Edwards would give her every support,' said Sheila. 'Her old cook has been with her for years, but now that her eyesight isn't as good as it once was, she can't cope with it.'

Granny shook her head. 'No.'

Aunt Daisy looked crestfallen and Sheila was disappointed, although it was clear that Granny meant well. What a shame. She might not manage the organizing and ordering, but cooking was well within Aunt Daisy's capabilities. Hadn't she been doing just that in Horsham?

Apart from the milk deliveries, the only other public service which came whatever the weather was the post. This may have been held up in the sorting office for a while, but Mr Turnbull, the postman, rarely missed his round. Sometimes Ronnie and Sheila would have a pile of letters and other times only one, but they saw their postman nearly every day.

The thaw was finally on its way when he delivered the letter which would knock Ronnie for six. In fact, he didn't even get as far as putting it into the tin they kept for the purpose by the garage door. Ronnie happened to be sweeping the forecourt of the last vestiges of snow when he came by.

'Lovely morning,' he remarked.

It was indeed a lovely morning. A watery sun struggled to warm the earth again and there was a rumour going round that today there would be a delivery of winter vegetables in the town. It would be a welcome change to eat fresh vegetables. For far too long, farmers had struggled to get them out of the frozen ground and in East Anglia some desperate farmers had resorted to using pneumatic drills.

'If I'd known you were coming,' Ronnie quipped, 'I'd have got the deckchairs out.'

He handed her the letter. He said something else, but exactly what he said didn't register. As soon as she saw the envelope, her heart lurched and the blood pounded in her head. She stumbled slightly.

'You all right, love?' Mr Turnbull's anxious voice penetrated the whirl of thoughts rushing through her mind.

'Yes,' said Ronnie, dropping her broom. 'Yes, I'm fine.'

Mr Turnbull watched her go. Dear, dear, he thought to himself. I hope it's not bad news.

Ronnie stared into space. How long had she been sitting here? And why was it that whenever she had an idle moment the memories came flooding back? They'd been so busy since the snow came, but now that it was beginning to thaw, the horrors of the camp were ever present. It was especially worse at night. She might get up to go to the toilet and she knew that once she'd climbed back into bed, she was destined to spend an hour, maybe two, thinking about it. Thoughts of Bruce came day or night. Funny how she thought of him as Bruce now. She'd only called him by his Christian name that one time. The day she'd called to say goodbye. He'd been sitting at his desk and rose as she walked into the room. It still made her blood pulse as she recalled him coming round the desk and taking her into his arms. She'd closed her eyes as his strong embrace pulled her close. She could smell his after-shave. She could feel his racing heart beneath his shirt. The feeling was wonderful, hypnotic, but it only lasted a second or two before she came to her senses. 'No, Bruce. We mustn't.'

The other memory that intruded all the time was of the day when he'd been reunited with his children. She'd arranged to meet him in a hotel rather than in the convalescent home. In her humble opinion, the girls had had enough of institutions. They needed to be aware that there were beautiful things in life as well.

Ruth had clung to him like a limpet and sobbed uncontrollably in his arms. Elspeth had hung back. Perhaps being that much younger, she didn't really remember her father. She'd pressed her back into Ronnie's stomach and trembled. Her father had crouched down and tried to coax his daughter to come to him, but Elspeth was reluctant. Eventually, he'd stood to his feet and looked at Ronnie.

'You kept them alive and brought them back to me,' he said, his voice choked with emotion. 'How can I ever thank you?'

'Your wife,' she'd said brokenly. 'I'm so sorry . . .'

'I know,' he said. 'Caroline told me.'

Ronnie had cast her gaze to the floor. Caroline. What else had she told him? She'd been the bane of all their lives for so long. They'd both been prisoners of the Japs together and, like Mrs Lyle, Caroline had been a real survivor. They had known each other for years and rumour had it that she had tried to seduce the Major more than once. In the camp, Caroline had managed to get more rations than the other prisoners and she'd gone into the huts with Mrs Lyle to 'entertain' the guards. When Mrs Lyle died, Caroline wanted

Ronnie to be her servant and she'd agreed to it for the sake of the girls. Ronnie would have done anything to get quinine when the children got malaria. Once it was all over, they'd ended up together in Perth. On the face of it, it seemed like a nice thing to do, to include her in the family plans, but with Caroline there was always another side of the coin, and now that Bruce was a widower, he was even more attractive. It was Caroline who arranged for him to come to the hotel and fetch his children.

Ronnie remembered seeing him out of the corner of her eye, drawing the girls away from her. She remained rooted to the spot, not moving a muscle as their father gently encouraged them towards the lounge where afternoon tea had been laid on for them. Then the door had swung shut and she was alone. She'd suddenly felt totally bereft. They'd been together for three dreadful years and now they were gone.

That hated voice intruded into her thoughts. 'You may as well go now,' said Caroline. 'Elspeth and Ruth will be fine.'

Ronnie had turned her head in shocked surprise. Mrs Lyle's best friend looked amazing. She remembered thinking that her clothes must have come straight from a Paris fashion house.

'I'd like to come back and see them sometime,' Ronnie had said.

'That's won't be necessary,' Caroline had said coldly. 'They won't need a nanny any more. Haven't you heard? The Major and I are to be married.'

And all those feelings of helplessness had come flooding back.

Ronnie had felt something drip off the end of her nose. She'd wiped it away with the back of her hand as the truth of it dawned. She'd never see the girls again. She'd never see Bruce again either. It was over. Gone.

Right now she was sitting upstairs in the bedroom. She could hear Sheila downstairs talking to a customer and she hoped she'd be there for a while. Fishing for a clean hanky in the chest of drawers, Ronnie sat down on the bed and looked at the letter in her hands. She recognized his writing, but how on earth had he got her address?

A car drew up on the forecourt and Nelson barked.

Ronnie turned the envelope over. His address was on the back: 8/146 Banksia Street, Tuart Hill, Perth, Australia. It was new to her. He must have moved to Perth after he'd married Caroline. Her hands were trembling as she picked up her steel nail file to use as a letter opener.

As she slit the envelope, Sheila's voice interrupted her. 'Ronnie, are you up there?' she called from the bottom of the stairs. 'Leslie's here.'

CHAPTER 32

Win and Daisy were walking arm in arm to the garage. The day was drizzly and damp. Elsewhere in the country the snow hadn't gone away, but because they were under the shadow of the Downs, Worthing hadn't had much fresh snowfall for a week or two. It had been cold and they'd had sleet, but nothing which hung around.

The past few weeks had been wonderful for Win. She'd let Daisy find her feet. Up until now, she hadn't pressured her to tell her about her experiences, but one thing really bothered her. Why had her daughter neglected her duty and run away? Had it all been too much for her? Win couldn't help being ill or being sent to a sanatorium far away, but surely Daisy must have realized how difficult it would be for her two younger sisters to cope without her – Basil never was much use in the home.

'Daisy,' she began tentatively, 'can I ask you something? Why did you run away?'

She felt Daisy stiffen. 'I can't tell you, Mum.'

Win chewed her bottom lip anxiously. 'Was it because of some boy?'

'Mum,' said Daisy, 'please don't. I'm ashamed of what I did and I'm sorry.'

Win squeezed her daughter's arm. 'Just remember this. I'll never stop loving you, no matter what you did.'

She felt Daisy tremble as she pulled her arm away from her to reach for her handkerchief. 'Oh, Mum . . .'

'Hello, sis.' Ronnie was surprised when Leslie put his hands on the tops of her arms and kissed her cheek. It was a perfectly natural thing to do, but they'd never been a demonstrative family.

Ronnie had never seen her brother looking so well. He was dressed in a chauffeur's uniform; grey with a double row of bright brass buttons down the front of the jacket. He had a peaked cap and his shoes were so shiny you could almost see your face in them. Parked on the forecourt was a Rolls-Royce. Impressive as all that might be, it was his facial expression which surprised her most. He no longer looked sullen and withdrawn. Leslie actually looked happy.

'I want you to meet someone,' he said brightly. He ran back to the car and opened the front passenger door to let someone out. 'Ronnie, Sheila, this is my future intended,' he said as he held out his hand to help someone out. 'This is my Effie.'

A small dark-haired woman stepped out of the car and Leslie tucked her arm through his as he walked her back to his sister and cousin.

Ronnie took in her breath. 'You're engaged? Oh, Leslie, that's wonderful!'

Sheila and Ronnie hugged both Effie and Leslie.

'Come inside,' Ronnie cried. 'You couldn't have timed it better. Granny and Aunt Daisy will be here in a moment. Oh, Leslie, I can't believe it. I'm so happy for you.'

Gerhard and Helmut were left in charge of the pumps as the two girls took Leslie and his fiancée upstairs. While Sheila was plumping up cushions and whipping things back into their rightful place, Ronnie put the kettle on. She was doing her best not to stare at Effie, but at the same time she wanted to take a good look at Leslie's fiancée.

'Have you come far?'

'We live in London,' said Leslie. 'A house off Park Lane.'

Ronnie's eyes widened. Park Lane. Her only personal experience of the place was from the Monopoly board. It was one of the most expensive squares.

While Ronnie made the tea, Sheila was trying to work out who Effie was. Could she be Leslie's employer, or maybe the daughter of Leslie's employer? She was smartly dressed in a brown-and-white herringbone suit with a military influence. Her slimline skirt was just below the knee and she wore a black shiny belt over the jacket at the waist. It was very attractive but hardly top drawer. She was a plain-looking woman with long straight hair tied back into a chignon and she had soft brown eyes and a clear complexion. She was the sort of girl you might pass on the street and hardly notice, but to see the way Leslie looked at her anyone would think she was as beautiful as Betty Grable or Jean Simmons.

Ronnie handed them their tea. 'So you're a chauffeur?'

'Not for much longer,' said Leslie. 'My employer –' he glanced at Effie – 'our employer changes her staff quite frequently.'

'Leslie is a very good chauffeur,' Effie chipped in, 'but he hasn't quite come up to expectations.'

They looked at each other and laughed, but they didn't share the joke.

'The thing is,' Leslie began, 'she's decided to move abroad. Her new beau likes to travel.'

Ronnie and Sheila glanced at each other, not sure what was coming.

Leslie looked slightly uncomfortable. 'I'll be all right, but it's Eff, you see.'

'She's asked me to go with her,' said Effie, looking at Leslie, 'but we want to get married.'

'We're afraid that if Eff goes with her,' Leslie continued, 'she won't be able to come back.' He paused. 'I know it's a lot to ask . . .'

'But she needs somewhere to live,' said Sheila, finishing the sentence for him.

The happy couple nodded vigorously.

'Oh, Leslie,' Ronnie cried. 'We've only got one bedroom here.'

'And Granny?' Leslie ventured.

Sheila pursed her lips. 'Aunt Daisy lives with her.'

There was a small silence. Leslie and Effie looked

disappointed and a little awkward as everyone sipped their tea.

'Can I see your ring?' Ronnie asked.

Effie held out her left hand. The ring was a very pretty violet sapphire gemstone between two diamonds, one on each shoulder. After admiring it, Ronnie glanced up at her brother.

'And before you ask, I bought it,' he said as their eyes met. 'My Eff wouldn't have anything that was nicked.'

Ronnie felt her cheeks go pink and looked away, embarrassed. He'd read her thoughts exactly.

'I'm a reformed character now, Ron,' he said. 'Being with Eff has changed me.'

Effie shook her head modestly. 'Oh, Leslie . . .' Her face was pink with embarrassment.

Ronnie immediately warmed to this little woman who had become so important to her wayward, angry brother. 'So tell me,' she said, 'were you employed as a maid?'

'Maid, housekeeper, chief cook and bottle washer,' Effie said with a chuckle.

'You can cook?' said Sheila.

Effie nodded and Sheila grinned.

Downstairs, the dogs were barking. 'Sounds like Granny's here,' said Ronnie.

Sheila glanced at her cousin. 'Will you do the honours, Ron?' she said. 'I've got to pop out for a minute.'

There wasn't much work done that morning. By the time Granny and Aunt Daisy had been introduced there was a lot of catching up to do. Leslie was shocked to hear about the fire and even more alarmed to know that at one time he'd been blamed for it.

'In the end, it turned out it wasn't arson after all,' Ronnie said. 'Just a faulty fuse box.'

'I was pretty fed up that night,' said Leslie. 'I admit I came up here, but the only person I saw hanging about,' he said, 'was that policeman friend of Sheila's. He didn't see me, of course, but I did wave to that old boy up at the window.'

'Benny Steadman,' Ronnie said sadly.

'I never did know his name,' said Leslie, looking across the road. 'Is he still there?'

'He died,' said Ronnie.

'Oh,' said Leslie. 'Anyway, I ended up in the bar in the Thomas A Becket and that's where I met Mrs Harrison-Vane.' He squeezed Effie's hand and smiled lovingly. 'They say every cloud has a silver lining.'

Sheila, hot and breathless from running, burst through the door. 'Effie,' she cried, 'how would you feel about cooking for twenty-four children?'

Mrs Edwards took to Effie straight away. She not only offered her the job as cook, but she also offered her a room. It was only a small room, but it was just off the kitchen and at present it was being used as a dumping ground. 'I'll get the workmen in to do it up for you,' she promised. 'What colour would you like the walls?'

They discussed a wage, less her board and lodging, and Effie was to start as soon as she could. The old cook was delighted to relinquish her post and Mrs

Edwards heaved a sigh of relief that the vacancy was to be filled almost immediately.

'Where are you going to live, Leslie?' Ronnie asked her brother just before they left. 'And if you give up chauffeuring, what will you do?'

'I'm still working on that one,' Leslie said with a grin.

Matthew had been doing some thinking. It was time he made his next move. Since he'd bumped into Ronnie at her grandmother's place, he had purposely kept away from Sheila. He had hoped to surprise her when she walked through the door, but as it turned out he was the one who'd got the surprise. He'd been shocked to find out that she'd gone back to that bloody garage. He'd felt sure that with everything that had happened she would have got it out of her system by now, but it seemed nothing had changed. And she still had that accursed Kraut working there. He'd have to do something about that. Still, it shouldn't be too hard. A word here, a hint there; he'd find a way.

He was also annoyed with himself that he'd got so het up in that cafe. Of course, it was all Sheila's fault. If she hadn't been so flippin' unreasonable, she would have known she was making a big mistake. As it was, he'd been ill after that incident, or at least that's what he'd told his landlady when he'd been forced to take a couple of weeks off. If Sheila had been at her grandmother's that night he would have told her how ill he'd been and she would have been sorry for treating him so badly. But she wasn't. At the time he'd been confident that Ronnie would tell her how much he'd wept and how he'd pleaded with her cousin to tell him where she was. Now it occurred to him the bitch might not have said anything because Sheila still hadn't come to him. Well, he wasn't having that. He'd stayed away long enough.

He sat at his small table with the writing pad in front of him. How should he begin this letter? Reprimand her or make her feel guilty for treating him so shabbily first? He could lay it on thick. Say how desperately he'd wanted her to visit him. How his heart had ached for her to soothe his fevered brow. He could appeal to her better nature that way. She adored him, of this he was sure. Of course, she didn't realize it yet because she was only a young girl with no experience of life, but once they were married, he would nurture her and change her into the woman he wanted. He began writing.

My dearest Sheila,

I know you must have been worrying about me. I'm sorry I haven't been in touch before now but I have been very seriously ill. In fact my doctor feared for my life but you mustn't feel badly, my darling. I know you would have come to me had you known. Don't worry. I am a lot better now. I shall come to see you as soon as I can.

All my love,
Matthew

He leaned back in his chair. Yes, yes. That ought to do it. That should bring her running.

Neville had invited Sheila for a meal to celebrate his twenty-eighth birthday.

'Of course I'd love to come,' she'd said, 'but why not have a party with your friends?'

'I probably will when Mother and the old man get back from their trip,' he'd said, 'but I'd much rather spend some time with you on the day.'

Sheila didn't argue. It was an age since she'd been out and she was looking forward to it.

It was a bit of a mad dash to get ready. The garage closed at five thirty and Neville was coming for her at six forty-five. She had bought him a present, one of those brand-new writing instruments called a Biro. At thirty-four and ten pence, it was quite expensive (although probably not by his standards) and it came with a refill unit for when it ran out. Sheila had seen the advertisements in women's magazines and been impressed. Who wouldn't want a pen with a velvet touch, that didn't smudge and whose ink dried as you wrote?

Sheila had bought a new dress as well. It had a plain aqua-blue fitted bodice with a matching patterned skirt in the same colours and to finish it off there was a collar and floppy bow at the neck in the same material as the skirt. When Trixie dropped by, Sheila had been complaining that her whole outfit would be spoiled because her only coat was so shabby. The next thing she knew, Trixie had taken the matter in hand and Sheila had borrowed a coat from Trixie's mum. It was lightweight and in a dusty blue with a drape coming from the shoulders across the back. It was very stylish and went perfectly with the dress.

There were no restaurants open at night apart from the occasional greasy-spoon type, which was why they ended up in Shoreham. Neville had found a hotel which had a jazz club in the basement. As soon as he told her, Sheila was even more excited.

The evening began over dinner. They had to surrender their ration books, of course, but Neville was definitely in charge. He ordered them both an aperitif.

'So how's it going at the garage?'

'Very well,' said Sheila. 'I'd say we're almost back to normal.'

Neville smiled over the rim of his glass. 'And what about your aunt? Is she settling down?'

Sheila sipped her Beaujolais nouveau. It was delicious. 'Very well. She and Granny get on like a house on fire.'

Neville raised an eyebrow and Sheila laughed. 'Wrong figure of speech, eh?'

'Probably,' he grinned. 'Have you found out why she was so upset about being in Findon?'

Sheila looked thoughtful. 'Actually, I haven't. I suppose I should have tried to find out, but to be honest, these past few weeks haven't been easy for any of us.'

'You might be right there,' he chuckled. 'I'm just

glad Mother and the old man have been in sunnier climes.'

'When do they get back?'

'Next week,' said Neville. 'They fly into Croydon airport on Wednesday.'

'Oh dear,' Sheila teased. 'What's he going to say when he finds out you've been wining and dining the opposition?'

Neville leaned towards her. 'When I tell him how delectable she is, I'm sure he'll understand.'

Sheila felt her cheeks flush. The hors d'oeuvre arrived. It looked like four swans on a bed of spinach. The cook had cut a slice from each side of a boiled egg and piped cream cheese over the top. The cut pieces had been stuck back on to represent the wings and an S-shaped pipe cleaner had been inserted into the pointed end of the egg to represent the swan's neck.

'What a clever idea,' Sheila whispered confidentially. She raised her eyebrows. 'And two boiled eggs each in one go.'

Neville grinned. 'Such decadence.'

'I haven't asked about you,' she apologized as the waiter left them. 'Is your business going well?'

'Yes it is,' he said. 'With all this snow, there are plenty of breakdowns to keep us going, so takings are up. In fact, the garage at East Worthing has been rushed off its feet.'

'I'm glad,' she said, taking a swan wing off and scooping up some of the cream cheese with it. 'Mmm, this is delicious.' Normally people didn't like it when a rival business did well, but she was genuinely happy for him. How could she be anything else but pleased for a man who had been so generously kind to her and her family?

'And what about your policeman friend?' he said, without looking up from his plate.

Sheila felt slightly uncomfortable. Should she tell Neville about the last time she and Matthew met in that cafe? He'd been perfectly beastly then and Ronnie had told her how she'd caught him in Granny's rooms. What he was doing there, she couldn't imagine, but Sheila hadn't seen him since. It was a relief to know he'd finally got the message. In the silence, Neville glanced up at her.

'I'm not seeing him any more,' she said.

'Should I be happy or sad?'

Sheila looked away. She didn't want to spend the evening talking about Matthew. 'It was my decision.'

'Then I shall be happy,' said Neville, turning his attention back to his plate. 'Are those German POWs still with you?'

'Not quite as much,' said Sheila. 'Mr Hurst needs them to help out with the planting now. Anyway, I suppose they'll be sent home soon.'

Neville nodded. 'Pity. A good strong man is always handy for the heavy stuff.'

'I'm not sure when they will go,' said Sheila, 'but when they get permission, I get the feeling that Gerhard will want to stay. He'll need a sponsor, of course, and me being a woman, I'm not allowed to do it.'

'I'd sponsor him,' said Neville, putting his knife and fork down.

'Would you?' cried Sheila. 'Would you really?'

Neville shrugged. 'I don't see why not. If he's as good as you say, he deserves a chance. What about the other one?'

'Helmut? Oh, he'll go home all right. He can't wait. He hates it here.'

'I'm not surprised,' Neville said with a chuckle.. 'He always did look a miserable sod.'

Sheila laughed. 'He can't bear it that Gerhard is happy either. He's always moaning at him. I can't understand what he's saying because he speaks in German, but I can tell by the tone of his voice and Gerhard's reaction that he's giving the boy a bad time.'

'You do know he's a little bit in love with you, don't you?' said Neville.

'What, Helmut?'

'Gerhard.'

'I can't think why,' said Sheila, slightly irritated to hear this again. 'I've done nothing to encourage him.'

The waiter came and took their plates away. 'Don't be cross with me,' said Neville when they were alone again. 'I'm only telling you what I see.'

Sheila felt her face flush.

'If Gerhard can't stay, will you employ someone else to help with the heavy lifting?'

'Well, we do have Malcolm,' she said.

'Malcolm?'

'He took Derek Milne's place,' said Sheila. 'He's

another one of Mrs Edwards's boys from the children's home. We're offering him an apprenticeship.'

Neville nodded his approval.

After their main course, neither of them wanted a pudding, so Neville took her down to the basement club. It was hot and noisy, but it looked great fun. There were tables all along three sides of the bare brick walls and the chairs had been fashioned out of old beer barrels. 'What a brilliant idea,' Sheila said as they sat down. 'Ronnie would love these.'

The jazz music was amazing and the dancers very energetic. Before long, Neville and Sheila felt compelled to join in. The place was very crowded, but they didn't care. They danced until midnight and beyond, and by the time Neville brought her home, the garage was in darkness. Sheila had closed her eyes and nodded off almost as soon as she'd climbed into the car, her head resting against his shoulder. He turned off the engine and shook her gently. 'Wake up, Cinderella. You're home.'

She opened a sleepy eye and murmured, 'And thank you, Prince Charming, for an absolutely wonderful and magical evening.' But the most wonderful and magical moment was still to come because that was the moment he kissed her.

CHAPTER 33

It wasn't until Sheila had set out on her date with Neville Webster that Ronnie got around to reading Bruce's letter. She'd kept putting it off. She knew whatever it said would change the course of her life, but would it be for good or ill? One minute she was eager to read it, imagining that he would tell her he'd made a terrible mistake in marrying Caroline, but a moment later she was terrified that this really was the last goodbye and that her heart would be broken. She had spent most of the day getting the shed at the bottom of the garden up to scratch. Having built shelving and a counter area when they'd first moved in, she had long wanted to turn it into a tool and machine shop. It would complement the garage to have car accessories and other goods on the premises, but because of the shortages and the added difficulty of transportation, it had taken a while to get enough stock together.

Ronnie waved as Sheila slid gracefully into Neville's car. Poor Gerhard had looked quite crestfallen when her cousin had sashayed through the garage door.

Gone were her greasy overalls and the turban around her head and instead of her usual coat, which Ronnie agreed did look rather moth-eaten, she carried a pale oyster-coloured clutch bag and looked absolutely stunning in Mrs Rodway's blue coat. Funnily enough, just after they'd gone, Ronnie thought she saw Matthew Keller cycle by. She half expected him to come back and ask her where Sheila was going, but he didn't.

Ronnie poured herself a glass of the brandy they kept for medicinal purposes before she finally took the letter out of the envelope. Once again she was filled with a mixture of excitement and dread and she would probably need a stiff drink by the time she'd finished. It began:

My dearest Ronnie,

Her eyes widened. She hadn't expected him to address her like that.

I was so delighted when Angela Lyons sent me your address.

So that was how he'd found out where she lived. Ronnie wasn't sure whether to be angry or grateful.

I hope you don't mind me writing to you. I keep thinking you must be married after all this time. I can't imagine anyone as wonderful as you staying single for too long.

Ronnie frowned. This was all very suggestive. What would Caroline make of her husband writing to her in this fashion?

The girls and I have been living in Perth. Ruth is nearly nine now and quite the young lady. She has masses of freckles and she's put on quite a bit of weight since you last saw her.

Thank God for that, Ronnie thought to herself. The poor child was all skin and bone when they came out of the camp.

She's learning to play tennis and she is an excellent swimmer for her age.
    Elspeth will soon be having her seventh birthday. She's more into animals than anything else. We have a veritable zoo of pets; a cockatiel, some rabbits, a dog and six chickens. She tells me she wants to be a vet when she grows up and I'm inclined to believe she'll do it. Her school grades are good and she's not afraid of hard work.

Ronnie smiled. Elspeth had always been the determined one. She turned the page.

For a while I was part of the team set up to implement the Tokyo War Crimes Tribunal. I also was seconded to help head up the prison guard in the barracks. We had to make sure the Japanese POWs didn't commit suicide

before they were brought to justice, as well as keeping
aggrieved relatives and disgruntled Imperialists at bay.
As usual the British army was piggy-in-the-middle.
When demobilization came, I left the army and came
back to Australia. Without you, I felt I couldn't leave
my children in the hands of strangers any longer. They
need at least one parent.

Ronnie took in her breath. Only one parent? Where
was Caroline then? Could it be that he hadn't married
her after all?

The trial didn't start until April 1946 and, considering
that it's still going on, I'm sure I made the right
decision.
My darling . . .

Ronnie's heart lurched. For a moment her tears
obliterated the words on the page. She swallowed hard
and sniffed into her handkerchief.

My darling, by the time you read this, we shall be in
England. We are visiting my mother who, as you
know, lives in Worcester.

No, no, I didn't know that. Oh, Bruce, you called
me darling . . .

She's too old and frail to travel to Australia to see us,
so it seemed providential that Angela's letter should

arrive just as we were leaving. I should very much
like to see you, just as a friend if you are courting,
engaged, or if in fact you married your fiancé. I have
no wish to disturb your life but you were so wonderful
to my girls and I know they would love to see you as
well. Caroline told me how ill you were and how
anxious you were to get back home to your fiancé so
I quite understand why you refused to see me in
Geelong.

What fiancé? And Caroline said what? I never refused to see you, my darling. The cow. The barefaced liar! Hot tears of frustration and grief spilled onto the page. The thought of being with Bruce again was the only thing that had kept her going through all those terrible years in the prison camp; that and making sure the girls stayed alive. When she'd dropped them off in Geelong that day, Caroline had told her how much he still missed Mrs Lyle. Come to think of it, that was probably a lie as well. This letter was three pages long and he hadn't mentioned the children's mother once. She turned the page again.

Please say you will meet me. My feelings for you
haven't changed. I promise not to make trouble for
you especially if you are settled with someone, but
the girls and I would love to see you just one more
time.
    My love, always and forever,
    Bruce

Ronnie sobbed for some time. When she had stopped and she could see again, she looked at the last thing he'd written. It was an English address and telephone number.

Mrs Harrison-Vane had a cold and was confined to her bed so Leslie took the opportunity to take the day off. She had given him notice and he was to leave at the end of the week. Mrs Harrison-Vane was to fly out of the country on Sunday and she had wanted Effie to go with her. There had been the most awful row when Effie refused and as a result they were both to leave without references. It was tempting to just walk out, but they were both owed several weeks' wages.

Leslie took the car on the pretext that he had to get a new brake-light bulb from the garage and afterwards he headed towards Croydon.

The card Mr Archer had given him before the snows came with a vengeance was for the Beau Brummel Male Model Agency, Cranmer Road, Croydon. At first Leslie had scoffed at the idea but, after a while, it appealed to him. Besides, with such short notice, he had to find another job quickly. What could be better than spending a whole day wearing beautiful clothes? He might end up as a male mannequin in some swanky department store or get photographed in exotic places. He'd get paid for it and handsomely too, if what Effie had told him was right.

Cranmer Road turned out to be only about ten miles from his employer and he found it quite easily. The house was in one half of a terrace. The rest of the road had been bombed. Like so many areas of London, it had remained untouched since the Blitz. Bizarrely, the only other remaining part of the terrace was a garden gate, now covered in ivy and bindweed in the middle of a sea of fallen bricks and splintered wood. Clearing bomb sites would take some time and it was tempting to think, what was the point? There was a chronic shortage of timber, bricks were rationed and every bombed-out area had its quota of unexploded devices waiting to be discovered. Not all the land was left unused. In some places, waste ground was turned into car parks. In fact, Leslie had been reading that a new company called National Car Parks had just bought a bombsite on Red Lion Square, a place synonymous with the body of Oliver Cromwell. Effie had introduced him to the joys of reading and encouraged him to read books. Until he met her he'd never read more than the *Daily Mirror* sports pages. He didn't take to reading stories, but he had discovered a whole new world in non-fiction books. That's how he'd found out that Oliver Cromwell's corpse had rested in Red Lion Square when, bizarrely, the new Royalist authorities had it disinterred from Westminster Abbey. Then they had posthumously tried it and 'executed' it at Tyburn. Leslie loved little bits of useless information like that.

He parked up and knocked on the door of the agency. It was opened by a man who was the spitting image of Mr Archer. For a second or two, Leslie was thrown. The man chuckled.

375

'I get that reaction all the time,' he said. 'You've obviously met my twin brother.'

'He gave me this card,' said Leslie, holding it out. 'Leslie Jackson.'

'Ah yes,' said Mr Archer number two. 'He mentioned that you might pass by although, I have to say, that was quite some time ago.'

'I get so little free time,' Leslie said apologetically.

'Not to worry, you're here now.' He led the way down a dingy corridor. It was all beginning to look rather seedy until Leslie found himself in a light and airy office. He felt a sense of relief. The office was nicely furnished. Mr Archer sat behind an impressive mahogany desk and Leslie lowered himself into a comfortable Chesterfield chair, albeit one which had seen slightly better days, opposite.

'I can see why my brother sent you,' said Mr Archer. 'You have a strong jawline and your skin is unblemished.' Leslie was grateful that the scars from his beating at the hands of Carter's gang had well and truly faded. Mr Archer put his elbows onto the table and pressed his fingertips together. 'May I see your hands?'

When Leslie opened his hands, he seemed impressed. 'Mmm, well-manicured and attractive. Very clean,' he murmured.

Leslie supressed a self-satisfied smile.

'If you would like to give this a try,' Mr Archer went on, 'I'll take some photographs of you and place your details on the books. The work is unpredictable and

I see by your uniform that you are a chauffeur. Will you have enough time off to model?'

'I won't be doing this much longer,' said Leslie.

Mr Archer asked him if he wouldn't mind showing him his feet. Leslie took off his shoes. 'What sort of things will I be modelling?'

'Anything the client wants,' said Mr Archer. 'You have wonderfully straight toes and very attractive hands. It might be gloves, socks, footwear or clothing, but I hasten to add, Mr Jackson, that this is a respectable agency. Nothing smutty.'

Leslie was tempted to say, good job, my Effie wouldn't have it any other way, but he held his tongue.

'I don't envisage you will have to wait long before you have a client,' Mr Archer added.

Leslie leaned back in the chair.

'There's an initial joining fee of fifteen pounds,' said Mr Archer. 'That covers your photographs, portfolio and publicity. After that, it's fifteen per cent of earnings.'

Leslie made no comment. Fifteen pounds was a bit steep, but he was happy to part with fifteen per cent of earnings. Something told him Mr Archer would be eager to find him work; after all, no work equalled no pay, equalled no fifteen per cent.

'You should be able to get at least ten pounds per photoshoot.'

Leslie tried to look nonchalant. Ten pounds, eh? Ten pounds! That was amazing.

'So,' said Mr Archer, 'shall I get the ball rolling?'

Leslie nodded and pulled out his wallet. As he opened

it, he looked at the picture of Effie taken at the church social. She'd dropped the photograph and hadn't noticed that it had slipped under the kitchen dresser. He did feel a tad guilty that he hadn't given it back to her, but he'd so badly wanted a little memento to keep with him at all times. It wasn't stealing, was it, not so long as he promised himself he'd give it back to her one day. He ran his thumb over her dear face and took fifteen pounds from the back of the wallet.

Sheila yawned. She was struggling to muster enough energy to do her work and it didn't help to be sent out on a false errand. They'd had a call-out for a broken-down tractor, but when she reached the farm, the farmer had no knowledge of the call.

Last night had been so fantastic and she'd enjoyed every minute. Ronnie had been all ears at breakfast time, but after less than four hours' sleep, Sheila could only manage a monosyllabic conversation. It was evening before they could sit down for a real chat. Ronnie had had a hectic day as well so they settled for fish and chips straight from the newspaper and sat down at the desk to eat them.

'So,' said Ronnie, dipping a chip into a puddle of HP sauce, 'spill the beans. How did you get on last night, where did you go and did he kiss you? And more than one word, please.'

'Whoa,' cried Sheila. 'Give us a chance. Now let me see. Very well, jazz club and yes.'

Ronnie chuckled. 'Okay, now fill in the blanks.'

'I've never danced so much, not even in the wartime dances at the base. Neville is a brilliant dancer. I reckon he could be in the pictures.'

'Ooh,' Ronnie teased. 'Regular Fred Astaire, is he?'

Sheila cuffed her cousin playfully on the shoulder. 'Are you seeing him again?'

'I hope so,' said Sheila. 'He didn't make another date, but I think he enjoyed himself as much as I did.'

'You really like him, don't you?' Ronnie observed. Her cousin was starry-eyed.

Sheila nodded. 'Yes, I do.'

'He certainly treats you better than Matthew.'

'Yes, he does.' Sheila smiled. 'Oh, Ronnie, I'm so happy. I wish you could find someone too.'

Ronnie screwed up her newspaper and stood up.

'Ronnie?' Sheila had noticed that her cousin's face was rather pink. 'What is it?' She gasped. 'You have met someone, haven't you? Why didn't you tell me? You sly old dog.'

'Not exactly,' said Ronnie. 'You remember I told you about a man in Australia?'

'Don't tell me he's got in touch.'

Ronnie nodded. 'More than that. He's in England.'

Sheila rushed to give Ronnie a hug. 'But that's fantastic.' Ronnie's body language was rather stiff. 'Isn't it?'

'Yes,' said Ronnie, 'and no.' Her eyes were glassy with unshed tears.

'Come on,' said Sheila. 'Sit down and tell me everything.'

They sat in the gloom of the office, not wanting to change their surroundings in case the moment was lost.

'He was my employer,' Ronnie said miserably. She glanced up at Sheila, expecting a look of reproof or disgust, but her cousin remained impassive. 'We didn't do anything wrong – not really wrong, that is.'

'I'm sure you didn't,' Sheila said reassuringly.

'Oh, Sheila, it was so hard even being in the same room as him. I loved him so much and Mrs Lyle was so awful to him. She had at least two affairs while we were in Singapore. I couldn't bear seeing him so humiliated. Everybody talked about it.'

'Lummy,' said Sheila, 'hardly the perfect wife then? Why on earth didn't he divorce her?'

'Because he adored his children,' said Ronnie. 'The courts would have given her custody as the mother.'

'Surely not if she was unfaithful.'

'She was a very clever woman,' said Ronnie, a hint of bitterness creeping in. 'She was the sort of woman who had men eating out of the palm of her hand. That's why she wouldn't go home at the start of it.'

'I thought you said she couldn't because the tickets went missing.'

'That's right,' said Ronnie. 'All I told you was true, but we had known the Japs were coming maybe four or five months before it all kicked off.' Ronnie blew into her handkerchief. 'But she wouldn't go because she had just started an affair with one of the other officers.'

'So you were captured.'

Ronnie nodded. 'Of course, we all tried to make the

best of it, the overcrowded boat, lousy food and sparse washing facilities. She hated it and went on and on and on about it. I can't tell you how embarrassing it was having her moaning and complaining all over the shop, and of course, I felt so guilty all the time.'

'But you hadn't done anything.'

'I went to his office. We promised each other when it was all over we'd be together. We kissed . . .'

'For God's sake, Ronnie, what's wrong with that?'

'He was a married man.'

Sheila rubbed her cousin's arm.

'You know the worst thing?' said Ronnie. 'For a moment back there when she died, I was glad. I feel so ashamed about it now, but I was glad.'

'Oh, Ronnie, don't make yourself miserable over something you can't change,' Sheila said stoutly. 'You're not a bad person.'

'All the other women in the camp hated her,' said Ronnie, lowering her voice. 'She used to sleep with the commandant.'

Sheila gasped. 'What! The woman sounds like a ruddy nymphomaniac.'

'She had a little hut away from the rest of us,' said Ronnie, the bitterness in her voice creeping back again. 'She had proper tea and real food. We were all in rags but she had whole dresses.' She paused and gazed into space. 'It wouldn't have been so bad if she'd slept with him for the sake of her two little girls, but she didn't. She did it all for herself, Sheila. All for herself: for a lipstick or a half-bottle of gin.'

Ronnie put her hands over her face and broke down.

They sat together for some time, Ronnie weeping and Sheila comforting her. Afterwards neither could remember what was said, but it helped. In the end, Sheila reminded Ronnie that she had brought two little girls back from hell and reunited them with their father. Ronnie nodded dully.

'Is he coming to see you?'

'He wants to,' said Ronnie. 'He's here because his mother is unwell. He goes back in a few weeks.'

'Then you must see him,' Sheila insisted.

'Oh, I want to, Sheila, but Mrs Lyle—'

'Mrs Lyle nothing,' Sheila said firmly. 'The woman is dead, Ronnie. You did your best but she's dead. You can't let the past ruin your future.'

'I still feel so bad about it.'

'Don't be an ass,' Sheila said. 'You've got a man who still loves you, a decent man and a ready-made family. Are you really going to chuck all that away because you feel bad about a woman who, quite frankly, sounds like an absolute cow?'

'I suppose if you put it like that,' Ronnie said cautiously.

'I bet if she were still alive she wouldn't give a toss about him or the girls, would she?'

'No,' said Ronnie quietly. 'I suppose not.'

'So what about them, Ronnie? What about their happiness?'

Ronnie gave her cousin a wavery smile. 'Thanks, Sheila. I guess you're right.'

CHAPTER 34

Matthew was livid. How could she do it? This was definitely a step too far. He'd waited for her at the garage only to see her dressed up like a dog's dinner and going off with that chap from Webster's. Worse still, he'd waited for her to come home and been stuck there in the bushes for seven hours. Seven bloody hours! He'd been frozen to the marrow and terrified that she wouldn't come home at all. Finally at around two in the morning – two in the morning! – he'd watched helplessly as that brute had mauled her around in his car before he'd let her go. He didn't go after her, although he'd wanted to. Webster hung around until she'd gone indoors. Damn his eyes. He couldn't let this go, could he? She would have to be punished. He had loved her for so long and this was the way she repaid him? Oh no, it wasn't right. She had to learn. She'd have to pay. She had to be punished.

Ten days later, Ronnie and Sheila opened the new shop. They didn't go as far as inviting a celebrity to come and cut the ribbon, but they did send a personal invitation to all their regular customers as well as displaying a large poster on the forecourt. If curiosity wouldn't entice them to come, Ronnie decided, the promise of a cup of tea and a piece of pie might do the trick, so she'd asked Aunt Daisy to do some baking. As always, Ronnie, the entrepreneur, had an ulterior motive. She secretly hoped that the pies would be such a success that Granny would allow Aunt Daisy to utilize the caravan on the forecourt to sell her wares. Both the caravan and Aunt Daisy were standing idle, something Ronnie felt should be rectified as soon as possible. In case Aunt Daisy felt overwhelmed by her customers, Trixie had been seconded to help behind the counter. The grand opening was scheduled for March 22nd, a Saturday, at ten o'clock, and fortunately the weather was good.

Effie had moved into the children's home and was settling in nicely. Matron felt confident to leave the running of the kitchen to her new cook and Effie had already sent one supplier, a butcher, packing. He charged a reasonable rate, but Effie decided his products were inferior. 'Growing children need good food,' she'd said with emphasis. Having prepared shepherd's pies for lunch the day before, Effie promised to be at the opening too.

Sheila had a couple of early-morning jobs; someone from Ferring had rung up to say their car wouldn't start and she had a tractor tyre to put on the air compressor, but she would be ready by ten. Ronnie wasn't expecting her back until about nine forty-five so she was surprised to see her cousin turning into the forecourt just after nine.

'That was quick.'

'Another false alarm,' Sheila said crossly.

'What do you mean?'

'I went all the way over to Ferring,' said Sheila, throwing her map back into the van, 'only to find that there was no Mrs Cranleigh and no car to be repaired. The man at the address said he'd never even heard of her and he'd lived in the same village for fifty years. What a stupid waste of time.'

Ronnie, who was putting Nelson on a long leash by the door so that he didn't bother the customers, frowned. 'Someone is doing this on purpose,' she said. 'That's the second time this week.'

'I know,' said Sheila. 'Somebody's idea of a joke, I suppose.' She threw her driving gloves onto the bench. 'I'm going upstairs to change.'

'What about the tyre?' said Ronnie. 'Mr Forester has already rung up about it.'

'I'll do it as soon as I come back down,' Sheila called as she took the stairs two at a time. 'I just need a couple of minutes to myself to calm down.'

When Ronnie got back to the shop, Granny and Aunt Daisy were putting the pies in neat rows on the table provided just outside the door. Trixie was already trying to memorize the prices. Milly set off in search of Nelson.

'They look amazing,' said Ronnie. And so they did. Aunt Daisy blushed modestly as her niece kissed her cheek. There were several different types all neatly labelled. Sausage-meat pie, vegetable, homity pie (cheese, leek and potato filling), leek and lentil pie, Kentish pasties (rice, cheese and carrot filling) and, of course, Daisy's famous Surprise Pie. All four of them had pooled their rations for the past couple of weeks to make sure they had enough ingredients.

It didn't take long for a crowd to gather and Aunt Daisy was doing a roaring trade. Pen Albright had come with her husband and two boys. Then there was Mrs Hargreaves and a few others from Pavilion Road, Elsie, and John and Grace Steadman from the house opposite.

'You've done a good job of this, Ronnie.' Dick Albright's praise was heartfelt.

'This is a grand pie, lady,' said John as he bit into a sausage-meat pie. 'You should do this for a living.'

As soon as she arrived, Effie bought and sampled a homity pie. She was impressed.

'I reckon you could teach my missus a thing or two about pies,' said Percy Bawden, wiping his mouth with the back of his sleeve.

'Here, you!' said Eva Bawden, giving him a well-aimed clout. 'I heard that.'

Several of the assembled crowd laughed.

'Can I buy one of them buckets?' said a voice. 'Mine has been mended so many times I can't tell which is the patch and which bit is the whole.' More laughter.

Several children had turned up without their mothers, but Ronnie doubted if they had come to buy. She didn't mind too much and, as long as they had a good look around, she was sure they'd be back another day.

Others had come with a purpose. Mr Spurgen, the retired teacher, said he was looking for a new claw hammer, and several members of the Christmas choir came with shopping lists.

'I love the shop, Ronnie.'

'Open at last! I never thought I'd finally see the day.'

'Well done, girls. Very impressive.'

The compliments came thick and fast. Ronnie smiled contentedly. After the terrible winter everyone had endured, this was a happy gathering.

After her quick wash, Sheila had changed into a clean pair of dungarees and she felt a whole lot better. She glanced up at the clock. Oh dear, two minutes to ten already. She hurried downstairs. She really should go down to the shop straight away. Ronnie had made it clear she wanted both of them at the grand opening, but Charlie Forester would be here any minute for his tractor tyre. She hesitated by the door. Go or stay? In the end she decided it wouldn't take long so she quickly laid the tyre on its side and reached for the compressed-air machine. Just as she plugged it in place, a shadow fell across her back, but she didn't look up. It didn't take much guessing to know who it was. 'Okay, okay,' she said as she switched the machine on. 'Just give me two minutes and I'll be ready.'

With no sign of Sheila as twenty past ten rolled by, Ronnie decided she'd better let everyone in.

They had been selling some of the stock in the new

shop well before Ronnie had created it, but now the variety was much better. The country's shortages may have meant that it had taken a while to get everything together, but they had carpentry tools, garden equipment, nuts and bolts, watering cans and such like. As well as the usual bicycle parts and a Tilly lamp, you could also buy a monkey wrench, a porcelain Prestone anti-freeze thermometer, an outdoor broom, a washboard or even a tin bath.

As everyone squeezed in to browse, Granny put her head round the door. 'Ronnie, love, put one of those clothes props on one side for me, will you? Ours is so wonky, I'm afraid it's going to collapse at any minute.'

Ronnie nodded as they both became vaguely aware that the dogs were barking. Granny frowned. 'Milly's a bit noisy,' she remarked.

'Probably because I've put Nelson on the leash,' said Ronnie.

After about fifteen minutes, the buzz of conversation was suddenly cut short by an almighty explosion. It was followed by two terrific bangs and the sound of something breaking. Everyone stopped talking and looked at each other in stunned surprise.

'What the hell was that?' Dick Albright murmured.

'Sounded like it came from the garage,' said Ronnie.

A child began to cry.

'Could it have been an unexploded bomb?' Effie suggested.

'There's no damage to the building,' said John

Steadman. 'If that was a bomb it would have taken the whole lot down.'

'We didn't have any bombs around here,' someone else said.

'Oh my God!' cried Ronnie, her hand flying to her mouth. 'The tyre! The tyre must have exploded. Sheila. Sheila's in there.' She pushed past them, and then, as if they were one man, everybody began to run towards the garage. A customer who had just drawn up to the pumps sat ashen-faced in his car.

'Steady, girl,' Dick shouted as Ronnie tore up the path. 'You don't know what you'll find.' As she drew nearer the garage, Ronnie slowed down and walked cautiously towards the open door. Nelson was straining at his leash, as if he was desperate to run. He was trembling all over with his tail between his legs. He was obviously in a state of shock, but Ronnie didn't think to comfort him. There was no sign at all of Milly either, but all her thoughts were towards her cousin.

Inside the garage was a scene of utter chaos. The big tractor wheel whose tyre Sheila had been inflating was in shreds. It was quite clear that the tyre had exploded. The wheel rim had been hurled upwards and hit the ceiling, leaving a large dent in one of the wooden rafters. Ronnie's gaze drifted down. The sound of something breaking must have been when the steel rim came down from the rafters and landed on the bonnet and windscreen of another car waiting for a service. The bonnet had caved in and the windscreen was smashed.

'She must have over-inflated it,' said John Steadman, coming up behind her. He picked up the rim. 'Not a good idea to leave it unsupervised, you know.'

Ronnie was still trying to take all this in. Sheila wasn't careless. She was always very conscientious in her work. She knew inflating big tyres was dangerous and for that reason she was always very careful.

'They always put big tyres in a cage in the garage up the road when they inflate them,' said Len Hurst. 'Less damage that way if they get too much air in them.'

'I read in *Tit-Bits* about some bloke in Australia being killed by an exploding tyre,' someone else said. 'They had a picture of the outline of his body on the ceiling.'

As if on cue, everyone looked up. Thankfully, apart from the dent in the rafter, there was nothing else.

'So where is Sheila?' said Effie.

'Is this her shoe?' Pen called from the doorway. She was holding up a black shoe, the lace still done up.

Ronnie's blood ran cold. Had Sheila been injured? Oh Lord, that must be it. She must have gone upstairs to lie down. Ronnie bolted up the stairs two at a time, shouting, 'Sheila? Are you up here, Sheila?' She flew around their flat, but there was no sign of her cousin. When she came downstairs, she could contain her tears no longer. 'So where is she? Where's Sheila?'

CHAPTER 35

'Could she have gone after Milly?'

Ronnie and her friends had spent the last twenty minutes hunting for Sheila. They had scoured every inch of the garage in case she had been thrown into some inaccessible corner and been covered by debris, but to no avail. They had even searched the hedge outside. With every other idea proving fruitless, Granny's suggestion certainly sounded feasible. Sheila could have been injured by the blast and gone after the dog in a confused state. She could be lying in the road somewhere or maybe she'd passed out. As Ronnie raced around the streets, she called and called her name.

Back at the garage, most people had gone home. Aunt Daisy had sold most of her pies before the shop was even open so with Effie's help she had packed up everything and shut the shop door. Trixie and Pen had lent them a hand too. After that, Effie made her apologies.

'I've got to get back to see to the children's lunch,' she said. 'I'm so sorry to run off like this, but I'm new to the job and I don't want to blot my copybook.'

'Don't you worry about that, my dear,' said Pen.

'Keep me informed, won't you?' Effie cried as she ran back down the path.

Granny had been trying to comfort Nelson. He was in such a nervous state he'd had diarrhoea and he was still shaking like a leaf. Until Ronnie appeared in the doorway alone, everyone was convinced that Sheila would soon return.

'No sign of her?' Granny asked anxiously.

Ronnie shook her head. 'I've been down every road,' she said. 'Highfield, Northfield, Chantry and Highdown Avenue. I even came back via Rectory Road, but she's nowhere to be seen.'

'It's a bit worrying that we only found one shoe,' said Pen, joining her in the garage. 'Does she have any other shoes?'

'Only her working shoes,' said Ronnie.

'Could she have gone out in them?' Granny asked.

Ronnie hurried up to the flat. Sheila's manky old working shoes were in their usual place at the top of the stairs. When she came back down again, shaking her head, she saw their disappointed faces.

'Who would go out wearing only one shoe?' said Pen.

'Who indeed?' said a male voice and they all turned to see Neville standing in the doorway. 'Good Lord,' he said, looking around. 'What happened here? This place looks like a bomb's hit it.'

As Ronnie filled him in, everyone became more and more concerned.

'Look,' said Neville when she'd finished, 'I'll take Mrs Peters and Daisy home and then I'll drive around a bit. Perhaps she got hurt and took herself off to Dr Rodway's surgery.'

Ronnie let out a sigh of relief. Of course, that's what had happened. Why hadn't she thought of that? 'I'll come too,' she said.

'Better if you stay here in case she turns up,' said Neville. 'She'll be glad to see a friendly face.'

'We'll take Nelson,' said Granny. 'You don't want to be worrying about him at a time like this.'

'Are you sure?' Ronnie asked.

'Absolutely,' said Granny, 'and if I'm not mistaken, I have a feeling Milly will be waiting on the doorstep.'

Ronnie gave the dog a hug and a pat. He was still a bag of nerves, but he seemed happy to go with them. Neville took him on the lead. Nobody wanted him to take off like Milly had.

With Granny, Daisy and Neville gone, Ronnie was only vaguely aware of Pen drifting away. She sat at the desk with her head in her hands. She didn't know how she felt. Numb, puzzled, hurt? Her feelings were all jumbled up. A little while later, Pen put a cup and saucer in front of her.

'Here,' she said. 'Get that down your neck. It's strong, it's hot and it's sweet. You've had a nasty shock.'

'I don't understand it, Pen,' Ronnie said, looking up. 'Sheila would never just run off like that.'

'People do funny things when they're in a state of shock,' said Pen.

'But that man who pulled up for petrol just as the tyre blew up said he didn't see anyone coming out,' Ronnie insisted.

Pen shrugged her shoulders.

'And why leave one shoe behind? You can't run far with only one shoe.'

Pen sighed. 'I feel exactly the same as you, love. I've been trying to think of a logical reason for all this, but you're right. It's very odd.'

Ronnie sipped her tea.

'Did you two have a row?'

Ronnie shook her head.

Pen pursed her lips and looked thoughtful. They heard footsteps coming along the path. Ronnie stood up eagerly, but it was only Neville.

'Any sign?' he asked.

Ronnie shook her head and sat back down.

'Nothing,' said Pen. 'We just can't fathom it out.'

'I've been all around the roads,' said Neville, 'but I couldn't see her. Has she ever done anything like this before?'

'Of course not,' Ronnie said crossly.

'She told me her parents were killed in an explosion,' said Neville. 'It did cross my mind that the tyre going off like that might have affected her mentally in some way.'

Ronnie stood up in a defensive manner.

'I think if she had been in the garage at the time,' said Pen, laying a calming hand on Ronnie's arm, 'she would have been injured in some way, but as you can see for yourself, there's no blood, no sign of injury, nothing.'

Neville nodded. 'You're absolutely right.' He picked up Sheila's shoe and turned it over in his hands. 'That only leaves one other possibility.' The two women looked up at him. 'Someone has taken her.'

Pen gasped and put her hand to her mouth. Ronnie lowered herself back into the chair. 'Oh God . . .'

'Any ideas?'

Ronnie shook her head.

'Now think carefully,' Neville went on. 'Have you noticed anything odd happening lately?'

Ronnie's eyes widened. 'Well, yes,' she began. 'Now that you come to mention it, some weird things have been happening.'

Neville perched himself with one leg on the corner of the desk. 'Go on. This could be important.'

'Well, early this morning, someone rang to ask Sheila to start their car. She went all the way to Ferring, but there was no car and nobody knew anything about it.'

'Oh, Ronnie,' Pen whimpered.

'And that wasn't the first time,' said Ronnie.

'But surely if someone wanted to kidnap her,' Pen interrupted, 'they would have done it then, away from the garage?'

'Go on, Ronnie,' said Neville. 'Then there was what?'

'The milk,' said Ronnie.

Neville frowned. 'The milk?'

'We kept getting sour milk on the doorstep,' Ronnie went on. 'Well, you know how cold it's been. So I waited for Armpit Price and challenged him about it. He pointed out that the bottles belonged to Coronation Dairies. Our milk comes from Oakland Dairies in Elm Grove.'

'I don't see what that has to do with anything,' said Pen.

'Someone was deliberately swapping our bottles,' Ronnie said impatiently.

'But why?' Neville asked.

Ronnie shrugged.

'Kids,' said Pen. 'Just kids mucking about.'

'Then there's the letters,' said Ronnie. 'We had several poison-pen letters, remember?'

'You didn't seem too bothered about them,' said Pen.

'They weren't very nice,' said Ronnie. 'I didn't want to think about them.'

'Did you take them to the police in the end?' Neville asked.

'Sheila gave a couple to Matthew,' she said. 'He said the matter was in hand, but nothing happened so we chucked the rest in the drawer.'

'Where are they now?' Neville asked.

Ronnie threw herself against the back of her chair. 'Destroyed in the fire.'

'Oh Lord, Ronnie, the fire!' Pen cried.

'That was caused by a faulty fuse box,' said Ronnie, her voice flat. She sat up again. 'But somebody reported us to the police. They came here twice to search the place.'

'Reported you for what?' said Neville.

'They didn't say,' said Ronnie, 'but they went through all the paperwork.'

Neville frowned. 'Have you told the police what you've told us?'

'Only Matthew,' said Ronnie, 'and like I said, nothing happened.'

'Anything else?' Neville asked.

Ronnie shook her head. 'Oh, apart from the oil leak,' she went on. 'We thought that was sabotage. Someone made a hole in the side of the drum and it went all over the place.'

Neville looked concerned. 'Right now,' he went on, 'we need to write all this down and anything else you remember, with dates if you can.'

'Why?'

'We're going to take it to the police.'

'They won't take any notice,' said Ronnie. 'Matthew said he tried but he got nowhere, and from the moment we told them about the break-in, they just weren't interested.'

'I think we all agree that one or two isolated incidents don't seem like much,' said Neville, 'but put them all together and it sounds to me like somebody has been making mischief.'

'You honestly think this has something to do with Sheila's disappearance?' said Pen. 'Stolen milk bottles and kidnapping hardly fit in the same league.'

'I suppose it could mean that the pranks have got out of hand,' said Neville, 'but . . .'

'Sheila would never just go off with someone without telling me,' said Ronnie.

'Exactly,' said Neville.

'So how are you settling in, Effie?'

Mrs Edwards was making a rare trip down to the kitchen. Her new cook looked calm and unruffled. She seemed very efficient too. It was two thirty and lunch was well and truly over. Everything was washed up and back in its place. In fact, the kitchen looked like a showroom and Effie was already preparing the teas. There would be sandwiches and cake for everyone.

She nodded. 'I think I'm going to like it here, madam,' she said, 'but I could do with a little more help.'

Mrs Edwards swallowed hard. More help would be more expense and the budget was tight enough already. 'You seem to be managing very well, Effie,' she said, looking around.

'I am,' said Effie, 'but like I say, I could do with more help. I'm on the go all day, with no time to do the shopping and even less time to do the books.'

'What shopping?' said Mrs Edwards. 'We have everything on standing order.'

Effie nodded. 'That's just the trouble, madam,' she said. 'In my experience, traders on standing orders take advantage. Did you know your butcher was charging you top prices? In my first week here he sent scrag-end of lamb and tried to charge me for shoulder. And Mr Mulberry, the grocer, is never on time with his delivery, which makes it very hard to plan the menus, especially when half the stuff I ask for isn't available.'

Mrs Edwards blinked. This was the longest sentence Effie had ever spoken. Her old cook had never complained, but if she was honest, she only cooked the same thing all the time. Everyone knew exactly what day of the week it was by what was dished up at mealtimes. Effie had brought some much-needed variety to the table.

'I have very limited funds for staff wages,' Mrs Edwards said apologetically.

'I realize that, madam,' said Effie, 'but with a few other economies, it shouldn't cost any more than you already pay.'

Put like that, how could Mrs Edwards refuse. 'Do you have anyone in mind?'

Effie thought back to Daisy's delicious pies. 'As a matter of fact, I do.'

'But there were no signs of a struggle?'

Inspector Sandgate leaned back in his chair with a rather tired expression. Ronnie and Neville had made their way into the new police station in Union Place and asked to speak to someone. Inspector Sandgate had volunteered to see them, but now he wished he hadn't. He had better things to do than listen to some fantastic yarn about a kidnap.

'There could have been a struggle,' said Ronnie. 'The trouble is, when we all heard the explosion, everybody came running. A couple of dozen footprints would have covered the tracks.'

'Umm,' said the inspector. 'I can see that you are concerned about your cousin, but she's hardly a missing person. She hasn't been gone long enough for a start.' Ronnie attempted to say something, but he put his hand up to stop her. 'She could have gone off by herself.' He glanced at Neville. 'Women do funny things sometimes.' He leaned towards him and added confidentially, 'You know, time of the month and all that.'

'Wearing only one shoe?' Neville challenged.

'There's no indication that she was wearing those shoes,' the inspector said patiently. 'You yourself admitted that you didn't see what she was wearing at the time.'

'She only has two pairs of shoes,' Ronnie said.

'She could have bought another pair you don't know about,' the inspector said.

His patronizing attitude was beginning to annoy Neville. He rose to his feet. 'This is a waste of time.'

'Look,' said Sandgate, 'if she's not back in forty-eight hours, come back and tell us. That's when we can start a missing person investigation, although I have to say, there may not be much we can do. People go missing all the time. Things get on top of them and they just take off.'

Ronnie sighed. She'd had a feeling this might happen. The two men stood back to let her go through the door first. 'Before we go,' she said, glancing sympathetically at Neville, 'could we speak to PC Keller? He and Sheila used to go out together. They were close at one time. He might know something.'

'Ask the desk sergeant,' said Inspector Sandgate, anxious to get back to some real policing. 'I can't say I can place the name, but then I haven't been here very long.'

When they asked him, the desk sergeant frowned. 'Keller? He was dismissed from the force. He hasn't worked here since January.'

Ronnie gasped. 'But I don't understand. Dismissed? Why, what had he done?'

'I'm not at liberty to say,' the sergeant said stiffly, 'but believe me, he's no longer a member of His Majesty's police force.'

'Then maybe you could help us,' said Ronnie. 'Matthew was investigating some poison-pen letters we'd been receiving. I just wondered if he'd found anything.'

'Poison-pen letters?' said the sergeant. 'First I've heard about it.'

'But he brought them here,' Ronnie insisted. 'He said, "leave it to me and I'll sort it".'

After checking through his report book, the sergeant called and a constable appeared behind him. 'Fetch last year's book, will you, Finchley?'

Having checked that one as well, the sergeant shook his head. 'Nothing about poison-pen letters has been reported in this station.'

Shocked and surprised, Ronnie allowed Neville to guide her out of the building. Her mind was in turmoil. Dismissed as long ago as January? But surely Matthew had been in uniform that day when she'd found him at Granny's? Come to think of it, she'd often seen him riding his bicycle in his uniform. Yes, she'd seen him outside the garage the evening Neville took Sheila to the jazz club. That was only a while ago. He hadn't acknowledged her, but it was definitely him.

'Excuse me, miss.' Ronnie and Neville turned to see PC Finchley follow them from the building. 'I couldn't help overhearing you at the desk.' He ushered them to the side of the pavement. 'Keller and I shared the same digs,' he went on. 'You obviously don't know what happened.'

'He used to go out with my cousin,' Ronnie repeated.

'I remember her at the New Year's Ball,' he said.

'He was asked to leave and he made a scene,' said Ronnie. 'It was all in the papers.'

'After that fiasco,' Finchley went on, 'he was sent on indefinite leave until he had to appear before a disciplinary panel. They fined him a month's pay.'

'Your sergeant said he was dismissed,' said Neville.

'Because he threw a punch at one of the panel,' said Finchley.

'Oh my goodness,' said Ronnie, putting her hand to her mouth.

'We all know what a pompous ass the chief super is,' he said, lowering his voice and speaking confidentially, 'but to lash out like that was asking for trouble. The thing is, Keller always did have a short fuse. I wouldn't like to be on the wrong side of him, I can tell you. Your cousin is well shot of him.'

Ronnie could hardly believe her ears. She'd never

liked Matthew, but the only time she'd ever seen him lose his temper was when she'd caught him in Granny's rooms, and she'd put that down to frustration.

'Does he still live in the same digs?' asked Neville.

The PC shook his head. "Fraid not. He got chucked out about three weeks ago. Didn't pay the rent. He even stopped washing. The landlady got fed up with it.'

'So where is he now?' asked Ronnie.

'No idea,' said the policeman. 'I haven't seen him around Worthing so I guess he's long gone.'

'Well, thanks,' said Neville, shaking the man's hand.

As they walked to the car, Ronnie was feeling quite down. She had hoped Matthew might have been able to make a suggestion as to where Sheila could be. 'So where do we go from here?' she said hopelessly.

Neville shook his head and sighed. 'I haven't the faintest idea.'

CHAPTER 36

Because it was Effie's day off, they had prepared today's lunch yesterday. Daisy just had to prepare the carrots, open a tin of peas and remember to put the macaroni cheese in the oven on time. It was no problem and the meals went into the nursery flawlessly. She was beginning to feel a lot more confident. Her heart didn't race in panic quite so often these days. Effie was a sweet girl and although Daisy was the elder of the two of them, she was never made to feel stupid.

Daisy took off her apron and crept towards the dining room where the children were eating their dinner. The door was slightly ajar so she watched them from the shadows. They sat at little tables happily tucking in to the nourishing meal she had provided. Daisy smiled and wondered about her own little girl. Of course, she'd be all grown up now, but maybe she'd once sat at a table like that. Or, better still, maybe she'd gone to live with a nice family, a mummy and a daddy who had loved her. A tear etched Daisy's eye and she sighed. That was one thing she would never know.

A footfall behind her made her jump and she turned to see Mrs Edwards.

'You like watching the children, don't you, Daisy?' Her tone was kindly, but Daisy was immediately thrown into a panic.

'Sorry,' she blurted out. 'I didn't mean anything by it. Sorry, sorry.'

'It's all right, Daisy,' said Mrs Edwards. She smiled and touched Daisy's arm. 'I was just wondering if you would like to feed one of the babies?'

Daisy stared at her, open-mouthed.

'Would you?'

Daisy nodded. 'Really? Could I?'

They walked to the baby room where six little cots stood along the walls. Two babies were playing happily with their toys whilst another was asleep. Two nurses were bottle-feeding two babies, but one baby was crying lustily.

'This is Michael,' said Mrs Edwards, picking him up. 'Oh dear, dear, Michael, you are a hungry boy, aren't you?' She turned to the nurse. 'Where's his bottle?'

'In the milk kitchen, Matron,' said the girl.

'Daisy and I are going to feed him in my office,' said Mrs Edwards. 'We'll bring him back when he's ready.'

Daisy, carrying the bottle in a jug of warm water, followed behind Mrs Edwards and the crying baby. In the office Mrs Edwards told her to sit down, then she put Michael on her lap. He squirmed and protested angrily until, having tested the milk on the inside of her wrist, Mrs Edwards handed Daisy the bottle. The baby drank eagerly. Daisy wasn't sure why – maybe it was the warmth of his little body or perhaps the memory of her loss – but she found herself struggling not to cry.

'I think you're trying hard to deal with something, aren't you, Daisy?' Mrs Edwards said. 'I have watched you since you came here and I think you have a painful memory.'

Daisy nodded. The baby had taken half his bottle.

'Sit him up now,' said Mrs Edwards, 'and rub his back gently to make him burp.'

Daisy did just that and Michael, after a few protests, produced a loud burp. He looked so shocked by his own effort that Daisy laughed and Michael's face dissolved into a lop-sided smile. She leaned him back against her arm once more and gave him the rest of the milk.

'I had a baby,' she said in a small voice. 'I was fifteen when she was born.'

She glanced up at Mrs Edwards, waiting for the scorn, the derision, the anger, but all she saw was a sympathetic smile, and for some reason she couldn't quite work out, Daisy told her everything.

When she'd finished, Mrs Edwards leaned forward. 'This was thirty-two years ago?'

Daisy nodded.

Mrs Edwards was staring at her. 'And your baby was born in Findon?'

'Yes . . .' Daisy said uncertainly.

'In April?'

'Yes.'

Mrs Edwards stood up and walked over to the window. Daisy shifted her feet nervously.

'And where did your father take the baby?'

'He said he had a nice family all lined up for her,' said Daisy. 'He said I couldn't hold her because I would want her. He said he'd take care of everything.'

There was a pregnant pause, then Mrs Edwards turned to face her.

'Daisy,' she began, 'it may be a coincidence, but I was a young nurse in this nursery thirty-two years ago. We had a baby brought in from Worthing hospital. She was very small and she'd had a rough start, but she grew into a beautiful child.' Mrs Edwards looked a little awkward. 'In this sort of job, you have to be very careful not to love the children too much. If you become too fond of them, when they move on, get adopted or go back to their parents, it tears you apart and it can be very upsetting for the child as well. I broke that rule when it came to that baby. I loved her as if she were my own child and in the end, although I am a single woman, when she was six I got permission to adopt her myself.'

Daisy was puzzled. 'I thought seeing as you're a Mrs, you were married.'

'The Mrs is only a courtesy title,' Mrs Edwards said. 'Anyway, that baby is Trixie's mother, April Rodway.'

Daisy gasped. 'The doctor's wife?'

Mrs Edwards nodded. 'Daisy, I think April was your baby.'

Daisy froze. Michael had finished his feed and was gazing up at her. She stroked his face and kissed his forehead.

'When I said April had a rough start,' Mrs Edwards went on, 'I mean to say that your father didn't find a home for her. April was discovered on Cissbury Ring by an old shepherd. He's long gone now, but he pulled her out of the bushes and took her to hospital. His quick action saved her life. All she had to identify her was a crocheted blanket . . .'

'Yellow and white and a bit wonky on the corners,' said Daisy.

Mrs Edwards put her hand to her mouth. 'So I am right,' she whispered.

They sat in silence for a moment, each lost in her own thoughts. Mrs Edwards was imagining how thrilled April would be to discover her birth mother, something she had always dreamed of since a child. Daisy was filled with a mixture of excitement and horror. That wicked man. How could he do such a thing? To abandon a baby like that was tantamount to murder. May he rot in hell.

'I had no idea you were April's mother,' Mrs Edwards went on. 'I just felt you had a heartache and I wanted to help.'

Daisy was rocking Michael. 'She's a lovely woman,' she said. 'And Trixie.'

'Your daughter and granddaughter,' Mrs Edwards said quietly.

Daisy turned her head away lest she saw her tears.

'I called her April because she was found in April,' said Mrs Edwards. 'Until I adopted her she was called April Charles because where she was found wasn't far from Monarch's Way, which was the escape route to Shoreham Harbour Charles the Second used after his defeat at the Battle of Worcester. Oh, Daisy, she'll be so thrilled.'

Daisy sat up quickly, making the drowsy baby start. 'No, no, she can't know. Not ever! I won't let that man destroy her life too.'

Mrs Edwards frowned. 'I don't understand.'

'Promise me,' Daisy said desperately, 'promise me you won't tell.'

'But why?'

'I haven't been able to give my daughter anything in life,' Daisy said fiercely, 'but this one thing I can do. As much as it breaks my heart, she must never know I'm her mother.'

'Why?' Mrs Edwards repeated.

Daisy looked up at the ceiling, her mouth contorted. A look of anguish on her face. 'Because her father was mine too.'

Leslie was really excited. He sat on the train rehearsing what he was going to say to Eff. It had been three weeks since he'd seen her; three weeks which had been almost unbearable. God, he'd never imagined that you could feel like this when you loved someone. She was never out of his thoughts and in his head he talked to her all the time. Life had changed beyond all recognition. Mr

Archer was quite right. He had proved very popular with the agencies and the work had rolled in.

The train was slow to enter Worthing station. He and Effie had agreed to meet at Worthing Central rather than West Worthing station even though that was the nearest to where Effie worked. In her letter, Effie told him she wanted some time to be together, just the two of them. He grinned excitedly. Imagine that!

He was standing by the door long before the train actually stopped. Frustratingly, someone else was just in front of him so he couldn't lean out of the window for his first glimpse of her. A slither of fear suddenly gripped him. Supposing she wasn't there?

The train stopped, the door flew open and the man stepped out. A second later, Leslie was right behind him on the platform and there she was. His heart missed a beat as she turned her head, saw him and hurried towards him, then she was in his arms and he was kissing her silky soft hair. 'Oh, Eff. Effie, my love.'

He stepped back and saw her face was shining. He held her head in his hands, then slowly brought his lips to hers. As they touched, he thought his heart would explode with joy. She didn't stop him so he kissed her hungrily.

'Hey,' she said teasingly, 'let a girl come up for breath, will you?'

And they both laughed.

They walked arm in arm towards the town. He told her about his modelling jobs and how he was so successful, he had to rush from one location to another.

'Mr Archer keeps me on the go morning, noon and night,' he laughed. 'And you won't believe how much money I've got saved already.'

She told him about the kitchen and the nursery. 'Your Aunt Daisy has been a great boon,' she said. 'I thought I was pretty organized, but she'd had experience of working in a really big kitchen. She knows more about bulk buying than I do and, between us, we've cut costs by a third.'

Leslie chuckled. 'That deserves a pay rise in my book,' he said.

'Actually, it pays your aunt's wages,' said Effie. 'Do you realize this is the first paid job she's ever had?'

They went straight down to the sea and Effie walked onto the stones. Leslie lowered himself onto the pebbles beside her. He kissed her ear. 'I've missed you so much.'

She turned to look at him. 'And I you,' she said softly.

'Oh, Eff,' he moaned.

Effie patted his leg. 'Soon, my love, soon.'

They gazed out to sea, each lost in his or her dreams.

'I brought you here for a reason,' Effie said eventually.

Leslie could tell by the tone of her voice that this was serious. His mind was thrown into a state of panic. Was she ill? Didn't she like her job after all? Were they treating her badly? He looked at her anxiously.

'It's about Sheila,' she began.

Leslie relaxed. 'Oh, so she's turned up, then?' he said brightly.

Effie shook her head. 'I'm afraid not. Everyone,

especially your sister, has scoured the town. They've put up posters, advertised in the paper, gone into barns and old RAF huts, but she's still missing.'

Leslie frowned. 'I don't understand,' he said. 'From what Ronnie said in her letter, I thought she'd just gone to walk about for a bit. You know, she'd let things get on top of her and wanted a bit of peace and quiet.'

Effie shook her head again. 'I'm afraid it's more than that, my love.'

Sensing something bad, Leslie gripped her hand. 'So what's it all about?' he asked and as Effie started to say something, he added, 'You'd better start at the beginning.'

CHAPTER 37

Ronnie was finding it hard to keep going. After a week of wakeful nights peppered with horrible dreams when she did finally drop off to sleep, she had little energy during the day. She seemed to be walking around with a permanent gnawing ache in the middle of her chest. She, Pen and Neville tramped the streets, putting up posters and stopping anyone who would give them a spare minute or two to ask them if they had seen Sheila, but nobody had.

They had gone back to the police station after forty-eight hours, but Ronnie felt the officers were simply going through the motions. Everyone was convinced that given the circumstances of her parents' death, Sheila, badly shocked by the explosion, had simply run away. Inspector Sandgate assured her that she would reappear when she was good and ready.

Just to be on the safe side, Neville decide to check all nursing homes and mental institutions in case she had been admitted with memory loss. Thankfully, or perhaps not so, he drew a blank. He'd even taken a trip to London to the area where her parents had died

413

with the vague hope that she'd become confused and gone back home. It was a fruitless exercise.

The garage was suffering too. Business was basic. With no trained mechanic to do the jobs, customers went elsewhere. Not that Ronnie cared anyway. She had lost her appetite for making a go of it as well as her appetite for food. Granny began to worry about her. She'd lost so much weight her clothes hung on her.

Sheila was in Ronnie's thoughts every moment of the day. If only she knew where Sheila was. What on earth had happened to her? And if she had been kidnapped, where was the ransom note? Ronnie rehearsed every move they had made on the fateful morning over and over again – the fruitless trip to Ferring, how annoyed Sheila had been when she got back, that wretched tyre – but nothing seemed out of the ordinary. Maybe it was just as they said and the loud noise had triggered some sort of delayed shock. She'd even sent a telegram to Leslie asking him if Sheila was there. Two days later, her brother had replied, 'Sorry. She's not here.'

Granny and Aunt Daisy were at a loss to know how to help Ronnie. Daisy brought her food in the vain hope that she might encourage her to eat, but although Ronnie was grateful and the food smelled delicious, everything tasted like straw and stuck in her throat.

Pen Albright was surprised how badly Sheila's disappearance had affected her boys. She had told them when they'd got up the next day that Sheila hadn't come back. At the time of the explosion, she'd simply comforted two frightened children and taken them home. When it became apparent that Sheila wasn't hurt, but had simply run off, she wanted to tell them herself before they heard some garbled tale from the other boys. After breakfast, she'd gathered them to her and tried to explain and it wasn't until then that Pen realized how much Sheila meant to them.

In the past Alan had spent time at the garage and Sheila had given him little jobs like helping to wash cars or sweeping the garage forecourt. Pen knew she slipped him a few pennies now and then. Of course, at six years old, Geoffrey was too young to do much in the way of helping but Sheila would give him sweeties and she was always ready with a hug. As the hunt gathered momentum, Alan helped his mother to put up posters in the area and that's when he'd asked all sorts of unanswerable questions: 'Why did Auntie Sheila run away?' 'Did she get lost?' 'Is it my fault?'

Pen answered as best she could, but she was as confused as everybody else. In fact, her own feelings were all over the place. One day she was worried, the next she was angry. That terrific bang had scared the life out of everybody, but once they'd discovered what had caused it, it was business as usual. Even if Sheila had been badly frightened by the tyre exploding, surely she would have realized how worried they all were and come home by now?

Her son Geoffrey was even more disturbed than Alan. When he woke in the morning his first question was 'Has Auntie Sheila come back?' and when he got home from school it was the same. This was the first time in his life that he'd seen an adult do anything out of the ordinary. It had unsettled him dreadfully and made him tearful and clingy.

After three weeks had passed, it looked as if Sheila was gone for good. Pen was still concerned but, apart from praying, she had exhausted her ability to do anything practical. She'd got into the habit of making a little extra when she cooked the tea for herself and the boys and taking it round to Ronnie, but that was about it. If the truth were told, Pen was more concerned about Ronnie now. This girl was a shadow of her former self. She had bags under her eyes and her hair was lank and greasy. The business had suffered because not only had Ronnie lost her mechanic but also her zest for life and her enthusiasm.

Pen decided to bring everything to a head. She called round one morning after she'd taken Geoffrey to school.

'Tell you what,' she said brightly as Ronnie appeared at the door still in her nightie, 'let me run you a bath and help you wash your hair.'

Ronnie looked a little surprised as Pen breezed past, but she let her take everything off the bath board and turn on the taps. Pen found some bath crystals in the bedroom and scented the water. While Ronnie soaked, she had a quick tidy round, gathered together some washing and stuffed it into a bag, and then found some clean underwear and clothes. Then when Ronnie reappeared, her hair washed and wrapped in a towel, she said, 'While you get dressed, I'll make us a cup of tea.'

By the time Ronnie came into the kitchen, Pen had emptied the bath and put everything back on the board. There was a boiled egg on the table.

'Thanks, Pen,' Ronnie said dully.

'I think it's time you let this go,' said Pen, pushing a cup of tea in front of her. Ronnie looked up sharply. 'And before you have a go at me,' said Pen, holding her hand up defensively, 'you've done the best you could. Nobody could have done more, but it's time to move on.'

Ronnie sagged as if she were a deflated balloon. 'I don't want her to think I don't care.'

'And she won't,' said Pen, 'but when she comes back, what is she going to come back to? You've let everything go.'

Ronnie bashed the top of the egg. 'I guess you're right,' she sighed.

Pen said no more. The two of them sipped their tea.

'I can't do much without a mechanic,' Ronnie said eventually.

'There's plenty of them around,' said Pen matter-of-factly. 'Advertise.' Ronnie nodded. 'Write it now,' Pen added, 'and I'll go with you to the *Herald* offices if you like.'

The advertisement for a mechanic would appear in the next edition of the *Worthing Herald* and run for four weeks. Although it had been a necessary trip into

417

town on the bus, Ronnie had enjoyed Pen's company and doing something different. She was still worried sick, but with Pen to chat to, she actually managed not to think of her cousin for a little while. The weather was pleasant. Not warm enough to be without a light-weight coat or a cardigan, but hats, gloves and scarves were consigned to the drawer until winter came again.

After they came out of the newspaper offices, Pen suggested going for something to eat. Lyons Tea Rooms would have been the obvious choice, but Ronnie fancied looking at the sea. They settled for the Sunny Seaside Cafe near the Dome cinema and ordered sand-wiches and a pot of tea. Ronnie chose a table in the window and they watched a few local strollers and some people in bath chairs going by. They made small talk, carefully avoiding anything to do with Sheila's disappearance, when all of a sudden Ronnie cried out, 'Oh my goodness, that's him!'

'Who?' Pen asked.

Ronnie was pointing out of the window. Pen followed the line of her finger and spotted a man walking on the opposite side of the road. He was wearing a heavy coat and looked rather down at heel. 'Isn't that—' she began, but Ronnie was already on her feet.

'PC Matthew Keller,' said Ronnie, grabbing her coat. 'I wanted to ask him if he might have any idea where Sheila could be, but he left the police force in January.'

Pen sprang to her feet as well. 'You go and catch him up. I'll see to the bill. Go, go!'

Ronnie ran from the shop. A bus had just pulled

up at the bus stop and was discharging its passengers. Unfortunately, Ronnie was caught up with them and struggled to get past. When she'd finally made her way through, Matthew was out of sight. She ran as fast as she could towards South Street and turned the corner. For the next few frantic seconds she was searching the crowds of shoppers until she finally saw him close to the town hall steps. She called his name, but he was too far away.

He was heading towards Chapel Road. She tore after him. There was a large lorry parked on the wrong side of the road. Matthew stepped off the pavement in front of the lorry, but he didn't see the bus coming in the opposite direction. She shouted again and he turned his head. Something flitted across his face; a look of surprise or was it horror? He quickened his step.

'Look out!' she screamed, but Matthew had stepped into the path of the oncoming bus. Ronnie spun round so as not to see and, as Pen ran towards her, there was a screech of brakes and a loud bang.

'Oh my God,' Pen breathed.

When Ronnie looked back, Matthew was lying partially under the wheels of the bus with a long thin trail of blood heading towards the gutter.

There was a moment of stillness, then panic everywhere. Some people were running away, some were screaming or frozen to the spot. Pen headed for the phone box next to the Midland bank.

For a split second, Ronnie thought he was dead, but

then she saw him move his head ever so slightly. She sprang forward and knelt in the road in front of him. 'Matthew, oh, Matthew, I'm so sorry. Help is on its way. Hang in there.'

He opened his eyes and fixed her with a lizard-like stare. Then, to her horror, his mouth curled into a superior grimace. His lips were moving, but she couldn't hear what he was saying. She leaned forward. He spoke with effort.

'You'll never find her. She's mine forever.'

CHAPTER 38

Win Peters held the door open wide to let Pen Albright in.

'How is she now?' said Pen, her voice lowered.

The doctor's given her a strong sedative,' said Win, taking Pen's coat and showing her into the sitting room. Two other people were already there, Daisy and Leslie. Pen nodded as they looked up.

'Sit down, Pen,' said Win. She waited until Daisy left the room to make some tea and then asked, 'So what happened? Ronnie was so distraught it was difficult to make head or tail of what she was saying.'

'She told you we saw Matthew Keller run over and killed?' said Pen.

'We got that much out of her,' said Win.

'The thing is,' said Pen, 'just before he died, he said something.'

Leslie lowered his paper.

'*You'll never find her, she's mine*, or some such thing,' said Pen. 'I didn't hear it. I was at the phone box.'

'But what does it mean?' Win was frowning.

'Ronnie is positive he knew where Sheila was. That he's been holding her captive.'

Win looked sceptical. 'Surely not?' she said. 'This is the twentieth century, not Victorian London.'

Daisy brought in a tray of tea and handed the cups round.

'As soon as the doctor pronounced him dead—'

'Doctor?' said Leslie.

'Somebody had run for Doctor Cromwell,' said Pen. 'He only lives in Ambrose Place. As soon as he said Matthew was dead, Ronnie insisted we go straight to the police. She told them everything, but they didn't believe us.' Pen lowered her head and fought the tears. 'Ronnie was very upset.' She sipped her tea. 'She was so convinced and the shopping didn't help.'

'Shopping?' said Leslie. 'What shopping?'

'He had two carrier bags of groceries,' said Pen. 'They spilled all over the road and the first thing we saw was the box of Black Magic.'

Win frowned. 'Sheila's favourite chocolates,' she said quietly.

'That's what Ronnie said,' said Pen.

They all sat silent.

'Look,' said Win, leaning forward confidentially, 'I don't think for one minute the girl is a liar, but did she really hear him say that? I mean, he wasn't a very nice man, but to hold someone against their will . . .' Her voice trailed.

'I don't know,' said Pen. 'I don't want to believe it

either, but if it is true, and we can't find her, Sheila is in very real danger and Ronnie feels responsible.'

'Don't be daft,' Leslie scoffed. 'How can she think that?'

'If she hadn't chased him,' Pen went on, 'and if she hadn't called his name, he might have looked where he was going.'

'That's not her fault,' said Win.

'But that's just it,' said Pen. 'That's exactly what she thinks.' After a few minutes, Pen spoke again. 'I came to ask if Ronnie was planning to go back to the garage tonight.'

Win shook her head. 'She's out for the count. Leslie is going back there in a minute to keep an eye on things. Ronnie can stay where she is. Daisy can sleep on the couch.'

'I knew you didn't have enough beds,' said Pen, 'so I wondered if Ronnie wanted to sleep at mine. I've made up the bed, so Daisy could come back with me if you like.'

Daisy hesitated, not wanting to offend her mother.

'You'll be closer to work for the morning,' Pen said encouragingly and Daisy nodded.

'Well, you can't come.'

The boys had decided to go back to Field Place. It was easy enough to slip away unnoticed. The grown-ups were still occupied by Auntie Sheila's disappearance. They gathered in little huddles and talked incessantly unless one of the kids was around, then they'd stop

423

and smile. They never said much in front of the boys, but Alan and Geoffrey weren't stupid.

Alan pushed his little brother in the back. 'You're too little.'

'No, I'm not!' Geoffrey protested loudly. 'I'm nearly as tall as you.'

He knew his reference to Alan's small stature would have the desired effect. If he wasn't allowed to play with the bigger boys because he was too short, he wasn't going to give up without a fight. As a young lad, Alan had suffered with a weak chest. There were times when he'd been forced to stay in bed and he'd struggled to breathe. He'd missed a lot of school too. He'd made up for it later on and for the past two years he'd been second in the class, but the illness had stunted his growth. As a result, he was small for his age and thin. Geoffrey, on the other hand, was a sturdy fellow, and despite being only half his age, he was almost as tall as his brother.

'You're only a baby,' Alan said scornfully.

'If you don't let me come,' Geoffrey shouted angrily, 'I'll tell Mummy where you're going.'

They had the inevitable scrap, but before he was thoroughly beaten, Alan said, 'All right. You can come but don't expect me to look after you.'

Defiant to the end, Geoffrey retorted, 'I can look after myself.'

The boys had arranged to gather in the grounds of the big house. The place was deserted, but since they'd last been there, several large KEEP OUT MOD PROPERTY signs had been put up. Hethy, Drew and Ian were waiting by the entrance to the tunnel. Steven wasn't with them. His family had decided to emigrate to some sort of tropical island thousands of miles away, so Hethy said. Drew reckoned they were going to look for pirate treasure. 'And he'll come back the richest man in the world.'

Hethy was none too pleased to see Geoffrey. He pulled Alan to one side and had words.

'If you come with us,' Hethy told Geoffrey when he'd finished, 'you've got to swear not to tell.'

Geoffrey nodded.

'If you say anything, the Field Place ghost will strangle you dead,' Drew said as he pretended to choke and gasp for breath before collapsing in a heap on the grass.

Geoffrey swallowed hard and shook his head vigorously. 'I won't tell, honest.'

The entrance was easier to find this time. It seemed someone had trampled the nettles and bindweed down. They soon found the iron ring and pulled it up. Alan went down first and the others followed one by one. Geoffrey was the last. His heart was in his mouth, beating very fast, but he didn't tell them. He wasn't a baby.

Once he got used to the gloom and having to hold a torch all the time, it was fantastic. They shouted down the tunnels and waited to hear the echo of their voices coming back to them. They put the torches under their chins and made monster noises to scare each other. They rode the bikes, two on one machine going very fast, and they fell off a couple of times. After some time playing German spies and tracking Hitler down, Drew said it was time to be getting back or his mum would come looking for them. There was a collective groan, but they all knew they had to go. Geoffrey felt sure of his bearings now and raced back up the tunnel. He hadn't gone far before he realized he wasn't in the right one. 'Oh, blow it,' he said aloud. 'I've come the wrong way.'

Just as he was about to turn round, he heard a moaning sound. Geoffrey froze, his heart pounding. There on the wall was a dim light which was growing brighter and larger by the second. He was so scared he dropped his torch and the light went out.

'Who's there?' said a raspy voice.

Thoroughly panicked, Geoffrey scrabbled about on the floor, but he couldn't feel the torch. 'Alan!' he yelled. 'Alan, I've lost my torch.'

Geoffrey heard a shuffling sound and the light on the wall became more concentrated. Then a croaky voice said, 'Geoffrey? Is that you?'

The little boy didn't wait a second longer. If the Field Place ghost knew his name it was bound to come after him. Screaming in terror, he ran back to the other boys as fast as his legs would carry him.

Neville had exhausted every avenue he could think of. At great personal expense he had employed a private detective, but after nearly four weeks of enquiries, the man came back with absolutely nothing. Neville had talked about Sheila so much he was sure his friends crossed the road rather than meet up with him. If Ronnie looked haggard and drawn, so did he. And now this business of Matthew Keller had come up. Ronnie was convinced Matthew must have been holding Sheila against her will somewhere, so Neville had thrown himself into finding out where Matthew lived. Through his father's police contact in the Freemasons he discovered Matthew had been living in a hut on the old RAF radar station at Durrington. He drove up there and had a poke around. The place was pretty dilapidated and a thorough search convinced him Sheila wasn't holed up anywhere on site. However, Matthew's lair yielded a few clues. The walls were hung with umpteen pictures of Sheila, all taken without her knowledge, so it would seem. Women's clothing was strewn all over the place. Some was drying on a clothes horse and some was neatly folded as if he was taking it somewhere. Neville didn't recognize any of it, but his heart almost stopped when he spotted Sheila's watch on the table. It was all very upsetting and worrying.

He decided not to say anything to Ronnie or her gran for the moment. What was the point of giving them even more grief? He remembered how distressing it had been when they'd told Ronnie's mum and dad, and that was bad enough. It was the sense of helplessness that made it worse, that and imagining what might be or had happened to her. He kept telling himself not to think about things like that, but his mind drifted back there all the time. What was she doing? Was she crying? Was she hurt? The questions gave him a perpetual headache and he was exhausted with it all.

His own parents had tried to be understanding, but

he was beginning to feel he couldn't share his fears and feelings with them any more. Quite frankly, they'd had enough and he didn't blame them. He knew he wasn't being rational or sane, but he just couldn't help it.

He loved her so much.

When Geoffrey's shrill, terrified scream pierced the wee small hours of the morning, Pen was out of bed and had her hand on the door handle before she was fully awake. Dick, who could sleep through a bombing raid, fell out of his side of the bed and began a frantic search between the sheets for his pyjama bottoms.

Geoffrey, still screaming, was sitting up in bed, his eyes wide open. Alan lay in the bed next to him with his hands over his ears.

'Shh, shh, darling. It's all right. Mummy's here.' Pen perched on the side of the bed and gathered her youngest son into her arms.

'What happened?' said Dick as he came into the room.

'He's had a nightmare, that's all,' said Pen. 'It's all right, sweetheart. It was only a dream. You're safe now.'

It was plain to both parents that this was no ordinary dream. Geoffrey was wet with perspiration and his screams had turned into heart-rending sobs. 'I saw it, Mummy,' he said, gulping the words out. 'I saw the Field Place ghost.'

Dick turned to go, but then he heard Alan say viciously, 'Shut up. Shut up, you promised.'

He frowned at Alan. 'Have you been scaring your brother again?'

428

'No, Daddy.' Alan's face was the picture of innocence.

'Then what did he mean?' Dick accused.

Alan knew he was on what Granddad would call a sticky wicket. If he said too much, his father would be suspicious; if he said nothing, he would also smell a rat. He did sometimes come over a bit heavy-handed with his little brother, but then Geoffrey could be very annoying.

'It was the ghost, Mummy,' Geoffrey blubbed. 'I saw it. I dropped the torch and then the light got bigger and it looked through the window.'

'What window?' Dick asked impatiently.

'He's making it up,' said Alan, but there was a desperation in his voice that made both his parents connect. They knew he was lying.

'Geoffrey, darling,' said Pen. 'I want you to tell Mummy and Daddy where you saw this . . . ghost. Take your time and tell us everything.'

'It was in the tunnels.'

Alan threw himself back on his bed with a groan and pulled the pillow over his face. Pen and Dick looked at each other, then Dick came and sat in the chair between the two beds. 'Tell us about the tunnels, son,' he said gently.

So Geoffrey did. He told them how the bigger boys let him come, how they'd climbed down, how spooky it was, how they'd shouted and heard their own voices coming back at them, how they'd ridden the bikes . . .

'You rode a bike?' Dick said incredulously.

Alan sat up. 'See, I told you. He's making it up.'

'I'm not, Mummy. I'm not.'

'No, he's not making it up,' Dick said sharply. 'The reason I know he's not making it up is because you're doing your best to shut him up.'

Alan looked down, shamefaced.

'So what's it all about, Alan?' Dick continued. 'Where did you take him?'

'To Field Place,' Alan said sulkily. 'Hethy found this tunnel so we climbed down.' His eyes brightened. 'It's fantastic, Dad. There's miles and miles of them.'

Dick looked at Pen. 'They must have found the old RAF radar place. Did they have tunnels there?'

Pen shrugged. 'They do say the house was used to store smuggling contraband back in the olden days.'

'Did you see this ghost, Alan?' his father asked.

'There is no ghost,' said Alan. 'Drew made it up.'

'But there is a ghost,' Geoffrey insisted. 'I saw it.'

'You couldn't have,' said Alan. 'I was with you all the time and I didn't see it.'

'It was when I went into the wrong tunnel,' said Geoffrey, beginning to get upset again. 'I saw the light on the wall and then it said my name.'

'What do you mean, it said your name?'

'Oh, Daddy, I already told you. It said, "Geoffrey? Is that you?" And when I ran away it said, "Geoffrey, Geoffrey, come back."'

Pen took in her breath noisily and put her hand on her mouth. 'Oh, Dick, you don't think—' she began.

'He's only saying that because he lost my torch,' Alan said.

'Shh,' Pen said sharply. 'Geoffrey, what did the voice sound like? Could it have been a woman's voice?'

'It said, "Geoffrey? Is that you?"' said Geoffrey in a rasping voice. He dissolved into tears again. 'Will it come back and get me?'

'Absolutely not,' said Pen, kissing the little boy's head.

'But Drew said it would get me if I told.'

'Well, it won't,' Pen said firmly. She began to settle him down to sleep again. 'Your daddy won't let it anywhere near you.'

Dick flexed his muscles and threw a couple of punches in the air, making them laugh. He turned to his older son. 'And no more talking when we've gone,' he said. 'You're not to scare him again.'

Alan nodded and Dick tousled his hair.

At Geoffrey's request they left the light on as they headed back to their own room. 'Oh, and Alan,' Dick said at the door, 'I don't want you going back to that place again. It belongs to the RAF and they've probably got guards and dogs patrolling the grounds. Keep away, okay?' He waited until he heard a muffled, 'Yes, Daddy,' from under the covers. 'Goodnight, boys.'

Pen was sitting up in bed when he got back to their bedroom. 'You don't think that could be Sheila down there, do you?'

'I shouldn't think so,' said Dick, 'but I think we ought to take a look as soon as it gets light, just in case.'

He climbed back into bed and switched off the light, but neither of them slept another wink.

CHAPTER 39

The next day Dick biked over to the Brighton Road to see Neville. By the time he got there, the garage had only just opened. Saturday was half-day closing. He went straight to the office where a pale-faced Neville listened as he told him what had happened the night before.

'Are you really sure she's down there?'

'No, I'm not,' said Dick. 'The lad could have made it up or imagined the whole thing, but he's only six and he was badly frightened.'

'Sheila would never have agreed to go underground,' said Neville.

'You're right,' said Dick. 'I think he must have over-powered her in some way and dragged her down there – if indeed she is in the tunnel.'

'But if the boys went down and came back all right,' said Neville, 'why can't she find her way out?'

Dick shrugged.

Neville slapped his thighs and stood up. 'But, yes, you're right. We can't just let it go. We have to take a look.'

'Shall I ring the police?'

'The police,' Neville said scornfully. 'A fat lot of good they've been. With the amount of help we've had from them they'd most likely take a week to get round to it. No, if that twat was holding her down there, he would have had to feed her. Ronnie told me he had a bag full of groceries when he got killed. If that was for Sheila, she must be low on supplies.'

'Good God!' Dick gasped. 'I never thought of that.'

'Let me make a couple of calls and I'll be right with you,' said Neville.

Someone came to take over the garage and, with Dick's bike strapped to the back of his car, Neville drove him home. On the way, they decided not to tell Ronnie and the others. 'Better not to give them any false hope,' Neville said.

They took Alan with them. His father explained that although he didn't want him going down the tunnels again, he needed the boy to show him the way. Everyone agreed Geoffrey should stay at home. He was far too young to be put through another ordeal. It was just after eleven when the two men and Alan set off. Pen watched them anxiously from the kitchen window. It was going to be a long morning.

Alan took his father and Uncle Nev to the entrance and uncovered it for what he knew would be the very last time.

'I reckon this is some sort of inspection shaft,' said his dad. 'It looks like a tight squeeze to me.'

'It's wider at the bottom, Dad,' Alan assured him.

The three of them climbed down. Uncle Nev had brought some smashing torches and Alan was allowed one for himself. As they walked behind him, he could hear the men talking.

'This must be some sort of bunker,' his dad said.

'Probably something to do with the secret radar station just up the road,' Uncle Nev agreed. 'I had a look round what was left of it when Sheila first went missing, but I couldn't find anything.' He paused. 'Did you know there are families living in those old huts?'

'Never,' his father exclaimed.

'As true as I'm standing here,' said Uncle Nev. 'They've got no tap water, no electricity, the places are running with damp and it's perishing cold. I wouldn't put a dog in one of those huts, but they're all homeless and got nowhere to go. It's a bloody disgrace.'

They came to the wider room. Uncle Nev shone his torch around the walls and glanced at the chart.

'I wonder if the lights work,' said his father. He threw a switch but nothing happened. Alan tried the same with another switch and the light in the middle of the ceiling fluttered for a few seconds before flooding the room with light.

'Blimey,' Uncle Nev gasped.

Alan looked around. What a pity they hadn't realized the lights worked when he was down here with Hethy. He gazed at the telephone, especially the red one, the maps, the funny-looking tables with knobs on. This would have made a fantastic space station to Mars.

'So come on now,' said Dad, bringing him back down to earth. 'Which one was the tunnel where Geoffrey lost his torch?'

'My torch,' Alan corrected. He turned round to face the two exits, but now he wasn't sure. 'That one,' he said, pointing. Uncle Nev stepped forward. All at once Alan was scared. What if he'd made a mistake? 'Or maybe it was that one.' His dad gave him an impatient stare. 'I don't know,' Alan said helplessly. 'I can't remember.'

'Don't worry, son,' said Uncle Nev with a chuckle. 'We'll check the both of them.'

They set off down the first tunnel and, as luck would have it, as they came to a slight bend, his father kicked Alan's torch. 'There it is,' cried Alan. It had fallen apart when it fell, and as he bent to pick up the pieces, he realized the two men were staring at the barred window of a door.

'Oh my God,' Uncle Nev whispered. 'Is she dead?'

His father coughed softly. 'Sheila, Sheila, love, are you all right?'

The window was too high for Alan to look in, but he heard a soft moan.

'She's alive!' Uncle Nev cried out. 'Sheila, hang on, darling. We're going to get you out of there.' He tried the handle of the door. 'Where's the key?' He began frantically searching around the frame. Alan's dad was running his fingers along the top of the door and they shone the torches around the walls. 'We'll have to break it down,' said Uncle Nev.

'Don't be daft, man,' said his father. 'You'll never break down that door; not in a month of Sundays. That's six inches thick and reinforced steel. No, we've got to get help.'

Alan heard a small moan and then a raspy voice said, 'Water. Water, please.'

Daddy looked down at him. 'Run home, son, and tell your mother to bring food and water. Tell her to be as quick as she can. Hurry, son, this is really important. Don't stop for anything.'

So Alan took off as fast as his legs could carry him.

The reception area of Worthing police station was crowded when Neville burst through the door.

'Excuse me, madam,' he said as he pushed past the woman at the counter.

She had been complaining that her purse had been stolen. 'Well, really,' she gasped.

'I'm sorry, love, but this is a matter of life and death.'

The desk sergeant looked up with a condescending stare. He'd heard it all before and it was usually something about nothing. 'If you would wait and take your turn, sir,' he said patiently.

'I can't,' said Neville. 'I need to see Inspector Sandgate. I've found the missing girl.'

'If you would sit down, sir,' said the sergeant. 'I shall attend to you in just a minute.'

'Didn't you hear what I said?' Neville demanded. 'She's in an underground cell and close to death.'

The sergeant rolled his eyes. Ah well, he'd never

heard that one before. A constable came from the back and lifted the gate on the desk to get out.

'I asked you to sit down, sir,' said the sergeant, raising his voice very slightly.

He went back to dealing with the woman. A moment later, as he turned to get the relevant form, Neville seized his chance. Lifting the gate, he raced down the corridor, shouting Sandgate's name. The inspector came from his office just as two constables were manhandling Neville back to the foyer.

'I've found her!' Neville was shouting. 'Sheila Hodges. She's alive but only just. You've got to help us. You've got to.'

The inspector motioned for the constables to let him go and Neville hurried towards Sandgate, explaining what had happened. 'We can't get through the door, you see,' he said as he walked into the inspector's office. 'It's too thick to break down. Did he have a key?'

'Did who have a key?'

'Matthew Keller,' cried Neville. 'When he died, did he have a key?'

When he finally grasped what Neville was saying, the inspector sent for Matthew's effects. A constable brought them in a brown cardboard box. They rummaged through the contents: a wallet, a handkerchief, a pair of motorcycle gauntlets, a photograph of Sheila, a fountain pen and an address book.

Neville's heart sank. What were they going to do now? It would take an oxyacetylene torch to get through that door, and by the time they'd mustered all the paperwork and the skilled manpower needed, it would be too late. When he'd shone the torch around the room, Sheila already looked half dead. She was sprawled across a camp bed with one foot on the floor as if she was too weak to put both legs on the bed. When he'd called her name, she'd tried to raise her head, but even that was too much effort.

The room, probably built as part of some living quarters in the event of an invasion, was very basic. There was a sink and a toilet and he could see a chair and a table. How long she'd been down there he couldn't imagine. If her captor had put her there on the first day she went missing, that was four weeks and two days ago. He didn't remember seeing any provisions in the room, so when did she last eat?

Inspector Sandgate was stuffing everything back into the cardboard box.

'Hang on a minute,' said Neville. 'Why would a man on foot need motorcycle gloves?' He picked them up and shook them. The left-hand glove felt rather heavy. Neville turned back the cuff and felt around. There was a hidden pocket along the seam. When he found access and pulled back the fold of fabric, out fell a large key.

Neville hardly knew how he got back to Field Place. He ran from the police station as if the devil himself was after him and then motored at speed along Marine Parade with a police car following close behind. He had to get to Sheila before it was too late. People can go without food for days, he told himself, but how

438

long can one go without water? Please, please don't let me be too late.

There was a St John Ambulance man waiting at the entrance to the tunnel and Neville recognized Tim Ogburn as an old school chum. Pen must have telephoned them, but there was no time for reminiscences.

Neville almost stumbled down the stairs, calling out to Dick to herald his arrival. Tim was right behind him and they met up with another ambulance man waiting with Dick at the door. Neville's hand was shaking so much, Dick had to take the key from him, and they all breathed a sigh of relief when the lock finally clicked open.

'Let the medics go first, mate,' Dick said gently as he pulled Neville to one side.

After a quick examination, Tim uttered the three words Neville had been desperate to hear. 'She's still alive.'

Tim put a flask of something to Sheila's lips. At first she didn't respond, but all at once she roused herself to take a few sips. Neville hurried to her side as she let out a slight moan.

'My colleague will get a stretcher,' said Tim, 'and then we'll get her to hospital.' But Neville had already scooped Sheila into his arms. As she felt herself being lifted, she opened her eyes and whispered, 'Oh, Nev.'

'It's all right, my darling,' he said gruffly, his voice thick with emotion, 'you're safe now.'

Ronnie picked up the telephone before the second ring. 'Hello?' she said eagerly. Behind her, Win Peters leaned forward to catch what was being said. 'Oh, hello, Dick,' Ronnie went on. 'There's no news yet, I'm afraid.'

Win turned away.

'What?' cried Ronnie. 'Where?'

Win searched her granddaughter's face and saw a mixture of emotions: surprise, anxiety, disbelief and something else she couldn't quite put her finger on. 'What's happened?'

Ronnie put her finger to her lips, then covered the telephone mouthpiece. 'They've found her,' she said. 'She's alive.' A wave of relief flooded through Win as Ronnie turned back to the telephone conversation. 'So she's in Worthing hospital?'

Win glanced up at the clock. Eleven forty. The bus would pass by at the end of the road in five minutes. Grabbing her coat and her bag, Win headed for the door. 'Tell them I'm on my way,' she called. 'I'm getting the next bus.'

Ronnie relayed the message and let Dick finish on the other end of the line. She thanked him for all he'd done and hung up. Sheila was safely in hospital, dehydrated and on a drip, but able to speak. Best of all, Neville was by her side. She stood for a few minutes, hunched over the telephone, and closed her eyes.

She sensed a movement by the door. Opening her eyes again, she said, 'Oh dear, did you miss the bus? I suppose for once it was early. It's always the way, isn't it? Never mind, the twenty-two goes along Rectory Road in ten minutes. It's a bit of a walk from Brighton Road, but you'll be with her before lunch.'

Her grandmother didn't reply, but the light level in the room told her she was still standing in the doorway. Ronnie sighed. She was in no mood for conversation or dealing with someone else's emotions. For the first time in weeks Ronnie realized how tired she was. In fact, she was exhausted. She couldn't laugh or cry. There wasn't an ounce of strength left in her body. She was completely numb.

Then a man's voice said her name and Ronnie caught her breath.

'Ronnie, my darling.'

She stretched herself up, but didn't dare to turn round. She could hardly breathe.

'Ronnie,' he said again.

Trembling, she turned her head slowly. She couldn't see his face, but she knew instantly that it was him and let out a strangled cry.

'Oh, Bruce, is that you? Is that really you?' She gulped for air and then the tears came. Tears of tiredness and relief and, most of all, tears of utter joy.

He came to her and held out his arms, and as he pulled her closer, she yielded herself to him in a way she had never done before.

CHAPTER 40

Glad to take the weight off her feet for a while, Win Peters lowered herself onto the bench. She fingered her corsage and looked around at the assembled people. This had been a perfect day and the happiest time they'd all spent together in a very long time. Her gaze drifted towards her daughter. Daisy looked far more attractive since she'd had her hair cut and set. It fell in soft curls around her curvette hat and blue was definitely her colour. She still had a trim little figure. Her V-necked dress with little cap sleeves was nipped in at the waist with two hidden pockets on the skirt seam. Curious, Win frowned. Why was Daisy staring at Mrs Rodway like that?

They were all in Dr and Mrs Rodway's garden, a lovely secluded area surrounded by trees and hidden from the road. It was typical of Mrs Rodway to open the garden for the wedding party. Like Mrs Edwards, her mother, she had such a big heart for the community. They had walked here from the church where Leslie and Effie had just been married. Win smiled again. How handsome her grandson had looked. She recalled the day Mrs Riley had handed her a knitting pattern. 'Here, is this your Leslie?' she'd said and Win had had the surprise of her life. Sure enough, there was Leslie on the front of a Sirdar knitting pattern. He was standing next to a mantelpiece decorated with holly and Christmas cards, holding a pipe and wearing a lovely Fair Isle pullover in two-ply wool. It would have taken ages to knit, but ooh, it did look smart.

What a difference a year had made – a year and dear Effie. The last time they'd all gathered together had been for Basil's funeral. She'd known from the moment he'd breathed his last that her life would be changed forever, but she'd never imagined she'd be here in this garden today. Of course, Effie was radiant. Her ankle-length white satin dress was perfect and she wore a lace veil which doubled as a train. Her bouquet was made up of roses from Mrs Rodway's garden and Dick Albright's allotment. Ronnie had put them together last night and they'd stored them in a bath of cold water until they were needed.

Ronnie smoothed down her bridesmaid dress. There was no doubt about it, the style suited both her and her cousin. The ravages of the past few weeks had all but gone. Sheila was still a bit pale, but the peach-pink bridesmaid dress gave her a warm glow. She'd been as weak as a kitten when they'd got her out of that hellhole Matthew had put her in. When Neville carried her to the entrance, they said she was barely conscious. A St John ambulance was waiting to take her to Worthing hospital where she was treated for severe dehydration. She'd eaten all the food he'd left her, but he hadn't counted on the water supply being cut off after the authorities decided to seal up the tunnels. Someone must have noticed that the water supply was still connected and turned off the stopcock. Sheila managed to get a dribble from the tap at first, but then it stopped altogether. It had taken her a while to talk about her experience, but once she'd opened up, she couldn't stop.

'I had just set up the tyre when he came into the garage,' she'd told Ronnie. 'I told him I didn't want to see him any more and we argued. I turned away and he came up behind me and put something over my mouth. I must have blacked out and when I woke up, I was in the cell.'

Ronnie hadn't realized that Matthew had been writing to Sheila for some time. Unfortunately, as soon as she'd seen his handwriting on the envelope she'd torn everything up without reading it. With hindsight he'd most likely hinted at what he planned, but that was something they would never know. In fact, a lot of things fell into place with hindsight. The fact that no one at the police station knew anything about the poison-pen letters probably meant that Matthew had written them himself. The petty irritations like the sour milk on the doorstep, false call-outs and tin tacks on the forecourt could have been down to him as well, couldn't they? By now Ronnie was convinced that Matthew was at the centre of everything. And even though the insurance company had paid up, she still had a nagging suspicion that Matthew had started the fire. While she was his prisoner, Sheila said he'd made it plain that he'd wanted her out of the garage, so perhaps everything they'd put up with was down to his jealousy and deranged mind.

When her cousin came home from hospital, Mrs Griffith had come round with Benny's diary.

'I'm sorry it's been so long in coming,' she'd apologized. 'I just don't know where the time goes.' Later that evening, the whole family thumbed through it.

'I wish we could have looked at this before,' Ronnie said, shaking her head. 'It would have put everything in a completely different light.'

It was all there. Benny had seen Matthew doing everything: dragging Nelson off after giving him a kick, damaging the oil drum, stuffing something into the petrol pump and spying on them from the bushes.

'Why on earth didn't the silly old man report it?' Sheila said crossly.

'Who would he go to?' Ronnie said quietly.

'The police, of course,' Sheila snapped.

'You're forgetting,' Win told her. 'Matthew was the police.'

The wedding guests moved around and chatted in small groups.

The sun was warm on her face so Win relaxed a little. The photographer was still taking photographs. At this rate, they'd have a drawerful before he'd finished.

Win glanced over at the happy couple. She hoped

they'd like the bone-china tea service she'd given them as a present and she'd stuffed an envelope inside the teapot with ten pounds inside as well. This year was going to be expensive with all these weddings. She pondered for a second over her Post Office savings book again. She hadn't looked inside it for years, but when Leslie said he was getting married, she'd decided to blow it all on him. When she'd opened the book, however, she'd had quite a surprise. Her twenty-two pounds had been drawn out and then put back again. Funny thing was, she didn't remember when she'd done it or what for. She shrugged. She must be getting forgetful in her old age.

Ronnie's young man – well, he was not quite such a young man, about forty – seemed a very nice fellow. He'd turned up the day they'd found Sheila. He'd been a great comfort to Ronnie, but he didn't stay long. Apparently he had to get back up north for the sake of his mother. He'd turned up again about a week later and brought his two little girls. Win loved them instantly and they clearly adored Ronnie.

Win had a feeling Ronnie wouldn't be around for long. She and Bruce were now engaged to be married. Their wedding was set for next month and they'd all have to travel up to Worcester because Bruce's mother wasn't well enough to come south. Win suspected that as soon as his mother passed away, Bruce would take Ronnie back to Australia. And why not? Everybody said it was the land of opportunity, a young people's country where a man could get on. The garage was up for sale and Neville reckoned they'd get a fair price. Ronnie and Sheila didn't want to keep it on. Too many bad memories. Win loved the way Neville looked after Sheila. It wouldn't be long before they got married too. She was sure of that, even though Sheila was a little cautious. Who could blame her after what Matthew had done, but Win was sure she was in safe hands with Neville. It saddened her to think that she might not ever see Ronnie again, but that was the way of things, wasn't it? So long as both girls were happy, that was all that mattered.

Daisy came over with a glass of fruit punch. 'You all right, Mum?' She handed her mother the glass and Win took it gratefully. After the terrible winter they'd had, everyone had enjoyed a blazing summer with temperatures in the nineties. Today wasn't as hot as it had been, but she tired easily these days. 'I'm fine,' said Win after she'd sipped the drink. 'I just needed a bit of a sit-down, that's all.'

Daisy looked back.

'Daisy, love,' Win began tentatively, 'can I ask you something?'

'Of course.' Daisy sat beside her mother on the bench and put her hand over Win's.

'You never said why you ran off that time,' Win said.

Daisy shivered and put her hand back in her lap.

'I'm sorry if I'm upsetting you,' said Win, 'but I want to know.'

'It's better left unsaid, Mum.'

'Was it because you had a baby?' said Win.

Daisy stared at her, open-mouthed. 'You knew?'

Win shook her head. 'I guessed,' she said. 'I got to wondering what would be so awful that you had to run away from home. That's when I decided it must have been because you were pregnant.'

Daisy looked down at her lap. 'Oh, Mum, I'm sorry.'

Win patted her hands. 'Don't be, love,' she said. 'I understand.'

They sat quietly for a moment or two. 'What happened to it?'

'She was adopted,' said Daisy.

'Have you seen her?'

Daisy smiled. 'Oh yes. She's had a good life and she's happy.'

Win followed her daughter's gaze. Without realizing it, Daisy was looking at April Rodway and somewhere deep in Win's mind a memory stirred. Of course! She'd heard stories about April Charles. How she'd got her name and how she'd been found all those years ago by Amos McCabe. She smiled inwardly. Lovely man, Amos. They said he sent money to the orphanage every year on the anniversary of the find until the year he died and Win was willing to bet that was on April's birthday.

'Does she know?'

'Oh no,' cried Daisy.

'You should tell her,' said Win. 'She's no snob. She won't mind the fact that you are working in her mother's kitchen.'

Daisy took in her breath, realizing she'd given the game away. 'Mum, you mustn't,' she said, rising from her seat. 'It's not what you think.'

Win pulled her back down beside her. 'Why won't you tell her?'

Daisy's eyes suddenly blazed with anger. 'Mum, just leave it. You don't understand.'

'Why, Daisy?' Win insisted.

'Because . . .' Daisy closed her eyes, imagining the onslaught, the anger and the disgust that would inevitably happen if she told her. Why pick on now? Why spoil Effie's wedding? She looked at her mother helplessly. 'Oh, Mum . . . I can't tell her because it was him. He was the father of my baby. My baby's father was my dad.'

Win gasped. 'What, Basil?'

'Yes. I didn't know what was happening,' Daisy said desperately. 'I was just fourteen and he said I should take your place. I'm sorry, Mum. He made me do it.'

Win had closed her eyes, but now they snapped open. 'But he wasn't,' she said.

Daisy held her breath. 'What?'

'Basil wasn't your father,' Win repeated. 'Didn't you ever wonder why he treated you different from the other girls? Oh, my darling girl . . . I had no idea that he . . . What a wicked thing to do to a little girl.' Win's eyes were bright with unshed tears. She leaned towards Daisy and said confidentially, 'I was already pregnant when I married Basil. He'd always wanted me and he said he'd give me his name and my reputation back.

Your father was a farmer's lad. He was killed when he fell into a threshing machine.'

They stared at each other for a few seconds, then Daisy whispered, 'Oh, Mum.'

Win grasped Daisy's hands. 'Basil always said I tricked him into marriage, but I didn't. He knew I was carrying before we were married. He was a terrible man and I was glad when he died. If that sounds wicked, I'm sorry, but it's true. The only good thing he did his whole life was to give me Agnes and Jean. Oh, Daisy, I wish I could right this terrible wrong. I'm so, so sorry.'

'Don't upset yourself, Mum.'

'But he had you put away,' Win said desperately.

'Everything all right here?' Pen Albright was standing in front of them.

Win whipped out her handkerchief from up her sleeve and dabbed her eyes. 'Oh, you know me,' she said. 'I'm an old softie. Weddings always make me cry.'

Daisy got to her feet. 'If you'll excuse me . . .'

The photographer was calling Win over. She downed the rest of the punch and stood up. Taking a deep breath, she squeezed Daisy's hand, then walked towards the bride and groom with a big smile. There would be time enough for tears and recriminations later. Right now, this was Leslie's wedding and she had to look happy for them. There was no need to pretend – she *was* happy for them. Jean and Bill stood next to their son and the photographer motioned Win to stand between Effie and Ronnie.

The photographer had already taken most of the family pictures. Effie's family, her parents and her brother had mingled with Leslie's family, clearly enjoying the occasion.

'You look fantastic,' Win said to the bride out of the corner of her mouth as the photographer went back to his camera.

'Do you think I look as pretty as the groom?' Effie said mischievously.

'Oh, go on with you,' said Win, giving her a playful nudge. 'Believe me, you're a beautiful bride. You look really lovely.'

'Look this way, please,' the photographer called.

Win looked out over the garden and, just beyond the photographer's head, she spotted Daisy standing beside Mrs Edwards. They were deep in conversation and then Mrs Edwards beckoned April over.

'Smile, please,' said the photographer.

Win smiled as she saw Mrs Edwards put her arm around Daisy's shoulder.

'One more time,' the photographer called.

And Win's small smile grew wider as Daisy, Mrs Edwards and April Rodway went inside the house and closed the French windows behind them.

*A*UTHOR'S NOTE

In January 1996, the *Worthing Herald* published two articles. The first, called 'Secret Under Your Feet' (January 5th 1996), drew attention to a wartime underground command centre under Field Place, now a popular wedding venue near Durrington-on-Sea station. During the 1939–45 conflict, the lovely manor house had been used as a billet for RAF officers connected with RAF Durrington, a top-secret radar station which operated from a building in what is now a school in Palatine Road. Rumour had it that there was a labyrinth of tunnels under the Field Place bowling green and that it had been part of a bomb-proofed bunker which was to be the local base for government in the event of an invasion.

In the second article, 'Hidden – But Not Forgotten: Town's Underground Secrets' (January 19th 1996), two men, Hugh Bartlett and the then greenkeeper, John Hammersley, said that as children they had played in the tunnels after the war. They had apparently gained access via a ventilation shaft in front of the manor house and stories of staircases, annexes and riding bikes through a honeycomb of passages emerged.

Some historians have disputed the tales, pointing out that the building of such a massive structure must have been noticed by the locals, but perhaps they are forgetting that what is now a heavily built-up area was just open fields until the 1950s.

In 2007, Graham Lelliott self-published an interesting booklet called *The Field Place Mystery* in which he sets out quite clearly the arguments both for and against the suggestion that the bunker and its tunnels exist.

Whatever the pros and cons of the matter, it fired my imagination. Apparently gaining access to the main entrance is covered by a seventy-three-year secrecy rule, so by my reckoning it's almost time to get the spades out.

ᴀCKNOWLEDGEMENTS

I should like to take the opportunity to thank all the staff at Worthing Reference Library for their help. I have spent many a happy hour up there researching for this book and the others before it.

I am also enormously grateful to my agent, Juliet Burton, and my editor, Jayne Osborne at Pan Mac. I do so admire your eagle eyes, which point out the things I've missed. Thank you, thank you . . .